Pound *for* Pound

ALSO BY F. X. TOOLE

Rope Burns
(reissued as *Million Dollar Baby*)

Pound
for
Pound

a novel

F. X. TOOLE

HarperCollins books may be purchased for educational, business, or sales promotional use. For information, please write: Special Markets Department, HarperCollins Publishers, 10 East 53rd Street, New York, NY 10022.

FIRST EDITION

Designed by Cassandra J. Pappas

Printed on acid-free paper

Library of Congress Cataloging-in-Publication Data

Toole, F. X., 1930–2002
    Pound for pound : a novel / F.X. Toole.—1st ed.
      p. cm.
  ISBN-13: 978-0-06-088133-7
  ISBN-10: 0-06-088133-X
    1. African Americans—Fiction. 2. Grandfathers—Fiction. 3. Grandsons—Fiction. 4. Domestic fiction. I. Title.

PS3570.O438P68 2006
813'.54—dc22   2005049508

06 07 08 09 10 WBC/QWF 10 9 8 7 6 5 4 3 2 1

For God,
and for my children—
Erin Patricia,
Gannon Michael,
Ethan Patrick—
whom I knew and loved in the womb,
and who saved me from an early death

And since I may not live long enough
to write and dedicate another one of these things,
allow me to express my great gratitude to, and respect
for, that distinguished man of letters himself,
Daniel Patrick O'Halpern,
the Ecco Kid.

LET ME AT LEAST NOT DIE WITHOUT A
STRUGGLE, INGLORIOUS, BUT HAVING
DONE SOME BIG THING FIRST, FOR MEN
TO COME TO KNOW OF.

—HECTOR

And when ye come and all the flowers are dying
If I am dead, as dead I well may be
You'll come and find the place where I am lying
And kneel and say an Ave there for me.

—"DANNY BOY"

FOREWORD

Boxing tempts writers.

It bids them to riff on the contained savagery of the prizefight. It entices them to explore the endeavor in terms of masculinity, race, and class. It lures them into an unapologetically all-male world. It taunts them with the knowledge that they do not and will not ever belong. It humbles them with the knowledge that they must remain circumspect and explicate that world from an outsider's perspective.

Writers approach boxing as idolaters, inquisitors, wannabes, and *manqués*. They see boxing as an enclosed society and a groovy, blood-and-guts lifestyle. The entry price is high. Non-combatants endure tedium and hitch themselves to stars that never shine. The fighters themselves chase an always-fleeting glory through the sustained cultivation and infliction of pain. Boxing levies high dues in return for short payoffs. Writers want to visit, but not live there. They come for the pathos and drama, then move on.

F. X. Toole was the exception. He worked as a trainer and cut man. He backstopped stiffs, trial horses, journeymen, and fringe contenders. He never brought up a titlist or cable-TV stud. He loved the fight game. He came to it as a non-writer and left it as the best boxing writer of his era. The fight world seduced him. He paid his dues and lucked into a high-end payoff. His fight-world transit led him to write—from the inside out.

His subject matter was preordained and rigorously circumscribed. He understood specific fight-game truths and their symbolic underpinnings as outside writers could not. The Fight World is the Outside World condensed and refracted. It is a world of great toil and pain. Definable laurels rarely accrue. Dubious laurels pale behind the heavy human cost. The satisfactions are prosaic and known only to the participants in the craft. The dividends are wholly those of witness. Perseverance, stamina, fidelity, and bravery come with the job.

F. X. Toole knew all this. I met him once, and knew that he knew it.

My literary agent and close friend, Nat Sobel, introduced me. We had lunch at the Argyle Hotel in Los Angeles. Nat knew that I was a long-time and fanatical fight fan. He had just sold Toole's short-story collection, *Rope Burns*, to an American publisher and wanted to hit me up for a blurb. I arrived for lunch. Toole and I talked fights for two hours—insider to outsider.

We discussed the craft. We covered great body punchers, shit-for-brains headhunters, our Mexican bantamweight–featherweight ten-best lists. We dissected vexing southpaws of the '50s and '60s, and mourned the early death of Salvador Sánchez. I brought up the first Archie Moore–Yvon Durelle fight.

It was December '58. I was ten years old. Moore defended his light-heavyweight crown in Montreal. Moore's age was up for speculation. He was at least forty-three. Durelle was a brutally strong Quebecois, down from heavyweight. He floored Moore four times in round one. Moore came back and stopped him in six. Their war made me a fight fiend for life.

Toole was thrilled that I knew the fight. I asked him what *he* was doing then. He dodged the question. He told me his fight career commenced years later. He only wanted to talk Fights. The Fights comprised his entire dialogue with the world. The World was the Fights and the

Fights were the World. The Fights mediated everything that he saw and felt. The Fights were the fulcrum for and the basis of all his notions of human drama. I read the stories in *Rope Burns,* and saw this single-mindedness strike gold. The book was dead rich in details that only a fight man could know. The book was savage and melancholy, and somehow heartbreakingly sweet.

I queried some fight-game acquaintances. They told me Toole's real name was Jerry Boyd, and he might have had some moniker before that. He looked fifty-five. He was closer to seventy. He held his mud. He didn't trash-talk other trainers or fighters. He might have a bum ticker. Close-to-the-vest didn't say it. With Jerry or F. X. or whoever he was, you never knew shit.

Rope Burns was well-published. It exceeded sales expectations and received fine reviews. The story "Million Dollar Baby" was turned into an Academy Award–winning film that won Oscars for all the principals. F. X. Toole did not live to visit the set or hug the stars at the premiere. The rumor was true. He had a bum ticker. He died with a single short-story collection behind him—and one big, fat, unfinished novel manuscript.

He carried it to the hospital. He was scheduled for emergency surgery and knew he might not survive. He was desperate to finish the book. He didn't. He bequeathed nine hundred pages to his three children and Nat Sobel. Nat and a freelance editor named James Wade shaped the draft into the finished novel you are about to read.

Toole's savage and melancholy tone only deepens here. It's a fully realized work, with a grace note of loss and elegy. It's musical that way. It's unaccountably soft. It's an unfinished symphony trailing off in minor chords.

F. X. Toole is dead. His short literary life was a notable one, and all about the Fights. To him, the World was the Fights and the Fights were the World. If there's an afterlife, I hope there's an 18-foot punchers' ring there just for him.

JAMES ELLROY

9/26/05

Pound *for* Pound

DAN

Chapter 1

In one way or another, Dan Cooley and Earl Daw had been partners for twenty years in the fight game, and co-owners for twelve in the body-and-fender business. Dan had opened the shop—Shamrock Auto Body—more than twenty years before Earl became a partner. Because of Earl's bad hands, and because his wife had urged him to stop fighting, Earl hung up his gloves permanently when his first daughter was born. Earl's deal with Dan was fifty-fifty, and they'd sealed it with a handshake. Like their friendship, the deal had lasted.

Earl Daw was a lean, dark-skinned black man who'd been born in the Nickerson Gardens projects in Watts. As a middleweight, with Dan as his trainer, he'd fought his way out of the projects and made money doing it. Because of Earl's many one-punch knockouts, he was given the fighting name "Captain Hook" by sportswriters who recognized the devastating power in his left hand. But fight guys, guys on the inside, knew that Earl had *soft hands,* hands that would break under the tremendous force fighters can generate. Fight guys are known for being realists. Earl's name in the gym went from Captain Hook to Softhand, but, because fight guys are also known to simplify, the nickname was shortened to Soff, and that stuck, as in, "Say, Soff!" What many didn't know was that Earl was a converted southpaw, and that under his father's, Short-cake's, instruction, he'd changed his stance to move his power from his rear, or defensive hand, to the hand closer to his opponent, his offensive hand. That change in stance often explained the knockout power of a big left-hooker.

Dan Cooley's skin was Irish skin, still had freckles on his arms if folks bothered to look, though age and the Los Angeles sun had darkened him some. If you looked closely at his face, you could see that something wasn't quite right with one eye, the result of an injury that had put him out of the ring as a boxer and into the corner as a trainer. Some fight guys called Dan and Earl Salt and Peppa.

Dan would answer, "Yeah, but I'm tired of this Salt bullshit. I wanna be Peppa."

Earl would add, "Yeah, an' I be tired a bein Peppa. I wanna be Salt so I can get all that white pussy out there."

"No good, Earl, I been with white women all my life," Dan would say, and point to his white hair. "Look at what they done to me, and I'm only twenty-eight years of age."

It was a show they'd put on, and fight guys, black and white, loved it no matter how many times they watched it.

Earl stood just inside the big roll-up door of the body shop and watched Dan get out of his truck, his movements slow and stiff, like an old man's. These days Dan would be fiddling with paperwork in his office upstairs one minute and then suddenly gone, destination unknown. Trouble was, Earl never knew when Dan might return. If indeed he would return—that worried Earl a lot, each time. But he kept his mouth shut. And waited.

That day it was hot and dusty, a typical early fall day in Los Angeles, but the grass was green inside St. Athanasius Cemetery. Greener still the

Connemara marble base of the Cooley family gravestone. Dan stood there just staring at it, his eyes moving from one name down to the next. All those dates were burned into his memory, as ineradicable as the letters incised in the stone.

BRENDAN CONNOR COOLEY   1963–1964

TERRANCE DECLAN COOLEY   1961–1985

MARY CATHERINE MARKEY   1965–1992

EAMON DERMONT MARKEY   1960–1992

Little Brendan, his second son, dead of acute lymphoblastic leukemia before his second birthday. Terry, his fireman son, buried alive when a retaining wall at a construction site collapsed as he worked to remove a trapped laborer. His daughter, Mary Cat, three months' pregnant with her second child, and her husband, both killed when their plane missed the runway in Acapulco.

He could still see the little boy, standing rigid as he looked at the two rose-covered coffins, his eyes aching and dry.

"But why did they put my mom and dad inside those long boxes?" Timothy Patrick Markey asked.

"Shhh, lad," said his grandmother Brigid. Her voice still had a trace of old-country brogue, thick and rich as Irish brown bread, and her eyes were so green they often looked purple. "Wait until after Father Joe's done."

The charred bodies of Tim Pat's mother and father had been flown back from Mexico in sealed aluminum tubes by the very same airline that had interrupted their second honeymoon when one of its aircraft crashed on final approach.

Tim Pat was six, bright as a new penny and full of life, but once he'd been told of his parents' death, the tears Dan expected him to shed never came, just a frightening stillness. It had taken over four weeks for the

Mexican authorities to identify and return the bodies to Dan and Brigid, Tim Pat's grandparents. They moved Tim Pat's bed into their bedroom, where he'd slept fitfully. He hardly spoke once he knew the bodies had arrived, and had said nothing at the rosary or at the funeral mass, but now he shivered like a cold pup and wanted answers.

The priest finished at the grave site, and Brigid had Tim Pat sprinkle a pinch of dark earth on each coffin. As they walked away, Dan gave the aging priest an envelope with the same thousand-dollar donation for a Tijuana orphanage he'd made too often, and then rejoined his wife and Tim Pat. The priest, Father José Capetillo, was pastor at Christ the King Church, a refuge for the soul located near the Cooleys' home in old Hollywood. Father Joe had lived and worked with his wetback *mojado* parents in Steinbeck's Salinas, but he had been born in the Spanish-colonial city of Guanajuato, in the state of Guanajuato, Mexico. His family had made sure that he would not spend the rest of his life in stoop labor in fields owned by other people. The Jesuits took him in hand when he was in high school and put him on the straight and narrow path to the seminary.

Father Joe would join the Cooleys at their home for the wake, as he had joined so many others at their homes, as he knew he would join yet more to come. He lowered his head. Almost daily, he went to what Miguel de Unamuno called the bottom of the abyss. *Lord, there is so much I cannot explain to my flock. From whence do they come? Why are they here? Where are they going?* Faith and hope would lift him from despair. *Lord, I love you with my whole heart and soul and with all of my mind.*

Dan Cooley wasn't so sure that he had any love left for the Lord. Maybe it had died along with all those he had loved and lost.

Once they had angled their way through the other gravestones and arrived at the mortician's limousine, Brigid cleaned the dirt off Tim Pat's hand with a white linen handkerchief. The boy turned and looked back. He saw but did not want to believe. Gravediggers were pulling away the squares of fake grass from the dark rectangles in the ground.

Tim Pat said, "Grandma, they're not going to put my momma and daddy in those holes, are they?"

Brigid had just buried her third and last child, her only daughter. Faith was all she had left to hang on to.

"They must," she said. "Yer mam and daddy've gone to God."

"The one up in heaven?" Tim Pat asked.

"The same," Brigid assured him.

"Will God send them back to me?"

His grandmother began to weep, her first tears since the call from Acapulco. "No, little one, He will not."

Tim Pat had an edge of something like anger in his voice. "But why not?"

Dan put his arm around the boy's frail shoulders. "Because that's not how it works."

Tim Pat looked up at his grandfather. "How does it work?"

Dan said, "Ah, God, I don't know how it works."

Brigid and Dan approached their new task of raising their grandson guardedly. They were careful not to coddle him, though that was hard, now that they had lost all of their own children. Both knew that safeguarding Tim Pat in a sealed bubble of their dread could be as lethal for him as a gunshot. They allowed him to remain in his old school up by Sunset Boulevard at first, but a few weeks following the funeral, they enrolled him at Christ the King. For two weeks, either Brigid or Dan walked him the four and a half blocks from their house on Cahuenga to his new school. Both explained that he should go by way of Melrose Avenue; both taught him how to use crosswalks and to obey the signal at Rossmore; and for another week, one or the other would walk a half block behind him to make sure he got to school safely. He was quick to learn, and enjoyed meeting other kids along the way and walking with them on to school.

Tim Pat had grown solemn, and having him walk to school alone was part of Brigid's plan to help the downhearted little boy back into the world. Dan took him to the shop and taught him how to spread body filler and use sandpaper, to clean spray guns. The plan began to work. The nuns were helpful, and Sister Mary Virginia excitedly phoned Brigid the day Tim Pat had his first scuffle over who would be pitcher during a noontime ball game. And while he continued to be Tim Pat at home, the growing-up part of him insisted on just Tim in school and the great world beyond.

Tim Pat's second journey to St. Athanasius was to bury Brigid two years later, dead from cancer. He knew to sprinkle soil on his grandmother's coffin, and as he stood up with the dirt between his fingers, he said, "Grandma won't be back either, will she?"

Dan could barely speak. "No."

Both of them stared at the name freshly incised into the gleaming green stone.

BRIGID ANNE MANAHAN COOLEY   1940–1994

Then Tim Pat asked, "But she's with Mom and Dad, and Uncle Brendan and Terry, and they're watching over us, right?"

Dan took ten steps before he could speak, and then it was his mother's, Nora's words, not his, that came from his mouth. "Sure, and why wouldn't they be?"

Dan sprinkled a few grains of loose soil on the green gravestone and hobbled to his truck. He dropped back down North Broadway to Chávez, hooked a right, and passed under the Pasadena Freeway, where Chávez becomes the Sunset Boulevard that leads west through Hollywood, Beverly Hills, and on to the Pacific Ocean. Dan stayed on Sunset until the fork at Santa Monica Boulevard, and then took it on into his part of Hollywood. Instead of pulling into the shop on Cole, he forced himself to drive past it a half block to Melrose, where he turned right after a block, to Wilcox, and circled back to park in front of the gym beneath the eucalyptus tree.

The gym was in an old building that had survived earthquakes that had destroyed prettier, newer buildings, and had knocked down segments of freeways, wrecked bridges, and tumbled hospitals. Behind the boarded-up windows at the front was an interior of high ceilings and exposed metal beams. Like a fighter's body, it was lean and spare. Places on the hardwood floor showed smooth, bare wood through worn varnish where fighters down the years had shadowboxed or jumped rope. There were circles of bare wood around the body bags and beneath the speed bags. There were sixteen-inch spit funnels crusted with years of dry mucous. Hoses ran from the funnels to five-gallon white plastic spit buckets on the floor. Neither ring had padding beneath its slick canvas. These were *boxers'* rings, no padding meant fast. A workout timer against one wall would mark off three-minute rounds and one-minute rest periods. Once fighters had been in the game for a while, they knew instinctively when the warning buzzer should sound, when the bell would ring. There were no stools to rest on. Fighters don't sit between rounds when sparring.

A hand-lettered sign on one wall read, "Good Fighters Don't Need Water and Bad Fighters Don't Deserve Water." Another read, "Learning's Hard, Doing's Easy." A third sign, "Remember the Easter Bunny," showed an amateurish drawing of a boxing ring scattered with faded Easter eggs. Another sign read, "The First Rule of War Is Don't Shoot Yourself."

The gym was located directly behind the rear of the shop. The shop faced Cole Avenue, while the gym faced narrow Wilcox Avenue, the next street west. Back to back, both buildings were part of what remained of an old Hollywood industrial/residential area. The gym could be entered directly from the back of the shop through the rear door. That's how the few fighters still using the gym entered it.

The address and main entrance to the gym were on Wilcox; a small, hand-painted sign that read "GyM" had once been nailed to the right of the front door. Until the day Dan tore it off and hurled it to the ground, under the huge eucalyptus tree that still afforded its gentle shade and pleasantly medicinal smell.

After he had fought off the idea of burning the place down, Dan had Centcor Security install a fire-and-burglar-alarm system in the gym. Because he had boarded up the front windows and door, the building looked like it had been abandoned. Anybody who decided to break into the place and trash it would find Dan Cooley confronting them with a twelve-gauge pump shotgun long before the police turned up. Dan lived, slept, and ate mostly in a room on the second floor. And he was a very light sleeper these days, when he slept at all.

Chapter 2

Dan was first-generation Irish, the youngest of five brothers—Cathal Michael, Liam Francis, Dermot James, Finbar Joseph, and himself, Daniel Aloysius. The first three were born five floors up in New York's Hell's Kitchen, the Irish slums west of Times Square; Fin and he were born in a converted first-floor loft on the Lower East Side. His mother told how she made the sign of the cross when she walked down the last flight of Hell's Kitchen stairs she'd ever have to climb.

Dan's father, Padraic Timothy, was from County Armagh; his mother, Nora Ann McGeough, from County Louth, counties whose borders touched, but they were married a few miles to the south at the massive, stone St. Pat's "chapel" in Dundalk, County Louth—"chapel," not church, because only the "churches" of the protestant Church of Ireland were called "churches" back then.

Ireland and its people were still scarred from the famine, the Great Hunger, which had begun in 1846. Work, good work, was hard to find and black poverty infested both town and countryside. Like thousands of others, Dan's parents saw America as the only way out and they worked day and night to save money for their passage. Nora was pregnant before they got on the boat for New York, and sick all the way across, but she kissed the ground of Ameriky when they landed, and both hoped they had reached salvation from hunger and fear.

Padraic was mad-dog crazy for Irish football and hurling, had played both and had the scars to prove it, but he instantly fell in love with boxing and baseball—he read every inch of the sports pages every day to follow the standings and batting averages—and he used baseball to improve his reading comprehension. He knew the records of Irish fighters, starting with the great John L. Sullivan as a bare knuckler. When there was money enough, he took his older sons to the fights at the old Madison Square Garden, and to St. Nick's in Manhattan, even took them all the way up to the Bronx Coliseum if the card was right. Nora had the kids, and thanked God from her knees, twice daily, that she hadn't lost any—so many children had been lost back in Ireland—and for the good man who labored so hard to put food on the table every day.

It was food hard earned in the early days, which included the bread lines of the early thirties. Padraic first supported his family as a roustabout, showing up at the docks or labor sites before dawn, hoping to be picked early and to work late. Then came steady work for New York City as a garbageman. When he got promoted to driver, he was able to move his family from the raging violence of Hell's Kitchen to their loft near the Bowery, where Jews, Ukrainians, Poles, and Italians were protective neighbors, and a decent girl could walk to school safely. Sidewalk justice was meted out to any punk who even thought of tampering with her. The loft was another step up for the Cooleys. It was where the last two boys were born, and it was in the quiet of the loft late at night that Padraic and Nora studied to become citizens.

The Cooleys would surely have stayed in New York but for the attack on Pearl Harbor and America's subsequent gearing up for all-out war. California suddenly had plenty of good-paying jobs and was short of men (and women) to fill them, so in mid-1942 the family moved by train to Los Angeles. They found a place to live in the old dock town of San Pedro, on the westerly rim of what would shortly become the massive Los

Angeles Harbor. Padraic found employment on the assembly line at the Douglas Aircraft plant in Long Beach. He worked twelve-hour shifts, sometimes seven days a week, and never missed a day. With overtime, and with Nora cashing every check and marking down every penny he earned and every one she spent, they lived well enough for him to buy his first car, a used 1934 Chevy four-door sedan for $165.00, a high price because of the war. Now he could drive to work like an American, instead of wasting hours a day on the bus like some Jerk McGee green off the boat. His children always had milk, and his family ate three times a day. That was why he had come to the United States in the first place.

The two older boys, Cathal and Liam, enlisted in the U.S. Navy, and though neither was wounded or won medals for valor, they hadn't been draft dodgers, either. By the end of the war, the number of two-car families had grown, but then the war plants closed down. Money was tight and jobs were scarce. Padraic used his experience at Douglas and the money he'd saved to open his own body-and-fender shop. Dan and his brothers worked for their father, Dan after school and on Saturdays, the older boys full-time until they went on to become policemen or firemen once they were sure the old man's business was successful.

"A man with a trade is worth two men," Padraic would counsel his sons at the dinner table, "and a man with a trade won't go hungry, not in this great land."

Nora would bump him with her hip to let him know who was the real boss, the one with the real trade. "Eejit, ya didn't like yer dinner, didja, nor the one yer not gettin tomorrow?"

Padraic would answer, his face solemn, "Och, there's nothin worse than a Dundalk biddy," but he'd always put his arm around Nora's waist and pull her back to him.

Dan learned that family meant you fought for and protected one another. As a little boy in a rough neighborhood in New York, he'd been insulated from harm by his big brothers. But in San Pedro, at St. Jude's school, there were no big brothers on duty—and he was a small freckle-faced kid who talked funny, weighed too much, and looked soft. Bigger

and tougher boys knew a mark when they saw one, and Dan was frequently bullied. He watched others tear into his lunch bag, take the pie or
cake, and scatter the rest in the street. In the beginning he tried to fight
back, but he was chubby and slow, and he quickly realized that he didn't
know how to fight. Dan finally quit fighting back, but never told the sis-
ters at school or anyone at home because he was ashamed of being fat and
weak. He withdrew into himself and began to play at home alone.

Nora was no fool; she knew something had gone wrong and followed
Dan to school one day. From down the block, she watched as two older
kids pushed him down and ran off with his brown bag. She wanted to
rush and comfort him, and then to spank the asses off the kids who had
abused her son, but she also wanted Dan to be the one to teach these bullies a lesson. And seeing her good food scattered on the street made her
even more furious.

The next Saturday she took Dan to the Police Athletic League gym
near the waterfront. There Dan met his destiny—a part-time boxing
coach, Sal Gallardo, who had been a professional fighter in his youth, but
like nearly all ex-fighters, he was kind and courteous, and wanted most
of all to be known as a gentleman. When he heard Nora out, he suggested boxing to her as a solution to the problem and pointed to the other
little kids he was training. She wasn't sure what to make of him, what
with his dark skin and his mashed-in nose. Gallardo added that boxing
might be best for Dan because the boys competed with others in the
same weight class. He explained how Dan's size wouldn't necessarily be
a disadvantage, and that he'd be able to build himself up at the same
time he learned boxing, the manly art of self-defense.

Nora was wary, but she liked the "manly" part, and sat with Dan to
observe how gentle Coach Gallardo was with his charges. Gallardo's little guys were lean and quick, and had learned how to fight—a glass cabi-
net full of Police Athletic League and Golden Gloves trophies testified to
that. Nora had never thought of boxing, had no idea how fighters became fighters, had assumed that the strongest fighter was the fighter
who always won.

Coach Gallardo explained that Dan would wear big gloves, head and body protection, and train to get into proper condition before he could box with other boys. "The worst that can happen, Mrs. Cooley, is that he'll lose weight."

Nora started Dan as a spectator, but nudged him gently into Coach Gallardo's care every Saturday before school was out for summer vacation. It wasn't long before Dan lost weight, and once that happened, he realized he was fast and strong for his size. Coach Gallardo was careful to make sure Dan understood and could execute fundamentals before he put him in with a suitable opponent—to see if Dan had heart. He did, he did indeed, and was he thrilled with his showing, thrilled with himself, and soon he was strutting to the gym alone.

Opening day of school the next September, he kicked the shit out of the first bully who came for his lunch. He had to fight three more days and got some lumps for it, but each day he was the one who ate his mother's pie or cake, and after the third fight, he no longer had to fight to eat. He'd earned the respect of his schoolmates, but most important, he'd earned the respect of his mother, and it was only after the semester began that Nora told Padraic how, with Dan's willing complicity, she'd kept the whole tale secret from him.

Padraic said, "Would it not appear that the lad's mother invaded the time-honored domain of the lad's own father?"

Nora placed the back of one hand to her brow in mock martyrdom. "The louts were stealin me pie."

"So, it's sympathy for yerself yer afther, is it?" he said.

" 'Tis," she said. "Because they stole me cake, too."

Padraic filled his pipe with cavendish. "So the lad's good with his mitts, is he?"

"Och, Paddy, he's wizard," she said.

Once Dan had put the bullies on their asses, he suddenly had friends who were Slavs, blacks, Mexicans, and Italians. When he began winning amateur tournaments and collecting fight trophies, those same friends invited him home to eat delicious meals prepared by their mothers, who seemed exotic to Dan. Though he was delighted by the food, and always had seconds, he was ever glad to return to the meat and *badehdahs* and the Irish bread he got at home. And pie.

Though he'd never be big enough to play on the high school football team, he was big and tough enough to fight. He got that way working his freckled ass off and eating the best Slav and soul food, and Mexican and Italian and Irish food in San Pedro, pronounced "Peedro" by the locals. Padraic was his greatest fan, and the more the kid had to train in order to win, the less he had to work in the shop. Nora had wanted at least one priest from her litter. Her other two sons would become cops and firemen, but Dan was her fighter, and sometimes she wondered, God forgive her, if he just might be her favorite because of it, her Brian Ború.

At eighteen, Dan was good enough to win the California Golden Gloves featherweight title at the Olympic Auditorium. Coach Gallardo turned him over to professional trainer Willie "Shortcake" Daw, Earl's father, and Dan made the trip in from San Pedro daily to train at the old Main Street Gym on L.A.'s skid row. It was there in the stink and spit that he learned to grow the nails on his thumbs and forefingers longer than on his other fingers, to better snag and remove adhesive tape from his hand wraps after sparring.

Shortcake Daw worked full time as a sorter in Los Angeles's old main post office across from Union Station. He also hustled football cards for a bookie on Central Avenue, and doubled his income among his fellow postal workers. If an inspector came sniffing around, Shortcake would slip him a few cards for himself. He made a lot of friends among government inspectors, who'd go out of their way to make social calls.

Under Shortcake, Dan developed into a slick and tireless boxer-puncher, and his black hair and handsome face reminded old-time fans of Irish Billy Conn, the great light-heavyweight out of Pittsburgh. The

Irish dubbed him "Connman" Danny Cooley to connect him to Billy Conn. "Connman" identified Dan with the cleverness of Billy Conn in the ring, but also hooked him to the "con" in the word "confetti"—Irish confetti—the old mick term for bricks.

By the time he was twenty-two, Dan had grown into a tall and wiry lightweight at 135 with a pro record of thirty-two and two, with twenty-one knockouts. He'd never been down, and most fight fans believed he was on his way to the world lightweight title. Because he stood five-nine, it was also thought that he would grow into a welterweight, and that he was good enough to hold both world titles at the same time.

But all those hopes turned to ashes when Dan sustained massive injuries to his right eye and the bone structure around it. The fight that was the one he needed to win to get his shot at being a champion turned out to be his last fight.

It was like déjà vu to Dan.

One evening, while they were washing and drying the dishes, Tim Pat said, "Grampa, I wanna start comin home for my lunch, okay?"

Dan said, "I thought you liked the lunches I make."

"I do, but I like eatin at home better."

Tim Pat had been brown-bagging for three years. Dan said, "Why do you want to eat lunch at home?"

Tim Pat said, "I just wanna."

Dan said, "Son, the shop's always busy at lunchtime. When my guys are all at lunch, and people come in for their cars and stuff, I have to be there."

Tim Pat said, "You could take my lunch to the shop and I could walk over there to eat."

Dan said, "Walkin would take time, and maybe I wouldn't be able to get you back to school for class. Besides, you couldn't play noon games with the kids, right?"

"Yeah, okay."

Dan didn't understand. Tim Pat had grieved following his parents' death, and after Brigid's. That was normal enough, but like most kids he was resilient, especially when he found abundant love from his grandfather, comfort from the nuns, and playful attention from Earl and the guys at the shop. All served to compensate for much of the boy's loss. He began to grow, to flourish, to break through the sadness and reserve of silence. He was particularly secure in his grandfather's love. He'd had his scuffles at school, like every other little boy, but no one had ever preyed upon him. He still walked to Christ the King School the way Brigid and Dan had taught him. Dan picked him up at school and usually took him to the shop, where Tim Pat would do homework or tinker with junk cars until closing time. The boy was good at team sports and liked to compete, but had never shown an interest in boxing, which was fine with Dan. Boxing was something you wanted, or you didn't, and Dan would never have pushed it on a son of his own, much less Tim Pat. Tim Pat liked baseball, was a good hitter, seldom struck out. Dan went to every game. Now things had changed. Tim Pat no longer seemed interested in baseball and Dan didn't understand why.

Earl said, "Watch the boy close, it could be his hurt comin back on him."

A week later, Dan noticed that Tim Pat had dark circles under his eyes. As a fight trainer, Dan was attuned to shifts. Tim Pat looked like he'd lost weight. A loss of a pound or two is nothing to an adult, but for a nine-year-old weighing sixty-four pounds at four foot six, it's a significant amount. Two pounds can be significant in boxing, as well. Should a 135-pound fighter come in at 137 at the weigh-in for a 135-pound fight, he'd have to make weight by sweating off the two pounds in the steam room or by doing roadwork. Having to lose weight so close to a fight would give the other guy the edge. Only the dummies showed up overweight. But this was about something more than weight.

Dan said, "Are you feeling all right?"

"Yeah."

"Then what's wrong, son?" Dan asked.

"Nothin."

Dan didn't buy it, waited a few days. The kid withdrew even more, looked cold all the time, went to his room.

Sister Mary Virginia called from school. "Is there something wrong with Tim Pat, Mr. Cooley?"

"Is he skipping classes, or something?"

Sister said, "It's not that. It's his schoolwork."

"Is he eating at lunchtime?"

Sister said, "I'm sure he is. No one has said otherwise."

Dan hung up. He could have kicked himself. "No one said otherwise" back in his own school days either—least of all him.

Dan waited for Tim Pat to leave for school the next day, then followed in the pickup from nearly a block back. Instead of going by way of Melrose, Dan and Brigid had taught him, Tim Pat dropped all the way down to Rosewood, then crept along the fence of the Wilshire Country Club. He danced through traffic on Rossmore, then headed for Arden Boulevard, and cut back again toward school.

Seeing Tim Pat weave through traffic had nearly stopped Dan's heart. When the boy got a short block from school, he slid behind a hedge and waited. He peeked through the leaves, and waited a few moments more. With his books and his lunch clutched to his chest, he began to run to school. Dan sped up, and as he drew closer, he saw two boys on the far side of Arden, one white, and a bigger boy, whom Dan thought was maybe Mexican. The bigger boy was several inches taller than Tim Pat. Dan judged him at ten to twelve pounds heavier, and maybe two years older. A size and weight differential like that were huge to someone Tim Pat's size and age.

The Latino boy ran across the street and jumped Tim Pat a half block from school. As other kids from Christ the King looked on, he knocked Tim Pat down, then bent down and yelled in his face. He snatched Tim Pat's lunch, as Dan suspected he would, and yelled some more. As the big kid walked away, Tim Pat caught up to him and tried to grab his lunch bag back. The bigger boy raised his fist, while the white boy kicked Tim Pat in the leg. Tim Pat backed off, fury in his little face and his fists clenched. Dan knew this wasn't the first time this had happened, knew that this wasn't the same as when he was a kid—now even children carried weapons. Tim Pat had done the right thing to back off. But backing off was what had caused him to lose weight, backing off was putting worry in his eyes, backing off meant he'd *always* have to back off.

Dan decided to fill in some blanks. He waited in the pickup and watched as the boy who had attacked Tim Pat crossed Melrose. Dan followed slowly as the kid sauntered up to Gregory Elementary, which was just two blocks from Gower Street and Paramount Studios.

Dan waited for school to begin, and then approached Mrs. Krikorian, the school principal, about the bully. She told him that nothing could be done because the alleged incident had occurred off school property.

Dan said, "Alleged incident. You think I'm lyin?"

"I didn't say that. Good day."

That night, just as they were finishing dinner, Dan looked Tim Pat in the eye and asked, "So what's this kid's name?"

"What kid, Grampa?" The boy was clearly at a loss.

"The one who is beating you up and taking your lunch."

Tim Pat looked down at his plate, as a blush of shame suffused his face. "I dunno—I mean I don't know his real name. The other kids call him Tiger."

Dan smiled and ruffled his grandson's hair.

"Tiger, is it? Well now, I knew a Tiger or two in my time, when I was just about your age. And I learned what you have to do about kids like him."

Tim Pat looked up, an expression of hope dawning on his face. There was also relief there. If anybody had the answer, it would be his grandfather.

"Only one way—you got to hurt this Tiger so bad that he will keep his hands to himself. You have to go at him. You can't walk away."

"But he's biggern me," said Tim Pat.

"You don't have to be big to win."

"I'm afraid."

"Afraid of what?" said Dan.

"Of Tiger."

"The worst thing he can do is kill you."

That shocked Tim Pat into silence, but it was something he would never forget.

Dan said, "The rule is, you must fight according to the rules of the aggressor. He punches, you punch. He fights dirty, you fight dirty, except you fight so dirty he crosses the street the next time he sees you."

Dan felt a thrill run through him when he saw a spark kindle in Tim Pat's eyes.

Though Tim Pat knew his grandfather trained fighters, until now he had never shown an interest in the fight game.

"Grampa, I want you to show me."

Chapter 3

Dan allowed Tim Pat to cock around in the gym on his own for a few days, wanted him to learn how much he didn't know about boxing. The boy put on beat-up old bag gloves and, without thinking, flailed at the heavy bag. He tore skin from his knuckles. He surprised himself by how quickly he pooped out and had to sit down.

When it was time, Dan and Earl gave Tim Pat his first set of wraps, taught him how to wrap his hands. They supplied a serviceable pair of used eight-ounce professional fight gloves, and would later switch to ten- and twelve-ounce-bag gloves once Tim Pat got into condition and punched with force.

Dan, as always with a new fighter, and just as often with an experienced fighter, began with the floor, with the feet, with balance. He would also make proper breathing part of the formula. Tim Pat learned that he could move *and* punch. He also learned that he didn't have to move excessively, learned that a quarter of an inch could be enough to slip a punch. Boxing was hard to learn, regardless of age, but once the fighter finds ways to mine boxing's secret treasures, the pain of learning is worth it, and good fighters keep panning for more—especially when that "click" travels up from the fist to the shoulders, and the opponent hits the canvas like a lead bar.

Once Tim Pat developed stamina on the big bag, and learned the mechanics of punching, Dan bought a set of casters and attached them to an old chair. Dan or Earl would sit in the chair to be at Tim Pat's level, using their feet to propel themselves around the hardwood floor while they called combinations and held the punch mitts for him. The boy developed a first-class jab and a cracking right, could go to the belly with it, or to the jaw. There wasn't time to teach Tim Pat more moves. But he wouldn't need them, not in a street fight, not if he stuck with what he was learning, and landed with power. On Saturday mornings, they took Tim Pat to a downtown gym, had him box with other beginners his own size so he would know what it was like to get popped. The little guys wore headgear and sixteen-ounce gloves that looked like leather balloons on them. Soon he and the Mexican kids became pals. They began calling Tim Pat "el Zorro Blanco," the White Fox. His first bloody nose didn't bother the White Fox one bit. Dan saw Brigid in his little face.

Earl had Tim Pat going three-minute rounds. Little guys his age only go one minute in competition. Earl was as tickled with Tim Pat as if the kid was his own.

Earl said, "We gone get respect, boy."

Dan and Earl put more pressure on the kid, tried to rattle him, popped him with the flat side of punch mitts upside his ear to see if noise would shake him, to see if he'd back down. Tim Pat kept coming.

Tim Pat was in his fourth week of training. His grandfather had been driving him to school every day. Dan sat him down.

"You're lookin good," Dan said, "but this deal with Tiger won't be easy, okay?"

"Okay."

"If he knocks you down somehow," Dan told him, "you got to get up quick so he can't kick you. Understand?"

"Yes."

"If you knock him down, don't kick him, but if he tries to get up, knock him down with your fists again before he's all the way up, and keep doin it until he doesn't want to get up."

"That's dirty fightin, Grampa."

"It's the way he'll fight you if he gets the chance, that's the way it is. Remember what I said about fightin by the rules of the aggressor?"

"But this is against the rules of boxing that you taught me."

"Fightin Tiger is not about boxing, okay?"

"Okay. But when are you going to stop driving me to school?"

"When I think you're ready."

A week later, Dan said, "Now you teach me."

"Huh?"

"You explain the jab to me."

Tim Pat made a face. "Well, first, see, you gotta stand like this with your dukes up and your chin down behind your left shoulder. Then you push hard with your right foot, off the ball, like this, and let the jab go quick, not hard. At the same time that you move in off the back toe, you make a quarter turn to the left; that lines you up again and makes him miss."

"If you do it right."

"If I do it right."

Dan said, "What if the other guy's moving, too?"

"You got to move with him," said Tim Pat. "You can't always throw a perfect punch, but if you got your balance, you can always throw a good one."

"Attaboy," said Dan. "What about the right hand?"

Tim Pat described it and did it. Dan held up his right punch mitt. He said, "One-two."

Tim Pat made the move quick as a whip. *Bang-bang*, gunshots. While boxing with the Mexican kids, Tim Pat had also learned the rudiments of how to catch and counter. He loved to train, became a student of the game, watched Dan's tapes of old fighters, sat with Dan and Earl and watched the new guys on TV.

"What about a one-two off a head fake?"

Tim did it. The fake was bait. Make the other guy think apple and give him an orange. Dan hugged his grandson.

"When can I walk to school again, Grampa?"

Dan dared to dream that this little kid might one day go where he had almost gone.

"Soon," Dan said, "soon."

The first day Tim Pat walked to school, he went the regular way, the Melrose way. He was already past the church and turning into school when Tiger made his move. Dan and Earl had taken Earl's van by way of Rosewood. They sat thirty yards down the way and faced the action from Tiger's side of the street.

Tim Pat was shaking. He hoped Tiger didn't notice. Other kids on the way to school made a loose circle around them and watched, waiting for the usual outcome. Some were bigger than Tiger, but none stepped in to help Tim Pat. In the past he had hoped for help, but now he was hardly even aware of the growing crowd.

Tiger said, "Gimme that bag, sucka."

"Take it away from me, punk."

"Huh?" Tiger grunted, taking a step back.

Something had changed, but Tiger wasn't sure what. The other kids were as astonished as Tiger.

Tim Pat started doing his footwork, circling his opponent, and said, "Go 'head on, thief, try and steal it."

Tiger threw a wild right hand at Tim Pat's face. Tim Pat was waiting for it, slipped under it. As Tiger turned to charge again, Tim Pat tossed his lunch bag at his feet. Tiger didn't know what to believe. When he looked down at the split bag, Tim Pat nailed him with a right-hand shot to the gut,

just like Earl had said. Tiger gasped, doubled over, rocked back. Tim Pat
hit him with another right lead to the chest bone. Tiger came back throwing wild, windmill shots, but they were arm punches that quickly tired
him. One of the punches caught Tim Pat on the cheek and split the skin.
When Tiger saw Tim Pat wipe at the trickle of blood, he was sure Tim Pat
would quit. The other kids thought the same as they milled around, yelped
and laughed. Tiger was able to grab Tim Pat, and tried to kick his legs out
from under him, but Tim Pat broke the hold and spun away.

Tim Pat gave a head fake like the one he'd given Dan back at the
gym. When Tiger went for it, Tim Pat hit him with a crisp one-two combination that bloodied the other kid's nose and sat him on his ass. Tiger
started to get up, but when he was halfway, Tim Pat cracked him in the
face again, knocked him back to the sidewalk, where Tiger watched
wide-eyed as his blood plopped onto his dirty sweatshirt. He made a
rush to tackle Tim Pat from the ground, but Tim Pat was too quick for
him. Tiger tried to stand again, but his knees wobbled, and Tim Pat fired
two stiff left jabs to his forehead that put him back down. Tim Pat's face
was flushed, his freckles had disappeared into the red. It had all happened in less than a minute.

Tim Pat said, "Get up and I'll knock you down again."

Tiger stayed down. Other kids, all colors of kids, felt Tim Pat's victory as their own, envied his scraped knuckles and swollen eye. Twenty-
plus high-fives, even from girls. Tim Pat was on his toes. He was King of
the Swings.

Other kids had lost lunches to Tiger, and two of the bigger boys
stepped in for their own revenge. They tried to kick him, but he managed to scuttle away. Dan and Earl saw it and raced over to shove the
kickers away. Tiger slumped onto his side. Tears streaked his cheeks.
Earl herded all the kids toward school.

Earl said, "Go on, now, or I'll tell Sister."

That was enough, and the crowd broke up. Tiger had never been so
glad to see grown-ups.

"Where'd you come from, Grampa?" Tim Pat asked.

Dan pointed. "Earl's van."

"Didja see me, Earl, didja?"

Earl said, "Boy, you made me proud to know the White Fox."

Tim Pat said, "You see my fast hands, Grampa? I didn't get tired one bit."

"You're the best, Timmy."

Dan nodded over to the van and Earl nodded back. He guided Tim Pat back to it and both got inside. Tim Pat was suddenly aware of his swollen left hand.

"I forgot and hit him in his head bone, Earl."

Earl patted him. "Now you know why fighters wear gloves."

"Did I really do it okay, Earl, did I?"

"Damn straight ya did," said Earl.

Dan helped Tiger up and wiped his face with a clean cloth from the van. The boy tried to keep from sobbing, but was unable to quiet his heart.

Dan picked up Tim Pat's split brown bag, wrapped the cloth around it, and turned back to Tiger. The kid was staring at the bag.

"You want this?" Dan asked quietly.

Tiger nodded, but didn't speak. Dan handed Tim Pat's lunch to him. Tiger looked inside.

"Why have you been takin these little kids' lunches, son?" Dan asked.

Tiger looked up, didn't blink. " 'Cause'm hungry."

Dan returned to the van. He had no feeling of victory, and knew Earl felt the same. At least Tim Pat had slain a dragon, and the odds were that he wouldn't have to fight to keep what was his anymore. Dan used Earl's car phone to call Sister at school. He told her the story. She was silent throughout.

When Dan finished, Sister said, "Sometimes that's what it takes. Our Lord told us to turn the other cheek—but we only have two."

Dan said, "I'm goin to put ice on my little guy, Sister, and if it's all right, I'd like to give him the day off."

"He deserves it," Sister said.

Earl drove back to the shop and Dan iced Tim Pat's hand and eye. The cut wasn't big enough to be a problem but would leave a little scar Tim Pat would be proud of.

"I whupped him, Earl. He ain't takin my lunch no more—ever."

Earl said, "Ain't nothin like winnin, baby."

Tim Pat asked, "Was I really good, Grampa?"

"Like a champ!"

Looking back, Dan thought, oh so many times, that it should have stopped there. But he was a trainer; he had a fighter to bring along. It was Tim (as he now insisted on being called, except by Earl and Dan) who said he wanted to fight in the next "kids' tournament."

The idea scared Dan, but it also pleased him.

"What do you think, Earl?" Dan asked.

Earl turned and looked at Tim Pat. "It's a hard row to hoe, boy."

"Not for me, Earl," Tim said. "You and Grampa are gonna train me, and we're all goin to the top."

Next day, ropes were whapping, bags were banging in the gym. The lights were up and the three-minute/one-minute timer was on. A dozen pro and amateur fighters were training. Five trainers, at one time or another, were yelling at them, either from outside the ropes during sparring sessions, or off in a corner trying to convert bad moves into good.

Tim Pat had warmed up and was sweating. His gloves were laced, and he was up on the balls of his feet. Earl fed off the kid's energy, and began to feel like a pup himself. He pulled the rolling chair over, slipped his hands into the punch mitts. Other fighters stopped to watch, some to smile. Many wished they had Earl in their corner. He called shots to Tim Pat, and the kid fired them nonstop.

"Jab. Jab. Double up. Do it again. Gimme three jabs. Jab. Three more. One-two. One-two. Three jabs. Again. Double up. Jab. One-two-hook."

Tim Pat got the one-two off, his shots quick and crisp, but he missed cranking the hook because his balance was off.

"Damn!"

"Don't cuss. Jab. Jab. Two of 'em. Jab. Three, do it quick, *bang-bang-bang*. Two more. Two of 'em."

Tim Pat's left shoulder was on fire.

"One-two-hook!"

Tim Pat missed the end of the combination again. He said, "What's wrong with me, Earl?"

Earl said, "Not a thing. Hooks is a bitch."

Tim Pat said, "You cussed."

Earl said, "I'm sorry, I won't do it again. Jab."

Tim Pat jabbed until his left arm began to droop. He looked quizzically at his glove, then moved off to the side before dropping it. Earl liked seeing Tim Pat move out of range before dropping his guard.

Earl said, "Don't worry about it, even small gloves are heavy for your size."

Tim Pat said, "How about me throwin a lead hook, Earl?"

"Too soon. Lead hook comes once you got the regular hook right. When you get it, the lead hook'll be easy."

"Hooks're hard, Earl."

"Jab."

Earl would stay away from the hook, let Tim Pat forget about it, would slip it in when Tim Pat wasn't ready for it. He kept the kid jabbing and throwing the right.

"Jab, jab, one-two!" Earl stopped at the bell and said, "Like your granddaddy says, be slick. Set the man up. Make him think right, then you go left."

Tim Pat said, "I got all that in my head, but I still can't throw the hook."

Earl said, "Watch. Bring the hook off the one-two, or off the jab, like this."

"That's pretty, Earl."

Earl had Tim Pat demonstrate the move in front of the mirror in slow motion. He got it right, and Earl had him do it faster. Tim Pat got it right again.

"Was I pretty?"

"Like a hummin bird," Earl said. "Now be pretty on the mitts for me. Set your guy up. Jab or throw one-twos, or mix your punches up, go to the body until he starts droppin his hands, or he oversteers on your head shots and brings both gloves in tight to protect that nose you been workin on. Let him think he's safe behind his hands and keep firin your shots into his gloves. He'll blink from the noise, if nothin else, okay? But once you got him thinking he's safe from the one-two, and he peeks out, that's when you throw it again quick as you can, *bing-bing,* and right then's when you unload that hook. You got to think it right to get it right, okay?"

"I got it."

Earl knew that Tim Pat would be in buzz-saw fights where the little guys flurried in one-minute rounds bell to bell. There were few knock-downs, and except for a rare nosebleed, nobody got hurt. He didn't ex-pect a boxing match out of Tim Pat, but he hoped that the kid could get off a few properly thrown punches in the upcoming competition.

Earl went back to the jab. "Let's go. Jab. Jab. Double up on him. Do it again. Jab, jab to the body. Jab to the head. Double up. Double up. One-two-*hook!*"

Tim Pat fired the one-two, *bing-bang!,* rocked back for balance and leverage, and *BOOM!*

Earl plopped to the floor as if knocked out, as so many had been, by the Brown Bomber himself, Joe Louis. Tim Pat threw both arms in the air.

"Yeow!" Earl whooped. "My baby boy!"

Chapter 4

It was six-fifteen on Saturday morning. Tim Pat had won his first fight the night before, in Carson.

Dan and Tim Pat were headed back to Carson. They made it in five minutes from home to the on-ramp at Melrose and Normandie, where they picked up the Hollywood Freeway heading downtown, then onto the 110 Freeway, and headed south. Dan was still sleepy, and had been so excited by Tim Pat's win that he'd been unable to sleep until three A.M. Tim Pat had already been out when Dan kissed him good night, but now the kid was wide awake. Every few minutes he proudly touched the slight abrasion at the side of his neck.

The 110 Freeway was nearly empty. Grandfather and grandson quickly moved past the coliseum, built as the Olympic Auditorium for the 1932 Olympics. Soon they went through South Central, and were heading to the 110-405 Interchange south of Gardena. Dan would swing the pickup east on the 405, and head for the industrial town of Carson. A three-day Silver Gloves Tournament for kids eight through fifteen was being held at the Carson American Legion Hall. The weigh-in was at seven A.M., and Tim Pat was scheduled to fight his second fight of the tournament at eleven. Like all boxers, Tim Pat had to make weight or he wouldn't be allowed to fight. Neither had eaten breakfast.

Dan and Earl had both worked Tim Pat's corner the night before, had been as serious as if the kid was fighting for a professional title. Because the shop was open a half day on Saturdays, Dan would work Tim Pat's second fight alone. Dan and Earl alternated, and it was Earl's Saturday to work. Dan had thought about closing the shop down so Earl could be there for Tim Pat's second fight, but Earl reminded him that they had customers coming in to pick up their cars.

Earl said, "The way the White Fox won last night, we'll all be there for trophy time on Sunday."

Tim Pat had gained nine pounds since he fought Tiger, and had grown two inches.

"We just might have us a classy white-boy heavyweight," Earl said, smiling.

Dan said, "His daddy sure was big and fast."

"Tim could be the one, Dan." He slipped into a black-folks accent. "White folks so hongry for a white heavyweight they like a welfare nigga wit a tapeworm."

Dan laughed, but the idea tasted good. "Wouldn't that be somethin after all these years?"

The night before, Dan and Earl had dressed Tim Pat in shiny gold trunks, a Kelly green top, calf-high white boxing shoes, and headgear that Earl had spray-painted a brilliant gold. Tim Pat fought novice. Kids in that division fought one-minute rounds, and most flapped and raged around like banty roosters. Dan touched his eye often, was so nervous he had to ask Earl to wrap Tim Pat's hands and to lace his gloves and tape the laces on his boxing shoes.

Dan got Earl off to the side. "You talk to him, my mouth's too dry."

Once Tim Pat was warmed up, Earl spoke quietly to him. "He's gonna come in like a windmill, okay? All little guys are like that when they first start."

Tim Pat said, "Not me, right, Earl?"

"That's right, Tim," Earl said, "not you, you're too smart. So instead of you backing up when he comes, you step to him, okay? Move inside his wide stuff, jab to his chest and neck, double up when you stick, forget about his head at first."

Tim Pat said, "Now he's tired."

Earl nodded. "Now he's tired because you made him tire himself out, right?"

"Right."

Earl said, "This is when you set him up with the jab and begin to fire your one-two at his head. You can even shoot the one-two and drop your hook on him if you think you got the shot." Earl made the move. "One-two-hook! *Bing!*, and then move outta there behind your jab."

Tim Pat made the same move so pretty that Dan had to turn away, had to rub his wet eyes with the backs of his wrists.

Earl said, "You won't forget, now?"

"I won't forget," said Tim Pat.

"You sure?" Dan asked.

"No way, Grampa."

Dan hugged the kid. This was the same little guy who, at bedtime, would hustle Dan to read *Winnie-the-Pooh*. Dan was an expert on grumpy donkeys and little bears who love honey. But now Tim Pat was eleven— and he was a fighter.

Tim Pat won by a unanimous decision in three rounds. He flurried like the other little guy, but he also got in some good shots. He missed with his hook, but Dan knew that hooks were a question of time and opportunity, and that Tim Pat had plenty of time ahead of him. Resting while Tim Pat changed into gray sweats afterward, Dan felt like he'd just gone fifteen rounds with Roberto Duran.

Dan could see their off-ramp up ahead. Carson was just off the San Diego Freeway, near oil refineries, and not far from L.A. Harbor and San Pedro, where Dan had grown up. Carson was a working-class town made up of whites, blacks, Asians, and Latinos, but there was a large Samoan community there as well. Many of the Samoans playing college football or in the NFL came from Carson. Tim Pat had been the only white boy in the tournament the night before. The other trainers with boys in Tim Pat's weight class thought he would be a *palomita blanca*, a little white dove. They didn't know how he'd handled Tiger, didn't know about all the months he'd worked hard with Dan and Earl, didn't know that Tim Pat was the White Fox.

The Friday-night crowd, mostly Latinos, with a scattering of blacks, was stunned by the little white boy's showing, the *gabachito*. It meant he'd fight the next day in the semi. If he won that, he'd fight Sunday for the first-place trophy. Men with beer guts and creased, brown faces smiled at the little *gabacho* as he and his trainers headed back to the dressing room. Balls counted, but so did skill. One of them called him *raza*.

Another said, *"Este chico sabe nadar y no mojar su ropa."* This little guy could go swimming and not get his clothes wet.

On Saturday morning, Tim Pat made weight, then Dan drove to a waterfront café in San Pedro that had served fishermen and lobster poachers since the thirties. Dan carbed up the kid, fed him S.O.S. on wheat toast, sliced tomatoes for potassium, a big glass of milk, and a piece of freshly baked berry pie with vanilla ice cream melting on top. Tim Pat cleaned his plate, sat back like a satisfied cat.

The waitress was a trooper, had a tobacco-and-coffee smile. "That's one heck of a little man you got there."

Tim Pat said, "I'm a fighter."

The waitress, Marleen, said, "You keep eatin like that, you'll be a world champ."

Tim Pat said, "This is my grampa. Him and me and Earl are goin to the top."

To pass time until nine-thirty, when they had to check in and get ready, Dan drove through his old neighborhood, though not much of it was left. He told Tim Pat about the hard times of his great-grandparents in Ireland. Tim Pat asked about his own mother and father, and Dan talked on, said that Mary Cat had been the prettiest and the smartest girl in school, told how Tim Pat's father, Eamon, had been a great defensive back in college.

Tim Pat said, "I fought last night's fight for you and Earl, Grampa. Today I'm fightin it for my mom and dad."

"You do that, laddie."

Dan wrapped and taped Tim Pat's hands and gloved him, buckled the strap of his headgear under his chin. Earlier, he'd also had the kid shadowbox and hit the punch mitts, made sure the little guy was warmed up. The kid had begun to sweat and appeared primed to fight. Tim Pat saw his shadowy opponent standing in the doorway of the opposite dressing room and suddenly his mouth went dry. He began to shiver despite the sweat. Gone was the confident little battler on the freeway, the one who sat forward on the seat and bounced with anticipation.

Dan had seen it before. You never knew when the cotton mouth or the empty ass would hit you. Fighters with twenty-five fights would sometimes have to take a scare pee after they'd been gloved and were already making their way to the ring. When it happened, Dan would pull a quick U-turn at ringside and run the boy back to the dressing room. He'd have to pull the boy's shorts and cup down, then aim his shriveled dick so he wouldn't piss on his shoes.

Tim Pat's opponent was a handsome little Mexican kid. He weighed the same seventy-five pounds as Tim Pat with his recent weight gain. The other kid was shorter and wider in the shoulders, and he stomped and banged his gloves in the far corner. *Cholos,* Mexican-Americans at ringside, made it two to one for the Mexican over the *palomita.* Old-timers who'd seen the *palomita* fight the night before took the wager. Fifty-dollar bets were not uncommon. Women with children were chosen to hold the bets, and they would collect a quick five dollars from the winners for guarding the loot.

Dan saw Tim Pat's eyes scurry. He cautioned, "When the ref calls you to the center of the ring for instructions, your guy'll try to stare you down."

"Why?"

"It's like Tiger. To give you the loose ass, to make you blink."

"Will I blink?"

"Hell, no," Dan said. "When he locks eyes, you lock right back. But while he's starin straight into your eyes, you're gonna look at the strip of skin just below his eyebrows and above his eyeballs. Keep starin at that eyelid skin. He won't be able to tell where you're starin. He'll be the one with the dry eye. When he blinks first, he'll start thinkin he's the pussy, not you. Got it?"

"Yeah, I do."

The ref waved Tim Pat and his opponent to the center of the ring. The stare-down began. Tim Pat followed Dan's instructions. The Mexican kid blinked.

Tim Pat said, "Pussy."

The Mexican kid flushed. *"Tu madre."*

The ref said, "No talking or I take points."

The Mexican kid, now pissed, which was just what Dan wanted, came out winging shots, tried to drive Tim Pat back. Tim Pat surprised him. He shoved off on that right toe and drove left jabs into his chest and neck. The other boy stumbled back. In the second round, Tim Pat stepped in with more lefts and a few straight rights, most of which connected. The other kid could not get set, was always on his heels. In the third, Tim Pat repeatedly landed with the one-two combination. Near the end of the round, he followed the one-two with his hook, *Boom!,* landed it flush on the other kid's chin, the hook as pure and tart and sweet as lemon pie.

The other little boy stumbled back again, hurt this time, but wouldn't go down. Tim Pat stalked him. The boy, still dazed, was unable to defend himself, but still wouldn't quit. The ref stepped in, pointed Tim Pat to the farthest corner. The ref turned to look at the hurt kid's eyes, then waved his hands to signal that he was stopping the fight. Tim Pat whooped and strutted and Dan had to calm him down, whispered to him to go congratulate the other kid for a good fight. By now, the fight over, the kids touched gloves and smiled. The outside corner of Tim Pat's left eye was pink and would swell slightly.

. Dan quickly removed Tim Pat's gloves and took his mouthpiece. The ref motioned both boys to the center of the ring. The announcer from ringside called Tim Pat's name as the winner, and the ref raised the *palomita*'s wrapped hand in victory. The crowd, winners and losers, stood to cheer him. Flashbulbs went off. One of the tournament officials, an old friend of Dan, congratulated him ringside.

The official said, "I got a good shot of him with his hand raised. I'll send you an eight-by-ten."

"Yeah, and here I was hopin for only a little one!" Dan said. He reached for his pocket. "Let me cover it."

"Naw, don't worry about it."

Dan said, "Thanks. Will you be here for the finals tomorrow?"

The official said, "I wouldn't miss it for the world."

It was close to one o'clock by the time Dan got back on the Harbor Freeway and headed home. Earl would hoot when he heard about Tim Pat's hook. The little boy squirmed in his sweat suit, Dan's precaution against catching a cold. It was Tim Pat's first time to warm down. It felt good.

Dan touched his grandson's hair. "You hungry?"

"No, but I'm still thirsty."

Dan pulled off the freeway at Rosecrans, where he drove to a minimart. "What do you want?"

Tim Pat said, "How about one of those lemon-lime frozen juice bars like I get from the ice-cream truck that comes by the gym?"

Lupe Ayala had parked the clinic's van at the rear of the horse corrals of the Santa Cruz Sports Arena. Lupe was on a field trip with five of her students, six- and eight-year-old deaf kids from the Boyle Heights Clinic for the Deaf, the CFD on Whittier Boulevard, near Euclid. Though not yet seventeen, she'd already been teaching part-time at the clinic for two years. This visit to the corrals was one she'd wanted to share with the children from the beginning, and finally getting her driver's license made it possible. The arena was a little over twenty miles east of Boyle Heights, located near the marshy Whittier Narrows in Pico Rivera, and close to the intersection of the 60 and the 605, the Pomona and the San Gabriel Freeways. Her driver's license permitted her to transport young passengers, and she usually dropped kids off at home after giving signing lessons, or following other events closer to the clinic. This was the farthest from the clinic Lupe had been allowed to drive the kids, and she felt honored by the trust placed in her.

The arena was a privately owned horse facility, but concerts and boxing matches were often held there as well. It was built like a *rancho del charro*, a scaled-down version of a bullring, but with one section open that led to the corrals, and it served mostly for *charreadas*, or Mexican-style rodeos. Horses were roped and bulls were ridden, and during breaks in the action, decked-out mariachi musicians outfitted in *trajes de gala* played trumpets and violins. Behind the brightly painted red and yellow structure, a long line of steel pylons ran south along the 605. Crackling high-voltage lines were strung between them. Puddles and pools of the shallow San Gabriel River stagnated beneath the pops and sizzles. Reeds and weeds and squat trees grew along the river's cement banks. Minnows and pollywogs flourished.

Riders and stable hands allowed the children to examine the saddlery, to touch the horses' big chests, to stroke their tender noses. The children had never seen or smelled a live horse, much less stalls and corrals full of them, and the kids' little fingers danced with excitement and awe as they signed to each other and played cowboys and Indians beneath corrugated roofs and turned the tubular metal fences into monkey bars.

Outside the arena were well-tended lawns, shade trees, and picnic areas. On the weekends, Mexican vendors stretched their stalls along narrow, curving streets to display everything from serapes to plumbing supplies.

Inside the corrals, Lupe wore boots and jeans, and taught her kids to feed and water the animals. Many of them were scrawny hacks and nags that were mercilessly knocked down during the arena's weekly rodeos. But there were glistening pintos and curried palominos as well, and big muscular bays and dark chestnuts that twitched and shone in the sunlight. Nearly all had owners who were too busy to groom them. Lupe paid for her riding lessons by grooming such horses there. And, riding sidesaddle in full, ruffled *Adelita* costume, she also appeared at the weekly shows, and broke hearts every time she did.

Lupe, the nickname for Guadalupe, as in *nuestra* Señora de Guadalupe, our Lady of Guadalupe, was just budding into womanhood. She wore her lustrous black hair in a *trenza,* a long, thick braid laced with colored ribbons that complimented her aristocratic features and hooked, Indian nose, her dark skin and almond-shaped eyes. She was a looker, moved with grace and assurance, had her daddy's straight white teeth.

Lupe lived with her mother, the widow Soledad Ayala, and Lupe's younger brother, Jesse. Mrs. Ayala's mother, Rosario, had been a seamstress in Guadalajara. She'd made the tiny white dresses for little girls receiving their first Holy Communion, and the "grown-up" gowns for fifteen-year-old girls celebrating their *quinceañera* rite of passage into adulthood. But Rosario had also specialized in ruffled riding dresses, and the traditional Mexican *charro trajes de gala* for men and women—the studded jackets and tight pants or long skirts—all worn with white shirts and floppy bow ties big as two hands, the fingers laced. They wore their moon-size sombreros like crowns above their dark faces.

Soledad had learned the trade from Rosario as a little girl in Mexico. From her home in Los Angeles, she produced the same Holy Communion and *quinceañera* dresses, but there was not much demand for the rest. She also worked full-time as a coffee-shop waitress at a major downtown hotel that catered to tourists, working the morning shift so she could be home when her kids got there from school and could be with them at night. She had good benefits from the hotel and made good money, including her tips, but supporting two kids alone, even on the "eastside" was tough. Living without her husband was tougher still.

Soledad daily served *gabacho* girls Lupe's age, observed how the white girls dressed and behaved, heard how dirty and rudely they talked, saw how many were pregnant but without wedding rings. *Airheads,* the whites had it right, thought Mrs. Ayala. Not her daughter. She didn't allow Lupe out with boys after nine o'clock, and then only when her deaf younger brother went along as a chaperone. Once word got out in the barrio, Lupe wasn't asked out much, but it wasn't because the boys didn't have their eyes on her. Mrs. Ayala's rules were unbendable, had to be. Lupe would sometimes sulk, would argue that the other girls got to stay out until midnight, even later.

Mrs. Ayala had lost too much of her family to risk losing her daughter, too. "As long as you live in my house, you will be a lady. You will not be like these little *putas* who give love away like it was a penny, little tramps who behave like boys between the legs, and have all of the disadvantages and none of the advantages of being real whores. Besides, I have to get up before *la madrugada,* before *dawn,* and I'm not losing sleep so you can be just another East Al-*Lay chola.*"

Lupe would make faces and huff, but underneath she depended on her mother, knew she needed her tough wisdom, loved her for being strict. And Mrs. Ayala knew that she'd better raise the girl right, or her beautiful husband, Jaime, her sweet Jimmy, would be waiting for her in heaven to divorce her, maybe worse, maybe slit her lazy throat. She wouldn't blame him.

———

All of Lupe's kids from the clinic were Chicanos, boys and girls; two were chubby, all but one was short compared to most white kids the same age. All signed quick as the wind because Lupe was their teacher, and they were inspired to learn because Lupe wanted so badly for them to learn. She herself had begun to sign as a child when her younger brother, Jesse, at six, lost his hearing because of a severe case of mumps.

Now twelve, Jesse had started at the CFD four years earlier, when Lupe was almost thirteen. In the process of helping her mother and brother learn to sign, Lupe became deeply involved in the world of the deaf. She took advanced courses in high school, and planned to study audiology and speech pathology in college. She worked part-time at the clinic, and attended seminars at the various facilities throughout the Los Angeles area. Her grades were excellent, and she was sure to get scholarship offers from the various Cal state universities to which she would apply. Her life was good, but it was also hard. When she grew weary, she drew strength from the little children, born forever trapped in silence, who struggled so bravely to learn to speak with their hands, who worked so hard to develop skills that others often squandered.

Aside from loving the horses, Lupe liked the arena because she could show what a good horsewoman she was. She could also flirt. She liked the way some of the older riders looked at her, how some tried to plant a little kiss on her neck. She liked *piropos,* too, the respectful ones, flirty compliments made in Spanish while a young man might clutch his heart tragically—¡Ay-yai-yai, no me dejes así morenísima de mi alma!—Oh, don't leave me like this, darkest beauty of my soul!

She would, of course, continue on her way, giving no sign that she'd heard, or that she was flattered, but she'd heard, all right, and was flattered. The *piropos* were said in fun and mostly by boys and young men who had known her as a little girl—and knew the great sadness that clutched at the heart of Lupe's family.

Chapter 5

Dan and Tim Pat passed through the heavy downtown traffic, then switched from the Harbor to the Hollywood Freeway. Traffic was still heavy, but the Melrose-Normandie exit wasn't far.

Tim Pat said, "I sweated up good, didn't I, Grampa?"

"You sure did."

Lupe and Jesse and Billy Tucker were also in heavy traffic, and Lupe drove extra carefully, not being accustomed to this part of the Hollywood Freeway. Billy had drawn a map, but Lupe checked it against the Thomas Guide, a book of street maps of Los Angeles County.

Billy signed that the Cahuenga exit was just ahead. As Lupe merged right, faster drivers honked at her, made her wish she was closer to home. Once at the exit, Lupe turned right, then headed south on Cahuenga. Dan's house was located some four miles down the way. Lupe ran into some traffic on Cahuenga, but there was virtually none on the residential side streets.

Lupe had to stop for lights at Hollywood and at Sunset Boulevards, but made it through Santa Monica Boulevard. Billy directed her to keep going south.

Dan and Tim Pat proceeded west from the Melrose-Normandie exit, turned right at the corner of Melrose and Wilcox, then headed north a half block. Dan parked under the splayed old eucalyptus tree in front of the gym. Most of the fighters had already finished up. Tim Pat raced inside and leaped into Earl's arms.

Earl said, "Lord a mercy, I been attacked by a grizzly fox!" Earl saw Dan's smile, saw his victory nod. Earl pretended to be a ring announcer, held a water bottle up to his mouth for a mike. "In this cawnah, fightin outta da Hard Knocks Gym in Hollywood, Califahnya; weighin in at two hundred an' toity-tree an' tree-quahtah pounds; wit a record of fifty-seven wins an' no losses, an' fifty-seven KOs; known troo-out da world as da White Fahx!; ladies'n'gen'lemen, da heavyweight *champ*ion of da worl! TimateeeePat-rickMahkey!, Mahkey!"

Earl made the roaring sound of a crowd, then tickled Tim Pat's ribs; he gave the kid a big kiss on his swollen left eye, and hugged him again. Momolo, who worked in the shop and was being trained as a fighter by Earl, came over to shake Tim Pat's hand gently and ruffle his hair. Momolo was a young middleweight from Liberia with miniature tribal scars across his shoulders and around his face. The name on the African's passport was Covenant Buchanan, Momolo his tribal name.

"You are a warrior," Momolo said.

His teeth were white and perfect, and his body had the incredible muscular definition of many West Africans. Earl liked to use the name Momolo instead of his given Christian name, Covenant, because of the African sound to it. Dan also liked the fact that Momolo had a Scots last name. Once they had seen how dedicated Momolo was in the gym, Earl and Dan gave him a job in the shop, where he'd proved equally conscientious. Besides, Dan liked the way Momolo talked.

"A warrior," Momolo repeated.

Tim Pat relived the fight. "I set him up, Momolo, made sure my feet were right, and then I went in there and I got 'im." He turned to Earl.

"But I missed you in my corner, Earl. I told our waitress about you and me and Grampa."

Earl said, "I'm proud of you, Tim, and I'll be in your corner tomorrow when you win that trophy."

"Last night I fought for you and Grampa, Earl. Today, I fought for my mom and dad. Tomorrow, I'm fighting for Grandma," Tim Pat told them.

Earl said, "Ain't nobody better."

Dan turned away, swallowed hard, and then turned back to the kid. "Show Earl that hook."

Tim Pat pranced up to a big bag, fired a one-two and came zinging back with the left hook. *Bang!* Tim Pat threw both hands in the air, did a champion's skipping jig.

Earl looked at the boy from Liberia. "See that? Now let's see you do it."

Earl held the mitts, but Momolo's hook was an arm punch. It was thrown with his weight on his front foot instead of the back. It was a hard shot because Momolo was so strong, but it was still an arm punch, which meant he was working too hard and would tire before his opponent. The hope was that he would learn, and that once he had it, it would feel so good that he would always have it.

Dan saw it. "He's not switching his weight."

Earl said, "That's what I figured, but I can't watch his hands and feet at the same time and maybe get hit. You show him."

Dan took the mitts, lined the African's feet up.

Billy Tucker directed Lupe past Santa Monica Boulevard. He signed for her to turn right at Willoughby, and signed again for her to go two blocks west, to Wilcox. At the Wilcox intersection, he signed for her to turn left and to park at the second house on the right. As Lupe pulled over, a candy-striped pink-and-white ice-cream truck passed her on the left as it headed south toward Melrose, the truck's loudspeaker blaring its signature invitation to kids, "Mary Had a Little Lamb." What Lupe couldn't know was that the ice-cream truck's usual route was from Melrose north, not south, that it should have passed an hour ago.

> *Mary had a little lamb, little lamb, little lamb,*
> *Mary had a little lamb, its fleece was white as snow.*

Momolo couldn't get the hook. "It is most difficult, this move. Is it so for all?"

"It is like a Ferrari," Dan said, mimicking Momolo's formal way of speaking. "If they were effortless to obtain, everyone would have one."

Momolo and Earl slapped their thighs and squealed with laughter.

Dan laughed with them. "Now we try it the other way around. Watch me. Instead of movin *forward* a step, this time I want you to go *back*. Push off your left toe, like me, see? But you gotta move both feet back the same short step, same as when you move forward. As you take the step, turn your hip like this. As your hip begins to turn, see it? As your hip begins to turn, *then* let the shot go. *Whip!*"

Momolo listened, moved slow as a sleepy snake until he felt it. He nodded and smiled that big smile. He executed at the speed of light, and *Boom!,* it was the best hook Momolo had ever thrown.

Dan said, "Now all we gotta do is get you to do it goin forward."

"Mr. Cooley, sir, I am indebted to you."

Momolo practiced moving backward and forward until he no longer had to think about his feet. Now the shots came like a drum out of Africa.

Mary had a little lamb . . .

The music came faintly into the gym, then grew louder. Tim Pat had heard it hundreds of times—at home on Cahuenga, and here at the gym. He was still thirsty, the fight having drained him of fluid and energy. Dan would feed him soon, and then send him off for a nap.

Tim Pat said, "Grampa, can I get another lemon-lime from the ice-cream man?"

Dan gave Tim Pat a five-dollar bill. "Here. But be careful when you cross the street, and don't forget the change."

"I won't."

"Then we head for home and some sack time. I want more ice on that eye."

Lupe delivered Billy Tucker to his mother, checked the van's rearview mirrors for cars, saw no one, and then edged carefully away from the curb. Down the way, she would pass the parking lot of the Department of Motor Vehicles, on the corner of Waring. Melrose was just a short block farther. She slowed from twenty-five to twenty at Waring, checking both ways for cars, then continued on at twenty. She'd noticed that the pink-and-white ice-cream truck had pulled to the right halfway down to Melrose, but her immediate focus had been on checking Waring for cars. Lupe felt happy. She'd soon be back on the Hollywood Freeway, and into familiar parts of Al-*Lay*. Her horses were less than an hour away. Thinking of them, she had to smile, could see Bobby and Tessie waving their heads for carrots. *Relámpago*, Lightning, would be sulking because she'd taken so long to get there. He'd make up once he got his carrot. Lupe smiled again.

As she neared the ice-cream truck, she checked her rearview mirrors again, slowed to fifteen miles per hour, and signaled to anyone who might come from behind that she'd be passing the pink-and-white truck.

Tim Pat held his change in his left hand. He was intent on getting at his juice bar, and tugged at its plastic wrapper with his teeth. The loud music was still playing. A young Hispanic mother with a toddler arrived to place her order with the driver. She noticed Tim Pat almost drop his lemon-lime bar when the wrapper tore loose. She would later testify that she saw Tim Pat bobble the juice bar, drop his change, and then stumble forward from behind the blind side of the truck, directly in front of Lupe's oncoming van.

Lupe hit him before she could get her foot from the gas to the brake, saw him fly into the air and hit the curb in front of the ice-cream truck. Even though she was driving slowly, it's one of the laws of physics: $F = MV$. The inertial force of an object is determined by the mass or weight of the object and the velocity at which the object moves. Lupe's van had a lot more mass than Tim Pat—and the velocity was just enough. She stopped immediately, placed both hands over her mouth, got out of the car, and ran over to Tim Pat. As she knelt down, the driver of the ice-cream truck turned off the music and sped away.

The lemon-lime bar remained whole, but had started to melt on the hot concrete, the gravel and pebbles of the old street showing through its chinked and sun-bleached cement. Dan's coins had rolled to one side, the bills were scattering.

Lupe screamed when she saw the impossible, skewed angle of the motionless boy's neck and the blood spreading in a widening pool from the back of his head. His eyes were wide open, filled with an expression of surprise. She didn't have to touch his body to feel for a pulse. The child was dead; she had killed him. She sobbed and she lost her breath, but she didn't feel the skin on her knees begin to tear as she knelt on the gritty street surface, bent over Tim Pat's body. She bent double, her head almost in the blood. She managed to sign to Jesse, who brought the clinic's cell phone from the van and kneeled silently down beside his sister.

"*Ay, Dios mío,*" Lupe said. Oh, my God.

Dan had heard the ice-cream music stop, waited for it to resume. He became curious when it didn't, then started for the street just in case.

Lupe dialed 911, her fingers stiff as chopsticks. She waited silently, hardly breathed, went more silent still. Neither she nor Jesse knew what else to do. When the operator answered after four rings, Lupe reported the accident and the address and the body. The operator took her information, then instructed her to remain at the scene. Lupe made the sign of the cross. Tears streaming down her face, she began to sign to Jesse what the operator had said.

Dan saw the little body instantly, saw it as if down a tunnel of whitest light. Shock hit him and a crushing weight pushed down on his chest as his heart rate soared. He felt himself go crazy, felt his feet flop on the pavement as he raced to the motionless figure. He slid to his knees, shoved Lupe and Jesse aside. He cradled Tim Pat.

Earl heard Dan's howl. He ran to the street. Dan was hunched over his grandson. His body was rigid, drops of Tim Pat's blood on Dan's lips. Dan looked again at his baby boy.

"I shouldda gone with him! Jesusjesusjesus!" Dan was sobbing.

"Dan, he's been buyin from the truck by himself for two years," Earl reminded him.

"I shouldda been with him."

But Dan hadn't, and now the last candle in his life had been snuffed out. Like some benumbed mother ape, Dan tried to shake life back into Tim Pat's little body. But Tim Pat was dead and that was it. Two lifeless eyes looked out at him, the dull film of death already starting to form across them. Dan tried to kiss Tim Pat again. His lips wouldn't move.

Earl bent down. He tried to get Dan to stand, wanted to get Dan someplace where he couldn't see what was on the ground. But Dan would always see what was there, would see it in flashes of morning light off of plate-glass windows, would see it in the pale faces of heart and cancer patients waiting to die, would see it in the astonished eyes of stroke victims at the hospital where Brigid had been treated. Tim's broken and bleeding body was the image he'd see in every red sunset, in every blood moon.

Earl saw Dan's eyes. Nothing was in there. Earl thought of Brendan, of Terrance, of Mary Cat, of Brigid, and now Tim Pat. He looked into Dan's eyes again. The brightness of life, the flame of the human pilot light, was burning dangerously low.

Earl said, "C'mon, Dan, c'mon, baby, here, lemme help you up."

"I'm fine here."

Earl saw Lupe clutching her cell phone. "You call 911?" he asked.

She nodded, then looked over at Dan. She saw the blood on him. "Is this little boy his?"

"Yes."

"I'm sorry. I was going slowly. I can't even say how sorry I am. I haven't words in English or Spanish, but I am dead inside. Please ask him to forgive me."

One siren first, then two more, the high sounds coming from two directions. The police units came down Wilcox, the ambulance headed up from Melrose. Jesse's face had gone gray. He began, soundlessly, to cry again. Lupe hadn't stopped. She signed to her brother as Dan glanced over.

It was an accident. The police will help.

Dan saw Lupe and Jesse clearly for the first time, saw their dark skin and realized they were Latinos. That didn't register, neither plus nor minus. But when he saw them signing, he thought they were throwing gang signs, and he went wild.

Dan looked up to Earl and wiggled his fingers. "What's this all about?"

Earl said, "I don't know."

"I do know," Dan said.

As the paramedics and police officers came up, Dan lowered Tim Pat and got to his feet. An officer said, "Sir?," but Dan didn't notice. He shoved past the officer, then swooped in on Lupe and began to choke her, lifted her in the air by her throat before the police could react. Earl pulled Dan off and wrapped his arms around him. Dan didn't struggle, but his body trembled with rage. He hissed.

"I'll kill her, Earl, I'll kill the little spic, and fuck the Fifth Commandment in the ass."

"Naw, baby," said Earl. "Don't be talkin that killin business."

"Christ is Satan, the son of a kike whore."

Dan gagged, nausea rising, pain flooding his chest. His hand went to his battered eye. He tried to die, but couldn't.

Chapter 6

Eduardo "Chicky" Garza y Duffy was five-ten, and, by the time he was seventeen, weighed in at 149, two pounds over his fighting weight. He was tall for a welter, and was sure to grow at least into a junior middleweight at 154, maybe even a solid middleweight at 160. Only a few Mexican fighters were that tall, and nearly all of those were raised in the U.S. From his mother, Rafaela, Chicky had inherited a light complexion, so you couldn't see the Mexican in him straight off.

Chicky was a nickname that had developed first from *chico,* and then *chiquito,* words meaning small and smaller still. The name stuck because he was small and sickly as a child. Because of his light complexion and green eyes, he was often taken for white, despite his dark hair. Even Mexicans would sometimes call him *güero,* a word used to describe light-skinned, or blond, people. Once he started fighting as a boy, some of the other kids called him Zurdito, Lefty, but that nickname never stuck. Being a southpaw had helped in the amateurs, confused other fighters when he boxed in ways they were unused to, but he preferred Chicky.

Garza y Duffy came from his grandpa Eloy's side of the family. The Duffy handle stemmed from way back, when immigrant Irish soldiers, abused under General Zachary Taylor's command during the Mexican-

American Wars, deserted to fight for Mexico. An annual parade is held in San Antonio to celebrate them. Many Mexicans proudly carry Irish blood.

Chicky didn't know who his father was. His mother wasn't sure, so she gave him her family name when he was born. All the kid knew was that he was Chicano, someone of Mexican descent born in the U.S., but he was also something else entirely: a Tex-Mex, a *pocho* Tejano, a Mexican *born* in Texas, and that was something to be especially proud of. Southside poverty and the slick talk of the lawless *vatos,* pronounced *bahtos*—the toughs of the project—quickly converted the little boy's gentleness into aggression and rebelliousness. Gang fights and *cuchillados* and *navajazos*, knife and razor wounds, were common and often fatal in the project. Jailhouse *pachuco* tattoos of a Christian cross located on the back of the hand between thumb and forefinger were commonplace. Chicky was caught riding a stolen bike. He was arrested, and a stern Tex-Mex judge named Herrera gave him a break because of his age, but promised him time in *el bote,* the can, should he see him in court again. The boy shrugged it off, thought of the slammer as a road to manhood and valor.

He was but a small package, and the darker-skinned kids teased him for his light skin, told him his father had to be a redneck GI from Kelly Air Force Base. Chicky refused to believe it. Some called him Whirlybird, and had to fight for that mistake. His resentment toward his mother, Rafaela, for his light complexion became so great that she knew she couldn't deflect it as long as he lived with her in the run-down Victoria Courts, temporary housing dating from the end of World War II. It was an anthill of danger and drugs and dirt where the *vatos* saw themselves as the baddest of the bad in San Anto, one of the long-standing Tex-Mex names for San Antonio.

Though Rafaela was far from an ideal mother, she feared the loss of her son to the prison system. She figured his only chance was for her to get him out of the project. She bundled his things up in a sheet one day and delivered him to her parents at their strawberry farm in Poteet. She said she was doing it for the boy. But her father, Eloy, also knew that she was doing it because of her part-time pimp, an over-the-road truck driver who aimed at increasing his income by taking her with him and working her at truck stops.

Chicky never saw her again. His respect and growing love for his grandparents, Eloy and Dolores, coupled with the responsibilities of the farm, would change him back into the decent child who at five had promised his mother to work hard and earn money and move them out of La Vica. Chicky could recall what she looked like only if he saw her photograph at an aunt's or uncle's house—there were no photos of her at the farm—but he was reminded of his time at La Vica whenever he heard of a stabbing or a drive-by shooting.

Amateur boxing would change the world for the scrawny little boy. His grandfather had been a fighter before he was a farmer, an amateur who turned pro and became known as el Lobo, the Wolf. Under Eloy's tutelage, the kid grew and got strong. He stopped wearing wife-beaters and baggy pants down to the crack of his ass, outfits designed by homeboys to trumpet their *cholo* toughness, their *valor mexicano*. Eloy had inherited fourth-generation Mexican-border poverty, but with the encouragement of his wise and hardworking parents, he had worked and boxed his way up through it, and he would not let it destroy his grandson.

Instead of turning to violence and drugs like so many other boys his age, Chicky, with his grandfather's encouragement, won several amateur competitions that were held for all kids of every background, ages eight to fifteen. From there he progressed to the open, or senior, ranks, and one wall of his room was gradually covered in trophies from every weight and age division he fought in. When Eloy told him that his green eyes and light skin came from the San Patricios side of the family, Chicky's shoulders relaxed for the first time since he was a little kid. He knew about the San Patricios from the parades.

"You mean I got the blood of those Irish men in me, the ones who fought for Mexico?"

"A huevo." Eloy grinned. "Just goes to show that the Irish will marry anybody."

By the time Chicky was almost sixteen, he'd already begun to take more responsibility for the farm. With his granddaddy always *pedo o crudo* from the booze, drunk or hungover, Chicky worried that some *gran chingadazo,* or enormous screwing, was on its way.

His grandmother Dolores had once attempted to make light of Eloy's alcoholism. She said that Eloy had swallowed the worm at the bottom of a *mezcal* bottle, and had to keep drinking so the worm wouldn't die. Realizing the depth of his grandmother's suffering, Chicky swore to her that he would never drink alcohol. That was tough in Texas, where roadies—ice-cold beer for the road—were as legal and common as bluebonnets. But despite offers from kids at school, girls as well as boys, Chicky had kept his promise.

After Dolores died in 1991, Eloy would get up sick every day, and pass out early. His foreman ran the farm for a couple of years, but got fed up and moved on. Chicky suddenly realized that he was his grandfather's caretaker and the boss of the farm. He took over as best he could, and he was glad to do it, but seeing pain in his grandfather was to suffer pain himself.

Eloy had his devils, but he was always protective of Chicky. The boy would not suffer the burnout so many youngsters experience when pushed too hard in any sport. Eloy would allow Chicky to train seriously only when upcoming tournaments were scheduled. Afterward, Eloy would lay the boy off for several months so Chicky could absorb what he had learned. Besides, there was football as well as other sports to play. But the kid was fascinated with boxing, wanted to be a fighter the way Travis, Bowie, and Crockett had wanted to hold out at the Alamo.

Since Chicky lived out in the country, this last year had been especially hard for him because he depended on Eloy to drive him to the gym. What he needed most was to spar. Without sparring, a fighter can't get sharp, can't become accustomed to pain, can't develop the speed and hand-eye coordination necessary to win. But now Eloy either sat around or slept. Chicky missed the workouts in their homemade gym, starting when he was brand new to the game. Eloy would talk strategy in his rough and funny way, and had even tried to get him to convert from southpaw to fighting orthodox, or right-handed. Eloy argued that fighting orthodox would give him the advantage of having a bigger left hook than most right-handed fighters. He also pointed out that right-handers, especially the pros, would do their best to "duck" southpaws, avoid them whenever they could, because facing left-handers was a handicap for most orthodox fighters.

"Come on, at least try it *huevón*," lazy big balls.

Chicky would laugh and try, but he felt better fighting as a left-hander. "I hit harder my natural way, Grandpa."

"That's because you don't practice at it."

The mischievous kid in Chicky would always stall the old man. He'd stumble purposely, or pretend he'd hurt his hand when he worked right-handed. "Maybe *mañana*," he'd tease, stretching the Spanish syllables.

"*Ay-yai-yai*," Eloy would say. "*Mañana* don't never come, you don't know that yet, *huevón?*

Chapter 7

C hicky and Eloy left the farm one afternoon in 1994 and drove to the San Ignacio Gym in San Antonio. Chicky operated tractors and trucks on the farm, but, at fifteen, was too young to legally drive roads and highways. As usual, he rode shotgun with his grandfather. The sun was bright as a white duck's bill, and he had to squint to see through the broken bugs and wings and yellow gut smears that nastied up the windshield.

Once they got to San Antonio, Eloy steered his pickup along Santa Rosa and into the San Ignacio parking lot at the corner of Travis. The Greyhound bus station and Crockett's barbecue were a couple of blocks east of the gym, the Cathedral of San Fernando a few blocks down from there.

"Made 'er," said Eloy.

Chicky softly closed and locked the passenger door of the truck, Fresita, Eloy's nickname for his pampered strawberry red 1981 Chevy pickup. "Fresita" was a play on the Spanish word for strawberry, *fresa.* His grandfather carefully locked his side. Chicky started for the nearby double doors of the gym, which was a sprawling, two-story enchilada red brick building located just up the street from the Santa Rosa Hospi-

tal. The gym dated from the late 1950s, and had originally been funded
by the Catholic Church. The far wing was an indoor basketball court
with bleachers on opposite sides. Basketball and boxing tournaments
were often held there, and drew large crowds. The gym was known to
the regulars as the "San Nacho," the nickname for San Ignacio. At the
door, Chicky looked back.

Eloy was still by the truck, his eyes sad. "Go on in and git to work."

Chicky didn't understand. "What about you?"

"Got to go to the hospital to see Doc Ocampo," Eloy replied.

"What's wrong?"

Eloy said, "Nothin's wrong. I had tests is all."

"You sick?"

"Naw, it's just tests," Eloy assured him.

"When'll you be back?" Chicky asked.

"Soon's Doc Ocampo does his checkup on me. So you gonna fish or
cut bait?"

Chicky said, *"Órale,* later," and started for the door to the gym, grateful to be training again, but worried about his grandfather. He looked
back once more, and Eloy was smiling. Things couldn't be too bad.

Chicky wished for times past, for suppers together when Eloy used to
tell him about traveling to far places and winning big fights. It was fine
even when supper turned into hastily consumed TV dinners once
Chicky's granny was gone. Chicky feared those times had slipped away
forever. So when Eloy had asked him earlier that day if he wanted to
head into San Anto for a workout at the San Nacho, Chicky said, "Book
it," unconsciously mimicking his grandfather's way of talking.

Chicky loved the old-timey Texas way Eloy spoke, his accent even
more pronounced than El Paso's great and charming golfer Lee Trevino.
Once Chicky began to wear boots and a wide-brimmed hat, he quickly
gave up the *vato* street talk of Victoria Courts to sound as much like Eloy
as he could. He soon sounded as Texas as guys with nicknames like Cooter
and Cotton. When Eloy let him drive the tractor alone that first time, the
kid thought he'd burst with pride, but he never forgot how afraid he'd

been when his mother left him to live at Eloy's farm that distant Thanks-giving Day, how he'd huddled in the thin little coat his mother had gotten from Goodwill. And he never forgot how his grandfather and grand-mother had made him feel as if he had lived with them always. When the Longhorns were playing the Aggies on TV, Eloy talked to Chicky as if he were a peer and it made him feel like a man, like an hombre.

Before their first game, they'd flipped a quarter for first pick of a team. Years later he realized that his grandfather had rigged the toss so Chicky would win. Chicky chose the Aggies because he liked the sound of their name, and thereafter would remain an Aggie. Eloy rooted for the Longhorns. They made a pact to watch the annual Aggie-Longhorns game ever after and had never missed one. Before she got sick, Dolores, nicknamed Mamá Lola, had served hot dogs made with Polish sausage, and sauerkraut and spicy mustard. Afterward, they ate homemade flan with strawberries. Lola made coffee she got from Nuevo Laredo.

Chicky and his grandfather had clapped and jumped on each play of the game. Whenever the Longhorns were behind, Eloy would clap his hands once and urge them on in that way of his. "All rat, 'horns, 'bout time t'open up a can a whip-ass."

If Eloy thought the referees had made a bad call, he'd rumble low in his throat, "Yessir, somebody got to the zebras."

It was Eloy's influence that made Chicky a throwback. It was because of Eloy that Chicky'd never cottoned to Lone Star *cholo*—Mex-American—rap like so many of his contemporary Tejanitos, why he liked *rancheritas* and polkas, and the honky-tonk music played in juke joints and ice houses.

Once Chicky had passed into the bright interior of the gym, Eloy crossed Santa Rosa against the red light, and walked slowly down the block to the hospital at the corner of Houston Street. Old at fifty-eight, and heavy for his height, he still walked like a fighter—short steps, chin tucked, shoulders slightly rolled forward. The Santa Rosa Hospital was where

Chicky had been born. It was where Dolores's cancer had been diagnosed and treated before she decided to go home. Now Eloy was going for a treadmill test, X-rays, and to get the results from previous blood and urine tests. They had been ordered by Dr. Rodrigo Ocampo, the family doctor of forty years, who promised a rush on the findings and that he'd be there to explain them.

"Somebody musta messed up here," Eloy protested when he was given the results.

Dr. Ocampo said, "Guess who."

Ocampo was nearly eighty years old, but looked sixty. His full head of stiff white hair and Zapata mustache gave him the look of a revolutionary, but his black almond eyes were those of a poet. He was one of the few who knew the truth about why Eloy's boxing career had effectively ended in a dreadful fuck-up, *desmadre,* out at the Olympic Auditorium in L.A. Ocampo had forgiven Eloy—what else could he do?—even if Eloy hadn't forgiven himself.

"We got to dry you out, pods. Your liver is getting as hard as a rock."

"I don't want to hear about no cures," Eloy said firmly.

"You know I saw this coming, right?"

"It ain't no big surprise to me, either, if you had any doubts," Eloy replied.

Ocampo slipped into a heavy *cholo* accent, "Come on, come on, goddamnit, this is the fuckin doctor's orders, man."

Eloy answered the same way. "Eloy Garza don't take no stinkin orders."

"What about the kid?"

"I'll last awhile." But Eloy knew he might not have a hell of a lot of time.

"He'll do better with you around longer than shorter," Ocampo told him.

"Doc, I'd'a changed a long time ago if I couldda."

Ocampo nodded. "You got my number if you change your mind, hear?"

Eloy swore Dr. Ocampo to silence about the results of the tests. The Wolf, his soiled T-shirt stretched tight over his distended gut, would never share the results with anyone.

The San Ignacio was a bustling gym, crowded primarily with Latinos, but there were a few blacks as well. No white fighters, though Chicky was often taken for one. There were two large, elevated rings and swaying body bags hung on cables and chains from the high ceiling. There were several rows of long benches near the entrance, and light from bright overhead lamps spun off the lime green walls as if dancing with the racket of the banging speed bags and whapping leather jump ropes. Some trainers huddled to whisper with their fighters, some moved through the commotion like monks gliding to evensong. There was one old-time white trainer who moved lithely despite his age. Some youngsters tried to teach each other, none of them teaching or learning much.

Two longtime trainers in the San Nacho, the brothers Trini and Paco Cavazo, went back almost to the day the gym had first opened. They always staked out territory near the back of the ring, and barked like jailers at their fighters on the premise that either discipline ruled or chaos would erupt.

Chicky took his time changing into his outfit—jock and T-shirt, sweatpants, and a sweatshirt with the sleeves cut off below the elbow. He wore dark blue gym shorts over the pants, and over the shirt he wore a kind of vest made from a faded black sleeveless sweatshirt. Layers meant perspiration. By the time he laced up his high boxing shoes, he figured Eloy would be in the gym waiting. He wasn't. Chicky wrapped his hands. He warmed up for three rounds, then stretched. He went on to shadowbox, and after three rounds had broken into a good sweat. It felt good, his sweat steaming him, his body feeling oiled inside. He was ready to work the punch mitts, but Eloy was still at the hospital, so Chicky worked the big bag. He took it easy for two rounds, wanting to save some gas for Eloy, still known around San Nacho as the Wolf, who hadn't returned.

Chicky cut loose, worked four hard rounds on the big bag, then went flat. He dogged it on the speed bag for two more rounds, painfully aware that he wasn't in the shape he liked to be in. He forced himself through only two rounds on the jump rope, then did a hundred sit-ups in four sets of twenty-five. Ordinarily, he'd do five or six sets of thirty. No Eloy.

Chicky showered quickly. He dried his close-cropped hair, then changed back into boots and jeans. Disappointed, and growing more concerned, he returned to the floor, which was nearly empty. Good fighters will go as many as fifteen, even twenty rounds nonstop in less than one and a half hours, then leave the gym promptly, no socializing. Chicky took a quick look around, nodded to the Cavazo brothers, Eloy's former trainers, and then hurried out to check Fresita, but the pickup was gone. He'd known from experience what to expect, but tried not to believe it. He waited ten minutes in the dark, then gave up and reentered the gym. He crossed over to where the Cavazos were finishing up.

"You seen my grandpa?" Chicky asked.

Trini, the older of the brothers, said, "You need a ride?"

Chicky said, "Naw, he's late, that's all."

Trini, the nickname for Trinity, as in the Holy Trinity, had also been known as Flash, but that was when he had a fine pro record of twenty-two and four, with sixteen KOs. Then the booze, the *chicas,* the gambling, and, finally, all the coke and the other shit he ingested made him a functioning addict. He thrived, became a dealer himself, and had maintained his habit for more than half his life. No street drugs for him, and none for what he referred to as his *GQ* customers, his uptown junkies.

Trini was a "thoroughbred," a dealer who sells only laboratory-pure narcotics. His current supplier was the civilian head of shipping and receiving at Lackland Air Force Base. Trini was able to obtain pharmaceutical-quality drugs for zip compared to their street value, and took the comfortable top piece of a 75–25 split. Trini's previous contact

had been a pale old junkie pharmacist at Kelly Air Force Base, before it
started closing down. Trini loved the flyboys. He loved to sing their song
as he drove out through the gate with sealed cartons of morphine sul-
fate, codeine, Demerol, and Dilaudid in his taco wagon. Very few tacos
were sold out of his gaudily painted vehicle, only enough to justify keeping his license and selling a few when he went on base. It gave him good
cover, made him a familiar figure. Pearly rosary beads dangled from the
rearview mirror, and the ragged fringe around his windows wiggled in
the rushing wind, as he belted out

> *Off we go, into the wild blue yonder,*
> *Climbing high into the sun!*
> *Down we dive, spouting our flames from under,*
> *La-la-laaaa la-la-la-laaaa!*

Trini never used a needle more than once. He would sometimes collect and toss them on a dope corner where junkies would pick them up
and use them. Dumping his darts this way made him feel superior. He
saw himself as a class act, the Cisco Kid of dope fiends. He ingested only
the best, none of that street shit. He used Dilaudid if he was low on morphine, but preferred "Miss Emma." Morphine didn't give him heroin's
hilltop high, but that dirty brown street horse was too hard to ride, guns
rode that nag, along with stumblebum spic violence, and there was AIDS
in that saddle as well. Demerol had a market, but it took six times as
much Demerol as morphine to get you where you wanted to be. Even
though his stuff was drugstore pure, Demmie often caused infection at
the point of entry, forcing people to go to the doctor. That meant someone might rat him out, so he trafficked less in Demerol than in the other
pills and liquids his uptown clientele delighted in. He focused on lawyers, stockbrokers, athletes, and media people. All they wanted was fresh
needles and the pure shit, clean and sterile, pretty pills and little tamper-
proof bottles. Trini's people had the money to pay for pure and sterile,
and pay they did when they met him in gas-station crappers, or some-

times right there in the courthouse of Bexar County. Athletes were his favorites. They had all that money and they were so big that they needed shit by the tubful. Besides, he got off on ruling those big mothafucks. Women were a trip, too, liked to score when they were sitting with Trini in their Beamers or Audis in car washes with the water going. Some, even the marrieds, offered to barter tits and ass and blow jobs.

Trini, the old-line junkie, would answer, "I don't even fuck my own wife, man."

Some would feel insulted by being turned down, some would laugh, but they all paid. He'd suck on lemon drops and watch the sheets of water flowing over the windshield while they dug into their purses for cash. One offered him two gold credit cards and said she'd wait a week before she reported them missing.

"Cash."

Chicky had known guys like this from the Victoria Courts, gaunt men who always wore long-sleeved shirts buttoned tightly at the wrist, the cuffs held in place by a loop of dirty elastic. He pegged Trini for a doper the first time he saw him. Eloy had bought morphine in squat little brown bottles from Trini when Dolores was in terrible pain at the end. Prescriptions written by Dr. Ocampo were not enough. Chicky had watched from the hallway when Eloy injected Trini's stuff into his grandmother's arm. He had heard his grandfather sob every time he shot her up. When Mamá Lola continued to linger in agony, Chicky wondered if maybe Eloy had started to use some of the squirt on himself.

Trini and Paco had trained Eloy his whole career. They had been in Eloy's corner the night Eloy had lost his title shot. But they were poor technicians who valued tough over fundamentals. They expected their fighters to stand Mexican style and take punches in order to land punches, yet they saw themselves as bold tacticians equal to Santa Ana in his cruel prime. Their relationships with all their fighters were strictly business, and they were quick to lure a boy from another trainer. They were equally quick to dump him should he lose a couple of fights.

Eloy had left the Santa Rosa Hospital in a hurry. Once Doc Ocampo confirmed that Eloy's heart and liver were shot anyway, the Wolf decided to have a few thousand *tequilazo* shooters with salt and lime, though he knew that the booze was what was killing him. He'd swallowed that idea the way he had swallowed a thousand *mezcal* worms, with a wince and a smile, but he wouldn't be able to smile his way through Chicky. And he knew it. How to tell the kid? He inhaled deeply from his third cigarette. Better not to tell the kid at all. Chicky had enough mud to haul as it was. If the kid was to be saved, it would be through boxing. He hadn't been working with Chicky at home in the improvised gym because he couldn't. He didn't have the gas. He was hurting every hour of every day. But the Cavazos could keep Chicky in the game. They weren't the best, but they weren't the worst, despite what they'd pulled on him, and on others. Trini's habit could make things tricky, but Eloy figured he'd be square with the boy, what with their having watched him grow up, and because they'd stayed tight with Eloy down through the years. It was a reasonable choice to Eloy, on the surface at least. He was too drunk to dive deeper, but for some reason he remembered the time he'd broken a knuckle in training. Trini had given him shots in the hand so he could fight. And in the years to come, more needles would follow.

Chicky motioned Paco Cavazo off to one side at the San Ignacio. "You know my *abuelito* a long time, right?"

"Yeah, hell yeah," Paco said. He was short and athletically built, had a pencil-line mustache like the old-time movie actor Gilbert Roland. He still combed his dyed black hair in a *pachuco* ducktail that was thick with pomade. He liked Lone Star longnecks, but he had kept in shape through the years by training fighters. He'd been the muscle, Trini the brains. To Chicky, his yellow-brown eyes were from dinosaur times. "Me'n my brother trained the Wolf here and in Houston, too. Almost got him the title."

"What went wrong with him?" Chicky asked.

"Lots a things, you know, he got old, couldn't do roadwork, that shit."

"Did he always drink?"

Paco stepped back, looked at Chicky sideways. *"Chico, chico,* you know how we are."

"Not this Mexican," Chicky said, pointing a finger at himself.

"Ojo," Paco said, "watch it, here he comes."

Chicky looked up and saw Eloy weaving toward them. Chicky glanced at Paco, who was grinning as if he and Eloy were *hermanos de leche,* brothers in milk, like they were screwing the same woman. Chicky knew that, at this stage, Eloy could hardly find his dick to piss.

Paco embraced Eloy, who then moved to embrace Trini.

Trini said, *"Hola, carnal,"* hello old buddy.

Eloy put on a show, got in a little dig. "Here we are again, the three Mousecateers."

Trini said, "Your kid's been waiting for you, homes."

"Had some bidness with a big outfit about my spread," Eloy said, thinking fast to come up with a plausible lie.

"You packin in the farm, *ése?"* Paco asked, using a word pronounced like the English "essay" and meaning *that,* or *that one;* but when used by the *vatos, ése* means buddy, or pal, or homeboy.

"Tal vez, could be, but only if the price is right, like on TV," Eloy replied, then laughed and tilted his hat to look prosperous. "They might want me to run one of their deals down around Rockport."

Chicky didn't believe his grandfather, but he went along in order to scheme on his own. He said, "There's good fishin down there, and soil's richer'n the Bush family."

Paco said, "But not much boxin down there, 'cept for Corpus or club fights in Laredo once in a while."

"I was thinkin the same thing," said Eloy. "What say you boys take over for me with Chicky? I know y'all eyeball him whenever he wins a tournament."

By now everyone knew Eloy was lying about selling his farm and working for someone else. But it was true that the Cavazos saw Chicky as a prospect.

"How'll I get to the gym?" Chicky asked.

Eloy said, "You'll be legal to drive Fresita in a couple of weeks, right?"

Driving the pickup on his own made the deal especially sweet for Chicky, and everyone shook hands on it.

"We'll take care a him good," Trini promised. "Down the line we're puttin on our own tournament over Uvalde."

"Book it," Eloy said.

Chicky had to drive Eloy home.

Chapter 8

Chicky missed the closeness he'd had training with Eloy. It was loyalty to his grandfather, rather than to the Cavazos, that kept Chicky training with them. He also felt trapped. Before the Cavazos deal, he had already decided to turn pro once he graduated from high school. Trini and Paco, for all their shady action, had over the years trained two boys from San Anto, and one from Nuevo Laredo, into world champions. They had the kind of juice with amateur officials and professional promoters Chicky would need, so he kept his mouth shut, partly out of respect for Eloy's judgment. Chicky had plans—and he wasn't quite ready to share all of them with his *abuelito*.

Education was important to Chicky. He was set on heading for College Station and graduating from Texas A & M. Like other local kids who had to work with their daddies, he would first attend Palo Alto Community College, just up the road from Poteet. Boxing, however, was as important to him as a college degree, and he figured he could do both. Not at the same time, but if he got knocked out of the fight game, an education meant he'd have a place to bounce to.

Graduating from A & M and using the skills he learned on the farm was Chicky's long-range goal. But no one, including Eloy, knew what

Chicky planned as a fighter. The last thing he wanted was to start out as a four-round prelim fighter at $100 a round. He'd lose 10 percent off the top for a trainer and another 33⅓ for a manager. Then there was a cut man to pay if the trainer couldn't double up as both. By the time Uncle Sam got his hooks into you, you went home with more lumps on your face than money in your pocket. There was a better way: Win the Nationals, and then win the Olympic box-offs for a spot on the Olympic team. Winning the gold medal would bring a professional signing bonus from big-time Tex-Messkin lawyers from Austin looking for the right homeboy. The next step was to win a professional World title. That would mean a good stake to invest in the sinking farm. Chicky figured he was four, maybe five years away from that title, and in between, he had to figure out some way to help Eloy. Chicky saw himself marrying the right *wifa,* retiring to the farm, and having a gang of kids. He'd teach them that soil was different from dirt. There was no way he'd ever let his granddaddy be put out along the side of the road with a little bundle tied in a bed sheet. No, sir, he had to fight and make it big for his *abuelito.* Soon as he had money coming in, he'd take care of his grandpa.

It was not as if Chicky had a choice. Eloy's local farmhands had been laid off. Mexican stoop laborers, in their seasonal sweeps through the South Texas harvest, no longer found work along the rows of red and green at Lobo Farms. Weeds took over the long rows where berries had grown. Some of the equipment was covered with frayed tarps, some stored in sideless corrugated sheds and wooden barns. The fragile sprinklers, once connected end to end to irrigate wide stretches at a single lick, were shoved together into a pile of rusting junk. The Mexicans saw what was happening to Lobo Farms and stopped coming.

Chicky kept order as best he could, remained a good student, and was hellacious as the best defensive back on the high school football team. But he could do only so much at the farm while Eloy continued with his daily *birongas* of Lone Star or Pearl, and his late afternoon launch into *pistos* of the hard stuff. Chicky worried about Eloy's drinking, knew it was killing him slowly. He also began to suspect that Eloy had closed down the farm to free him from his chores. Equipment was sold to pay bills.

None of Eloy's suffering, his slide into dereliction, made sense to Chicky. The old man had achieved his dreams, and more. He couldn't grieve for Dolores forever. He had to get on with life. But what could a boy say to his grandfather, the man who had saved and loved him? What could he do but endure and stay loyal? Chicky did it, but he let fury loose on the football field and in the gym. It would be the same during tournaments. Chicky could punch, Eloy had taught him well. Other young fighters swallowed hard when they thought about facing Chicky Garza.

Living in Poteet and driving to the gym six days a week got old quick for Chicky, but he did it. At first Eloy made the trip north with him, but more and more he stayed at home. After busting his hump in the gym, it was no fun to come home to Eloy snoring in front of a blaring TV set.

Chicky knew he had to focus on the Cavazos' shitty tournament in Uvalde. He had started running again, having learned from his other fights that he had to be fit, inside the ring and out, physically and mentally. Being ready was the key, but sometimes fights with other southpaws were his toughest fights. It was often that way for left-handers. Because lefties came at each other differently from right-handers, and because southpaws fought many more right-handers than lefties, left-handed fighters became used to fighting right-handed fighters. But being left-handed also made boxing seem easy sometimes, especially when Chicky'd see the look of confusion in right-handed boys with little or no experience with left-handers. In any case, should he get cocky and lose concentration, either while sparring with an orthodox fighter in the gym or duking it out in a fight, the Cavazos were there to push hard and relentlessly.

"All right, you fuck, what's this bullshit?"

It was one of the many ways they began a criticism, especially if a fighter got tired. Chicky had to give them credit—they got their fighters in shape, or else. Fighters came to the Cavazos because of their reputation as winners, and had to be ready to absorb personal assaults for a chance at the big time. Being dropped by the Cavazos was like a dishonorable discharge from the Marines.

When the day of the tournament came, Chicky drove and Eloy rode shotgun. They took the 173 up to Devine and then hooked a left on the 90 down to Uvalde. The tournament was held in a church community center that had a small playground for kids and a senior center. A ring was set up in the auditorium. Farm boys, white and Tex-Mex, as well as boys from the other side of the border made up the card. Amateur boxing would change from three three-minute rounds to four two-minute rounds soon after Chicky left the amateur ranks, but on this day, Chicky and the other amateurs would fight the usual three rounds. Chicky won his class easily, took every round, and got a unanimous decision. The Cavazos were smugly silent after the victory, but Eloy hugged Chicky to his beer gut and hooted.

After the Uvalde fight, Chicky went on to win in several tournaments in other towns around San Antonio, sometimes fighting as low as 142 pounds in the 147-pound classification. He tried to get below 139 in order to fight in a lower weight division, but couldn't lose the weight and stay strong. He also tried to gain weight, but remained the same, and usually had to overcome the disadvantage of being lighter than most of his 147-pound opponents. He was awarded the winner's trophy for a two-night tournament when he won the second night by a "walkover," a free ride. Walkovers occur when one of the scheduled fighters can't make weight, doesn't pass the medical exam, shows up late, or for some reason decides not to fight. When that happens, his opponent simply walks across the ring for the win. The boy Chicky was to fight on the second night failed to appear once he'd seen Chicky kick ass the first night. It was an easy trophy, but Chicky had wanted to win with his gloves, not by default. He'd been pumped with adrenaline, and it took him a night and a day to calm down.

An amateur fighter can default for a number of reasons: a medical problem; failure to present his passbook; a flat tire on the way to the arena. To coordinate the complex details of bringing a large number of young fighters together, the weigh-ins are usually held several hours before the matches are scheduled. Fighters must pass a medical exam each day they fight. They must also present their passbook or they are not allowed to participate. The passbook identifies them, and also contains the complete record of their fights. The passbook was designed to show a boy's record—not only to document his experience, but also to indicate how he'd won or lost. A boy losing by a knockout is not allowed to train again for thirty days, depending on the circumstances: In certain cases, a boy could be prohibited from training for as much as 180 days. The passbook is primarily there to protect the fighter. If a fighter doesn't have, or fails to present, his passbook, he cannot fight. It contains his photo identification, his date of birth, and other pertinent information. Boys' participation in tournaments that could place them on the U.S. Olympic team must also prove United States citizenship.

Chicky's next big fight was against a big-boned boy at the New Braunfels Wurtsfest, where there was a large German community. A polka band was brought over from Germany, and tubas boomed loud and deep through the town. Many in the community turned up in outfits imported from the fatherland. They ate sausages, drank beer, and did the chicken dance, a line dance that included old ladies, towheaded kids, and much sweat.

An outdoor ring was set up for the tournament, and the German boys were ready to fight. They kicked about as much Mexican ass as the Mexicans kicked German ass. In the first round of Chicky's fight, the German kid knocked Chicky down with a right-hand body shot that made Chicky's guts spasm. It was Chicky's first time to hit the canvas. He wobbled to his feet when he heard the Cavazos cursing him in Spanish, calling him a punk for letting the *gabacho* white-boy kraut mothafuck put him on his ass.

"*¡Anda, desgraciado puto ojete!*" Come on shameless faggot butt-hole!

In amateur boxing, a knockdown doesn't have the same import as one in professional boxing, but Chicky was furious with himself because he had taken the square-headed white boy lightly. As in all his fights, because of the style he'd been taught, Chicky had to fight the German shit-kicker face-to-face. He didn't know what angles and distance and the laws of physics could do for him. Not knowing cost him a rib separation.

The aching ribs made breathing a bitch, would force him to sleep in a chair for a month, would keep him from sparring for two months, would keep him out of tournaments for three. He nonetheless came back in the second round of the fight to down the white boy. Because he was left-handed, Chicky had the advantage over his inexperienced opponent. Because his opponent had a rock-hard chin, it took a series of big right hooks to drive the German kid to his knees. Afterward, Chicky wasn't sure which shot had put the blond boy away, but it was a vindication. The shit-faced Germans cheered them both. Once the ring doctor checked both fighters, Fritzie was up and bouncing on his thick legs as if nothing had happened.

Chicky, however, the winner by KO, was the one left to lick his wounds at midnight, the one who had to figure out precisely what he'd done wrong. Sometimes he could, sometimes he couldn't. The Cavazos had begun to strut to and from the ring when Chicky fought. They were quick to take credit for his punching power, forgetting that it was because of Eloy's training that Chicky could hit so hard. They didn't do anything about the limitations of Chicky's style because they thought tough was enough.

———

Chicky continued to train and win, and was rewarded with more tro-phies to add to his wall. His record included eighteen Junior and Silver Gloves wins from his kid fights, starting when he weighed ninety-three pounds. Overall, his record totaled fifty-six wins and seven losses, with twenty-nine clean KOs. To fight guys, twenty-nine knockouts in the am-ateurs meant that Chicky could dig to the body and crack to the head well enough to knock an opponent out despite headgear and a hovering ref. There were periods when Chicky would fight often, in fights at the San Ignacio, or in nearby towns, or even Austin. There were other tour-naments that were too far to travel to. Chicky would also take time off from boxing because he had other things to do—keep the farm looking decent, football, exams that had to be studied for. With one exception, he'd always return to the San Nacho with his legs and lungs in shape from several weeks of roadwork. Now, for the second time, he stopped running. He told himself he just didn't have the time, had too much work to keep the farm in one piece. The truth was that he had no one pushing him. Eloy was out of it most of the time. Trini Cavazo didn't give a shit whether he ran or not. All he wanted was for Chicky to keep punching hard. Common sense being the hardest sense of all to learn, he would acquire the common sense of roadwork the hard way.

Eloy said it best. "If you won't run, you can't fight."

It was after a knockout that deposited a boy flat on his face on the canvas that Chicky had taken a month off. He went back to the gym cocky. Stamina had never been a problem, so what was one lousy month? His string of impressive wins had made him overconfident. He sparred suc-cessfully with the local boys in his weight class he'd worked with previ-ously. He knew their moves and faults, which made it easy for him to dominate them. It wasn't long before no one would get in the ring with him. The Cavazos found a tubby little Indio with a flat nose who looked like a pushover. The tubby pushover, Chicky would learn, was an old pro from El Chuco—El Paso, that is—the original home of the pachucos of the 1940s, slick-dick dudes who wore zoot suits with reet pleats and drape shapes. Watch chains looped down to their ankles, and they kept their ducktails in place with Tres Flores pomade. Their cap-toed oxblood shoes had two-inch soles, the heels thick as a brick. Chicky had heard of them, had seen photos. He found them amusing, but he also felt a kinship with them. Who wouldn't have some sympathy for a droopy-eyed *carnal* out there willing to shoot craps and play taps in the *yanqui* world?

Chicky would soon realize that the fat man from El Chuco might well have slipped across the toll bridge to Ciudad Juárez to turn pro at fourteen, that he'd had eighty, maybe a hundred fights. The Indian flat-out whipped Chicky's ass.

Unconsciously, Chicky tried to use southpaw footwork to turn the right-handed old man of thirty-two the "wrong" way, move him to his right instead of allowing him to go to his left. That would make him vulnerable to Chicky's attack, but the pro knew Chicky's game and reversed it on him, made him go to *his* left. That immediately put Chicky on the defensive, took his confidence, left him open for a lead right hand and a follow-up left hook. Chicky tried footwork repeatedly to cut off the ring and to control the direction of movement. He failed to get his right, or front, foot outside his opponent's front foot. It was the pro who consistently got his left foot outside Chicky's right. That meant that Chicky was forced to defend himself from angles he was unaccustomed to. Chicky knew he was being taken to school, and lost his temper. He began throwing wild "arm" punches. Instead of having the torque of his hips behind his shots, he was using only shoulder and arm muscle to generate force, and this drained him of energy.

Not having done his roadwork, he tired quickly and began to gulp air around his mouthpiece. He tried to stand and fight, but the middle of his chest felt scalded inside and his arms came down. The *gordito,* the fat man, kept coming, not hitting hard, just relentlessly. He nailed Chicky with right-hand leads that knocked him back, and kept him moving in the wrong direction. Fatty's right leads forced Chicky to cover his face. Exhausted in body and mind, Chicky unthinkingly exposed his body to the *gordo's* liver shots, hooks that sometimes wandered around to kidney shots like poisoned swords. At ringside, the Cavazos winked at each other, let it go on until the middle of the fourth round. Chicky wanted to finish the round, but Trini waved him off. Chicky felt doubly degraded.

Chicky remembered Eloy's words: "If you won't run, you can't fight." He now understood that tired means you can't think. He never made the mistake of not running again.

The pro wasn't the first to teach Chicky how much he didn't know. The kid realized clearly that what he lacked had something to do with feet and floor. He also understood that there was a whole load of shit that the Cavazos did not know. He had gone to them with questions, but they treated him like he was looking for a way out, instead of in.

Trini said, "Somethin wrong with your tittie, *ése?*"

Chicky couldn't go to Eloy. His granddaddy had been the first one to pass the Cavazos' tough-guy system on to Chicky. Besides, his *abuelo* was shit-faced all the time.

Thanks to the work with the little pro, Chicky was able to control a right-hander easily in his next fight, and the next as well. Then he fought two speedy black fighters from the Eastside, winning both matches by a split decision. It scared him—not fighting blacks, but what it would be like to fight top-ranked blacks for a shot at the Olympics. And how would he handle them as a pro?

The better he got, the better his opponents got. Now all his fights were hard fights. He began going home with some of the lumps and black eyes he had sent other boys home with. He continued to win, but puzzled over why he had to fight so hard, why he got winded despite his roadwork. The clever boxers, even the boxer-punchers, did not have to grind out wins the way he did. He'd heard it said that there was a finite number of punches a fighter could take. Each fighter would have a different number, but they all had a limit. Chicky didn't believe in a limit at first. Now he wasn't so sure.

There were other aspects of boxing that troubled Chicky. Being left-handed had always given Chicky an edge with right-handers. Punches from southpaws bewildered them, especially the jab, because it came at them from the same side they used to throw their jabs. He'd tried to set up his usual attack with the El Paso pro, but the guy knew how to handle a lefty and made Chicky aware that being a hard-hitting southpaw wasn't enough. Now he had to learn consciously what he had instinctively done in the past. He must seek to *agarrar la onda* of boxing, to dig to the depths of the sweet science and seize its hidden truths. Part of that was to strip the opponent of what he did best, take his very fight from him—take his balance, limit his ability to punch, drain him of power. Chicky knew, in his gut, that there had to be more, starting with his own spread-eagle stance. The El Chuco Indian also made him wonder if he could keep fighting as a pro, when he'd have to go twelve blistering rounds in a title fight. *¡Híjole!*

As Chicky began to meet better fighters, he found that he could only land punches within the distance of his own, limited reach. Even at that range, he'd sometimes miss openings wide as a barn against slick fighters "on their bicycle," boxers who continually bobbed and weaved, guys who baited him in so they could take him out. With such fighters, his punches would come up short, usually by inches, but sometimes by half steps as well. Those black fighters from San Antonio's Eastside had given him fits, though he didn't like to admit it. Range and distance were a problem the Cavazos' style of fighting would never help him solve. It meant, bottom line, that he had to stay close and trade shots. He'd been hit hard, so he knew he could take a shot. He knew he hit harder than anyone he'd ever fought, but he also knew that power couldn't always save him. Knew that there had to be others who could punch as hard as he, maybe harder. What if he had to face some black bird who could move him to his left and hit like he hit? It cost him sleep.

Chicky watched how the Cavazo brothers taught newcomers, and listened to them as they called instructions to experienced fighters. When he finally broke the code of their style, he almost laughed. The Cavazo style was no style. Essentially, it was street fighting—plant your feet wide apart and swing hard, homeboy, and forget that your face will fucking wear out. *Ay, madre de Dios,* Chicky thought. It was a style that worked well when fighting Mexicans who fought the same way. What you had to do to beat most of them was to absorb more punishment than they. And there was the Cavazo hook, the same big, wide Mexican hook used famously by Mexican executioners like Castillo, Olivares, and Pintor. The problem was that their style of hook left you as wide open as the Texas sky, made you take shots to land shots. Chicky wanted to fight like Salvador Sánchez, clean, classically, a fighter who fought only as hard as he had to fight in order to win. If it took a knockout, he could put you to sleep, too. The Sánchez and the Julio César Chávez styles were made of the stuff Chicky'd need to beat the black lightning that was sure to fight him for an Olympic spot. Black fighters often beat Cavazo fighters. Chicky thought about getting a black trainer, but decided against it. He knew Eloy would have to put up with shit from the Cavazos about betrayal; shit about all the work and time they'd wasted; shit about *raza,* Mexican blood and solidarity, though they didn't give a dead duck's dick about *raza.* Chicky was just another investment for them.

And if a fighter didn't produce a return on that investment, then *adios, chico.*

Chapter 9

As Father José Capetillo finished saying Tim Pat's funeral mass at Christ the King, yellow sunlight changed to pink as it beamed through the stained glass above the altar. Except for the old priest, two altar boys, Earl and his wife and Dan, the church was empty. Dan was oblivious to the priest's eulogy and final blessing.

Father Joe was near retirement. He'd often had dinner with Dan and Brigid at their home. Through the years he had followed boxing on TV and bullfighting through the Spanish-language newspapers he subscribed to. It was his interest in the fight game that had jump-started his close friendship with the Cooley family. He became a frequent and welcome visitor and often had a shot or two of top-shelf bourbon with Brigid, who preferred it to Irish whiskey. He would sometimes have more than two shots when he came by after watching an old friend or a newborn die, his eyes filled with pain from a lifetime of hearing and seeing what most couldn't bear for a day.

He was grateful to God he'd been called to the priesthood, grateful that he'd met and served people like the Cooleys. He'd loved to listen to Brigid's brogue, and knew that what remained of his Mexican accent pleased her as well. He'd wept at her funeral mass, said in Latin, as she had wished. Now, saying this mass for Tim Pat, and seeing Dan's dry, desolate face in the empty church, Father Joe barely suppressed a sob when he said *Dominus vobiscum,* the Lord be with you.

There was to be no wake, and Dan chose to drive alone in the Caddy to the cemetery. "No offense," he said to Earl. "I just want to be alone behind the hearse."

Dan had the top of the Caddy up because he didn't want anyone to see his eyes. He followed the hearse as it headed east on Sunset. The ride was a quick one, the motorcycle patrolmen clearing the intersections, and soon Sunset became Chávez. Earl and his wife followed. Father Joe drove his own car, said he had stops to make at retirement homes and at Cedars. Shortly thereafter the small procession moved left onto North Broadway and up to St. Athanasius.

Dan burned with a passion for vengeance—not mere justice, but vengeance. Tim Pat had been murdered, hadn't he? Once the police put the little spic whore away, he'd be free of her. The men in blue were on his side. He'd seen the cops fill out the police report, hadn't he? Even though they'd placed him in handcuffs inside the patrol car for choking her, he'd heard her say that she'd gone *around* the ice-cream truck, hadn't he? The diagram would prove it. The bitch was going down. Nothing could make up for what she'd done. But at least a long stretch in the slammer was something; at least some kind of *justice* would be done; at least some kind of *respect* would be shown for the death of a little boy at the rotten hands of this fucking gangbanger whore *beaner.*

Dan blinked his dry eyes as he got out of the car. Father Joe prayed. Dan looked away. After the service, Dan took a pinch of soil and sprinkled it across Tim Pat's short casket.

There had not yet been time to incise the last name on the stone:

TIMOTHY PATRICK MARKEY   1986–1997

Not wanting to talk to anyone, Dan turned quickly away and started for his car. Some of the paint had faded; there were small chips where careless drivers opening their doors had dinged it; there were hairline scratches on the fenders; faint patches of rust worked at the big bumper. The car had only sixty-eight thousand miles on it and still handled like a dream. Sunlight reflected off the windshield. Dan stopped abruptly. Was that Brigid in the car, Tim Pat in her arms? Were those shamrocks and roses in the backseat? Dan's vision grew dim, and he felt as if he was about to pass out.

"Dan," said Father Joe, lightly placing his hand on Dan's arm.

Dan pulled away.

Father Joe offered Dan his card, with a number on it that had been penned in red ink. "I got a cell phone last week. Not ten people have this number. If I can't reach you by this evening, please call me. Wherever you are, I'll be there."

Dan gave him a bitter grin. "Father Joe, Jo-Jo, dear old family friend."

"Dan?"

"Don't *Dan* me, Jo-Jo," Dan said, reaching for an envelope in his back pocket. "You came over for this, right?"

"I don't expect anything. You know that."

"That's good, then," said Dan, his face suddenly mottled with rage. " 'Cause you ain't gettin nothin." Dan tore up the envelope, threw the pieces in the priest's face. "That was a grand in there, Joe, same's always when my family gets stuffed down holes."

The priest tried to touch Dan's arm again. "Why don't we go have a drink? There's plenty of places on Sunset. There's that Irish place, right?"

Dan's eyes filled with rage. "Do you, as Christ commanded, love God with your whole heart and soul, and with all your mind?"

"What a question," said the priest. "Come on, I'll drive."

"Well, do you believe, or don't you?"

"I wouldn't be a priest if I didn't."

"You never have no doubts about Ab'ba?" Dan asked.

The priest pleaded, "Let's have that drink, the two of us."

"It was for the boy, for his mother, and for my wife, but only out of respect for them. Here's what I think of your god, with a small *g*." Dan handed the priest three pennies. "One for your heart, one for your soul, and one for your god, two cents more than your fuckin god's worth, small *g*."

"Ah, Dan, don't, please, don't do this to yourself."

"Fuck god."

Father Joe hung his head, his face twisting, but he didn't leave. Dan waved Earl off.

Earl had heard it and stepped in. "You're still comin to our place, right?"

Dan got in and closed the door of the Caddy. "You go ahead. I'll see you in a couple of days."

Dan drove away. Earl went over to Father Joe. "You all right, Father?"

"I'm not sure," he said.

Dan took Chávez-Sunset Boulevard all the way to the sea. At Highway 1 he turned north. In Malibu he filled up the tank and put the Caddy's top down. He had intended to drive to San Francisco, maybe all the way to Canada, what the fuck, maybe never come back. No, he couldn't go that far. There was a certain matter that had to be handled through the LAPD. He drove calmly for a stretch, managed to keep his mind blank, but then grief bored in and he started to weep. He pounded his forehead on the steering wheel.

The wind off the sea distracted him for a time, and driving comforted him as he moved along the scrubby brown mountains and barren beaches south of Point Mugu. He began to feel sick to his stomach. He tried to make sense of so much death to those he loved, all of them younger than he. Yet here he was, an old man, his heart ticking away, while his other five hearts were still, in boxes, down holes. There was a time when he could have blamed all this on god, but now there was no god. He wanted to blame it on Satan, but since there was no God, there could be no Satan.

That left him with nothing. He was speeding along the beaches and rocky retaining walls north of Ventura when he started retching. He pulled onto the weedy shoulder of the freeway and threw up.

By the time Dan got up to Santa María, he'd pulled over three more times to vomit, but by Solvang he had the dry heaves and only tears, bile, and snot came out of him.

At Pismo Beach, he said, "Fuck Canada."

It was well past dark when he got back to Malibu, and twenty minutes later he headed for the Santa Monica Pier and the merry-go-round. He watched kids and moms, and lowered his head so they wouldn't see what was going on in his eyes. He wanted a drink. He wanted twenty drinks. Instead, he chose a fish shack, thinking that he could keep down a broiled fish dinner with steamed potatoes. He ordered halibut, his favorite, but when it was served, his appetite vanished. He paid the check, left the table, and went to a nearby bar. He drank too quickly and he drank too much. He became rude and loud and got himself eighty-sixed. In the parking lot he kicked the left-rear white sidewall of the Caddy. He stopped at a store for a quart of milk and a package of Mother's cookies. He chugged half, then spewed all of it back up. Between spasms, he remembered something about the women who'd come for the little gang bitch who killed Tim Pat. But he promptly forgot them as the dry heaves doubled him over again.

He got home sick but almost sober and pulled into his driveway. He backed out immediately. He would never be able to sleep at home again. He didn't want to check into a flophouse or dirty-underwear motel, so he drove to the parking structure of the Los Angeles airport and slept in the car.

The next day, he ate cold cereal and cottage cheese and cantaloupe in an airport hotel coffee shop. From the phone booth near the shoeshine stand, he telephoned the Hollywood division of the LAPD, which was located on Wilcox and De Longpre. The phone was answered by a woman who identified herself as Officer Carneros. Dan explained that he was calling to request a police report.

"What kind of report?"

Dan gave the details of Tim Pat's death, and asked if he could stop by in an hour to pick up a copy of the report. The officer informed him that cases like Tim Pat's were automatically processed by the West Traffic division of the Wilshire area regional facility, located on Venice and La Brea.

Dan said, "But this happened on Wilcox, only two miles down from you."

"I know, but West Traffic handles all traffic-related homicides," the lady cop said.

Homicide, Dan thought, *yeah, the cops call these things by their rightful names.*

Officer Carneros added, "But give it at least a week before you make your request."

Time. How could he speed up the sunrise, how could he shove down the sun? Each night, late, he pulled the Caddy into the shop and slept in the car, used the shop toilet, but would leave before the crew arrived. He didn't shave or brush his teeth. He knew he was gamy, but didn't care. He began to wear a Dodgers cap and dark glasses, and only kept in touch with Earl by phone. Sometimes he'd drive all day, choosing to poke along the old streets of as many Mexican communities as he could think of, hate in his head. Riding under the front seat was the 12 gauge that he'd taken from the shop. The shotgun was a holdover that Earl had brought in during the Rodney King riots. Dan knew how to load the gun, to aim it, and to shoot it. He knew where the safety was. As far as he was concerned, that was enough. *Boom-boom-boom-boom-boom.* Perfect aim wasn't what shotguns were about.

Somehow he always managed to turn around and find his way back to the shop.

————

Dan telephoned West Traffic a week after Tim Pat was killed, sure that the police had already nailed the little bitch, sure that justice would be done. It wouldn't bring Tim Pat back, but at least there would be a consequence for a *homicide*. He wondered how they'd charge her. Assault with a deadly weapon? Could a van be a deadly weapon? Vehicular manslaughter?

An Officer Singleton answered Dan's call. He listened patiently, then told Dan that the report was not yet available.

"But since there was a fatality, what you might need to do is contact Detective Rall Nájera on this." In saying "Rall," Singleton had used the Anglicized pronunciation of Raúl. "But when the report's ready, you can order it here at the desk."

"Right," said Dan. "So if she's not already busted, she will be, right?"

"Was she driving under the influence, or speeding, or both?"

"I don't know."

"Reckless driving? Did they arrest her at the scene?"

"No. Uh, I don't really know. I remember some Mexican women, is all."

"I see," said Singleton. "Are you sure the investigating officers didn't arrest the driver?"

"Not that I saw. To tell you the truth, I don't recall." Dan didn't add that the police had handcuffed him and placed him in the back of a patrol car once Earl had pulled him off Lupe. Nor did he mention that the police, sympathetic to his grief, cut him loose. He assumed that Earl had said he'd be responsible for getting Dan off the street.

Dan said, "How much longer before I can get the report?"

"Give it a few more days."

Dan said, "We're talkin right and wrong here, aren't we, Officer?"

Dan waited another day, but then couldn't wait any longer. He showed up at West Traffic on four days in a row before the report was available. Dan paid the fee, expecting to get the report at that time, but

Officer Singleton, a big black man with a creased face, told him the report would be mailed to him in about a week.

"Has the driver been arrested, or what?"

Singleton checked the computer. "It looks like this was determined an accident."

Dan exploded. "Accident! We got a murdered kid here!"

"Apparently not in the view of the investigating officers."

"I want to see that Mexican detective you told me about."

"Rall Nájera," Singleton said. "I'll check his schedule and make an appointment for you."

Dan didn't know what to do with himself. He bought new clothes rather than go home. He checked into a whorehouse motel so he could shower and shave and brush his teeth. He showed up at West Traffic the next day. He was sober, but his hands were shaking. He had to wait fifteen minutes. Then Detective Nájera came out and led him to a reception room off the hallway.

Dan said, "We got a murdered kid here, Detective."

Nájera was in his fifties. Most thought of him as a Chicano, but he had been born in El Paso, and though he'd lost his Texas accent as a child, when his family moved to California, he still considered himself Tex-Mex, off duty wore boots and a Stetson. His home was near the Santa Cruz Sports Arena, where for several years club fights had been held. He had done his share of boxing, and he often went to the sports arena to have a few beers, talk with some of the old guys he had known since his boxing days, and unwind. What was left of Nájera's balding hair and clipped mustache was salt-and-pepper gray. At five foot nine, he weighed close to 190, but Dan could see he was solid. Nájera's nose was flat and there was scar tissue in his black brows. Dan felt like he was with one of his own.

Nájera shook hands gently, the way fighters do who have nothing to prove. He noticed Dan's eye, smiled slightly, and nodded. "You know me," said Nájera.

Dan said, "That right? From where?"

"From Daw, your middleweight. Earl retired me after my fifteenth pro fight. You're Dan Cooley the trainer, right?"

"Yeah, I remember you, you were big for a Latino fighter in those days," Dan said. "That was like thirty pounds ago."

Nájera smiled broadly and nodded.

Dan added, "You knocked Earl down in the second. You always had to gain weight because the forty-seven-pounders wouldn't fight you. You had a big hook."

"Yeah, but Earl had a bigger right hand. That's when I became a cop. What can I do for you, Mr. Cooley?"

Mollified, Dan spoke barely above a whisper. "It's about my grandson."

"Which one is that?"

"The Markey kid, Timothy Patrick."

"Oh, I'm sorry. Jesus. I didn't make the connection you were that Dan Cooley."

"You arrested the bitch who did it, right?"

Nájera cleared his throat, watched as Dan's eyes went from green to black. "Could you call me tomorrow, Mr. Cooley, so I can get the whole file?"

"I been waitin a long time. I made an appointment."

"I wasn't told specifically what this was about. Our error. Or I could call you?"

"No, no," said Dan, "I'll call you."

"I'll wait to hear from you."

"Just so we're pullin on the rope in the same direction," Dan said, "we're talkin Justice with a big J here, right, Detective?"

"Mr. Cooley, I'm backed up here. Tomorrow, okay?"

Dan went to his car feeling even more unsettled than before. Maybe he was just being jerked off.

He put his key into the ignition. "They better put that bitch away, they fuckin better." He reached down to touch the eighteen-inch barrel of the shotgun. "These fuckin dicks better help."

Dan called Nájera several times daily, three days running. He left the number of his cell phone, but Nájera didn't return his calls. Dan was living on coffee, aspirin, and bourbon.

Dan drove the streets of East Al-*Lay*, and other points east. He was on automatic pilot. One day he found himself at East Fourth and Mathews, at Theodore Roosevelt High School. One side of the school was blocked to through traffic, but he drove along the three open sides several times, cruised at ten miles per hour, all the while looking at the predominately brown faces of the students, especially the girls. He didn't realize that he was less than four blocks from the pink-and-green house of Lupe Ayala. And he did not know that she and her mother had knelt to place two dozen roses at Tim Pat's grave.

On the fifth day of his peregrinations through inner L.A., Dan found himself parked in the lot at Eighteenth and Grand, at the Olympic Auditorium. It had been painted pussy colors, was now known as the *Grand Olympic Auditorium*, the name changed by order of the International Olympic Committee. Dan replayed his fight there, relived every one of the blows that had wrecked his face. He touched his eye. His cell phone rang. He fumbled with the phone, dropped it in his lap. It got caught in his sweatshirt. He answered during the third ring. His voice was hoarse.

"This is Cooley."

It was Nájera. "Could you come by?"

"Where? When?"

"I'm at West. I'll be here the rest of the day," said Nájera.

"I'm on my way. Twenty, thirty minutes."

Nájera said, "No rush."

"Yeah, there's a rush."

Dan fought traffic, then picked up Freeway 10 west and raced to the La Brea exit. Fifteen minutes. It took him another ten minutes to get to West. He checked in with the front desk, and Nájera came out to meet him.

Nájera said, "I know how important this is to you. So I read the report front to back. I interviewed all the officers on the scene. They stood by their call, that it was an accident. Even so, once I read that the ice-cream driver had taken off, I located the company he works for and chased him down."

"He was the Mexican guy, right?"

"Yes. I interviewed him in Spanish. He's going to lose his job for taking off from the scene. Up to the DA if he gets prosecuted."

"The chickenshit," Dan said. "You think he will?"

"Probably not, since he wasn't involved in the actual incident. But here's the point. He confirmed the statement given by the woman who was a witness at the scene, and by the young driver and by her brother, who was with her. The ice-cream guy was very clear about it. The victim tripped and stumbled directly in front of the oncoming vehicle."

"And the *victim* was my little one, right? We ain't talkin fender-bender, right?"

"No, but the girl's vehicle was going only ten to twelve miles an hour."

"She shouldn't a passed the truck."

"It was parked adjacent to the curb, Mr. Cooley."

Dan leaned forward. "Reckless don't have to mean speed."

Nájera said, "True, but there's no skid marks, no liquor, no drugs."

Dan said, "I don't care if she's the Virgin fookin María! My little guy's dead. I want the justice he's due. I want the driver arrested for murder!"

"I'm sure you know I'm in your corner. That's why this took me so long. I know how you must feel."

"No, you don't."

Nájera said, "But I do. My youngest son was drowned in a neighbor's pool. He and our dog wiggled under the fence. My son was three."

"Was she Mexican?"

"Mexican? What does Mexi—"

Dan interrupted. "Was the female witness Mexican? Were the investigating officers Mexican? You're Mexican. The ice-cream driver's Mexican, right? So who paid you off, Officer?"

"This interview is over, Mr. Cooley. Go."

"I want the fuckin chief of police."

Nájera said, "Please. I know your loss is enormous. Believe me, I do. But the Ayala girl is innocent of a crime. Another tragedy won't make the first one right."

"She's a gangbanger, don't you get it? I saw her and the boy doin the finger-signal gang shit." The urge to kill came over Dan; all he lacked was the shotgun. "So how much did you get to sell out my little guy?"

Nájera flushed under his dark skin. He was on the verge of reaming Dan out, but he remembered what he'd felt when the paramedic looked up to tell him that his little Rudy was dead, remembered how he had grabbed the man by the throat.

Nájera said, "The investigating officers gave you a break, Mr. Cooley. You could have been charged with assault with intent to kill. Three were fuckin Mexicans, okay? And one officer was white. They could have nailed you, but didn't. The girl, the one you tried to strangle, she said not to."

"Fuck her, too."

"Mr. Cooley," Nájera said, about to lose it himself, "I think you'd be wise to quit while you're ahead."

Dan pushed through the heavy door.

"Ayala!" Now he had a name.

He stumbled and nearly fell. He gulped deep breaths, but didn't feel like he was getting air. He leaned against a front fender of the Caddy. His shadow fell across the long hood of the car, made him think of death. He clawed at it at first, broke several fingernails. Then he began to bang on it with his fists. He tore off a windshield wiper. He used the metal part to dig into the paint. He got up on a fender and dented the top of the hood with his right fist. His hand swelled, he barked his knuckles. His bruised hand and wrist bones would ache for weeks. He broke the middle knuckle of his right fist. He kept cracking the hood.

"Fuckin, fuckin, fuckin dicks shouldda done right."

On the ride back to the shop, Dan felt pressure in his chest. He couldn't seem to catch his breath. He didn't care. He couldn't go home. He couldn't keep sleeping in the car.

When Dan pulled up at the shop, Earl saw the Caddy's scratched paint and dented hood.

Earl said, "Somebody hate Cadillacs?"

Dan showed Earl his hands. Earl walked him up to the office while the crew watched.

Dan said, "Remember Rall Nájera? Knocked you down? You retired him?"

"His left hook got me."

"Yeah, well. He just retired me and Tim Pat, the fuck."

"I don't get it," Earl said.

Dan explained what had gone down.

"Damn!" Earl exclaimed.

Dan sat at his desk. He looked down. His hands were swollen; one knuckle was bleeding. He looked up to Earl, who was standing in the doorway.

"I got nobody," Dan said. "You take over the shop. It's yours."

Earl shook his head. "No good. A handshake made us partners back when you trained me, and when I worked for you, and when we trained fighters together, and when I bought in as a partner. No paperwork, just somethin between you and me. Ain't partners if we ain't in it together." He slipped some black into his talk. " 'Sides, man, I'd feel like I was pimpin off you, and pimpin ain't my style. Now 'ho'in, that be somethin else."

Dan smiled despite himself. "Earl, you're all I got."

Earl said, "I'd feel empty as you if this happened to one of my little girls. Just try to go a little easy on yourself."

"Was it my fault, Earl? Did I cause it?"

Earl said, "No, no, this could happen to me, and you know how I watch my kids."

"I'm runnin like a lost dog."

Earl said, "Maybe you could sleep upstairs in the gym? Fixin up that room'll give you somethin to do. Don't worry about the shop. All the guys can work a little extra. I'll handle our fighters, so don't worry about the gym."

"Somebody's gotta pay for Tim Pat."

"Long's it's not you."

Dan fixed up the upstairs room. It took him a week. Once it was finished, he hardly left it except to buy booze and TV dinners. He took tranquilizers so he could sleep, but he didn't tell Earl that he washed them down with booze, that he gulped whisky from a water glass. He could no longer see colors, only battleship gray. It didn't matter. All he wanted was to live long enough to get justice. After that, he didn't care.

But his anger was often undercut by doubts and a slow seepage of guilt. Why had he allowed Tim Pat to go to the ice-cream truck alone that day? Dan tossed back the last three ounces from the Jim Beam bottle. The hit felt as if he'd taken a right-hand shot to the heart. He fell back on the unmade bed. Then, mercifully, he passed out.

Chapter 10

The police report arrived in the mail. Dan took it to his room. He read it, silently shook his head. He drank. He ate two dry doughnuts with black instant coffee. He opened another bottle. Ten High, bottom-shelf sour mash. Only two weeks before, he drank Old Granddad and Old Forester. Now it didn't matter. Later on he had pretzels. After that it was Cheerios and evaporated milk. He kept reading the police report. He drank more whisky and passed out. He slept fitfully, finally woke at four-thirty in the dark morning. His mouth was dry, tasted like the bottom of a birdcage.

He drank some grape juice for the potassium and the fructose. He read the police report again, but this time he crumpled it and tossed it in the trash, spat on it, then took the trash down to the Dumpster.

"Good riddance to bad rubbish."

The next four days were more whisky and pretzels. He thought about blowing his head off with the shotgun and being done with it. That would be consequence.

He looked for the report. Didn't remember that he'd tossed it. He put on all the lights. Tore up the place. Panting, he sat down, cupped his face in his hands. He poured more whisky in the water glass. He crumpled the brown bag from the liquor store. As he tossed it into the empty trash can, he remembered the report and having taken out the trash. He grabbed a heavy-duty flashlight from the shop and ran back to the Dumpster, terrified that the trash had already been picked up. He lifted the plastic lid. The Dumpster was full. He climbed in, went through every piece of trash. He was halfway into the soggy mess when the wide beam of the flashlight flicked across the report. Dan squatted down, hoping that the coffee stains and milk and garbage had not erased the full name and address of the driver.

He left the trash on the ground and went to his room. He spread the report on the table and smoothed out the soggy wrinkles. Searched letter by letter, number by number, line by line. And then he saw it. Guadalupe Ayala. Breed Street. He washed and dried his hands. He searched the Thomas Guide for the right map. There it was. In fookin Boyle Heights. It was near where he'd circled the high school, Roosevelt, home of the Rough Riders. He'd been right there. He'd fookin go back. And finish it.

Dan showered and shaved for the first time since he'd met with Nájera. He backed the Caddy out of the shop, then picked up the Hollywood Freeway at Melrose. When he got to Breed, he slowly drove by the pink-and-green house. He circled back around. He parked on Breed, on the same side of the street as the pink house down the way, but north of Sixth so he could have a 180-degree view of the action. He waited. It was six-thirty. The black sky had gone rosy to the east. Time was back on the clock. He wished he had coffee. He lit a Montecristo, needed the bang. He waited, smoke hovering inside the car despite the open windows. He began to understand how snipers felt. It felt good. He had the shotgun beside him on the leather seat. He'd get her on her way to school. Even if someone picked her up in a car, it didn't matter. He'd kill her if she was going to confession.

But it didn't work out that way.

———

He took up his position for four days. The gun was cocked. The push-button safety was built into the base of the trigger guard. He made sure it was off, meaning that the trigger was ready. Four bullets for her, one for him. On the first day, at five after seven, two boys and two girls, all Chicanos, rounded Inez Street and walked north, toward Dan. They stopped in front of the pink house. One of the boys whistled. A moment later, another girl joined them. The others greeted her, and then all crossed Breed at mid-block and walked toward Sixth Street and Dan. It was the Ayala girl. Pretty as a brown dove, a *palomita*.

The other kids chatted, but she remained silent, her dark eyes down. There was something about her that stopped Dan for a moment, made him rethink what he was about to do. He blinked several times, drew on his cigar, then decided he couldn't do it here, not with her friends around. No. He'd have to catch her alone. He had time, all the time in the world. But he noticed that none of these kids wore a gang outfit. That confused him.

Dan waited until they turned east. He also waited until they had crossed Soto, wanted to be sure they were heading for the high school. As they turned up Mathews, he followed slowly along Sixth. From the corner of Mathews, he saw them turn into the main gate of the school.

"Gotcha."

He soon established that this was the route she would take every day. Now all he had to do was call the school for the schedule of classes. Say he had to pick up his grandson.

"Classes start at seven twenty-five and end at three-fourteen."

"Three-fourteen? Really?"

"That's correct. I assume you are registered with us as a relative."

Things had changed since Dan had gone to school. It didn't matter. He'd be there each day, and he'd find her all right, find her all by her lonesome little self. He began to eat properly. He slept well. He cut down on the hooch. He was, so he told himself, almost back to normal.

Earl had noticed it. "You're lookin better."

"Feelin better."

Dan watched as the Ayala girl's friends stopped by for her each morning at the same time. One morning her brother stuck his head out of the
door. He and the girl played little gangbanger sign games.

"Play on," Dan whispered.

Dan started to wait for her after three in the afternoon. So what if
there were witnesses? But, if she walked home, alone or otherwise, she
didn't take the same route that she took to school in the mornings. Dan
decided that some gang punk was giving her a lift somewhere. Probably
to get fucked.

The following Monday morning, Lupe Ayala was accompanied by the
same four friends. That afternoon, Dan found a parking place on Mathews
near Roosevelt's main gate. At three-twenty, the same van that had run
down Tim Pat showed up. It was driven by an older woman, who greeted
the Ayala girl with a hug. Dan followed the van east through the afternoon
traffic. They passed the Nichiren Buddhist Temple at Camulos Street. The
van crossed Evergreen, kept going one more short block to Euclid, and
turned right. It proceeded along Euclid to Whittier Boulevard. It made a
right and then a quick right into a stucco mini-mall a few doors from fire
station number 25. The small businesses in the two-story mall were draped
with banners and posters and signs in Spanish advertising bargain prices.
Sandwiched between them was a covered stairway leading to the second
floor. Above it were signs advertising a dental clinic and a lawyer. There
was another sign, initials only: "CFD," in large black letters.

Dan watched as several cars filled with children entered the driveway of the mall. He could only see the children's heads because of the
many cars in the parking lot. His view of the stairway was blocked. He
would wait on Breed. He would wait on Mathews. He would follow the
van here. He would follow the girl home.

Dan waited until eight o'clock, but the van didn't leave the parking
lot. Except for the taco joint and the guitar store, everything else on the
ground floor was closed. Upstairs, the lights were out. The same thing
happened the next night. The girl, Dan concluded, must have different
people driving her home.

Stalking became an obsession. Part of what made it interesting was that Dan's opponent didn't know he was on her tail. His only problem was that his ass was getting sore from all the sitting. By parking on the other side of the street in front of the CFD, he learned that Lupe and eight to ten little Latino kids were going up the stairs leading to the second floor. Maybe it was a private school that taught English, or even Spanish. He sure as hell couldn't track the girl upstairs, not with all those kids up there.

Dan stayed with the pattern. School in the morning, then wait in front of the mini-mall. Fire trucks would head out from time to time, but mostly it was same-ol'-same-ol', except he'd park the car in different spots. He'd see the girl, but she was never alone.

At eight o'clock the following Saturday morning, the older woman picked the girl up at her house. He lost the van at a red light when it made a left turn on Whittier Boulevard. When he got to the school, the van was gone, but Lupe Ayala was standing alone at the driveway. Dan drove by, saw that Lupe wasn't watching him, then circled back. He parked in the red zone next to the fire station and got out of the car, thirty yards from the girl. Let them tow the car, let them have it. He wouldn't be driving again after the next half minute. He pushed the safety button to off.

He removed his Dodgers cap and dark glasses, wanted the girl to know who he was. He held the gun down, pressed it behind his right leg. His heart began to race, as if he'd been holding his breath. He breathed deeply from the diaphragm, but he wasn't getting oxygen. He felt woozy, but not enough to force him to turn back.

The girl glanced at him, then turned away to look up the empty street. People were sleeping in after a boozy Friday night. He walked slowly, didn't want to draw the attention of the few who were out, the shopkeepers, the firemen polishing their truck. His eyes focused on the girl's neck. He'd shoot her there and watch her fookin head come off. As he got closer, his vision cleared.

When he was ten steps away from the girl, she looked back in his direction, and noticed him for the first time. She recognized him. He pointed the gun from his waist. He saw the hurt in her sloe eyes. She saw the gun and she looked away and made the sign of the cross and lowered her head. As he closed on her, the older woman pulled into the driveway in her van. Eight little kids tumbled like pups out of a cardboard box, grinning and signing and hugging Lupe's legs. The girl did something with her fingers, and pointed toward the stairs. The kids paid her no mind, continued to scramble around her. She tried to place herself between Dan and the children, but they continued to circle her.

It was now or never. Dan knew she'd recognized him, would call the police if he didn't take her head off while he had the shot. Maybe he could order her behind the wall so the kids wouldn't see. But something was wrong. There was no noise, only absolute silence, only the kids' wiggly fingers and their adoring eyes as they looked up at the girl. Dan stopped, still as a stone. He focused on her hands and fingers. He took himself back to Tim Pat's death there in the street. Dan realized that the girl had been talking sign language to the kid. What he had taken for gang signs was a young woman comforting a deaf child.

Dan backed away. He did a 180, pulled the shotgun down along his leg again, and plopped into the Caddy. The girl dropped to her knees and covered her face. As Dan floorboarded the Caddy out of there, he saw the children pulling playfully at Lupe's fingers.

Dan took surface streets, expecting to be red-lighted by the police. It was over. Finally. He'd commit suicide by cop. He'd point the shotgun at the police, shoot over their heads, make them kill him. He couldn't blame the girl for calling in the cops. What he could not know, as he left Lupe in front of the Clinic for the Deaf, was that she felt she didn't deserve to live.

Dan drove to the Hollenbeck police station on First Street, where he parked in clear view of entering and exiting patrol cars. The Hollenbeck gym for amateur boxers was off to one side. He waited a half hour. When the heat didn't approach him, he drove off. He had a double Wild Turkey at the first bar he came to, chased it with a bottle of Beck's. He stopped at more saloons. He circled police headquarters at Parker Center. The boys in blue didn't pull him over. He had more boilermakers. The brand names no longer mattered. He drove back and forth in front of the Hollywood station. Nothing. He was drunk by now, but no one noticed.

Driving drunk was stupid, he knew that. And it was criminal. He knew that, too. His mind was clear, he saw all the points. Connecting them was the task. He watched himself as if through a microscope. He was a speck of shit. He was to blame for Tim Pat's death, bottom line. The girl killed the kid, Dan could never forget the horror of that. But he'd never go after her again. He'd never get the chance now, even if he wanted to, not if the cops caught him drunk with a riot gun. No, the girl would never have to worry about Dan Cooley again.

If only he'd gone with the little guy to the ice-cream truck. Dan was supposed to be the kid's watchdog. The kid was Dan's *fighter*. Trainers are supposed to take care of their *fighters*. It was a rule. Dan had broken his own rule. He dug at his eye.

He started to gag, his eyes began to run. He couldn't stop himself, so he pulled into a gas station. That made him stop, just going through the motions, other people moving around, pumping gas. He filled the tank. He rode the freeways for the rest of the day, sometimes counterclockwise, sometimes clockwise, stopping only for more gas and liquor. He got back to the shop sick of himself and sick to his stomach. Drunk, he wasn't sure and he didn't care. He ate some heavily sugared lemon cookies and drank evaporated milk.

He went back downstairs to the cement floor. Cement was easy to hose down. He sat on a bench, then straightaway set the black polymer stock of the shotgun on the cement floor and pressed the barrel against his forehead. He exhaled. He pressed the push-button safety, felt the *click*. Because of the booze, and because of his haste in running from the Ayala girl, he had forgotten that the safety had already been in the off position. He exhaled again, then hit the trigger with his thumb, shoved down on the curved trigger with all his might.

Nothing happened. He checked the gun. Fookin safety was *on*. He sat there blinking. He pushed the safety to the off position. He placed the tip of the barrel in the middle of his face. He exhaled. He waited. He exhaled again. But he didn't have the courage for a second go. He started to howl, stumbled to his feet, and pumped five shots into the Caddy. He blew out the windshield and tore up the rag top and upholstery and blew out a headlight and ripped into a fender and a tire. He was blinded by the spurting light, and deafened from the booms that reverberated inside the garage. It was done, all of it. He began to choke on gun smoke. He began to weep.

Earl saw the car first thing in the morning. Then he saw what lay on the floor next to it. He locked the shotgun in the back of his van. He went to Dan's room.

Dan told him the whole story, told him what he'd been up to for the past weeks, right down to the fuckup with the safety. "I'm ashamed of myself."

Earl said, "At least you're both alive."

"I hit bottom."

"Only way now's up."

"I coulda done evil," said Dan. "I'm supposed to be dead."

Earl said, "Well, you didn't and you ain't."

"I couldn't even blow myself away."

Chapter 11

The change of seasons in Los Angeles can slip right by you. July and August are usually hot, but it can stay hot on into October. January first can get hotter for the Rose Bowl game than the Fourth of July. But Dan was as oblivious to the weather as he was to everything else.

At his gym in Hollywood, Dan would stare at himself in a wall mirror and wonder if he'd gone brain dead.

"Might as well have."

He struggled with whisky every day. He'd be drunk for a stretch, then not. Drunk, he'd lie up in his room, racket from the shop and gym drowned out by the liquid candy in his head. When he was sober, he'd work in the shop, but Earl could see Dan's hands tremble. He knew Dan was only going through the motions, and that Dan craved the very thing that was killing him. Then Earl took a shot at breaking the pattern. Momolo was booked for a fight and Earl needed a cut man in the corner. When he asked Dan, to Earl's amazement Dan said yes without giving him an argument. Then Earl started to worry—had he made a mistake? Would Dan be sober when the day of the fight came? And even if he was sober, could he handle it?

The days passed slowly. The gym remained open, but Earl, working alone for the most part, couldn't give fighters all the time they needed, and some moved on to other trainers. No hard feelings on either side. The fight game was black and white. You could or you couldn't. You did or you didn't.

During the brief stretches when Dan was on the wagon, he would keep the gym clean. He'd also go back home and clean the house until it squeaked. Windows, tile, rugs, hardwood floors. He'd polish the mahogany tables and chairs, and wipe down the clear plastic that covered the sofa and overstuffed chairs. He'd change the bedding and towels, though they were never used. He wondered why he bothered. He wondered, too, if this would be the place, as it had been for Brigid, where he would put his head down for the last time.

He could never sit down in the house, no matter how tired he got. Being there just brought back too many memories. He saw Brigid pregnant her first time. He saw his kids playing and praying. He saw little Brendan in his tiny coffin. He saw Mary Cat the night of her first date. He saw Terry's closed coffin, his body too broken to show. He saw Tim Pat alive at Carson, saw him dead in the street.

Dan heard the slow grind of an old lawn mower. Cuco Corrales was the same Mexican gardener that Bridey had hired nearly thirty years before. He was stooped and gray now, but he still kept the place neat and pruned. Dan thought of Lupe Ayala, thought of all the shit things he'd said and thought about her.

"I blew it with Nájera, too," Dan said out loud.

Dan had to drink beer for breakfast just to get out of his room in the morning. He worked in the shop when he could, even managed to tear down the "GyM" sign and board up the front windows and door of the gym so no other little kid could ever die because of it or him. Fighters and trainers could still enter through the rear door.

Each night he had drunk himself unconscious by eight o'clock. Once again he let the gym get dusty, the floors unswept, neglecting it the way he had in the weeks after Tim Pat was killed. It didn't matter—more

fighters drifted away to other gyms. They were uncomfortable in an at-
mosphere permeated with Dan's grief and dereliction. It was pretty much
down to Momolo and Earl using the gym. Dan brooded silently. Suicide
came back to taunt him—he didn't have the guts.

Pain in his chest began to flick on and off, would then flare like a
gasoline fire. The pain increased daily until Dan was pressing the butt
of his right hand hard above his left tit, this after only going halfway
up the office stairs or climbing the steps to his room. He tried to help
Earl in the gym, but he'd have to beg off the punch mitts after thirty
chickenshit seconds. Walking at his regular pace through the parking
lot of a supermarket, he'd be out of breath before he got to the front
door. He'd seen the same things happen to his mother and father.
Modern medicine and surgery had not been available to them. He had
no doubt about what was going on inside him, but he wasn't sure he
wanted any of the cures. Booze seemed to offer a better solution,
didn't require a prescription and was sure to lead to a permanent
cure.

Earl saw the symptoms. He knew what they meant because he'd seen
some of them in his little girl. He waited for Dan to do something about
them. When he didn't, Earl took Dan by the arm one day and drove him
to Dr. Milton Kogon's office in the Cedars-Sinai Towers. Earl knew the
cardiologist because he had saved the life of his daughter Orla, who suffered from congenital heart disease.

Kogon ran the tests. His eyes were kind behind thick glasses, but Dan
could see that he was strong—a solid 147-pounder under his white coat.
Earl stayed beside Dan, because Dan looked like he might bolt. Blood
pressure. X-rays. EKG. The sonogram didn't look good.

Results of the blood work took two hours. Piss test. Dan loved the
instructions for women on the wall of the crapper: *With one hand, spread
the external lips* . . .

Treadmill. Dan pushed himself to prove the other tests wrong, but
pain remorselessly built inside him. He had to quit at ninety seconds.

The nurse gave him a squirt of nitro under the tongue. Kogon nodded, and she gave Dan another squirt. Kogon took Dan into his office.

Dan winked at Earl. "I'll catch a cab."

Earl understood Dan's need for privacy. "See you at the shop."

Kogon said, "Angiogram for starters, Mr. Cooley. We go in at the right side of the groin so we can take pictures, get you on tape. But if the tests we've taken are right, as I judge them to be, I'm sure we'll end up doing an angioplasty."

"That's the balloon you hook to the hardware you run up my vein."

"Up the femoral artery. If we discover arterial blockage during the angiogram, we then go back in with the balloon, as you call it. At the point, or points, of obstruction, we expand the balloon, then deflate it and remove it with the catheter. Now the blood can flow like it's supposed to. Your pulse is strong, so the problem's not with your heart."

If he only knew, Dan thought.

Dan said, "When does the atrocity begin?"

"Tomorrow morning, unless you want a heart attack tomorrow afternoon. You check into the hospital *this* afternoon."

Dan said, "How long's this catheter thing you run up into me?"

Kogon said, "Hundred centimeters, a yard, more or less."

Dan said, "The hell with your hundred centimeters. I could die on the table, right?"

"Yes, you could," Kogon admitted. "But without it, if you don't get on the table, you'll die sooner rather than later."

"I got a fight to work day after tomorrow."

"You should be out by then," Kogon said.

"So, it's okay I work the fight? I gave Earl my word."

"Is the fight local?"

Dan lied. "Yeah."

Kogon cleaned his glasses. "Ordinarily I'd say no, but barring complications, you could. We have to make sure your circulation is restored and the incision has closed. The femoral artery opens and you're dead.

So as my *bubba Manya* would say, it couldn't *hoit* to rest. Except that hard-heads like you will always take the chance, right?"

"Ain't no romance sleepin by the phone, Doc."

"None in a casket, either."

Dan said, "Ain't no pockets in a shroud, Doc." He liked Kogon.

Chapter 12

In Fredericksburg, Texas, a good lick outside of San Antonio, Chicky fought another left-hander like himself, Tommy Farrell, a ropy-armed white-boy Army corporal stationed at Fort Sam Houston. Farrell was pumped and pissed and there to clean Chicky's clock. By now Chicky knew what to expect from a southpaw. He "switched" from left-handed to orthodox, trying to get his left foot outside the lefty's right foot the same way the fat Indian had finessed him. It was the same move Eloy had tried to teach him, going all the way back to the Juniors. Chicky could see the change in the white guy immediately, saw his steely eyes go on double alert. But fighting as a right-hander still felt awkward to Chicky. He lacked power, the one thing he'd always depended on while fighting as a left-hander.

Trini shouted at him between the first and second rounds, ordered him to fight as a lefty, said to go out and give it to the *puta madre,* the whore mother.

Farrell was a savvy, hard-eyed, twenty-two-year-old Irish boy out of New York's Hell's Kitchen. The *irlandés* brought with him a record of seventy-two wins and twelve losses. Twenty-five of those wins were by knockouts. Chicky got tagged hard and had to go right-handed again to keep from being dropped by the more experienced New Yorker. Farrell drove lead lefts to Chicky's solar plexus that knocked the wind out of him and made him half brain-dead. His roadwork had led to superb physical conditioning, and that kept him from folding, but self-doubt butt-fucked him for the first time in all his fights, and he forgot most of what he knew. Between rounds, it was Paco who yelled at Chicky, called him Chickenshit Chicky.

"Then you go fight that blond *gabacho* sumbitch," Chicky told him.

Chicky lost the fight, even though halfway through the third round he dazed Farrell when he switched back to southpaw and with raw power tried to go kamikaze do-or-die. The Cavazos blamed him for the loss, said it was because he wouldn't listen to them, said going from left to right had cost him the fight. Chicky saw it otherwise, knew that going right-handed had kept him from being knocked clean fucking out. He didn't like the truth, but there it was. He'd just been beaten, not by much, but the truth was the truth. After the last bell, each fighter went, as always, to the opposite corner to nod to the seconds. At mid-ring they met and shook hands. Both said, "Good fight." The white boy winked and touched his jaw, acknowledging that it had been a tough fight.

Chicky said, *"Eres un pinche gallo de pelea,"* you're some fuckin fightin cock.

"Huh?" said the mick, his pale skin mottled and scraped.

Chicky said it in English. "You're one tough white-ass."

Farrell snorted. "Ey, Mex, you ain't so bad yaself."

Something was happening to Eloy. He'd stopped eating so much junk food and was losing weight. The puffiness in his face had lessened, and there was some spring in his step. He still had the swollen gut, but he started going to the gym with Chicky again. He shadowboxed after a fashion, and even did some light work with the weights. He also did some stretches, and very few squats, but it was better than nothing. Chicky was proud of him. He'd even cut down on the booze, or so it seemed. At least Chicky couldn't smell it on him. Even so, Eloy would sometimes nod off to sleep in the time it took Chicky to go to the kitchen and back. What Chicky didn't know was that Eloy had been buying those squat little bottles from Trini again—not to get high on, just to get by. *Morfina*.

In Poteet, he'd hung out with white and Tex-Mex boys, and dated a few Anglo girls, but he felt best with the *Tejanas*. He liked to joke with them in Spanish, and dance to *norteña* music, and be invited home for Mexican dinners. Most fathers of white girls didn't think much of boxers, and Chicky couldn't blame them. Fathers of Mexican girls admired him for boxing, looked at him with squinty grins when he came home a winner, but even they would not want their daughters to marry a pug. That would change when he got his degree from Texas A & M. One of the fathers got drunk, wanted to fight Chicky to demonstrate how tough he was. Chicky declined, modestly saying that he was sure the old man could whip his ass. Then Chicky went out in the field and screwed the old man's daughter in the cab of daddy's brand-new, big ol' green-and-yellow John Deere tractor.

A month after Chicky graduated from high school, a date in mid-September was set for the Senior Division of the Texas Amateur Boxing Regionals. They would be held at the San Nacho complex, a location that fit Chicky like a wet shirt. The San Antonio region was one of five in the state of Texas. There was a gang of boys of all colors and sizes in all five regions stomping at the bit to kick ass and take names in San Antone. The Regionals were serious business, one link in a long chain. The first link was made up of more than fifty Local Boxing Committees located throughout the U.S. Winning in the Locals moved you to the Regionals. Win there and you went to the Nationals. A win in the Nationals meant you fought in the Olympic Box-Offs. A win in the Box-Offs and you had a shot at the Olympic team. It would be a long grind, but Chicky was as sure as tar melted on the road in July that he'd make it. If not with power and the kind of slick he hoped one day to learn, then with heart and will, *a huevos.*

He had been running regularly. Now he ran daily, and felt he could run to the moon. He'd gained a little weight, and remained between 144 and 145 pounds, or just below the welterweight division's top of 147. Chicky drove into the San Nacho and trained every afternoon. No girl trips, not even to nearby Leming. His record had increased to sixty-two wins with nine losses and thirty-three KOs. He was an experienced, hard-hitting, hardheaded Mexican boy with a dream. The last day of the finals would be held on his eighteenth birthday.

Chicky's punches added to the harsh echoes of the San Nacho gym. He stuck the mitts and banged the bags. The Cavazos pushed him hard—that was their job. Their job was also to get sparring partners for him, but amateur sparring partners were scarce as hen's teeth. Yet the San Nacho was filled daily with local fighters, as well as fighters from as far away as Bandera and Seguin. One boy said he was from Pawnee. Most were Latinos who weighed 135 and less. The Anglos were bigger, and usually weighed 160 and more. When no one else was available, Chicky would work easy with the little guys for speed. But he had to work hard with the middle- and super-middleweights whether he liked working hard or not.

Trainers of local fighters in Chicky's class were reluctant to let their charges work with him—either because he was a lefty, or because their boys were gun-shy about Chicky's punching power. The best that competing trainers could hope for was that Chicky would get hurt, or maybe knocked off before their kids would have to fight him.

The scarcity of sparring partners at his weight often meant that Chicky had to work with pros, or with the bigger amateurs, if he wanted to test himself. Sometimes he was sharp, sometimes flat and dull. It was that way with everyone. But when Chicky had to give up a fifteen-pound weight advantage to inexperienced amateurs, boys who thought they had to throw punches at max power at all times, it could take its toll. Chicky wouldn't notice the hurt until after the sparring session. He'd be forced to take days off from sparring to heal, and cuss himself for being a punk. But he came back, many times while still hurting. When boys in his weight class from out of town came in looking to spar, he'd take them on, but they were usually in San Antonio for only a day or two. Even though they used the sixteen-ounce sparring gloves that amateurs and professionals usually wear when they "work," the out-of-towners would pass when offered a second shot at Chicky the next day.

Chicky sparred with pros and did well, but professional boxing tends to be slower than the amateurs because the pros fight more rounds and must pace themselves—and because the gloves are smaller, meaning they have less padding and do more damage. For 147 pounds and less, pros wear 8-ounce gloves. Above 147, including heavyweights weighing 260 and more, pros wear 10-ounce gloves. Padding in professional gloves is distributed well above the wrist, meaning there is less over the knuckles. Amateur gloves weigh 10 ounces for weights below 147, and 12 ounces for weights above, and are designed with more padding over the knuckles. Pros' hands are wrapped differently, as well. They use the same amount of gauze as amateurs, ten yards; but amateurs are only allowed, give or take, thirty inches of tape, depending on the size of their wrists and hands. Pros are allowed ten yards, though the guys in the heavier divisions are given the leeway of a few more yards. Wrapped and taped properly, the pro's fist is a lethal weapon. Hands wrapped by a coyote corner man can lengthen a fighter's reach on each hand by as much as three-fourths of an inch *inside* the glove. Fires ignite and blackouts occur when those fists land. Getting hit wears you down.

Pros also go to the body more. Punching power, as well as the number of punches landed, will score points in the pro ranks. In the amateurs, scoring is determined solely by the number of punches landed. A knockdown is scored equally with a powder-puff jab. Working with pros got Chicky in good condition, but he knew he needed to increase his speed and the number of punches he threw. He wished he had someone like Farrell to work with, only a right-hander. But he also hoped the Irish boy would be in the tournament so he could avenge his loss, something that stuck in his craw. Winning was what all this was about.

None of the usual fighters in Chicky's weight from the San Antonio region worried him. He had heard about them, or had fought and beaten them, and each day he felt more confident. Waiting to fight, especially when tournaments were scheduled well in advance, and when so much was riding on them, was tough on everyone. Chicky was anxious to get it over with, and especially anxious about meeting Farrell again.

What concerned Chicky most was fighting a hardhead, someone who would put his life on the line the same as Chicky. It would be like two bulls at the watering hole, where the odds for victory or defeat could be even. Either fighter could lose or win, but even the winner would be damaged goods, maybe permanently. Fighters who fought like bulls usually had short careers. Those who could take big punches were usually the ones more likely to walk on their heels and talk funny through crushed sinus cavities. Chicky knew he needed a good, long look at the tactics that the great boxers and their trainers did their absolute best to keep secret from other fighters and trainers.

Chapter 13

While Chicky was learning how much he still had to learn, another fighter, Cyrus "Psycho" Sykes, began to get the attention of the fight people of San Anto. He was on parole, and had fought some local fights around Houston and Galveston since his release. He had recently moved to San Antonio from the hellhole of the Fifth Ward of Houston to live with an aunt. He got started boxing as a junior in the smokers that were held regularly by the various fight clubs in and around Houston. He had a record of sixty-seven and seven, with twenty-six wins by KO. He had fought six southpaws, and four of his losses came from fighting them. Two of those losses resulted from his intentional fouls, fouls he committed to keep from being knocked out. He didn't like left-handers, felt cheated by them. He didn't mind hitting low, or any of the other dirty moves, if that's what it took. Scraping the laced and taped portion of the inner side of a glove across his opponent's face was a favorite.

Sykes said, "Muhfuh leffies come at you backwards."

He had fought in a few competitions in the joint, where he did sixteen months for aggravated assault. He'd beaten up his youngest sister, who had sold some of his rap CDs for crack money. While she lay knocked out on the bathroom floor, he used her burning cigarette to char two capital letters, "HO," high on the inside of her left thigh. Though he walked around several pounds heavier, Psycho Sykes would fight at the same weight as Lobito Chicky Garza.

Sykes, at twenty-two, was blue-black, had purple in his gums, and shaved his head smooth. His dead eyes languished behind the latest Oakley sunglasses. His drug of choice was hydrocodone cough syrup, Tussionex, because once high, he could maintain it with little sips from the bottle. Use of a glass crack pipe was not uncommon. He wore expensive 'hood clothes and $150-dollar Nikes. His fight gear was all brand-new Reyes stuff, Mexican, top of the line.

He trained under old George Hanks at Hanks's Gym on the Eastside, dark town. The old man stood erect at five foot eight and 162 pounds. He had white hair cropped close. Most men wished they had his arms and neck. He had fought some in the fifties at 135, but had a family to support and soon went to work. He opened a small gym and trained some good professional fighters along the way, but once he got them started, someone quick and dirty would always lure them away with a coin purse full of dollars and a suitcase full of lies. Because of the respect he'd earned through the years, white and Latino fight guys always called him "Mr. George," while blacks called him "Mist Jawg." He had retired from the San Antonio school system as a gardener, had stopped training pros altogether, and now worked with kids as young as eight. The hope was to give them power and self-respect as they moved up through the amateurs, and that both would serve them in the world of education and commerce. His boys usually made the finals, and often won. They were gentlemen fighters, and were always welcome and respected in every part of Texas where they fought. What brought Sykes to the San Nacho gym was that Mr. George did not have fighters at his gym big enough, or with sufficient experience, to deal with Sykes's relentless pressure.

Chicky had seen Sykes a few times, but had never watched him work. Either Sykes had just finished, or he had come in while Chicky was finishing up on the rope or doing sit-ups. Chicky refused to play stare-down games with Sykes, since he stayed behind his Oakleys, but Chicky knew he would have no problem meeting him in the middle of the ring once the shades came off.

Paco Cavazo said, "They say he's one bad nigga."

Chicky said, "Bring the bitch on."

Paco saw Sykes as a serious threat. Once he learned Sykes's schedule, he purposely brought Chicky in at a different time to guarantee there would be no pretournament flare-ups between the two. Out of sight, out of mind, and Chicky forgot about Sykes. Word in the gym on Sykes was that he could bang, fight guys gave him that; but they also shunned him because he always tried to play gangsta games. Local amateur trainers refused to let their boys spar with him.

Convinced that he was a black avenger who could walk through any punk who doubted his badness, Sykes didn't care what others thought or did. The pros waited for their chance. They'd work with him all right, but he'd have to pay.

Sykes behaved as if he was the undisputed champion of the world. "Muhfuhs, what I care they be suckin dolla' bills from my black ass? Ain't my money."

Mr. George forked over ten dollars a round. Everyone knew Mr. George didn't have money. That meant Sykes had backers. It was illegal by amateur rules for someone to sign a fighter to a professional contract until the fighter finished his amateur career. But there were those in boxing, as in every other business, who felt that rules made to level the playing field were for chumps. Sykes's backers were two local white-bread criminal lawyers, Toby Redding and Seth Laurel. Both had graduated from the University of Texas and then gotten their law degrees from Georgetown. They were pampered yuppies raised on country-club bourbon and branch. They fancied themselves legal gladiators, but had never shed a drop of blood in anger or fear. By hooking up with Sykes, they looked to lay claim to some tough by getting black gym sweat on their Armanis. Backing Sykes gave them strut. They'd heard of Sykes's jailhouse record and reputation, and with the testimony of bought-and-paid-for headshrinkers, brought Sykes to San Antonio in the name of rehabilitation. Power in professional athletics was what they were after, and they saw Sykes as their way to becoming agents and promoters without having to spend too much for an education in boxing.

Unknown to Mr. George, Sykes's backers' first choice of trainer had been Trini Cavazo, who had declined because Sykes was sure to come down to welterweight, and he already had Chicky. It was Trini who had referred them to Mr. George.

Paco said, "Our *cholo* boy won't go for a second pair of eggs in the same tepee."

"What if Garza doesn't win the tournament?" Toby asked.

"Then you bring Sykes back to me, and fuck my dear old friend Mist Jawg," Paco said with a big grin.

"Suppose," said Seth, "that something happens to Chicky, just supposing, and you take over for us? Are you sure Sykes'll listen to you?"

"Once Psycho learns I'm a badder psycho than he is, the mothafuck will," Paco assured them.

Toby and Seth went to Mr. George and pretended they had located him through big ol' Lamar Steuke, the manager of the San Nacho gym. Steuke wore an ink-black wig over his bald head, and ran amateur boxing in San Antonio. The lawyers offered Mr. George a hundred dollars a week to get Sykes ready for the Regional tournament, and added that they were paying that much because of Mr. George's solid reputation.

Seth said, "The way we see it, you can get our boy the Olympic gold medal, and that means you get bigger paydays down the line."

Mr. George knew that nobody could guarantee anything in boxing, but a hundred dollars was more than 99 percent of what the other amateur trainers got, and most pro trainers, as well. Mr. George understood that when these men talked about the Olympics, they expected a gold medal. They probably thought that a black trainer would get along better with a black boxer. Mr. George wasn't sure about the deal, especially with Sykes being the head case he was, but that hundred a week meant he could buy new equipment for his little guys. He listened and nodded, but only promised to take on Sykes until the tournament was over.

"That's when we know if we be happy wit each other, and we go from there." Mr. George turned to Sykes. "If you can't do what I show you, that be one thing. If you won't do it, that be somethin else, you undastan' I'm say?"

Sykes said, "What, I look like I talk Vietnam?"

"We'll see what you look like soon enough," Mr. George replied. "What you weigh?"

"A hundred fifty-four, and still goin down from one sixty-four when I was eatin joint food."

"He could fight as a one fifty-six," Toby suggested.

"No good," Mr. George said. "He still got fat on him. We'll fight him at forty-seven."

Toby and Seth kept Psycho in clothes and cash, and sported his belligerent ass at political socials. They were careful not to actually sign a contract with Sykes, and that kept them within the law. But they had Sykes sign an undated contract, one that only lacked a day, a month, a year, and their own flourishing signatures. Toby and Seth knew the right judges, had defended Trini successfully against drug charges over the years. It was Trini who told Seth to tell Mr. George that Lamar Steuke had recommended him as a trainer for Sykes. Ol' Lamar was happy to help. He'd done bidness with the Cavazos before.

The two months Mr. George had to work with Sykes seemed like plenty of time in the beginning. Sykes got down to 146 in two weeks. He was cooperative, and appeared to apply himself, but his biggest problem was that he didn't seem able to retain even the simplest fundamentals. As the Regionals approached, Sykes's impatience with his progress increased, and he began to revert to his slam-bang jailhouse style, one based on strength and virtually no brainpower. It was a subtle shift at first, but there it was, little refusals about minor things. The direction was clear. When Mr. George called Sykes on his lack of attention, or reminded him that he was not executing properly, Sykes would feign innocence. Pussy games was the way the old man saw the little rebellions.

The boy also had a smart mouth that Mr. George thought would one day cost him his teeth. He'd seen it happen, when a boy went to the ER from an aluminum baseball bat to his face. Mr. George came to think of Sykes as a gold front tooth over a root canal, all puff and shine on the outside, but everything dead inside.

Sykes had a compact body at five foot seven, all cuts and grooves and shine, but he wouldn't run as he was supposed to. When called on it, he'd hold up his gloves and say that it was the other boy who would be doing the running.

"I got def in bof hands."

He threw a good shot, Mr. George admitted, but not as good as Sykes thought he threw. What Mr. George liked least was that Sykes had a temper like a wild dog—worse, like a bitchy child. Mr. George called Sykes's backers, ostensibly with a progress report, but it was more to complain that things weren't going right, and that he didn't want the mess dumped on him.

Mr. George told Toby, "Sykes a fuckup. He see a cat sleepin, he got to kick it, see I'm sayin? He a boil ready to bust."

Toby said, "There's still time. If anyone can fix it, you can."

Mr. George hung up, wondering how someone could be such a fool and still be rich.

As the days ticked off, the pressure increased. Sykes would lose himself, as if hypnotized, in repetitive, full-force banging on the big bag. Old-timers were reminded of Sonny Liston and George Foreman before their fights with Ali. Punching as hard as he could, time after time, served to feed Sykes's grand impression of himself, but hitting a stationary target meant nothing to Mr. George. If he tried to improve on the mechanics of Sykes's punching or footwork, Sykes would stomp off and pout. A good trainer starts looking for a way out the door when that kind of shit comes down.

Sykes was even worse in the ring. He'd become frustrated with his pro sparring partners, who made him miss; he'd storm for the dressing room, calling it quits for the day.

In the shower, he'd bellow, "Stan' still and fight me now muhfuh, or watch you muhfuh back on the street. Check it out!"

Other fighters would double over, trying to keep from bursting out in open, derisive laughter. When Chicky heard about it, he laughed along with them, but he laughed out loud. Mr. George could only shake his head. Meanwhile, Sykes would play the wronged-brothuh game.

"Muhfuh don't play fair wif me, why I pay a muhfuh?"

When Sykes acted as if he didn't care what others thought, wiser folks knew better—a fighter is a performer, after all. But by then, those whom Sykes wanted to impress didn't care at all.

Toby and Seth often came by the gym. Watching Sykes rip into the big bag, they were thrilled by what they considered to be his primal force. They became so convinced of it that they incorporated, calling themselves Primal Force, Inc. They began to show up in, and to hand out, PF baseball caps, and PF T-shirts. They had leather jackets made at $400 a pop for themselves and Sykes in the University of Texas's longhorn orangey-tan. On the backs of the jackets, in bold white letters outlined in black, was "PF Boxing." Guys in the gym decided that "PF" stood for Palm Fuckers.

Sykes, meanwhile, who had, at least, pretended to listen to Mr. George in the beginning, began to rage through his workouts like a bug-eyed nut. The closer to the tournament, the worse he became. The more he raged, the softer he punched, his power squandered foolishly. Mr. George saw how Sykes might be able to intimidate amateurs, but also how easily the pros jacked him around—how they slipped his punches, how they caught them, how they countered his punches with their own. But they didn't hit him hard, not hard enough to run him off, just hard enough to make him think they were earning their money. The pros winked at each other, but kept silent. Picking up an easy forty to sixty dollars a day in beer and nachos money was good duty, and they joked about how they had the *mayate* shit-bug pussy lapping up their whipped cream. Mr. George wanted to give Sykes a bitch slap.

Yet he knew his job was to get the boy in shape one way or another, maybe even teach the hardhead something, so he kept putting Sykes in with the pros, who by now loved Mr. George, referred to him as "Don Jorge." He knew what they were up to, and couldn't blame them—he was doing the same, and didn't kid himself. He nonetheless worried about Sykes, and regretted that he had been unable to reach him. He wondered if a white or a Mexican trainer wouldn't be better for Sykes, since the dummy wouldn't listen to one of his own. Now he was rejecting everything he didn't already know, and that was a hatful. Mr. George couldn't see Sykes taking the tournament from a fighter like the Garza boy, and that would be the end of any hope of Sykes getting a place on the Olympic team. Experience also told Mr. George that PF Boxing would go out like a cheap cigar in a piss trough.

With three days to go before the first of the three days of the tournament, Mr. George instructed Sykes to go for a light run, and then rest until fight time. He wasn't surprised when Sykes showed up at the San Nacho that afternoon whacked out of his head. Mr. George doubted that Sykes's cough syrup would make him that goofy, so he could only guess at what he'd taken. He watched regretfully as Sykes would strut a few steps, like a mechanical chicken, then crank his head back and forth, his eyes wide and unblinking, first in one direction and then the other. Then he'd strut and crank again. Mexicans in the gym understood immediately that the chicken strut and head movements were a crack-cocaine tip-off. The *vatos* had an expression for it:

Homeboy's chickidín.

Sykes talked as if he were already on the plane to the Olympic Games, held up a fist, then did more chickidín. Mr. George wanted out right then, but he still had stuff to buy for his real fighters. Besides, he sensed that his paydays would be over soon enough, probably on the first night of the tournament. He also knew that you could never count a fighter out before the ref did. Maybe Sykes was the avenger he thought he was. Mr. George tried to imagine Sykes winning the tournament, but couldn't.

Chapter 14

Fighters arrived in San Antonio for the Regionals from as far away as Amarillo and Jasper, and would fight in weight classifications ranging from 108 pounds to super-heavyweights, for which there was no weight limit. The lesser of the two heavyweight classes topped at 201. But as a *super*-heavy, a boy could weigh 201 pounds, plus a fraction of an ounce, and find himself fighting someone as heavy as 265 or more. Fighters would weigh in and be paired according to a blind drawing. If there were eight fighters in a given classification, the numbers 1 through 8 would be written on bits of paper. Once they were drawn, numbers 1-3-5-7 would be paired with numbers 2-4-6-8. If there was an odd number of fighters in a weight class, one would draw a bye and advance to the next round without having to get hit.

Two rings had been set up to keep the action flowing. Each had a red and a blue corner. Half of the contestants would fight from the red corner and wear red gloves with white knuckles. The other half would fight from the blue corner and use blue gloves with white knuckles. It was a system followed in every weight group. There could be as few as two entrants, but in the Regionals there were typically many more. In Chicky's classification, there were sixteen fighters. They would be paired according to standard drawing procedures, and being in a lower weight division would be some of the first to fight each night or day of the tournament.

Tournaments can go on for days, but are never static. The crowd swells and shrinks according to how many fighters are entered at a given weight, and how many friends and relatives have come to support their champion. Children and grannies are there, as well as the parents of the fighters. Spectators are racially mixed; in San Anto, the crowd would be mostly Latino.

A good ol' boy in the crowd stood up and shouted, "Remember the Alamo!"

It got a good laugh from everyone, and a Mexican fan slapped him on the back.

The food stands sold hot dogs and potato chips, but there were also tacos, tamales, nachos, and enchiladas. There were soft drinks and coffee, but it was clear that some of the *raza* had smuggled in bottles of their favorite adult beverage. A huge U.S. flag stretched across one wall, but there was also the Texas Lone Star flag and a Mexican flag. Several vendors offered T-shirts, caps, boxing equipment, and gaudy posters. The most popular were those of Muhammad Ali and Julio César Chávez.

The officials, headed by Lamar Steuke, were mostly folks from San Antonio, male and female, but there were officials from other parts of Texas as well. Officials wore white uniforms, but because of their big butts and hanging guts, they looked foolish next to the finely tuned athletes. Various boxing teams wore shorts and tank tops that blazed with primary colors. Chicky wore his Aggie colors, maroon and white, and Farrell wore the same green and gold shorts with a white top that he'd worn when he'd cleaned Chicky's clock. Sykes wore pearlescent white, and greased himself to make his body shine.

Sykes smirked, "I like white."

The fighters were frightened, fearless, worried, and bored, depending on experience and who their opponent would be. The sixteen fighters in Chicky's classification ranged in age from seventeen to twenty-eight.

There would be eight bouts in the welterweight division on Friday night, and eight of those sixteen boxers would be eliminated. There would be four bouts on Saturday afternoon, which would eliminate four more fighters. The two bouts Saturday night, the Semifinals, would match four boys who had already fought once that day. Fighters would be getting tired, some might be fighting hurt. The two winners of the Semis would fight in the Final on Sunday afternoon. Depending on the number of fighters entered, the same process would play out in all twelve weight classifications. Winners of the Finals would go to the Nationals in Colorado Springs. The losers would have long rides home, whether all the way to the Panhandle, or just down the block. Folks in these parts called it nut-cuttin time.

There were two open-area dressing rooms, each fifty feet square—one for the red corner, one for the blue. Each had a chalkboard with the schedule of matches as determined by the drawing. Officials had matching bout sheets. Xeroxed programs were handed out at the door, where admission was $5. Fighters in the lower weight groups would go first. A few girls were part of the show, and they would be matched with other girls. All females had to present their passbooks. Once a fighter won the Semis, his passbook would be kept locked overnight in a tin box to prevent screwups on the day of the Finals. Taking home a passbook marked with a win in the Regionals was better than a brand-new Chevy four-by-four with ten-inch subwoofers going full bore.

The national anthem was dutifully sung, and the bouts proceeded quickly, some lasting the scheduled three three-minute rounds. Others lasted less than a minute of the first round—fights would be stopped when a referee decided that a fighter could not defend himself, but there were a few outright KOs, as well. Chicky would have to beat four opponents to win the tournament. Two could be Sykes and Farrell, and if so, Chicky knew that both would be knock-down, drag-out affairs. He was elated by the prospect of facing both, because, by beating both, it would move him to the Nationals, where everyone would know he was a badass.

On the first night, Sykes said, "This Chicky-dickie punk ain't nothin, right?"

Mr. George sensed Sykes's fear. So he couldn't be faulted later, the old man said, "This Chicky-dickie a whup-ass Messkin boy who will fight you three minutes of every round."

Sykes said, "Who hit hardes'?"

Mr. George lied. "You do."

"What it is!"

Mr. George watched Sykes dress for his bout. Psycho was sober, as reasonable as he would ever be, and his weight was right. *At least,* Mr. George thought, *crack don't make a muhfuh hongry. Goddamn weed make a boy go through a gallon of rocky road watching dirty movies. Onlyest way he stop playin wit his dick be eat more ice cream.*

On the first night, Chicky fought at 145 pounds. Many of the boys in his weight class had trained down eight and more pounds to make 147. Because Chicky had worked with bigger fighters in the gym, he felt comfortable against his heavier opponents. As expected by nearly everyone in the know, Chicky was pure search-and-destroy. He beat his first opponent by a comfortable margin. Eloy was elated, but Chicky's opponent had clipped him with some wild shots. It made Chicky realize he was short on defense. Out of respect for the other boy, a fireplug of a Tex-Mex kid from Abilene, Chicky shook hands mid-ring.

Chicky said, "Good fight."

Abilene said, "Y'all'll win the whole shitteree, you watch."

Sykes knocked out his first opponent in two rounds, a white farm boy with a near Oklahoma accent, from up in Wichita Falls. Once the boy recuperated, Sykes refused to shake his hand. The ref warned Sykes that he would not raise Sykes's hand in victory until he did.

Mr. George growled at Sykes, "You do the right thing, or you be all alone out there doin the wrong thing, you hyuh?"

Sykes didn't like it, but he went to the beaten boy, whose eyes were still half goofy. The most Sykes would allow was to pound one of the other boy's gloves.

"Yeah," Sykes said. But under his breath he muttered, "Cracker, I get you dawg-mess momma, too."

Mr. George heard the last part, and said, "Ain't this a bitch."

He would be glad when the tournament was over, so he could quit Sykes's common ass altogether, and get back to his real fighters. By now, the only reason he stuck was because he'd given his word to the lawyers to see Sykes through the tournament.

Farrell had a tough fight with a left-hander like himself, but won by unanimous decision. Chicky went to Farrell's dressing room to congratulate him.

"You did good, pods."

"You, too," said Farrell, and added, "Who's this Sykes dirtball?"

"Some jailbird hails from Houston."

"He's built like a brick shithouse, awright," Farrell said, "but can he handle sout'paws?"

"He'd best."

The next day, Saturday, the second round of the tournament followed weekend procedures. Weigh-ins were at eight A.M., and included a physical exam. That gave boys time to eat and rest before the first fight at noon. Out-of-towners would return to their motels and cheap hotels. Some stayed with relatives. Eloy and Chicky had gone home the night before, and at dawn the old man had used the last of his morphine. He had a pocketful of money and would see Trini later that day for more painkiller. He was calm as he drove into town, but after the weigh-in that morning, his habit began to jitter through him. He'd wanted to make a buy, but Trini had taken off.

Trini said, "Later."

"But what about my you-know?"

"Later, *damn!* What don't you understand about *wait?*"

Eloy began to fret as he drove Chicky to the Cattle Drive Hotel. He fed the kid what was billed as the "Longhorn Breakfast" at Crockett's All-Nite Barbecue Palace downstairs. Fear of pain and his growing need for the Lullaby Lady had him talking to himself, had him picking at dried-up gum stuck underneath his side of the booth.

"Eat," Eloy told the boy, though he couldn't even think of food. "Put some meat on your ribs."

He checked Chicky into a room upstairs after breakfast, and had to sit down. Chicky would drink iced tea with lemon and rest until eleven-thirty. Eloy had grown sicker over the last year, but had stayed away from Doc Ocampo—there was no way he'd cop a plea about being strung out to the old man. He knew that what ailed him could not be cured. *Son cosas de la vida,* fate, destiny, whatever. As he sat in a brown overstuffed chair, the view of his beloved San Anto through the hotel room's window was blocked by a newer, taller building. He felt sick as a gut-shot buck, but tried to remain calm.

Afraid that he'd vomit, Eloy left. "Rest," he told Chicky. "I'm walkin down to the cathedral, light us some candles."

That was a lie. He tried to phone Trini as soon as he was out the door, but there was no answer. He drove over to the tournament, but no dope dealer. He went to his truck and drank Popov vodka from a paper cup, and hoped no one would smell it on his breath. He chewed a handful of Rolaids, hoping to make sure, then swallowed half a tin of Mexican *aspirina.*

The tournament was packed. At one forty-five P.M., Sykes overwhelmed a boy who had come all the way from Texarkana. He had a good record, but he'd had easy fights. Unprepared for Sykes's onslaught, he was first put on his heels, then flat on his back. The ref didn't bother to count. Mr. George urged Sykes to go say something sportsmanlike to the beaten boy. Sykes went over, but when he didn't look at the boy as he banged his glove, the audience saw Sykes's bad manners and hooted him. He started shouting back, but the ref stepped in front of him, and, shaking his head, ushered Sykes back to Mr. George.

In the dressing room, Mr. George took Sykes aside. "Didn't you mamma teach you nothin?"

"I won—what you want?"

"Yeah, you did, but you lose sometime and you watch you lawyer money dry up like a dead skunk in the Pecos sun."

Sykes held his taped hands up and boasted, "I'ont worry about it, I got these."

Mr. George said, "Don't never leave 'em home."

Following Sykes's fight, Farrell also had it easy. His opponent had the chinky-shaped blue eyes the Poles had brought into Texas, eyes donated way back by Genghis Khan and his golden horde. He was a farm boy from Bandera, and had worn his dusty black cowboy hat outside the ring while standing by. He was proud of it, and of everything it represented, but because of Farrell's two left shots to the liver, he was unable to meet the bell for the second round. The boy's daddy was his coach, and stomped on the black hat when his son could not continue.

"I tried, Daddy."

The boy's daddy had immediately realized the hurt he'd unintentionally caused, and cursed himself for one dumb redneck sumbitch. He quickly hugged his boy to him, kissed his neck, and said that he was proud the boy had made it this far. It was hard for him to talk, but he gritted it out. "What say we head for Paris Hatters, and after we git you a new Stetson, we could get us a few thousand Pearl roadies for the ride back home and some of Momma's venison steaks?"

"I'd like that a lot, Daddy."

Chicky was next to fight. He had a tough opponent, a typical fast-moving Eastside black fighter who made Chicky miss more than he was used to. Chicky stood in the center of the ring after the last bell, and worried a ton while waiting for the decision. He got the win by a slim margin, and said a silent prayer of gratitude. He hadn't been rocked at any time, and was never worried about the other boy's power, but Chicky's dug-in, stiff, wide stance had limited his ability to navigate the cardinal points of the squared circle, and he was unable to corner his slippery target and explode on him. He knew he wouldn't have to go looking for Farrell or Sykes, and was grateful for that. Dissatisfied with his showing, he was nonetheless grateful for his power, and felt he had more pure juice than Sykes. Farrell was another thing. He had power to burn, plus experience. Being a left-hander like Chicky would make it tough for both of them. A short, stocky boy named Sal Torres from Eagle Pass would be included in the final four opponents going to the Semi. Torres's left hooks to the body had separated ribs and temporarily paralyzed his first two opponents. He was considered the dark horse to win.

Chicky took a shower and weighed himself. He was down to 141, but still in the 147-pound classification. He needed carbohydrates and potassium. While he was dressing, Eloy sought out Trini. Trini knew what Eloy was after.

"When can we have a sit-down?" Eloy asked.

"I'll wait around here. Go take care of our boy."

Chicky walked the half mile to Crockett's barbecue with Eloy. He skipped a meat dish, and ordered two glasses of grapefruit juice. After that, he had double servings of corn bread, beans, and bread pudding that was made with cinnamon and raisins and served in a lemon sauce that reminded him of his granny's lemon meringue pie.

"You still miss her?" Chicky asked. He didn't have to explain who *her* was.

Eloy picked at his uneaten fried chicken, and slurped up his sugar-laden coffee.

"All the time ever' day, 'n more n more. She's what kept me honest."

Eloy's transactions with Trini humiliated him, but without them he couldn't get through the days or the nights. He'd croak if Chicky ever learned what he was up to, so he seldom spoke to Trini when Chicky was around. Just as he thought of Dolores daily, he constantly thought of ways to aid and protect Chicky. One of those ways was to keep Chicky from knowing how little time he had left to live, and his nasty ritual with a needle. *Shame,* he thought, shame was what his Lola had told him he'd lost. But if he'd lost it, why did he still feel it? A *sinvergüenza* was someone who was without shame. In Spanish, being called shameless was worse than being called a whoreson, a motherfucker, and a *puto* cocksucker to boot. *S-s-sinvergüenza* made Eloy stutter, but once he had Chicky resting safely in bed, he went searching for Trini at the San Nacho.

Eloy didn't see Trini's bust-out '78 Monte Carlo lowrider in the parking lot. Hoping for a note from Trini, Eloy checked under Fresita's windshield wipers, then went inside the arena.

"He better come through, he's gotta come through."

The tournament was winding down for the afternoon, and the clean-up crew was already preparing for the Semi scheduled for that night at seven o'clock. Eloy had the all-overs and started to sweat. He checked everywhere for Trini, and when he didn't see him, the all-overs got worse. He went back to the parking lot and found Trini sitting in Fresita. Eloy was sure he had locked the truck.

Eloy said, "What the fuck's this?"

Trini smiled. "What's what?"

"How'd you get in?"

"Tricks of the trade, *ése.*"

"Don't fuck around. You got my *arrullo,* my lullaby?"

Trini shook his head. "I made calls all over town. Looks like things is dried up for two more weeks, *ése.*"

"Things never dried up before," Eloy protested.

"Things is tight, my nigga. When it opens up, the price'll be jacked way up and there's no tellin when it'll cap out."

Eloy stayed as calm as he could. "You got to have one *pinche frasco,* one fuckin vial."

"Not even for myself, baby, just that rank, dark shit from Mexico, that's what I'm sayin, my brother. I'm sick, too."

"Who else got some?" Eloy asked, a note of desperation in his voice.

"Nobody, *nadie, nadie,* fuckin *nadie,*" Trini replied. "Go see your croaker to write you a scrip."

"He wants me to go to detox and eat fuckin green vegetables."

"These fuckin doctors is cold."

Trini loved these scenes. He'd been on the wrong end of enough of them to know how Eloy felt. So fuck Eloy, the *cholo* prick. Trini hadn't made any scratch off of Chicky yet, so he had to get paid somewhere, right? Bidness was bidness. Besides, he could see from Eloy's yellowing eyes that the sick puke wouldn't be around for long. Trini was just joking about raising the price. He had to have some fun; that was only reasonable. The more Trini thought about it, the more righteous he felt.

Eloy said, "How 'bout I see you later?"

Trini said, "I'll keep my feelers out, but only because we go way back, you and me. But things is hot, okay, *mi Lobo Tejano?*"

Eloy said, "See you at the fight. Take care of my boy."

"Be cool," said Trini.

"Yeah," Eloy muttered. Something inside his liver was blinking on and off, and breathing got hard, and puke stung the back of his throat.

Trini got into his car and drove off, the muffler hanging loose. Once he was around the corner, he began to laugh. "Dumb fuckin Messkin."

———

Passbooks had been turned in, the weigh-in was over, names had been drawn, procedures had been strictly adhered to. The most important thing was to protect the fighter, and Lamar Steuke was there to guarantee it. Chicky and Sykes would fight the Semi from the red corner, but in different rings, and both would share the red dressing room with a score of other fighters. Sykes drew Farrell from the blue corner, and would go first. Chicky, going second, got Torres from the blue, and the Cavazos got busy with Chicky on how he could nullify Torres's body shots.

Mr. George and the Cavazos kept Sykes and Chicky occupied to prevent any sudden ignition between them that could disqualify one or both before the Semi began. Sykes was the kind who could find something wrong with moonlight, and was deep into being poor little Cyrus.

"Why it be me gets that wrong-handed white boy?"

Mr. George had been trying to explain the proper way to move on a southpaw, but Sykes was unreachable.

"It the luck a the draw," Mr. George explained.

Sykes snarled, "Fuck a draw, nigga, I suppose to have that right-hand beaner boy."

Mr. George tried one more time to get through to him. "Listen at what I'm sayin 'bout feets."

"Fuck you feets, I been set up!" Sykes looked like he was on the edge of a meltdown.

Mr. George decided that Sykes just didn't get it, never would.

Sykes and Farrell were the first of the welterweights, and it soon became obvious that Sykes had trouble with the left-hander. Sykes tried to make a street fight out of it, but Farrell kept his right foot outside Sykes's left foot, controlling him. Farrell pasted him with jabs and wasn't there when Sykes came blasting in with both hands. Farrell was ahead on points with all the judges after the first round.

In the corner, Sykes was breathing hard. Mr. George tried to calm him first, then tried to get him to think. Sykes first had to establish who was boss of the canvas, and then throw right-hand leads, and come back with his hook. It was too much for Sykes, who had only one way to go—

reverting to the streets and attacking more like a gangbanger than a boxer.

"I'ma kill that honky and his dawg."

The bell rang, and he charged from the corner like a mini Mike Tyson, but Farrell pivoted out of the way. When Sykes came around, Farrell hit him with a quick right-left-right combination that knocked Sykes down, his first trip to the canvas ever. He tasted blood from a cut lip and began to shake. Mortified that a white boy had knocked him down, he let loose a high, keening wail that bounced off the hard walls. The crowd keened back. He took the mandatory eight count on his feet, and roared back at Farrell, who continued to pepper him with jabs. Sykes tried to wrestle him down at one point, and the ref was there to step in and penalize Sykes with a one-point deduction. The crowd hooted at Sykes and went into a frenzy of whistles and spit. They hated the *mayate* black shitbug for the crappy sportsmanship he'd shown in all his fights.

"*Hipócrita!*" a stooped old Southside farmworker shouted. "Hypocrite!"

Sykes didn't know what it meant, but knew it was bad. "What?" he shouted back.

Sykes went into his pout, and Farrell knocked him down again, hard this time, hard enough to ring his bell. He looked to Mr. George, who tried to signal to him, but the signals were too complicated for Sykes, who got up cursing. The crowd cheered Farrell. Near the end of the round, Sykes briefly trapped Farrell on the ropes, but Farrell spun free and won the round going away.

Chicky, already gloved and warmed up, watched the action from his stand-by position near the dressing room, and saw how Farrell outclassed Sykes. It appeared that Chicky would be fighting Farrell—good, thought Chicky. Sykes and his temper would have been the easier of the two to beat, but Chicky liked going against Farrell again. It would decide who was boss between them.

———

In the third round, with one eye starting to swell shut, Sykes came out firing to the head. He suddenly dropped down, and with Farrell's body blocking the ref's view, intentionally came up full power with a head butt to Farrell's chin that knocked his head back. Sykes, during the same lifting motion, came up with the heel of his glove, which caught Farrell at the base of the nose, breaking it. Sykes's fouls happened so quickly that the ref and most of the crowd missed them, but not Chicky, who wanted to squash Sykes like a bug. To Farrell, the nose shot sounded like a bat breaking at Yankee Stadium. Water flooded his eyes, and blood spurted down the front of his white top. He couldn't see except for smears of light and dark. He didn't care about the blood, but his face was on fire from the broken bone and he could barely keep his eyes open. He was punching at blurs and shadows, but still managed to whack Sykes so hard that the brother's eyes fluttered and his mouthpiece cartwheeled across the ring. Sykes grabbed and held, and the ref crossed to separate them. When he saw how heavy the flow of blood was, he understood it meant a broken nose, and right then stopped the fight.

Farrell cut loose, "Nooooo, I had 'im, I had 'im!"

Chicky caught up to Farrell on his way to the dressing room. "Sykes beat you dirty, pods."

Farrell squeezed blood from his nose. "Yeah, he did, and the ref missed it. But now you got a shot. Bust up that fuckin dinge for me, okay?"

Chicky touched Farrell's bare fist with his glove. "I'm gonna tear him a new asshole."

Before Chicky's fight, Eloy had motioned Trini down a hallway and around a corner.

Trini looked over his shoulder, whispered, "I been callin my guys."

Eloy asked, "You got some, right?"

"No way," Trini said, but gave Eloy eight hard, sixty-milligram number four white codeine tablets. "It's like from my own stash because I know you're hurtin, homes. You can gag 'em, or you can cook up, but your face might swell."

Eloy left Trini standing there, went at a half run to Fresita, where he chewed four of the pills and downed the bitter paste with cheap vodka.

It was five minutes later, and Chicky was in the ring. He looked nervously for his grandpa. Eloy entered and waved from the main entrance. Chicky nodded, felt safe again, and went to the center of the ring for instructions from the ref. Moments later, he returned to his corner, dropped to one knee to make the sign of the cross. He banged gloves with Trini and Paco as the bell rang. Eloy was feeling better already.

Torres came out and quickly tried to go to Chicky's liver and ribs with his wide left hook, but Chicky's jab and foot position took it away from him. Torres saw he couldn't get the hook off, and tried with a straight right behind three stiff jabs. He was a good and quick fighter, and Chicky saw that he must watch his every move, slip or block Torres's every shot.

Chicky was winning the first round on jabs to the body as well as to the head. Halfway through the round, Chicky unloaded with a left-hand lead, then came back with his right hook. The simple but crushing combination cold-cocked Torres, who lay on his face, his lips twisting involuntarily up from his teeth, his eyes twittering. The ref called the fight immediately, and the doctor sailed into the ring. It was several minutes before Torres revived and Chicky went to him as he slumped on a stool in his corner.

"You okay?"

"No, but I'll make her."

They shook hands.

Sykes had seen the KO, saw how the boy dropped like a bank sack full of nickels, and saw how the crowd came roaring to its feet. Mr. George watched as Sykes blinked, watched as Sykes's eyes jittered toward the green EXIT signs.

Good, thought Mr. George, *boy has earned him his ass whippin.* Mr. George also watched as Chicky and the Cavazo brothers and Eloy were whooping. Seth and Toby watched them, too, had seen the devastating KO, and had seen Sykes's scurrying eyes.

"Sheee-it," said Seth.

Toby said, "What now?"

"Well . . ." Seth tried, but he couldn't go any further.

The referee raised Chicky's hand. Chicky and Sykes were proclaimed winners of the Semi. They would meet the next day at noon.

"Sheee-it," said Seth, repeating himself. His first instinct, lawyer style, was to cover his ass. For the first time since he'd passed the bar, he didn't know how.

Toby felt the same. "This is bogus, man."

Both had known that six of Sykes's losses had come at the hands of southpaws, but being new to the game, and not understanding its geometry, they'd decided the losses had been quirks. They had believed that proper training by Mr. George would solve the problem with lefties, but Sykes hadn't improved, so they decided that it must be Mr. George's fault. Now that they'd seen what Sykes had to do to beat Farrell, they realized that their plans for getting to the big time were about to go down the tubes unless something could be done with this badass southpaw Garza kid. They wondered how much the Messkin would charge to take a dive.

On the way to the dressing room, Trini massaged Chicky's neck and shoulders. He said, "You hit like the Wolf, kid, right, Lobo? Yeah, he hits like his *abuelito,* right?"

Eloy had calmed down from the vodka and the spreading codeine, and smiled. "Hits harder'n me, *más recio, mucho más recio.*" A lot harder.

Dressing rooms are the best places in the world when you win. But they knew that they still had to win the Final.

Paco looked at Chicky. "It's comin up nine. Eat good first, but I want you in the sack before ten-thirty, okay? No dirty movies."

Chicky nodded. The pressure was on, and he knew from past tournaments that he'd be dreaming all night. He'd see himself punching in slow motion while his opponent would be firing on him full blast and at will. He'd wake up a dozen times before the alarm went off.

"Weigh-in's eight o'clock," Paco reminded them. "I'll be there early."

"I'm sleepin in," Trini said.

"I'll be early, too," Chicky promised.

Trini asked, "Both you stayin in the hotel?"

Eloy looked at Trini. He had schemed on his own. "Chicky is. I'm drivin on home, make sure everything's still where I left it."

It made sense to Trini. Traffic would be zip that time of night, and the same coming in the next morning. Being rid of Eloy's motor mouth would be a relief.

"You got my cell phone number if home don't answer?"

"Yeah, yeah, and you got all my numbers," Trini assured him. "What time'll you be up?"

"Early," Eloy said, confident that Chicky had no idea of the real meaning of this conversation. "Sunup."

"Why don't you call me at nine and we'll all have pancakes?"

"I could call earlier."

"Yeah, do that, I might as well go to the fuckin weigh-in with y'all."

"Don't hang me up, hear me?"

Trini sucked on the wooden end of a blue-tipped kitchen match. "Would I do that?"

At Crockett's, Chicky drank water, more grapefruit juice, more water, and then ate Mexican-style scrambled eggs with beans and corn tortillas. He had more bread pudding, and two glasses of milk. Getting their business square at the arena had taken an hour. Chicky was hungry and dug

into his food. Eloy looked on, sipped coffee he'd loaded up with four sug-
ars. He noticed that Chicky had dropped in weight. Eating and the fluids
had taken another forty minutes, but food and drink meant the lost
weight would come back on.

They went to Chicky's room, and Chicky took a quick shower. His
hair was clipped almost to his scalp, so drying off was quick.

"Why you goin all the way home, Grandpa?"

Eloy already had his lie. "It's the ranch. We been away."

Chicky said, "But you'll be here tomorrow in plenty of time?"

"I'll come back and get you up at seven. We'll feed you early, and then
again after the weigh-in."

Eloy could see the boy was tired, but was sure he'd be fine in the
morning, even if he would toss and turn getting to sleep. He was proud
of the boy. He saw much of himself in Chicky.

"You're gonna be better'n me, verás, you'll see."

Chicky smiled, "You betchum, Red Ryder." Without thinking, he repeated what Eloy had said to him a thousand times, going back as far as
Chicky could remember. Chicky squinted. "You able to make it home
okay?"

"Hail, yeah, ol' Fresita knows the way by heart."

The Wolf made it to the street, his body damp. He hardly shit these
days, and almost never pissed, and he could no longer tell if the alarm
bells ringing in his body came from his pickled guts or from his desperate need.

Chapter 15

Following the Semifinal, Toby and Seth pulled up in front of Sykes's aunt's house. They told Psycho to be ready at seven-thirty the next morning.

Sykes said, "My knee be hurtin'n, my foot, too, where the honky muhfuh step on me."

Mr. George knew Sykes was lying. Seated next to him in the rear seat, he yawned and said, "Put ice on 'em, you be fine."

Sykes got out of the BMW and started for the door, but then returned. He pursed his lips and rubbed his thumb and forefinger together like a tailor feeling fine wool.

Sykes said, "Need some more you-know."

Toby, the driver, said, "We gave you two hundred before the tournament."

"My awntie a big eater. She don't get it this way, she get it robbin you house."

Seth forked over another hundred. "Stretch it."

Sykes turned away, and spoke as if he were talking to a prison guard. "Stretch some a this," and walked toward the house.

Seth said, "I don't get it. No matter how much we do for him, nothing makes him happy."

Mr. George said, "Sykes not be happy if he'as white."

Mr. George pulled down the armrest and settled into the buttery leather of the backseat. One more fight, and one more hundred-dollar bill to go. He'd already bought four pairs of sixteen-ounce sparring gloves, some new punch mitts, and three new speed bags. Helping his little guys was the only upside.

Toby drove in the direction of Mr. George's gym, located in a warehouse district off of East Houston, near Cherry. Once his wife had passed, Mr. George lived alone in two windowless back rooms. He was surprised when they got to his gym but drove on by.

Mr. George said, "You passed where I live."

Seth muttered, "We need to talk."

"Talk back at my place."

Seth said, "We'd rather keep moving, if you understand what I mean."

I understood all along, saltine.

"Look," said Toby, watching Mr. George in the rearview mirror, "you saw this Garza tear the head off that husky boy."

"Uh-*huh!*"

Seth said, "Sykes didn't like what he saw."

"Sykes ain't gittin paid to like."

"Just what is his problem?" Seth asked.

"The boy a fly—he love shit same as sugar."

"But can he go all the way?" Toby asked nervously.

Mr. George was having fun. "All the way where?"

Seth said, "Win tomorrow and beyond."

"That depend on him."

Toby pressed. "Can he beat Garza?"

"Sykes, he a badass. It can be good when a fighter a badass. But a badass same as everybody else, all he got to do to beat the other boy is whip him."

Neither lawyer wanted to deal with that germ of truth, and that made it all the more fun for Mr. George.

Eloy stayed in San Anto instead of driving back to the farm. He'd planned it that way since early afternoon, when Trini was unable to get him his goods. Eloy's problem was where to stay—clearly not with Chicky, and maybe puking or having to take off in the middle of the night if Trini called. He took North Broadway to the cheap motels past Mulberry and out near Brackenridge Park. It had been years since he'd been in that part of town at night, and he was wary. Streetwalkers with bulging fake tits and their crotches near to hanging out patrolled the sidewalks and preened at corners. Transvestites wore feather boas. Eloy drove past as the hookers waved and whistled at him. He decided that maybe a South-side motel was best after all, but then he saw cruising cars and pickups pull over suspiciously in front of motels and under dying oak trees. When they immediately pulled away, Eloy realized that they'd made a quick score from the shadows that moved in and out quick as cats. Eloy thought fast, made a plan. He'd check into a nearby motel, head for the shadows under the trees, and then go back to his motel to shoot up. He had sterile, disposable needles with him, so that was no problem. He'd score just enough to get him through the night. But then he realized that he had to face the tournament the next day. He decided he'd better go for two days. But what if that shithead Trini let him down? Eloy decided that he'd best try to score for five days. Fuck it, if all he could get was some Mexican shit, he could always steal a spoon from a coffee shop and cook it. He came to a decision and made a U-turn.

The Maverick Motel dated from 1947, just after the boom of World War II. It had three floors, plus stairs and parking on both sides of the building. The faded old stucco needed eight coats of paint, and clusters of dry weeds hugged its flaking walls. The Thai owners had let the whores take over, but were stingy with clean sheets and supplied one frayed towel per trick. For thirty dollars, a john could rent a room for an hour. He was usually out and gone in half that. Eloy paid $43.37 for the night. Nocturnal creatures in human form had slithered away from his headlights, then watched from shadows and through narrow openings in blinds as he went to his room on the ground floor. A cricket sang his hardy love song behind the patched wall next to the toilet. Eloy gagged back a spurt of vomit and felt bile burn the back of his throat.

"Lordy."

Eloy wanted to score—but his body wanted something else. You can abuse major organs like the liver and kidneys only so much before the body revolts. Pile on top of that the stress load that comes when the body is screaming for a fix. Eloy suddenly felt as if the floor had disappeared from beneath his feet. His legs refused to move. He slowly collapsed and lay on the floor. His eyes closed, his breathing became slow and shallow.

Toby drove the BMW out onto the 410 loop—no more stoplights meant no carjacking niggers to worry about. Mr. George had his hand on the ice pick in his pocket. He calmly watched the cars go by as the BMW circled close to the International Airport, and near both the Lackland and Brooks Air Force bases. Planes were flying everywhere in the dark night.

Toby said, "There's a reason we need to talk."

"Uh-*huh*," Mr. George muttered.

Toby explained that he and Seth weren't concerned for themselves, or because any money that could be lost on Sykes would in any way cost them. No, they were concerned for the investors whom they had promised a fair return on their money—old friends, even relatives, folks who cared about the plight of African Americans, decent folks who revered the Reverend Jesse Jackson and put their faith in the idea that Sykes was someone fundamentally good who needed and deserved a second chance.

Toby pleaded, "They need your help."

Mr. George said, "Sykes be the one to save them po' rich folks, not me."

"But you're the trainer."

"Dass right, but dass all."

Seth broke in. "True, but winning is the real issue, wouldn't you agree? And sometimes the downtrodden need a little help to win, a little head start, you know, like a bootstrap deal. So think. Isn't there maybe something you know about, with all your years in boxing, that you could do, let's say, to somehow influence the outcome of tomorrow's fight in your fighter's favor?"

"He you fighter. You wanna fix the fight, up to you to do it."

Mr. George had smelled weasel sweat from the time they'd gotten on the loop, and he smiled to himself.

Toby was getting pissed. How dumb could one old jigaboo be? He tried again. "It would be very much to your advantage if you could ensure a win for Sykes tomorrow."

"Ain't no big thing, win. Jus' tell you boy to go out there and knock that muhfuh Messkin out."

Seth, hating to say it outright, said, "Just how common is it, you know, for someone to fix a fight?"

Mr. George sat back. " 'Bout as common as a nigga wit a snake."

Toby tried to be patient, but he was starting to sweat and felt slightly sick to his stomach. "Boxing is like every other business, Mr. George. There are ways, and there are ways. What we're talking about here is maybe somehow putting something on Sykes's gloves, or in Garza's water bottle, you know, or maybe something in his food?"

"Fool, that not how it done."

"Okay, fine. How is it done?" Seth asked impatiently.

Mr. George said, "Like this hyuh."

He reached up and lightly twisted Toby's ear. Toby nearly ran off the road at sixty-eight miles per hour.

"Whoa!" said Toby, finding the brake pedal. "Whoa!"

Mr. George twisted ever so lightly. "Y'all goin take me home now, or what?"

Toby made a beeline for Mr. George's place.

Seth said, "Of course it's understood that you'll get paid your final hundred dollars after the fight tomorrow."

They drove off and Mr. George stood on the curb, thinking, *God surely didn't make lawyers to be what they'd become.*

He went to bed in his stuffy room. He couldn't sleep. Maybe he should go to Lamar Steuke about all of this, but he had no proof. He could go to crazy-ass Trini Cavazo, but what might that dope-head nut do, shoot Sykes? Shoot the lawyers? Maybe blow him away, too? He could tell Chicky what he knew and urge him to go for an early knock-out, but coming from him, Sykes's own trainer, it could spook the kid right out of his jock. Should he place a call to Eloy? But shit, this ain't gonna come to nuthin. How would those two dumb peckawoods fix a fight on their own?

Trini lit a cigarette as he watched an infomercial about roasting two turkeys and making corn bread at the same time. It was past eleven. Like always, he couldn't sleep.

Toby and Seth hadn't yet cleared the Eastside when Seth fingered his cell phone. It rang once.

Trini said, "Wass up?"

"Seth."

Trini said, "My brother Seth, *ése.*"

Seth said, "Here's Toby."

Toby came on. "Yeah, Trin, hey, level with me, okay? How high are Sykes's chances to beat Garza tomorrow?"

" 'Bout as high as a Chinee dwarf."

Toby said, "That bad?"

"Chicky'll kick the shit outta him."

"I want Sykes to win," Toby told him.

Trini asked, "How bad?"

"Bad enough for you to meet us at the Hilton Palacio on the river."

Trini didn't like that idea. "Parkin costs too much, and I'll stick out over there. How's tomorrow?"

Toby said, "You saw how Sykes had trouble with that lefty. We got to talk before it's too late."

"Late is right now, for chrissake."

"It'll be worth it," Toby promised him.

Trini squashed his Marlboro Menthol in a coffee lid. "Crockett Barbecue's got good coffee, and over there us spicks can mix with y'all and not draw a look."

"Thirty minutes."

Toby and Seth were already at Crockett's when Trini got there. He walked past them to the counter to order coffee. Toby and Seth sat midroom in the near empty barbecue joint, drank Evian water, and tried not to be noticed.

Lame brains, Trini thought.

Bright overhead lights shone through the big plate-glass window and turned the sidewalk yellow. Trini ordered coffee at the counter. Loading it with sugar, he took his time to check the room for any fight people. He knew they'd all be crapped out like a burned tortilla by this time, but his years on the sly had taught him that there was no such thing as too careful. He'd have preferred meeting these two *gabachos* in the daytime at the old red courthouse, or out in the mesquite, but they were anxious and he sensed that he could make a meal of these little white mice. The room was clean, so he ambled over and sat down.

Trini said, "Say it quick."

"Can you make it so Sykes wins tomorrow, yes or no?" Toby asked.

Trini let them have it hard. *"Claro que sí,* clearly, but it'll cost you five big ones."

Toby was surprised it was so cheap. He wanted clarification, but played it dumb. "Five hundred seems a little high . . ."

Trini said, "Toby, baby, remember the Nina Simone song? Maybe it's before your time? Something like, 'Oh, Lord, I don't want to be good, just don't let me be misunderstood,' some shit like that?"

"You said five, right?" Seth asked, already knowing the answer.

"Yeah," Trini said, "five *beeeeg* ones."

Toby said, "Why so much, dang? Who we dealing with here, the Federales?"

"I got to split with my people, don't I?" Trini smiled, his eyes droopy. "But when Chicky goes down tomorrow, you boys best be clear that I'm the man who'll be training Cyrus shit-bird Sykes from now on, ain't that right?"

The lawyers hesitated.

Trini said, "Is that a yes?"

"It's a yes," Seth said, "you're Sykes's trainer, assuming Sykes wins tomorrow."

"He'll win."

"You sure Sykes'll listen to you?" Toby asked.

"Once Psycho learns I'm a badder psycho than he is, he'll listen all right."

"But is Sykes worth it down the line?"

"Oh, yeah," Trini replied. Down the line didn't matter to Trini either way, but he wasn't going to say it. "Sykes is a tough nig. Not as tough as my Chicky right now, but when we turn him pro, Sykes don't fight no left-handers, and that's how that's handled."

"Awesome," Toby said, and belted down some more Evian.

Trini followed the lawyers in his car and waited up the street and out of camera range when they drove into their secured chrome-and-glass office building. They were back on the street in less than ten minutes, and followed Trini's car to a deserted market on the Southside. Through his passenger window, Seth handed Trini twenty-five hundred-dollar bills taped in a sealed envelope from the United Way.

Trini said, "If this don't count out right, no deal, O'Neill, and I'm keepin what's here."

"It's all there," Toby said. "It's twenty-five now, twenty-five tomorrow."

Seth said, "When you plan on getting it done?"

"If the bread's all here, it's already done."

"Nobody gets hurt on this, right?" Toby asked nervously.

"Only Garza, unless I don't get my other twenty-five."

"You'll get it, so long's we don't get let down."

Trini smiled. He'd have his dick in these white-bread *bolillos'* ears for the next five years.

Trini drove off in one direction, Seth and Toby in another. Heading for home, Trini pushed the two buttons on his cell phone.

After quite a few rings, a sleepy, pissed-off voice on the other end said, "Yeah, who is this?"

Trini said, "Me."

"Why the fuck you callin me? I got to get up early."

"It's bidness. You gon be five hundred dollars richer tomorrow. And 'at's it. Don't push me, or it goes down to two-fifty."

Eloy came to in the dark, then saw the faint gleam of light through the blinds. It took him a few minutes to figure out where he was. He crawled over to the bed and stretched out on it. Sweat seemed to be oozing from every pore and his hands were shaking so much that he could barely punch in the number on his cell phone.

Trini knew who it was, decided to let it ring forever. But he'd done good with the *gabacho licenciados,* the white-boy lawyers, his *partners* in his five-year plan, and changed his mind. Besides, he'd just had himself a little taste, so for old-time's sake he could afford to be nice to his good *cuate*, his buddy the Lobo, who'd be down for the count soon enough. Trini pulled a Marlboro butt from the coffee lid, lit it, and picked up the phone. "My nigga."

Eloy was counting his money. "Tell me you got it."

Trini sucked through his teeth. "The best, man, it's the most righteous shit like you never seen, like it was first processed in Switzerland, man, before it was packaged here, but like I said, you know."

"How much?"

Trini's eyes fluttered, but he could still think, he could always think. He'd piece Eloy off with 20 milliliters, 200 milligrams. Divided by fifty or even 60 milligrams, it was enough for three or four good pops at most. By Sunday night, he'd have sweat dripping from Eloy's dick again.

This here's like things is supposed to be, carnal.

Eloy said, "You still there?"

"Yeah, yeah, I don't desert my friends."

"How much? How much you got, and how much it cost?"

"Well," Trini said, pronouncing it *oowehl*, "sorry to say, just enough to get you through the next day for now, but I gots a ton coming in on Monday, Monday's my delivery day, *formal*, depend on it."

"So, how much more does it cost, goddamnit?"

Goddamnit? He talks like that to me, this scum? Trini kept his cool, but he bubbled inside. "Oh, that, yeah, I lucked out, this load I got it for *tantito más*, for a little bit more than normal, so for you it'll still be cheap, like always, like you'll only be doin say eighty or ninety or maybe a hundred a day from now on, that's all, you're my Lobito, *ése*, and if that gets to be too rich for you, all you got to do is cut yourself back down on your own, and then you're down to forty or fifty a day, no big thing." Trini knew a junkie cut *up*, not down, knew Eloy's eyes rolled when he heard *cut back on your own*.

Eloy didn't like having to pay more, but he was grateful, "I owe you, Trini, you don't know how sick I got." He cleared his throat. "How soon, pods?"

"Whatever time is comfortable for you, *mano,* my brother," said Trini, sounding like a counselor at Planned Parenthood.

Eloy said, "I'm on my way now."

"Ride, cowboy."

Eloy counted his money again, his palms wet. He thanked God he still had plenty of cash left, but when would this shit end? He knew for sure that one day it must, that he must die like the crud he was, but he couldn't imagine how or when. The sooner the better, he thought.

Chapter 16

Dan put his cut kit together before he drove the pickup to the hospital. The "local" fight was to be held outdoors during the Del Mar Fair at the Del Mar Racetrack, ninety-five miles south of Los Angeles and located between the 5 South and the Pacific Ocean to the west. Dan's kit contained tape and gauze and grease, as well as stainless-steel tools and ice bags that kept swelling down. Dan usually stuck with a vasoconstrictor, adrenaline chloride 1:1,000 for cuts. But as a backup, he also brought along a form of thrombin, a freeze-dried white "bovine" powder and a dilutent of 10 milliliters of sodium chloride, each in small vials to be mixed together before use. In surgery, thrombin is used on big bleeders, things like livers and spleens, to cause hemostasis, clotting. With adrenaline 1:1,000, it is the effect of vascular constriction that stops the blood flow. If a sizable vessel was severed, Dan would sometimes use both in hopes of stopping the blood flow.

Stopping blood is a precise skill, one that makes a cut man feel like a champ. Adrenaline was twenty dollars and change for 30 milliliters. If any unadulterated solution is left over, and if stored in a refrigerator, it can be used subsequently. Thrombin costs sixty plus for what amounts to 10 milliliters, and can be used only once. Dan would use adrenaline in

Del Mar, since Momolo was in a four-round fight. Bad cuts are usually stopped by the ref in preliminary fights as a matter of course, so Dan would probably not have reason to mix the thrombin. Were this fight a ten- or twelve-rounder, Dan would have the thrombin ready by fight time, mixing the two vials in the dressing room. Because adrenaline is cheaper and the leftovers can be used again, some cut men mix their own concoctions, say equal parts of 1:1,000 and its illegal counterpart 1:100. This makes a more potent solution than the straight 1:1,000, but it can sometimes sizzle tissue and cause serious scarring. Stopping blood is battlefield business, where every second counts, and is not meant to be anything more than a stop-gap procedure. Even so, Dan never went on the cheap, and none of his boys ever lost fights or had slabs of scar tissue because of him. If Momolo needed thrombin, Dan would mix it ringside.

Dan checked into Cedars-Sinai at four-thirty P.M. His carpeted room felt more dead than alive. It looked clean enough, but it felt a long way from antiseptic. Dan didn't like having a carpet, preferred tile or hardwood floors in hospitals, saw hospital carpets as germ farms. Jails had better TV sets. His prefab meal was served in individual containers, had a metal taste, had been nuked into tasteless slop.

It had been the same for Brigid in the cancer ward. "And at these prices, shouldn't there be some Frenchy Jean-Claude himself dishin up the biscuits?"

Except for the watery applesauce, Dan left it all on the plate, and then called Earl about the angiogram. Earl stopped by at seven-thirty to give Dan a rundown on the shop and gym. He said, "You know, I can get someone to work the corner with me in Del Mar if this mess is a problem."

Dan said, "Naw. Kogon said I'll be out by tomorrow afternoon."

Earl said, "I only said something because me and Momolo got to show by eleven tomorrow morning for the noon weigh-in."

Dan said, "You two go first. I'll take the pickup and meet you at the hotel."

Earl said, "You'll be okay?"

"Piece a cake," said Dan. "What time's the fight go off?"

"Fight time's two o'clock, outdoors. No TV."

A Filipino male nurse fussed in at eight o'clock with water and a pill. He sized up Earl. "Mr. Cooley needs quality-time rest, so you'll soon have to say bye-bye."

Dan said, "What's this pill?"

"For seepy-seepy night-night."

Dan didn't like the idea, but he took the pill. Earl smiled, shook hands, and said he'd see Dan at Del Mar.

Dan was starving by nine-thirty. Bum TV made things worse. He wasn't one to read magazines.

"Screw this."

He waited until the nurses were away from the desk down the hall, then unhooked himself from the heart monitor. He dressed quickly, slid into an elevator, and went down to a Japanese restaurant on Third Street for sushi, hot sake, and a bottle of cold Kirin. He got back to his room at ten-thirty. The male nurse was pissed off. Dan told him to get the fuck gone.

Early the next morning, Dan had the right side of his groin shaved, and was then wheeled into a pale gray, high-ceilinged room. There were several pale gray machines. Electrical cables dangled from overhead, connected to the machines, which silently moved in and out of position. Dan had been medicated slightly with Valium, but he was alert.

A dimly lit screen covered a large portion of one high wall, and a technician operated controls from inside a glassed-in booth. Two nurses slid Dan from the gurney onto the operating table. He could see the screen and the technician, who sat like a pilot in the green light of the booth. Nurses in blue scrubs moved about, each with a task, each as silent as the moving machines.

Kogon, also in scrubs, came in and went to work. "See that screen?

We'll be doing echocardiogram imagery during the procedure, and I'm going to put you on the silver screen, just like in the movies. We need you conscious so you can talk. Once we're inside, and we inject dye through the catheter, you're going to feel like your name is in lights."

A faint network of bones and other things came into focus on the dim screen.

Dan said, "That's star quality if I ever saw it. Me and Marilyn Monroe."

Kogon said, "Three things. One, stretch your arms back over your head, and keep them there unless I tell you to move them. Got it?"

"Yeah."

"Two, you will experience slight discomfort in your chest, but you've been through worse, so I don't want to hear you bitch. Three, if you feel significant pain, I want you to tell me."

"You said not to bitch."

"There's bitchin and there's bitchin."

"What's this balloon doohickey again?"

Kogon said, "The greatest thing since penicillin for clap. Once inflated, it depresses any collection of cholesterol, plaque, and fat against the walls of coronary arteries. Removed, it allows blood to flow properly, and you're back in business."

A nurse dabbed alcohol at the right side of Dan's groin. Dan felt a needle prick.

Kogon said, "That's to numb you locally before we make the small incision to go inside."

"Do you ever have people jump off this rack halfway through the deal and run screamin out the door?" Dan asked.

Kogon nodded. "A few have tried. That's why we have restraints, and why that IV's in your arm. Two milligrams of Versed does the rest."

Dan perceived rather than felt something move up and through him. It made him gag, but not throw up. This wasn't something he'd ever felt, and he didn't like it at all, not at all, but he wasn't about to go dog—the time to haul ass had been back at Kogon's office. Dan focused on breathing, and waited to see if he'd die or pull through.

Kogon said, "You doing all right?"

"Spinnin like a top."

Dan felt more movement inside his thorax. At first, he imagined the catheter as a metal caterpillar maneuvering the twists and turns of his circulatory system. Onto the screen came what looked like a cheap gray ballpoint pen that was inching through him. A misstep that punctured an artery would mean death in quick time. He wasn't sure if he'd care one way or the other. You slipped the shot and countered, or you didn't.

Kogon said, "Watching the screen?"

"I'm watchin, but there's not much to see. What's the dye all about?"

"It will show blocked coronary arteries," Kogon explained

The dye hit the screen like a whip, and Dan's arteries suddenly looked like black spiderwebs in a winter tree.

"Yow!" Dan said.

Kogon jimmied out the catheter. "Three bad arteries, as I thought. You game for the bubble?"

"Do I have a choice?"

Kogon said, "Not unless you want me to tear up the release form you signed."

"What's this going to feel like?"

"A little more in and out, that's all."

"You mean you'd tear up the release if I told you to?" Dan asked.

"No. But I won't proceed if you say to stop."

"That means I'd have to go dog."

"Precisely."

Kogon finished the angioplasty quickly, with the nurses and another doctor backing him up. He stood beside Dan. "The blocked arteries are absolutely clear. We've placed sandbags on your groin. It's standard. The weight will cause the femoral to close. I slipped you a little hop so you don't move around and paint the walls red."

"How long with the sandbags?"

"Each case is different."

"Doctors bullshit worse than lawyers," Dan said. "Ballpark."

"An hour, anyway, maybe a little more to make sure you've closed properly."

Dan said, "Will you be around?"

"Your nurse will be watching you carefully," said Kogon. "I've got some more procedures to do down the hall."

Dan wanted to ask another question, but he faded to black before he could put the words together in the right order.

Woozy, Dan awoke in some kind of storeroom lit by overhead fluorescent lights. A still body rested on another gurney across from him. Hand movement. A sigh. Stacks of long, gray cartons two inches by six inches by forty-plus inches leaned against two of the walls. Nurses entered by two doors. They selected different cartons, then departed, sometimes by the same door, sometimes through the other. It took Dan a while to remember why he was there.

His head was not entirely clear when a nurse entered and lifted one of the sandbags and moved the other. Dan could see that the bags were covered in canvas, and slick from use, and looked like small pillows. The nurse replaced the sandbags.

"Not yet."

She was out the door before Dan could speak.

An older man, who looked like a doctor, entered and checked the other patient. "Good, very good. Now it's back to your room."

Dan waited patiently, thinking he'd soon be rolled to his room. He became aware of severe groin pain caused by the two eight-pound sandbags. He wanted to move them, but thought better of it. He spoke to the next nurse who came in for cartons.

"What's in the long boxes?"

"Catheters."

"Tell somebody to get these bags off of me, okay?"

The nurse said, "Someone'll be in."

A nurse wheeled the other patient out.

Dan waited. The bags, bearing down into his groin, had Dan talking to himself. A different nurse came in to check on him.

"Not yet," she said.

Dan said, "How long have I been here?"

"A bit."

Dan said, "This should have closed, right?"

"We'll give it a little more time."

"How much more?"

"A little."

Dan was sure Kogon didn't know what was going down. He held his hands out, palms up. "I get the feeling that no one knows I'm here. That, or nobody gives a shit."

The nurse huffed out. Dan looked at the walls. He realized without surprise that he didn't care whether the femoral closed or not. He figured that dying itself wouldn't be so bad, might even feel good. All he wanted was someone to get rid of the slick and greasy sandbags. Another nurse came in for catheters. Dan asked her what time it was.

"Not late," she said, and hurried out.

Dan waited another hour. It felt like four. Another nurse came in and checked the incision. "Not yet."

Dan said, "Get a doctor in here now."

"I can't just go get a doctor, sir. We have procedures."

"Well, you just got a new procedure. Bring a croaker in here now or I'm getting my ass up and walkin the fuck out."

The nurse hurried off. Five minutes later, three large men entered. One of them, the oldest, was the one who'd checked on the patient who'd been wheeled out.

Dan said, "You guys croakers, or from the goon squad?"

The oldest said, "We're staff doctors. Maybe you should go a little easy on your nurse."

Dan said, "I already took it easy now for, what? four, five hours? I could bleed to death between the times these nurses come in to screw with the bags."

The youngest doctor said, "You mean you haven't had the same nurse?"

"Hell, no," said Dan.

The youngest doctor lifted the first sandbag, then the second. A shot of spurting blood arced thirty inches into the air. Two more heartbeats launched two more red rainbows onto the tile floor.

Dan said, "Why not mix up some thrombin and be the fuck done with it?"

The oldest doctor said, "So, you know about thrombin?"

Dan said, "Yeah, doesn't everybody?"

The femoral closed immediately with thrombin plugs; plugs were something Dan had no previous knowledge of, though he knew that coagulants could be used in different forms. After forty-five minutes, he was wheeled back to his room. His leg and groin were hurting and felt bruised. He bitched. He was given a tiny white pill.

Bing!

He woke near midnight and rang for the nurse. Some patients loved the effects of drugs, but he hated the woozy feeling.

Dan said, "You got anything to eat this time of night?"

"Fruit. Apple. Orange."

Dan said, "I got to take a leak. Do I need one of those bottle things?"

The nurse said, "You're okay to use the toilet, if you want."

Dan got out of bed. He was unsteady. He checked the incision, which had closed, but was still partially soft instead of hard with scab. He turned to the nurse.

"Is this hole in me closed for good?"

The nurse said, "Barring complications."

Dan said, "When will Doc Kogon be in?"

"Someone will check you again at four A.M., and then again between seven and eight. You doctor will also be in later, since there was a problem."

Dan said, "When'll that be?"

"Before he starts his procedures tomorrow, say around one or two?"

"I want to leave now."

"No."

She gave Dan some kind of capsule to swallow with water. He tried to figure out a scheme for the next day. The fight was at two. Kogon wouldn't be in until one at the earliest. No good. Dan got fluffy. He crashed before he had a plan.

He was woozy again at four, but alert when he woke at six A.M. He checked how hard the scab was and if it was dry. For breakfast, he ate cereal and an apple, and drank chamomile tea because they wouldn't give him coffee. A fuzzy-cheeked intern did an examination at seven.

"Looks good, old fellow."

Dan said, "You talkin to me or to my dick?"

The intern blushed and got out. Dan rang for a nurse, then began to dress. A grumpy, bleach-blond nurse came in. She was losing her frizzed hair but had great-looking legs. She stopped cold when she saw Dan in his pants.

"You get back in that bed this instant!"

Dan said, "I don't mean to be a pain in your you-know, but please tell those in charge that I'm outta here."

The nurse said, "Sir, you could break open."

"I'll buy some Kotex."

"Kotex? You can't just get up and leave, clown, we have to inform your physician!"

"He's already worked it out."

Chapter 17

The right side of Dan's groin was black and blue. Walking to the parking lot, he felt like he had a groin pull. He fired up the truck, then set the thrombin pack beside him on the seat. He purchased a box of Kotex maxi pads on Melrose, then stopped on Robertson for pastry and strong coffee at a French bakery. He finished at nine o'clock, then stayed on Robertson down to 10 East. When he hit downtown, he veered onto 5 South. Two hours later he was at the hotel in Del Mar.

The fair was in full swing when Dan and Earl and Momolo pulled into the parking lot at eleven-thirty.

Sweetly, politely, Momolo said, "You have the proper equipment and the necessary medications, am I correct?"

"Pardner," Earl said, "he's got the whole world in his hands."

Momolo was a Christian boy from a missionary school that had been destroyed by civil war. He got the reference and smiled.

The bright, overhead sun made for short shadows. The breeze off the rolling breakers a mile away kept the temperature in the mid-seventies.

Food stands were set up. Smoke and grease mixed with the smells of oregano and cilantro and garlic and ginger and cinnamon. Italian, Texas barbecue, Thai, Mexican, a coffee stand, Greek, corn on the cob, cotton candy, fish and chips, lemonade, ice-cream parlor, and Mom's Pies.

The horse crowd was there, Western and English. There were families of every color, speaking many languages. Surfers, dopers, old folks, military, teenagers in Future Farmers of America jackets. A cheap carnival was up and running, and the Ferris wheel was turning. The boxing ring and folding chairs for a thousand had been set up in the middle of the vacant acreage outside the apricot structure of the old racetrack. Dust from the massive parking lots moved with the breeze through the narrow valley.

Earl and Dan sniffed the food, while Momolo checked in with the Boxing Commission doctor. Momolo returned to say there was some kind of problem, his eyes moving from left to right.

Earl said, "What kind of problem?"

Momolo said, "I am not clear on this. We are to see the official."

Earl said, "Best see Jolly Joe."

They headed for Commissioner Johnson, who sat at a makeshift desk ringside. José Maximiliano "Jolly Joe J. J." Johnson was the son of a Mexican mother and a black man from Houston. He weighed close to three hundred pounds, and had a smile as big as his ass. His round head was shaved, and his midnight eyes laughed whether he was eating or in a fight. He was known alternatively as Jolly Joe and J.J. He had his mama's straight black hair, and spoke passable Spanish with his daddy's Texas drawl. He liked working with Earl and Dan, saw them as stand-up guys who played straight with their fighters. He called Dan "Big D."

When he saw them, he said, "Say, Soff! Happenin, Big D?"

Everyone shook hands the old-fashioned way.

Earl said, "What's this business with my man Momolo here?"

Jolly Joe said, "That right, bro. You fight fell out."

Earl said, "Say what? Our opponent was talkin shit in Mexican like he was Marco Antonio Barrera!"

Jolly Joe spread his hands. "His trainer called in a hour ago sayin once his boy thought about your African, he up an' run to mama."

Dan said, "Where's mama live?"

"Way the hell down Ensenada someplace."

Earl said, "The promoter get us a stand-in?"

Johnson said, "We bof tried, even if I ain't supposed to get into it. But it too late for locals in you weight, an' too far down here for nobody else."

Momolo looked like he was going to cry. "I still receive my compensation, do I not?"

Dan shook his head. "See, the deal's not made until you actually sign the contract. Fallouts are why lots of promoters don't let prelim boys sign until just before the fight. That's in case something like this goes down—so they don't have to pay the fighter who does show. This promoter is usually able to put together solid fights. That's why me and Earl took the chance on him. Promoters'll even try for if-come with ten-round fighters, if a boy's hungry enough to go for it. It's not just you."

Dan could see that Earl was pissed about the fight falling out, and that Momolo had already spent his purse.

Momolo said, "These are crafty fellows."

"Yeah, they are," said Dan. "But they got to cover their asses, too. See, there was a time when fighters who lived a long way off would cash in their plane tickets, and that could cost promoters big bucks. That way, the bunko punks could collect, and never have to fight."

"Would the authorities not arrest them?"

Dan shook his head. "What promoter's going to sue somebody in another state, much less another country?"

"The boxing life is a treacherous one. My father warned me."

"Yeah," Earl told him, "but it's the only life where you can become champion of the world."

"Yes," said the African, "that is of importance."

Jolly Joe Johnson had seen it happen too often in his twenty years with the Commission, and for twenty more as a fighter and a trainer.

He'd begun as a successful middleweight at 160, fought in the amateurs when Dan was already a pro. But he realized that his place in boxing was outside the ropes, not in. When a low-level Commission job opened up, he grabbed it, then worked his way up. The California Commission under Johnson was ranked with Nevada and New York. Jolly Joe's personal file on boxers started the day he began work for the Commission, and contained the records of every fighter in every fight since, national and international.

Anytime some manager or promoter tried to bullshit him about a boy's record, J.J. would smile, his black eyes merry. "My man," he'd say, "I'm big like a elephant, an' I remembers like one."

Now, gazing calmly at Dan, Earl, and Momolo, Johnson scratched his ass, then wiped sweat from his jowls with a clean white handkerchief. "You boys takin off, or you gon hang around like civilized folk?"

"I don't know about these two, but I'm headin back to town," Dan replied.

"Why should we stick around for nothin?" Earl asked.

Jolly Joe said, "Hail, there's always *somethin* when friends socialize. Don't all got to be bidness."

Dan started laughing. "J.J., I broke your code a long time ago, you don't know that?"

J.J. said, "What shit you talkin, man?"

Dan said, "You're a cheap-ass mooch, that's what I'm sayin. Notice that I didn't say a shameless mooch."

Johnson brought his fingers innocently to his bouncy chest. "Mooch? *Me?* A man of my station in the community?"

Dan laughed and said, "Oh hell, why not? I'm gonna take you out to dinner, J.J."

Momolo looked outraged. This was the man who had just taken away his fight, and now Dan and Earl were going to buy him dinner? As they were leaving for the restaurant, Earl pulled Momolo aside and said quietly, "You know your Bible, so you gonna remember what it say about castin yo bread on the waters. Well, we gonna cast some bread and one of these days Jolly Joe give you a break. Forget the fight falling out. Happens all the time. We'll give you a raise at the shop, make up for some of dat purse you would have gotten knocking that Mex on his ass."

They had a blow-out meal. Dan paid. But he did wince when Jolly Joe placed his order.

"Let's see. Baby-back ribs, beans, slaw, corn bread, sweet potato pie, *an'* I'll need some that peach cobbler wit a little vanilla ice cream, yeah, that ought to do it. An', uh, I think I'll have me one a them double lattes, too."

"You want a half slab of baby back, or you want a whole?" Dan asked.

"Half? Half?" Jolly Joe laughed. "Damn, you chislin on me after all what I done of old Salt and Peppa? Half? Sheeuh, I want the whole slab, man! You didn't know that?"

Dan knew that fat was bad for arteries, but he ate barbecue anyway. He checked the incision several times throughout the day. There was some leakage at one point that he stopped with adrenaline. He covered it with a sanitary pad, but he never mentioned the incision to Earl, and Earl had the sense not to ask about the angioplasty. Later that day, when Dan called Kogon, the cardiologist said that he hadn't been surprised by the way Dan left the hospital. Kogon liked the type As, being one himself.

Dan saw Kogon two days later. He examined the crusted incision and then checked Dan's heart. He said, "So far so good. Did you win?"

"Fight fell out. I upset your people for nothing."

Kogon said, "At least you proved I do good work."

"Doc, I got a problem," Dan said, his eyes scanning the Santa Monica Mountains. "I've noticed that I don't care about anything anymore."

Kogon said, "You think it's because of the angioplasty?"

Dan looked back at the doctor. "Truth to tell, it's been comin on. But when the fight fell out, I noticed that I wasn't pissed. I wasn't even disappointed. Nothin."

Kogon said, "It's not uncommon, say, for bypass surgery to radically affect someone's moods. Some go into serious depression and stay there awhile. Some break down crying all the time, men as well as women. Others come out of their depression quickly. Some experience little or no negative emotional effects. To a large extent, it depends on the individual—that and a number of variables, medical and otherwise. Some in cardiology attribute negative effects to the heart-lung machine. Others claim it is the trauma of the surgery itself."

Dan said, "Always an upside, always a down."

"But it's also a matter of degree and duration," Kogon said. "In your case, you might be experiencing a kind of hangover from the medication. It could simply be trauma, physical as well as mental. But I don't think any of these things are likely in your case—not after the way you left the hospital. Dan, it's mostly to do with you, not the procedure."

"So what am I supposed to do, roll over and die of the mopes?"

"From what you and Earl have told me about your family situation, especially that tragic thing about your grandson, and now you learn you have heart disease, you just might need time to grieve and heal," Kogon advised him. "An extended rest would not be a bad idea if you can afford it."

"I got the money," Dan said. "But I never was one to quit."

"Resting and quitting aren't the same. And you've got to rethink your lifestyle. Your chances of surviving depend on that. Whether or not you change—eat right, get plenty of sleep and reasonable exercise—depends on how much you want to live." He wrote Dan a prescription for Xanax, 0.5 milligram. "Just make sure you stay in touch—in another week, then a month, then three, and then at least twice a year so we can catch any new obstruction."

Dan hadn't mentioned his drinking. "What if I don't keep in touch?"

Kogon smiled. "It's your funeral."

Dan didn't check back with Kogon. His moods and energy fluctuated radically during the next three months. He hit the pit mentally, but when he took his pulse, his heartbeat wasn't irregular; its rate kept up with his watch. He hardly ate. He took Xanax six at a time. He got out of bed to urinate and defecate, but he wondered why he bothered to get up at all, wondered what was so bad about sleeping in piss and shit. He'd go three weeks without a shower and a shave. He lost seventeen pounds. He was aware that he was drinking himself to death. He began to wonder why it was taking so long. He had no plan. He kept drinking.

He switched from cheap bourbon to low-down vodka. Alcohol became Dan's job. Earl continued to work a twelve-hour day, but still split the profits a buck for a buck. Dan sat Earl down.

"You got to stop cuttin me in when I don't work."

"I'm just waitin for you to make a comeback."

Dan sighed. "This ain't gonna change, Soff."

Earl said, "You got too much goin for you to buy into that mess."

Dan shook his head. "Naw, baby, my black thoughts own my candy ass."

When Dan ran out of tranquilizers, he cleaned up and drove the pickup to Tijuana and bought five hundred pills from three different TJ pharmacies. He also bought Seconal and Nembutal, fifty each, out near the Auditorio, TJ's boxing arena—fighting at the Auditorio was like going a hundred years into the past.

On the Avenida de la Revolución, at *gringo* prices, he bought two Cuban Romeo y Julieta Churchills in an upscale *tabacalero* that stocked only Cuban leaf. For lunch, across from the Frontón Palace, he ate *camarones al mojo de ajo,* garlic shrimp in butter, and sopped up the thick sauce with freshly baked rolls. He washed lunch down with two bottles of Bohemia, ordered a snifter of Hennessey XO, then took his time smoking half of one of the monster Churchills. He arrived at the end of the long line of cars waiting to cross the border, half-whacked and still smoking the cigar. By the time Dan worked his way up to the front of the line, the border guard had already used his computer to check with the DMV for any outstanding warrants against him. Dan knew that if his truck was searched, and the pills were found, he'd be in deep shit. He didn't care. But he went through the border check as easy as pie.

Instead of heading back up 5 North through the city of San Diego and Orange County, Dan immediately exited the freeway in Chula Vista for a bottle of vodka. He took a long pull in the parking lot, and several more in quick succession, then maneuvered back toward the 5. But he gradually lost any sense of where he was headed until he found himself at the casino at the Pechanga Indian Reservation in Temecula, seventy miles north of the Mexican border. He and Earl and their boys had won four fights out of five at Pechanga, two of them main events. Dan fogged out. He nearly ran into a ditch thinking how little those big wins meant to him now. As dust swirled up and around and through his stalled truck, he realized he was too drunk to drive home. He got a motel room and continued to drink. He flirted with the sleeping pills. He opened the kidproof plastic orange bottles. He poured them onto the bedspread. He sucked eighteen, maybe twenty into his mouth. They were slippery as snot. He went into the crapper for a glass of water. He saw himself in the mirror, looked at himself closely in the blinking pink light of the motel sign. He spat out the pills, then flushed the rest down the toilet. He stomped on the little orange bottles. He was damned if he'd die like Marilyn Monroe.

Chapter 18

Dan woke up at four A.M., his heart banging off his rib cage. He didn't know where he was. He called the front desk, and when the operator told him he was at the El Paraíso Motel in Temecula, he remembered all his wrong turns and felt brain-dead.

The pink sign of the Paradise Motel blinked on and off. Dan heard the sound of a fist against flesh and bone from down the hall. A woman began to shriek. "Don't spit on me there, don't spit on me there!"

Dan took a hit from the glass full of vodka next to his bed. As he fell back shuddering into the tangled bedclothes, the plan hit him fully formed—simple and crisp. Dan felt his forehead for fever. His hand was hot, but his head was cool. Sometimes madness brings a sudden clarity of vision and purpose. He had a perfect plan.

No one would ever know, especially Earl. It was important that Earl never know.

Dan slept fitfully and was fully awake when the sun came up at six. He took a shower, checked out of the motel, and went to a coffee shop for a big breakfast, his first food since lunch in TJ. He slipped vodka into his orange juice to slow down the tremor in his right hand. At seven-thirty, he used his cell phone to call his lawyer's office. He left a message with the answering service for Robert Plunkett to meet with him at ten A.M. concerning an emergency.

He arrived at Plunkett's office, 1 Wilshire, at nine forty-five.

Dan filled Plunkett in on his heart condition, exaggerating as he went along. He then instructed Plunkett to draw up the necessary documents to transfer all of his property to Earl—Dan's share of the business, his house, his two apartment buildings in Westwood, the gym and everything in it, his vehicles and personal effects, his life-insurance policies, and his savings and checking accounts.

Bobby Plunkett had known Dan from their days together at St. Jude's in San Pedro. He knew more was going on than Dan admitted to, but he couldn't figure out what. Plunkett, known as Bobby P to his criminal clients, cleaned his glasses with a linen handkerchief and picked at a patch of flaky skin on his bald head. He folded the handkerchief and returned it to the breast pocket of his three-piece gray flannel suit.

Plunkett said, "You don't look your usual pink self, but are you positive your condition is so critical that you need to do this thing right now?"

Dan lied, but it was also the truth. "I live from day to day."

"Jesus, Danny, I had no idea."

"How long for the paperwork?" Dan asked.

"Is a week okay?"

"Sooner. Get on it full-time, and have a check ready for me to sign to cover everything I owe you. But remember, Earl is not to know anything about this until I die, or if for some reason you don't hear from me in three years."

"Why wouldn't I hear from you?"

"Just set it up so it clicks into place three years from today, regardless. That way, it'll be a done deal and Earl won't be able to back out."

Bobby P said, "In three years, you could change your mind."

Dan said, "I'm doin it this way just in case. Heart patients can check out anywhere and anytime. I'm thinkin of goin to Ireland. What if I end up buried in the Ould Sod somewhere, and nobody here would know for ten years?"

Plunkett said, "I'm sure they'd notify the American authorities over there."

Dan hated doing it, but he lied again. "I didn't tell you. Because my mother and father were born in Ireland, I went ahead and got Irish citizenship and a mick passport."

Bobby P said, "I was thinking of doing that, too. Let me know what it's like over there."

"Roight," said Dan, sounding like his father. "How many days'll this take?"

"Give me five, maybe four, but I doubt four." Plunkett scratched his bald head again. "What if something happens to Earl before it happens to you?"

Dan said, "Leave half to Earl's wife, and the other half to the American Cancer Society, in memory of Brigid."

Bobby P smiled wanly at his stricken friend of so many years. He, too, could talk in the old way. "So what'll you be afther leavin me?"

Dan answered, this time sounding like Brigid, "What Oy'll be leavin ya is for good."

Plunkett had his own tremor. He reached into the credenza behind his desk and brought out two glasses and a bottle of Booker's eight-year-old 126.5 proof. "Sure and doesn't Mrs. Plunkett's little boy Bobby feel like pissin the day away?"

"One drink, laddy-buck, then it's on to the clock with ya," said Dan. The deception sickened him, but he didn't want his old friend to suspect that this would be their last drink together. Each sip of Booker's made Dan wince, but not Plunkett.

Dan stopped at a liquor store. He bought another bottle of vodka, and a copy of *Autovender,* a magazine offering nearly five hundred pages of photographs of privately owned cars for sale. He drove to Hancock Park. He sat at a table overlooking the pond.

Dan leafed through the magazine. He was looking for an original owner wanting to sell a twenty-year-old car that had a hundred thousand or so miles on it. He wouldn't need it for long, but he would need it for sure. A Cadillac Seville, or maybe a Mercedes 300 diesel. *Autovender* offered a dozen choices, all under thirty-five hundred dollars. A Mercedes diesel seemed best, a workhorse car that could take him anywhere he wanted to go. Dan got on his cell phone and called to make appointments with the closest three. He withdrew forty hundred-dollar bills from the bank, and placed thirty of them in an envelope under the driver's seat of the pickup. He put the other ten C-notes in his wallet for his trip. Should he have to negotiate a price, cash spoke to all persuasions.

The first three cars were in poor shape. Dan telephoned three more numbers. He left his name and number on the answering machines of the first two, along with the message that he was calling about the cars advertised in *Autovender*. He was in the process of leaving the same message on the third answering machine when what sounded like an elderly lady picked up the phone.

"Hello, Toussaint residence."

Dan gave his name and explained that he was interested in the car she had for sale. She answered his questions about the condition of the car, and they agreed to meet in an hour and a half, after Mrs. Toussaint asked for Dan's land-line phone number and address. That way she could check him out in the phone book.

"Can't be too cautious these days."

Dan said, "I understand."

Right on the dot, Dan rounded a curve in the 4400 block of Palma Road, and saw a tomato green 1979 300D parked in front of a stucco house. A red and white "For Sale" sign was in the front window of the car. An old woman with thinning blue hair stood cleaning the car with a long-handled red duster.

Dan introduced himself to Mrs. Toussaint, an eighty-year-old who shook Dan's hand firmly.

She said, "This was my late husband, Maurice's, pride and joy, bought it new." She indicated two boxes on the backseat. "Records go back to day one. Maurice worked at the old main post office across from Union Station, don't you know. He and I were the only ones who ever drove this old heap. Now my eyes are shot. I guess you'll want to chisel me on the price."

"Not necessarily," Dan said. The exterior and the leather interior of the car were in excellent condition. Tan sheepskin seat covers protected the front seats. "You're asking twenty-six hundred. That's on the high end for a diesel this old, but it's fair enough if the car's in good shape."

The old lady snorted. "Mercedes diesels're the best cars ever made, so why wouldn't this one be? It's got only ninety-some thousand miles on it."

"I see it's got good tires."

"They're a month old, so're the brakes and battery."

Dan's quick check under the hood confirmed his favorable first impression. He asked for and received permission to take the car on a test drive. But only after he left his wallet with Mrs. Toussaint. Her mamma didn't make no foolish babies.

Dan quickly got down the hill and onto the Arroyo Seco Parkway. The car checked out to be exactly what he wanted. He'd been gone eight minutes by the time he returned the car.

Mrs. Toussaint said, "You took longer than you said."

"I apologize, and I'll buy the car."

"Well, all right."

The transaction took two more minutes. Dan handed over the money, and she handed him the signed pink form.

Mrs. Toussaint squinted at him and said, "Now you drive carefully, hear? You got a good car. Don't wreck it!"

———

Dan dropped the car off for a lube and oil change that same afternoon.
He had a complete tune-up, including filters, glow plugs, belts and hoses,
new wiper blades, and new shocks. He added freon to the AC, also had
new head- and taillights installed. Since he didn't plan to register the car
in his name, he didn't want some cop pulling him over because of a
blown taillight.

The Mercedes was set to go the day before Plunkett called to tell Dan
to come in and sign the documents.

When Dan got back from Plunkett's office, Earl was looking under
the tarp that covered the shot-up Cadillac. He'd loved that car almost as
much as Dan. Watching his partner waste away was killing Earl. *How do
I tell a grown man what to do when I might be doin the same thing he is?*

Earl ignored the carnage inflicted on the Caddy and asked Dan,
"What about doin some more fights? Get back into the game." He paused
and then said, "You ain't got no life, livin this way."

"Listen to me," Dan whispered. "I don't care anymore if I win or lose.
Maybe I need a change."

Earl said, "Hell, yeah! You need a rest, that's all."

Dan said, "All I know is that you got a family, and that you're workin
too hard."

Earl said, "My wife understands. She said that gettin your butt out of
town for a spell might do the trick. You'd feel different in no time."

"I been thinkin about takin a long drive, you know? Maybe see some
of the country I've only flown over. Maybe take the coast route all the
way up to Washington state."

"Yeah. Stop and visit somebody you know."

"I got nobody."

"Then go to Ireland. You always wanted to go to Ireland."

"I don't even care about Ireland, Earl," said Dan. "I'm not goin away
for all that long. And I don't want you workin so hard. Hire somebody in
my place. You'd have more time for your family and the gym. Bring in
another trainer."

Earl tried to smile. He said, "You spoiled me, Coach." He didn't remind Dan that business at the gym was mighty slow these days.

Dan hesitated, then measured each word. "I can't go back on the floor no more. I see flashes of Tim Pat in the mirrors."

Earl touched Dan's shoulder. Dan shuddered, choked back a sob, then broke all the way down. Earl let him go on, patted him like he patted his little girls when they hurt. Dan gagged, but couldn't weep. Earl got paper towels.

"Wipe and blow."

"Look how low I've sunk."

Earl thought about the mirrors and the voices. He looked into Dan's haunted eyes. "I don't know any other way, so for now, I say we close the gym to outsiders."

"No, that's not what I'm sayin," Dan said. "You don't have to close down on my account."

"I'll keep workin with Momolo. He's good in the shop, and he's got heart. His dream is to return to Africa as a champ and open a powdered-milk factory. Kids over there don't get milk."

"Ain't nothin better than a dream."

"I'll tell trainers and their fighters that I don't have time to run the gym alone, and that you're quittin the game."

Dan hung his head. "That ain't no lie."

"Course that don't mean you can't come back, right?"

"Right," Dan lied. His mouth hardly moved. His eyes revealed nothing. "Yeah, I think it's about time I took that drive."

"You sure you're up to driving all the way to Washington?"

"Oh, yeah," Dan replied. "I've always wanted to get me a potful of Dungeness crab right out of the water."

"When you takin off?"

"Tomorrow or the next day."

Dan bought a road atlas that had maps of all the states, the kind that included illustrations and descriptions of points of interest. He bought a sleeping bag, thinking that it would allow him to sleep in the car, thus minimizing the number of people who would see and possibly remember him. He left his room in the gym clean as a monk's cell. He stayed away from his home on Cahuenga.

Everything Dan needed, including the booze, was locked in the trunk of the 300D. He hugged Earl and shook his hand. Both choked up. Dan promised that he'd call that night, and then at least every week. It meant one, maybe two more phone calls before Dan's plan went into effect. Dan eased the green diesel Merc into traffic without looking back.

Dan had driven the I-10 through Texas several times while campaigning as a young fighter, and knew exactly where to head. He'd told Earl that he'd be driving north, but instead he'd aim for some hidden spot in the dry Davis Mountains off the I-10 a hundred miles or so east of El Paso. Late some night, while parked in a remote valley tucked between the mountaintops, he'd fill five plastic one-gallon bottles with gas from one of the five-gallon cans he had locked in the trunk. He'd line a cardboard box with several layers of aluminum foil. He'd spread part of a bag of charcoal briquettes, also stored in the trunk, across the foil, then place the gas-filled water bottles and the five-gallon gas can on top of the briquettes. He'd place the loaded cardboard box in the backseat of the car, and sit next to it. He'd use one razor blade to cut a hole in the crotch of his right pants leg big enough to expose the pink scar left from the angioplasty, the thumping femoral artery just millimeters beneath the skin. He'd use a second razor blade to sever the femoral with one stroke. Then he'd have a drink.

While the blood was spurting across the back of the front seats—but before Dan felt light-headed and passed out from loss of blood—he would ignite several of the slow-burning briquettes a few inches from the bottles filled with gas. He'd be unconscious by the time the flame of the first burning briquettes ignited the adjacent briquettes, which, in turn, would melt the nearest bottle of gas. Once the first bottle melted and the escaping gasoline roared out like a Molotov cocktail, the other four bottles would go up like an atom bomb. The remaining five-gallon plastic can would also melt, and more gasoline would flood the car, the interior now a crematorium. The beauty of the "plan" was that the flames and smoke would be gone by daybreak. Dan was pleased that there would be nothing left of him. No face. No gold inlays. No fingerprints. No ID. Nothing. Any edible slush that might remain would be worked over by land scavengers and carrion birds. There was a good chance that his bare black bones would lie there for years. If found, small-town police would do a routine report. If anyone bothered to trace the vehicle to Mrs. Toussaint, she would probably have thrown away his phone number. The case would be closed, satisfactorily or otherwise. Earl and his family would be taken care of. Ashes to ashes.

Dan took the 5 North over the Ridge Route and then swung to the right at the 99. A half hour later he pulled into Bakersfield. In a kicker beer joint, he sat thinking of his fights at the old Strongbow Arena all those years ago, the wooden seats so close to the ring there was no place for the corner men to work. Heat from the cotton fields and heat from human bodies made the slick walls sweat. Dan had lost eight pounds during one Bakersfield fight.

He called Earl that night and lied some more, said he had stopped at the town of Harmony on Highway 1, which was actually over on the coast, just down from the Hearst Castle at San Simeon.

"The ocean's beautiful, and things are cheaper here than up near the castle."

Earl sounded worried to Dan. "What'd you have to eat, some of that good fresh fish they got up there?"

"Had some fresh, charcoal-broiled halibut, salad, baked potato, the works. Coffee and pie. No booze." He'd eaten a ham-and-cheese sandwich he'd gotten back on the 5 when he stopped for gas at Gorman. Dan said, "Give my love to the family. I'll call you in a week."

"Don't forget," said Earl.

"Not me."

Earl hadn't believed a word Dan said. He didn't know why, but he hadn't.

Chapter 19

Sunday, the last day of the tournament, Lamar Steuke presiding. Weigh-in. Physical. The bout sheet was drawn up according to weight class, the lightest going off first. Chicky would fight seventh on the program. Fighters were told to be back by ten-thirty, no later than eleven. Hands wrapped, they were to be ready to fight at twelve. Passbooks, all filled out, would be handed back to them as they left the ring with their trophies, losers as well as winners getting trophies.

Eloy was on time and Chicky was already up. Eloy could see he had gained some weight, but was still under 147. As soon as the kid got his boots on, Eloy took him down to Crockett's for biscuits and gravy with a little fresh salsa on the side, an order of sliced tomatoes, a cinnamon bun with raisins, and two glasses of milk. Once he'd taken a healthy dump, Chicky weighed in at 145. Eloy was pleased that Chicky might not have to give up much weight to Sykes. In fact, Sykes had lost his appetite completely, and instead of pushing 147 at the weigh-in, he came in all eyes and scared shitless at 144. Toby and Seth looked the other way. Mr. George knew something had gone down, even if Sykes didn't.

Finished with the weigh-in, Paco went with Chicky and Eloy back to Crockett's. Chicky had two glasses of grapefruit juice, oatmeal with cinnamon and raisins, and corn bread with butter and honey. Trini had slept in, after all, gotten more sleep than Eloy for sure.

Paco said, "Don't worry, Trini'll be pumped at fight time."

It was nine-fifteen when Chicky finished eating his second carbohydrate meal that morning. Paco told them they didn't have to show up until eleven-fifteen, because the tournament, as always, wouldn't get started until twelve-thirty or so.

"So you're all set?" Paco asked.

"Ready, set, go."

Eloy could see that his *nietito,* his grandbaby boy, was sleepy from the rich food, and from fighting all night in his sleep, so they went right upstairs to Chicky's room. It had been three hours, going on four, since Eloy had medicated himself after connecting with Trini. He felt his scalp dampen, and a trickle of sweat slipped down the crack of his ass. That hit hadn't lasted the way it should have, but he couldn't let on that he was in trouble. Chicky finished getting his equipment and fighting togs together, then sat on the bed.

"You hit the pillow, I'll git you up."

Chicky crawled under the covers. "Where'll you be?"

"Doin the mess-around over at the show, but I'll be back for you a quarter of."

Chicky was almost asleep. "I love you, old man."

Eloy touched the boy's cheek, was swallowing hard as he left the room, but his tight throat was not only from the love he felt for his grandson. He wondered if his last shot of lullaby had been as strong as usual. Might he have injected less? Naw, he knew that this was doper-think.

Eloy would have to get off good and do it soon or he'd never make it through the tournament. At least he wouldn't have to cook up, thanks to Trini. He could do himself quicklike right there in the truck if he had to, but if he parked on the street somewhere he wouldn't be able to enjoy it afterward, wouldn't be able to listen to the sound of snow falling on the moon.

He still had his room until noon checkout at the Maverick, so he headed Fresita for it as fast as the law would allow. He pulled up at the far side of the building, walked in fast, trying to get past the office and to his room. But the owner was on alert and tapped on the bulletproof window of his stall.

"You pay me mo'."

"I got till twelve checkout."

"No, you pay me mo' now."

Eloy barked, *"Toma por el culo, pinche chino mamón,"* in your ass, you chink suck-off!

The old Thai pulled his green-and-blue-flannel plaid shirt tightly around his neck and slinked out of the office as if running from the sun. Eloy unlocked the door to his room and went in, his eyes sifting the gloom. He didn't have much time. He pulled off a boot and damp sock. He loved the little brown bottle morphine came in, loved its blue and white and red label.

He slipped the needle into a fat vein so he wouldn't blow the fix. It wasn't long before his skin tingled and his pupils clamped down. His hacking cigarette cough stopped dead. Moments later, he settled back to float in three-quarter time.

Chicky's gear bag, packed and ready, rested on the floor in front of the door to his hotel room. His fighting shirt and shorts hung from a hanger on the doorknob. There was no way to lose or forget a thing.

Chicky's second meal in the morning had affected him more than he'd expected. Because of the rich food, his system sent a large quantity of blood to his abdomen, facilitating digestion, but also drawing a goodly amount of blood away from his brain and inducing sleep. Chicky had planned on a quick nap, but tired as he was from the previous night, he'd allowed himself to fall completely away, secure that Eloy would wake him at ten forty-five. That would give them plenty of time to get to the Finals, and be dressed and wrapped on time.

A key, tapping repeatedly on his door, woke him. He sat up, refreshed and energized. He expected Eloy to walk in, but instead, a Mexican chambermaid peeked around the corner of the door. She excused herself, saying she'd been told the prepaid room was supposed to be vacant.

Chicky's eyes snapped to his watch, and he was alarmed to see that it was 11:10. Eloy should have been there almost half an hour earlier. The maid apologized and left. Chicky dressed immediately, then stood still, hoping to hear Eloy approaching from down the hall. He didn't know what to do. He was expected at the tournament in five minutes, but he couldn't leave without his grandfather. What if Eloy was sick along the road, or maybe in a wreck somewhere, the truck turned upside down on him?

Chicky rushed down to the lobby, hoping for a message. None. He waited until almost eleven-thirty, then telephoned Eloy's cell phone from a pay phone. When Eloy didn't answer, Chicky left word that he was leaving for the San Nacho. He left the same information for Eloy at the front desk, then ran over to the tournament aware that he was burning energy he'd need against Sykes.

He checked in at the fighters' entrance, where he was told he'd drawn the red corner dressing room again, Sykes the blue. He hurried, removing his shirt along the way to the dressing room. Eloy was not there. Chicky started changing, and as he finished lacing his second high-topped shoe, he asked one of the old-time trainers to wrap his hands. Still no Eloy.

Chicky was queasy with worry. Having worked up a sweat running to the arena, he now felt a chill, and hoped it didn't mean that something bad had happened to the old man. It wasn't until the other trainer was ready to wrap him, and asked for gauze and tape, that Chicky realized that the Cavazos were not there either.

"You ain't seen Trini or Paco?"

The trainer shrugged, and said, "They was around earlier."

No Eloy, no Cavazos? Chicky's anxiety doubled. He could make no sense of it.

The first fight went off at 12:20. Chicky was frantic. He was sure Eloy was in trouble, but didn't know what to do to help him. He edged right up to full-blown panic, hovered there, wondered where Trini and Paco were, wondered how he'd fight without his seconds in his corner, without his granddaddy in the stands.

The matches had proceeded up through the 119-pounders, and still no Eloy. Chicky looked out into the crowd, but there were no Cavazos anywhere.

Chicky turned to one of the other fighters, a San Anto homeboy. "You seen Sykes?"

"He's over in blue."

One of the local officials shouted into the dressing room, "One twenty-five pounds on deck!"

The 125 boy left at a run. The gloved 139-pounder began to bang the mitts held by his trainer. Chicky, his head on a swivel, his hands wrapped and ready, went out into the crowd. Moving through people who cheered and patted him, he felt lost for the first time since he'd gone to live with Eloy. He approached the officials' desk ringside and spoke to Lamar Steuke.

Chicky said, "Mr. Steuke, sir, excuse me, but y'all seen my corner?"

Steuke didn't look up. "Which izzat?"

"Cavazo brothers and my granddaddy."

"Oh, yeah, that, uh, they're up in my office. You better hightail it on up there."

"Why?"

"Git goin, boy," said Steuke, "I'll be rat up."

Chicky sprinted up to the second floor where he could see Trini and Paco in Steuke's glassed-in office. Chicky shoved open the door.

"What we doin up here?"

"You're late," Trini snapped.

Chicky assumed that being late was the problem. "Granddaddy didn't wake me up on time."

Trini said, "Where's he at?"

Chicky, thoroughly confused by now, asked, "Don't you know?"

"Why'd I know?"

"I'as just hopin you might."

Paco looked Chicky up and down, shook his head disgustedly, then looked away. "Boy, you messed up good."

"No, we still got time if we hurry," Chicky insisted.

Trini said, "Not just messed up, you fucked up."

Chicky rocked from one foot to the other. "Not me, I don't fuck up, c'mon, let's go."

"Where's your passbook?" Trini asked.

"Where it's supposed to be, officials got it until after I fight," Chicky replied.

"You sure about that?"

Chicky considered the implications of a lost passbook, his mind computing lickety-split as Lamar Steuke entered the office. Chicky turned to him. "You got my passbook, Mr. Steuke, tell 'em."

Steuke said, "I ain't got it, what'd you do with it?"

"I gave it to you, same's the other boys, you kept 'em after the Semis."

"You didn't give it to me."

Chicky said, "To one of the officials."

"Which one?" Steuke asked.

"One of them outta towners, I don't know just who."

"We have no record of that."

"Y'all had it at the weigh-in this morning."

"You sayin I had it?" Steuke asked, looking Chicky straight in the eye.

Chicky was wild inside. "Somebody had it, otherwise they wouldn't a weighed me and give me my physical."

"Well, it's gone, and it's up to you to provide it before you can step into the ring."

Chicky's tongue was thick. "Y'all had it in the box with the others."

"I know about the others," Steuke said. "What'd you do with yours?"

"I never had it once y'all had it!" Chicky shouted.

Steuke said, "Wait now, I never did have it, not me."

Tears were in Chicky's voice, but not in his eyes. "We'll find it later, okay? Only now I got to git my gloves on so's to be ready—we're runnin outta time."

Trini lit a cigarette and coughed. "That's what's he's tellin you, *chico*."

"Nobody ever has to tell me to be ready, I'm always ready, I'm ready now."

Trini inhaled again, let smoke out as he spoke. "No, you don't understand. He's tellin you to forgit about gittin ready."

Steuke looked down at his desk and moved some papers around. "Cain't fight, you ain't got no passbook, you know the rules."

Chicky yelled, "But you already got it!"

Steuke said, "Calm down, boy, no, I don't, and I don't know nobody what does, that's our problem here."

"Come on, Lamar," Paco broke in. "You know this kid, this kid ain't no fuckup, this is Chicky Garza, for chrissakes."

"Yeah," said Trini, standing up as if he was ready to fight. "Waive the rule, this kid is local, his granddaddy is the Wolf, and this here boy could go all the way."

Steuke shook his head. "No, no, can't waive no rule, start that rule-waivin stuff and now we're on a terrible slippery slope."

"Then issue the kid another passbook, that's all," Trini suggested.

Steuke got tight-jawed. "Can't do that without no application, no weigh-in, no physical, no birth certificate, and no photo ID."

Chicky had begun to sink into despair. "It's too late for me to git all that."

Steuke said, "Don't I know it?" He slapped Chicky on the back and smiled real friendly. "Better luck next year, son, I'm terrible sorry."

"You sayin for real I can't fight, Mr. Steuke?"

"It's a rule," Steuke said, ending the discussion. He looked at Trini. "The one thirty-niners'll be started, so I got to git me back to preside."

"So what happens to me, Mr. Steuke?" Chicky asked forlornly.

"You lose, automatic," Steuke told him.

"What about Sykes?"

"Sykes wins on a walkover, automatic," Steuke replied, a note of impatience in his voice.

Trini turned to Chicky. "You know how that works."

Chicky said, "I ain't sure if I do or I don't."

"Well," said Steuke, going out the door, "you boys work her out."

Chapter 20

Lamar Steuke left his office and hurried back to the fight. He had to grunt *huh-huh* in little puffs at each step down the metal stairway, but the climb up had been worth it, and he snapped his fingers as if he was listening to Ernest Tubbs. Nothing beat making a few bucks on the sly. *Yessir.*

Eloy, meanwhile, felt himself rising up through shades of gray water and splashes of white and yellow light. He held back, wanted to stay gone, wanted to dive down into his dark place. Something shook him. Again. Shook his body.

"Hmumph?" he grumbled.

He woke staring directly into the lens of a bright flashlight. He squinted and turned away, sure it was the police. He desperately tried to come up with a way to talk himself out of the fix he was in.

Stalling for time, Eloy said, "I didn't do it."

A dark form moved away and the flashlight went out. The only light left was what filtered through the blinds, which were jerked open. Eloy could see that the day had gone gray, saw that rain clouds had formed. The dark form he'd taken for the police was the old Thai motel owner, and Eloy was momentarily grateful. The old man swooped back to bed-side, held the long metal tube of the flashlight like a club.

"You not dead. You pay mo' now."

Eloy swung from junkie panic to outraged citizen whose privacy had been invaded. "Whoa, I got to twelve o'clock here, and you got no cause and no right to be in my room!"

The old Thai said, "Today start all new day, you pay me 'notha forty-three dollars, thirty-seven cent now."

"I ain't payin nothin, you old skinflint slope."

The owner pointed to Eloy's dark Emmy bottle, and the discarded spike. "You no pay now I call cop in hat. I call cop in hat on you Messkin shit."

Eloy collected his works in one swipe. He was ready to throw punches until he looked at his watch. It was 1:18. "God, no."

Eloy tossed three crumpled twenties on the bed, and stumbled as he ran to his pickup. Racing back to town along Broadway, he checked his cell phone for messages, and found one from Chicky. The pain and con-cern and incredulity in Chicky's voice were clear.

"God, no," he repeated.

Cyrus Psycho Sykes was standing in the blue corner, his arms draped on the upper ropes, his "PF Boxing" leather jacket on display. Steuke gave a wave to the ring announcer. As Sykes's name was called as the 147-pound winner in a walkover, he sauntered slack-limbed to the red corner, Chicky's corner. Chicky was still in Steuke's office, and couldn't hear the half-hearted applause. The Cavazos had left Chicky alone and returned to the arena with a sense of accomplishment. Their cut from working twenty four-round prelim fights wouldn't be what they got from a fix like this. Trini was proud of how smoothly things had gone. Check and mate, as in jerk and off.

Gots to be slick, gots to be quick.

As Steuke watched Sykes accept his trophy in the ring, someone from the stunned audience shouted, asking what happened to Chicky Garza. Steuke looked away.

Sykes, who had no idea that the fix was in, shouted back, "Chicky Garza got dawg in him, dass what!"

People hooted, but it would be Sykes who moved on to the Nationals, not Chicky.

Mr. George stood watching Toby and Seth. Neither had acknowledged him. Now they celebrated with Sykes. When Mr. George saw the lawyers and the Cavazo brothers laughing together, he had no doubt about what had happened.

"Muhfuhs ruin a boy an' feel good about it."

Mr. George approached the jubilant Toby and Seth, who were shaking hands with Trini and Paco. Toby raised Sykes's hand as if he'd just unified a world title. Mr. George got closer, and Toby tried to look away, but Mr. George wouldn't let him.

"Yassuh, cap'n, you for sure got you that win."

Toby said, "Yeah, right, isn't it great?"

Mr. George talked more down-home than usual. "Yassuh, it be so great you can pay me my las' hunna-dolla bill an' I be gone."

Toby said, "Oh, yeah, that." He offered his hand in a courtly way, and Mr. George took it friendlylike. Toby shook hands harder than a fight guy would. He said, "Yes, well, since you were unable—and/or unwilling—to help us out, per last night's conversation—"

Mr. George interrupted Toby with his own squeeze. Mr. George said, "You means the conversation we had what never happen?"

The crowd milled around, moved near, kept Mr. George up close to the lawyers. Toby didn't like it, but neither did he want to create any sort of scene that might tarnish Sykes's victory. He tried to remove his hand from Mr. George's grip, but couldn't. Mr. George's eyes had become darker than black.

"Look like to me you got all the he'p what you needed, yassuh," Mr.

George told him, making no effort to keep the contempt out of his voice.

"No comment on that," Toby said.

Mr. George applied more squeeze. Toby's voice trailed off, his knuckles colliding like icebergs, his fingers starting to creak. He cleared his throat before he could speak. "See here," Toby said, "my partner and I, on behalf of our many investors, concluded, as a result of your lack of full participation in project Primal Force Boxing, that you had defaulted on your commitment to those investors. Accordingly, our position is that you are not entitled to further compensation."

"Uh-*huh*," commiserated Mr. George, who waited a split second, then cranked down double hard.

Toby's face went from cocaine pallor to drained white. He reached over with his left hand and grabbed Seth by the back of his collar. Toby said, "Why don't you just go on and give Mr. George here his hundred."

Seth said, "I thought you said fuck the old booger."

Mr. George clamped down another ton.

Toby hissed as loud as he dared in front of witnesses. "Give him his hundred, damnit."

Mr. George squeezed some more. Toby thought his bones were ruined. He smiled through his clenched teeth. "Give him two fuckin hundred, now!"

"Two or one?"

"Two, goddamnit!"

Seth peeled off two worn, stinky C-notes and Mr. George got his due. He tipped his cap politely as Toby backed away rubbing his bloodless hand.

Mr. George said, "Y'all be fine gennemans, yassuh, *fine* gennemans." He left by the front door and never looked back.

Eloy parked, and noticed Paco's blue-gray Chevy pickup on the far side of the San Nacho parking lot. Next to it, Trini's taco wagon had been backed

into another space. Once inside the arena, Eloy was immediately aware
that the light-heavies were fighting, the 178-pounders, three classifications past Chicky's. He hurried through the crowd looking for the kid
and for Trini. As he passed the ring on the way to the dressing rooms, he
was surprised to see Trini and Paco standing close to the lawyers who
were backing Sykes. As Eloy eased toward Trini, he saw one of the lawyers flopping one hand around like it was a fish on the end of a line. Eloy
also saw the second lawyer slip something white to Trini. Trini immediately took off for the men's room and Eloy followed. As he went through
the door, he saw Trini standing facing the toilet in one of the stalls. When
Eloy got close, he also saw that Trini was counting a thick stack of bills.
Trini sensed something behind him, and when he saw Eloy he quickly
stuffed the bills back into the white envelope and stuck it up under his
arm and down into the sleeve of his jacket. Eloy didn't understand. If the
lawyer was Trini's drug supplier, then Trini should be the one making
the drop, not the lawyer. Trini pretended he was about to piss.

"Chicky still here?"

Over his shoulder, Trini said, *"Creo que sí."* I guess.

Trini's answer confused Eloy further. "Chicky whipped the loud-
mouth's ass, right?"

Trini said, "He'll run it down to you."

Eloy said, "But he didn't lose, did he?"

Trini zipped his fly, and turned to leave the stall. "I don't speak for
Chicky no more."

"Since when you don't speak for my kid?"

"Since I started trainin Sykes."

"What!" Eloy reached for Trini's jacket, but Trini jerked away, and
was out the door. Eloy went directly to Lamar Steuke, back in the
arena.

"What's goin on?" Eloy asked.

Steuke had been waiting for Eloy, prepared for whatever was going
to go down. He reached over to the runner-up trophies, and he handed
one to Eloy without looking at him. "Here."

Eloy couldn't believe no runner-up. "What's 'is?"

"It's Chicky's," Steuke replied.

"He come in second?" Eloy asked.

"Runner-up's more'n second."

"Sykes's in the Nationals, not Chicky?" Eloy asked in a tone of utter disbelief.

Steuke nodded. "Chicky knows it."

Eloy said, "What dressin room?"

"Red."

Eloy carried the trophy to the red room. The trophy was made of plastic, and painted silver, but to Eloy it felt like a six-foot crowbar. The dressing room was nearly empty, most of the fighters from the lower divisions having changed clothes and gone. No one knew where Chicky was, but one of the trainers pointed to his gear bag, and boots. Eloy stuffed Chicky's things in the bag, and with the trophy in one hand, went looking. He found Trini talking to Steuke.

Eloy was urgent. "¿Pues, qué pasó?" What happened?

Trini and Steuke spoke at the same time, "Sykes won."

Eloy knew something smelled bad, but couldn't decide where the stink was coming from. "Where's my kid?"

Trini said, "Last I seen him he was in Lamar's office, up on the second floor."

Eloy found Chicky still standing in Steuke's office. His chin was on his chest, and his eyes had a stunned look in them.

Chicky looked up. "You missed the big event."

"Looks 'at way," said the Wolf, who felt like a cur.

"You was supposed to take care of me. It's my birthday."

"I know, I know, and tomorrow I was fixin for us to go on over to Paris Hats and pick out something good to celebrate." Desperation made for inspiration. "But my truck had this here flat tar."

Chicky shook his head imperceptibly, and whispered, "Truck did, huh?"

"Had to have it towed," Eloy explained, sick from all the lying. "Had to find a tar guy open on Sunday, you know how that goes."

"Yeah, I do," said Chicky, "a tar guy open on Sunday."

When Chicky talked Eloy through the missing passbook deal and told him how Sykes had won on a walkover, Eloy put the fix together. Trini counting that money in the crapper downstairs; Trini to train Sykes. *Chingones*. Fuckers.

Jesus, if you want to be an outlaw, go rob Frost Bank, or rustle cattle, but don't do this to a trusting kid with his heart in his hand—and sure as hell do not do it to Eloy Garza's kid. That was absolute.

"Ain't this a bitch," Eloy said. What he didn't say was that he'd be into Trini's back-stabbin ass like red on a strawberry.

"It's a bull bitch," said Chicky. It took him a lick before he could say the rest of what he had to say. "I figure you was drinkin, Granddaddy."

"No, I swear on your grandma's grave, boy."

That was another lie to add to the rest. But there were worse things lurking—those little brown jugs he lived to embrace four to six times a day. Chicky had to know that something was seriously wrong. The kid hadn't figured out the details yet, and Eloy was grateful for that, but to God's eyes they had to be clear as a pumpkin moon across a cotton patch. But how could he ever tell Chicky the real reason he was late?

"I shouldda been here," said Eloy. "It might a helped."

"Wouldn't a made no never-mind," Chicky said. "I just didn't much like doin her all by my lonesome on the day I turned eighteen."

A rush of misery flooded Eloy. It was as tangible as the rush from a fix, but the needle squirting this rush didn't make the hurt go away. Fed up with himself, he wanted to blurt it all out, but he wasn't about to spill that all to nobody. Certainly not to his grandson. He needed to dip.

"You got some cope?" Eloy asked. *Cope*, like *dip*, was down-home for snuff.

Chicky produced a flat, round can of long-cut Copenhagen from his bag; beside the brand name, the embossed metal top read "Fresh Cope" and "1822." He handed his can over to his granddad, and Eloy slipped a pinch up next to an eyetooth.

Eloy watched the kid settle his snuff, and wondered again if maybe it was best to just go head-on and tell Chicky. Bad as the timing was, at least the kid would know who held the ribbons that dangled him. He could tell the kid he was deep sorry, and if Chicky dumped him, then he'd have no bitch, because if anyone deserved to be dumped, he surely did—when you loved a needle more than your own kin, you were indeed shameless. !Ay!, that word again, sinvergüenza.

Chicky saw how uneasy his grandfather was. "You sure you wasn't drinkin?"

There!

Chicky gave him the chance, the shot, the opening. In the ring, Eloy would have taken it quick, but now his moral reflexes failed him, as did his fighter's heart.

"No, no booze, *mi querido nieto, te lo juro,*" this I vow.

"I keep goin over it, 'n over it, but it just don't figure."

It figures, all right, Eloy thought.

Once again, Eloy tried to rat himself out, but all he could say was, "I shouldda been here."

"Yes," said Chicky, quietly.

Dark saliva was collecting behind Eloy's lips and under his tongue, and sweet murder chugged through him. He thought about the difficulties of killing both Cavazos, thought again, and decided that getting them both at the same time was no big thing. He'd just bring along his pump-action Mossberg Persuader 590 to the gym instead of the over-under, and go *bang-bang* as often as it took.

"Can we go on home, Granddaddy?" Chicky asked.

"Rat now," Eloy said, giving him a grin, but his contempt for himself and his hatred for Trini were about to choke his heart. "Let's hook 'em."

"*Eee-hah.*" The kid grinned weakly back, letting the old man know things were okay between them, but down inside Chicky felt hollow, and in that empty space where his heart and lungs used to be, things were going every which way.

As Eloy left Steuke's office to go back to the arena, he asked Chicky to get into his street clothes and then meet him down at Fresita. There was no point in going for Steuke yet, not until Eloy knew for sure if ol' Lamar was mixed up in the fix. If he was, he'd have to find a way to kill Steuke, too. There was no doubt that Trini and the lawyers were in it up to their snouts. He wanted to make Trini look him in the eye. He knew what he'd see, and that's why he knew his plan for the next day in the gym was the right way to get the deal done.

Two black heavyweights, weighing 228 and 237, were standing toe-to-toe in the ring, the last match of the tournament. Flying slobber reached the ringsiders, who laughed and swatted at it. Steuke was there fussing with the passbooks, but Eloy couldn't see Trini or Paco. Neither one of Sykes's lawyers, either. They had to be part of it. He'd light up the Cavazos in the San Nacho first, then drive on over to the lawyers' offices and blow those cocksuckers away, too, have himself his own mini Texas Tower deal. Now that he had worked it all out, he calmed some.

He knew he was a dead man anyhow, just a matter of time, so what did it matter if he zigged or zagged, or maybe did both? Putting Toby and Seth on the ground made sense, but it was Trini he wanted to kill first.

The tournament was nearly played out and cars were leaving the parking lot. Trini and Paco sat in Trini's car, which faced the lot. The motor was running, and they had the windows down for fresh air because exhaust rose up from the leaky muffler. They could watch most of the arena's doors, and carefully looked for Eloy among the fans leaving the arena.

Paco said, "What if Lobo's packin?"

"He'd a been shootin by now if he was," Trini assured him.

In Paco's hand, in the pocket of his jacket, was a hot little .38, a hundred-dollar Hi-Point compact, a hide-away gun cheap enough to make disappear if Paco didn't want anyone to know he'd used it—all he had to do was wipe it clean of fingerprints, and leave it with ammunition in the phone booth of some old Southside *cholo* bar, *yip*.

Paco said, "I still think it's best I stay."

Trini said, "Naw, circle around the block and park back down the street there by the ivy. Follow us if we leave."

Paco said, "You didn't say you was leavin."

Trini said, "I ain't fixin to."

Paco said, "What if Eloy gets cranky?"

Trini said, "I'll pump my brake pedal a bunch so you'll see my stop lights blink. So take off before the Wolf*cito* shows."

Trini knew what Eloy had to be thinking, and that he would be bent on killing him. But he also knew that Eloy would always try to protect Chicky. Trini had already worked out how he'd use his hoppers to play Eloy's feelings for the kid against the old man himself.

¡Ay!

Paco had gone to his pickup truck, and was driving from the parking lot as the Wolf moved out through the arena's wide doors. Eloy saw Paco's truck scoot off, and thought Trini might be with him. *Tomorrow,* he thought. He tossed Chicky's gear bag into the back of Fresita, then turned and noticed that Trini's car was still parked in the lot, right next to the taco wagon. He squinted against the sunlight. He couldn't be sure if he could see Trini because of the dark interior of the car, but he thought he could see him behind the steering wheel. Eloy's *indio* eyes showed no emotion, but inside he was doing whirligigs, and right quick he forgot all about his plan to blow both brothers away with his Mossberg the next day.

The part of Eloy that was still rational warned him not to kill Trini in the parking lot. It would be better to get Trini and Paco inside the San Nacho, get them defenseless and both at the same time. But here was an opportunity. Kill Trini on the spot. The idea got so good, he forgot about his nausea, forgot everything except squaring things for Chicky. He tapped his right-rear pocket for his Buck jackknife, a solid 6.8 ounces of honed steel, brass, and antler.

Eloy's new plan was to go back into the building, exit at the rear, and slip up behind Trini as he sat in the car. One quick move was all he needed. If the car door was locked and the windows up, he would slash all four tires, and use the butt of the open knife to break the driver-side window. He'd stab Trini two fingers down from the bastard's breast-bone, then gouge around to sever the aorta. Blood would cover the dash-board, then clot on the upholstery and floor mats. Afterward, he'd go looking for Paco, catch him some way, somehow. He'd go to the liver, or lungs, or slit his throat and watch him spurt and gurgle.

As he was choreographing the slaughter, Chicky came up behind him, and touched him on his shoulder. Eloy almost jumped straight out of his boots.

"*Yaaah!*"

Chicky asked apprehensively, "You all right?"

"Yeah, I'm all right, why?"

"Oh, nothin," said Chicky. "What tire went flat?"

Eloy wondered how he'd get out of the flat-tire lie, and decided to stall. "I'll show you when we get home."

From his car, Trini saw Chicky and leaned forward for a better look. Chicky being there messed things up.

As Eloy caught his breath, he also caught a quick look at Trini's scum face inside his car.

Chicky said, "Ready to go?"

Eloy said, "Soon. But you got to go on over to Crockett's."

"Huh?"

"Go on, git, I'll be there shortly."

Chicky said, "You said we was to head home."

"I'm gonna talk to Steuke about the walkover, see about filin a protest."

"You think she might work?" Chicky didn't sound too convinced.

"Never can tell. Now you git. Go eat."

"I ain't hungry," Chicky said.

"*Boy,* eat anyway."

Chicky heard *boy,* and the tone Eloy used meant there was no room for mess-around. Chicky thought of baby back ribs, a whole rack, and salivated. He started off for Crockett's. Paco cruised into position, but Chicky's mind was on the walkover, and he missed Paco's move altogether.

Trini slid down in his seat when the kid started in his direction. He didn't understand what was going on, but it was good that Chicky was taking off.

Eloy watched as Chicky walked away. His grandson was still in a fog. He almost fell when the toe of one boot hit a crack in the sidewalk.

Chicky turned a corner, saw that the Sunday downtown streets were nearly empty. When he was sure no one was looking, he edged into the doorway of a failed travel office, and went down on one knee. He covered his face with his hands so no one could see.

"Ahh, God."

He cried out once, his voice high and helpless, couldn't help himself, but he wasn't about to give in to no wet-eye.

Chapter 21

Once Chicky was out of sight, Eloy turned and made his way through the departing spectators, his plan still to head for the dressing room exit at the rear of the building, and then go get Trini. That done, he'd quick find Paco someplace, and finish him before he knew what had happened to Trini. But as he was about to enter the building, he remembered Chicky's gear bag in the back of his truck, and was afraid someone would steal it. He moved swiftly to the bag, and unlocked the passenger side of Fresita.

Trini watched Eloy with the gear bag, then turned to make sure that Paco was back by the ivy. Eloy was still by his truck, so Trini dropped his transmission into low gear and hit the gas. He was across the parking lot before Eloy realized what was happening. Trini punched the brake and skidded up to Fresita.

"My nigga," Trini smiled, "git on in."

Eloy was surprised by how calm he felt. "You goin to stab me in the back, too?"

"Don't talk shit," Trini said.

"Where we goin?" Eloy asked, trying to keep his tone level.

"We ain't goin, we're stayin."

"Turn off the key, and put it up on top of the roof," Eloy told him.

Trini chuckled for Eloy's benefit, but turned off the ignition, reached out the window with his keys, and dropped them on the metal roof above his head. "What, you don't trust your brother after all these years?"

"Shit," Eloy said. As he opened the door with his left hand and got into the car, he slipped his right into his back pocket for his Buck, the curved back cuddling into his palm. He could open it with one hand, *click*.

Eloy could also see that Trini's bony hands were on the steering wheel. There were no weapons in sight, and Eloy wasn't worried about a fistfight in or out of the car. With the Buck open and resting alongside his knee, Eloy didn't fear Trini or anyone else, but he knew that he had to keep his guard up against Trini's underhanded brain.

"*Bienvenido, mi hermano.*" Welcome, my brother. "I'd offer you some Zijuatanejo jump rope, but I know you don't like no hemp."

Trini had heard the click. He was not surprised that Eloy had a knife.

"Talk to me, talk to me," Trini said, "but put that machete away, okay? What the fuck."

"I'm gonna put it away in you, unless you can jump short *cholos* in a single bound." Eloy moved his knife hand from beside his knee to rest on his right leg. "You ruined the one thing I got in the world."

"Why don't you go ahead and close that ol' cutter?"

Eloy jerked the knife up shoulder high, was ready to slash and plunge. He wanted Trini to cringe and struggle, wanted to justify cutting Trini's head clean off. Trini didn't move. Eloy waited. When Trini didn't even beg, Eloy grabbed Trini by the throat with his left hand, and raised the knife to get his shoulder into the downward stroke, but he snagged his hand in the sagging head liner.

"Stumblefuck," Trini said. "You're lucky I ain't somebody wants a new hole put in your ass."

Eloy drew back again, but Trini leaned in and calmly took a steady bead straight on into Eloy's eyes.

"No matter you kill me nine times, you fuck, you'll be hurtin your kid more'n he's already hurt. Talk to me, think. You do me, Paco does you."

"No, I kill Paco, too." *Depend on it, you piece of shit,* Eloy thought.

"But what if Paco gets Chicky first?"

"No," Eloy said, feeling the knife clutched in his hand. "I get you here, and easy as pie I go get Paco."

Trini shrugged. "So you get me. Listen close now, I'm tryin to help, okay? So you get me, right? Maybe you'll be doin me a favor, ever think on that? And say you get Paco, okay, big deal, but let's say some *chickidin cholo* with big round chicken eyes sets Chicky's head on fire for a nickel bag of Kibbles 'n Bits if we get dead? There's nothin you can do about that, and that deal's already been done with a devil, unless I call it off. It's snake eyes no matter how you roll 'em, *mi rey.*"

"You hurt the kid again," Eloy said, "you best kill me first, or it's your head what gets torched."

Trini waved his hand in a dismissive gesture. "Nobody wants to hurt your kid, *ése,* and let's say nobody torches nobody, okay? Only way to butcher me and Paco so's Chicky'll think you did right is to tell him why you done us in the first place, *¿no es verdad?*" Ain't that right? "Are you sayin Chicky don't feel bad enough already? Eh, *hermano,* one thing if they put you in the death house in Huntsville. But you want Chicky to know the inside truth so he can trigger-happy himself all the way to Huntsville, too?"

The parking lot was almost empty. Trini knew what Eloy needed most, and it wasn't revenge. "Lighten up, think, talk to me. What's important here? It's important I made some scratch, okay? I ain't made dick money on Chicky, you know that. Chicky's nickels and dimes, he's if-come at this stage, like every other amateur, right or wrong?"

Eloy said, "Except he ain't just anybody's grandkid, and he couldda been *some*body."

Trini said, "Yeah, and he still could, so?"

Eloy saw that he had only two cards left in his deck. He pictured both as blank, but he could still bluff. "You'll know he's somebody when I report you to Lamar Steuke."

Trini said, "Ol' Lamar's in on this up to his nuts, you didn't figure that? Unless you got a wire on you, and I don't figure you're smart enough for that, then you got no proof on me or on anybody else."

Eloy tossed in his last card, the remaining blank. "I'll go to USA Boxing in Colorado Springs."

Trini said, "Shit, ol' Lamar'll put on his white outfit and swear on a stack of Bibles the whole deal was a simple fluke done by a unknown party or parties. You think they won't believe him over you?"

Eloy said, "Chicky'll believe me."

"Sure, oh, hail yeah," said Trini. "Are you sure you want Chicky to believe? How about he finds out all about you and your needles, too?"

That stopped Eloy like a stiff jab on the way in. He could see Chicky loading up the Mossberg, and packing the over-under along for backup. He wouldn't let that happen to Chicky, no matter what the Cavazos did to him. He held the Buck up, thumbed the safety, and closed the blade. He was about to slip it into his back pocket when Trini nodded.

"Okay, that's better, now that's important, and yeah, I fucked the kid over, okay? That's the truth, but he ain't dead, right? And the way I see it, job one is to make sure he don't get hurt no more."

Eloy's voice was deep and the words hard. "I want you hurt, *sinvergüenza* cocksucker *puto maricón* queer faggot, that's what I want, and this ain't over yet."

Trini didn't let nobody call him cocksucker. It was time to bring in his hopper from back down the street. He tapped the brake pedal, as if musing on what next to say and do, but he already knew what to say and do. Paco saw the blinking brake lights from his place next to the ivy, reached for his gun, and raced for the parking lot, the 9 millimeter out and cocked.

Trini said, " 'Cocksucker,' 'faggot'—them's fightin words what could take you and Chicky both down a rat hole on the far side of the Río fuckin Bravo you say 'em to the wrong *vato*, right? Listen close, 'cause way I see it, we both gotta protect Chicky. That's our job." Trini sighed, shook his head. "That's why Chicky's gotta up and leave San Anto."

"*Chicky* leaves town, you pimp!" roared Eloy, his hand trembling on the Buck. He went to flip it open, but it slipped from his sweaty hand and fell between his knees to the cluttered floor mat. As he fumbled for it, Trini started up like a crazy man.

"Okay, fuck it, you dumb fuck. Here!"

Trini ripped open his shirt to expose his bony chest. Buttons clicked off the windshield as Eloy got hold of his knife.

"Do it!" raged Trini. "Get yourself off! Then who you go to for your drugstore pure? You think them hustlers out there don't know a little punk boy-virgin like you when they see 'im? Little *virgencitas*," Trini spat, intentionally ending with the *ita*, the feminine form.

Eloy backed against the door, addled by Trini's hollering. Things had gone all haywire, and the noise rocking through the car and crashing in his head kept him from working them out.

Paco's truck squealed up alongside, and Paco was out and the 9 millimeter was out and stuck into Eloy's neck, and Eloy had nowhere to go.

"¡Déjalo, déjalo!" Trini shouted across Eloy to Paco, the noise loud like gunshots to the Wolf. "Leave him alone, Paquito, ¡déjalo!"

Paco yelled back, his words tearing into Eloy's eardrum. "I'll kill this shit piece of fuck asshole *culero!*"

Trini waved Paco off. "No, git back into the truck, git!"

Paco sat down sideways in his truck's driver's seat, but both arms were extended straight down between his legs, the gun held tight. All he had to do was raise his hands, cop an angle away from Trini, and squeeze his trigger finger.

Trini whistled one soft, high note, settled back, then spoke awful quietlike. "Things's gettin real radical here? In case you ain't happened to notice?"

As happens in San Antonio, fat raindrops suddenly came down big as your thumb, banged on Trini's car like buckshot at a turkey shoot. Trini reached up for his keys. He and Eloy rolled up the side windows, and

Paco pulled back into his truck. The inside of Trini's windows fogged up as if they'd been sprayed with WD-40.

Trini carefully dried off each key. "Uh, remember that guy you fought out in Al-*lay?* You know, that *bolillo* dude you fucked up so bad?"

A wave of shame choked Eloy, and Trini had him by the balls for all time.

Eloy knew it, but he tried to play innocent anyway. "What fight was that?"

"The big fight in Al-*Lay*. The Olympic Auditorium, *ése*. I figure Chicky don't know nothin 'bout what you did that night, right?"

"*We* did it, *we*," Eloy said, but it didn't make him feel any better.

Trini puckered his lips, blew a little kiss. "Chicky could find out all about *you*, the way I see it."

"Aw, screw you and the whole deal," Eloy said. Capitulating, he held the Buck out so Trini could see it was still closed, then inserted it down the leg of his left boot.

Trini sat there spider-eyed, said, "That's the first smart thing you done. But do I see you thinkin on comin back on me so's to fight another day?"

"Not hardly," said Eloy. He had to piss, but wanted to do it in an open field somewhere, because his pee was so stinky and dark. Then some more gut-nasty came up to his throat, and he swallowed several times to get it back down where it belonged. He needed some Rolaids. "You got my word on it."

Trini spoke as if to a child. "That means you don't go hog wild on me no more ever, right?"

"You know my word's good."

Trini said, " 'Cause now I'm gonna reach down for a present for you, somethin special I got right here under the seat, okay, *carnal?* Say *okay*."

Eloy twitched hopefully at the sweet sound of Trini's baby talk. "Okay."

Trini leaned slowly forward, nodded once, then came up real careful-like out from under the front seat with a doubled-over brown market bag. Trini jiggled the brown bag so Eloy could hear the bottles clink. "This here's a ten-day supply, needles and all, and it's free of charge for my Wolf*cito*." He presented Eloy with the bag of morphine bottles and a few hourglass ampoules. "Now, soon's Chicky gets his ass out of town, there'll be more where that come from, and the price'll be right, *¿comprendes?*" You get me?

Eloy held the brown bag to his chest, his head down. "Yessir."

"Where'll you send him to?"

Eloy didn't hesitate. "College Station, so's to make somethin of the farm."

"And he stays there until this blows over."

"Yessir."

Trini and Paco took off in the downpour. Eloy was clutching Trini's brown bag under his jacket as he ran to Fresita. He dropped his keys twice before he got the door open. Drenched and breathing hard, he fumbled in the bag for a throwaway spike and a 20-milliliter brown bottle. The rain smeared his windshield. He felt safe inside. He selected a vein, and administered what was now a light hit for him, enough to stop hurting for a while, but not enough to keep him from driving home.

He sat stick still, his knee up while he pressed his thumb against the oozing puncture left by the needle. When the blood stopped, he licked his thumb clean, liked the chemical taste. His body had gulped the morphine, and his brain had come back again to hang plumb. All he could think of was how lucky he was—rain meant mud, and mud on his wheels meant that Chicky couldn't check around Fresita's tires and rims to see if there had been a flat tire for real.

Chapter 22

C hicky sat in Crockett's picking at his bread pudding. He'd eaten half his baby backs, and the rest were on the table in a doggy bag.

Eloy came through the door swatting rain from his hat and jacket. Thirty minutes had passed from the time he'd called Chicky *boy,* but it felt like thirty years.

Chicky gave him no time for small talk. "Did you file the protest?"

Eloy lied. "Tried my best, but Steuke said the walkover's a done deal."

Chicky fiddled some more with his pudding. "Was I set up, Granddaddy?"

Eloy said, "What? Hail no, why'd you think that?"

" 'Cause I never heard a such a thing."

Eloy hadn't either, but was sure it had happened. Everything happened in boxing, just like in everything else. "Shit happens."

"What in the name of rotten cotton am I supposed to do now?" Chicky asked.

Eloy didn't answer right away, acted like he was pondering. This was like heart, brain, and eye surgery all rolled into one. "Well, you *could* sign in for a couple of years at Palo Alto CC like you always talked about."

"But I'm a fighter now."

Eloy had to use reverse English on the kid, had to say one thing and hope he would bounce opposite. "With good grades and all, couldn't you later transfer up College Station? Study all that tricky new plant stuff at A & M?"

Chicky looked at him like he was a nut. "That was for later."

Eloy tried another gambit. "You could come on back from A & M and turn the farm into somethin again, you could be the strawberry king of South Texas. A course, that might not sound so good now, but in a few years, with hard work, you could be playin golf and raisin Ayrab horses."

Chicky's dreams of the Olympics were scattered on the canvas of that ring.

He gathered his thoughts and said, "Why don't I just turn pro?"

"I s'pose you could do that," Eloy sniffed, "but you'd have to start out in four-rounders at a piddlin hundred a round."

"Have to start someplace. Once I start knockin heads, my price'll go on up."

"*If* the pro boys'll fight you, what with you bein a southpaw," Eloy shot back, sending the words in like shots to the solar plexus. "Amateur boys have got to fight lefties, but pros don't."

Chicky's innocent eyes clouded, and as they darkened, so did Eloy's heart. Chicky said, "Trini and Paco got the juice to get me fights, right?"

Eloy took in a deep breath. "They done dropped you. They's trainin Sykes from now on."

"*Psycho* Sykes?"

Eloy tried not to blink. "Trini said so, when I went to Steuke about the protest. Said it was bidness, nothin personal."

Chicky said, "Well, if that don't beat the baby's butt blue. Who'll train me?"

Eloy said, "That's why I got to thinkin about you goin to Community College. Hail, it's just down the road from home."

Eloy paid the bill and they headed for the farm. Rain was banging down outside. The more Chicky fancied himself turning pro, the better

Eloy liked it, because he saw how he might use the kid's fancy as leverage to move his grandson out of town. But he couldn't let the kid know
that.

Eloy said, "See, pros ain't like amateurs, it ain't enough to bang, you
got to box. Boxin right'll let your body boil like it's supposed to, but it'll
keep your brain icy, and your face pretty, that's why a pro's got to be
trained by the best."

Chicky said, "I could get Mr. George to train me."

"He's good, but he don't train no pros."

They rode in silence a long ways, and then Eloy had to swerve when
three deer flew across the road.

"Whoa!" Eloy exclaimed. "That was a close'n."

"Everything's close," Chicky said, "except the Regionals, and I missed
them by a large ration of snakebit."

"It's all for the best, you got to think that way."

"Tell the truth to me, Granddaddy," Chicky pleaded. "Say the fight
was fixed. I just need to hear it so I can go do who I gotta."

Eloy stonewalled. "*Boy*, don't you contaminate your mind thinkin
like that."

Chicky ignored the *Boy*. "It was Trini, right? I know he was in on it."

"Listen to me," said Eloy. "It was one a them bad-luck deals, that's
all."

"I never had bad luck before."

Eloy's jaws got tight. "Chicky-*boy*-Garza, what I say?"

Boy worked this time and Chicky said, "You're right, but this is like
dyin, Granddaddy."

"I know what you mean."

Eloy also knew that even if he hadn't caused the stink with Trini, the
passbook fix would surely get loose anyway—someone would get to
bragging about it, someone like Steuke, if not the lawyers. Soon as
Chicky got wind of it, he'd go hunting with the Mossberg sure as there
was stink on shit.

The rain let up to a light drizzle, then stopped all of a sudden. The round black sky was filled with stars all the way to Brownsville.

Eloy said, "We're comin up on the Palo Alto now."

"Yeah, well, I ain't about no Palo Alto." Chicky was digging in his heels.

Eloy pulled Fresita into the school's big parking lot. He needed to take a pee real bad. As they passed through some deep mud, Eloy felt safer and safer. He rolled down the windows to cool things off, and to keep the windshield clear.

"Talk to me, talk to me," said Eloy, realizing that he was echoing Trini. "I know these last years's been hard, but the farm's paid for, and I got some money stashed Uncle Sam don't know about. Look how my face got all busted up. Maybe this San Antonio fight bidness ain't for you after all?"

Chicky went for it like a bay redfish after a lure. "What if I was to go fight somewheres else?"

"Whoa!" said Eloy. This was the opening he'd hoped for, and this time he went for it like a pit bull. "You ain't talkin about leavin town on me?"

"Course I wouldn't go," Chicky said, "if leavin'd cause a mess of boogers and hanks."

"You don't think I can cut it? You didn't know I was fixin to plant again next season?" said Eloy. "You ain't seen my weight come down?"

Chicky said, "Yeah, I seen it, but I'd have to know you was okay inside."

Eloy got out of the truck, went to some bushes to pee. As soon as he got back in the truck, he said, "Weeeell, Corpus Christi ain't all that far."

Chicky said, "Corpus ain't got enough fights or trainers, and I'm fed up with Texas. I was thinkin on New York or Philadelphia. Philadelphia's got good fighters."

Eloy pretended to hesitate. "Yeah, but who'll train you? How'd you live?"

"I'd find a trainer, I'll get me a hotel busboy job."

"Only problem's they ain't got that many of us back there."

"They got Porto Ricans, ain't they?"

Eloy said, "Yeah, but the way they talk Spanish ain't hardly worth listenin to."

"There's always Los Angeles," Chicky suggested.

"Yessir," Eloy said thoughtfully. "That dawg might hunt."

Chicky was warming up to the idea. "I can always come back and go to school. And if you get to feelin poorly, I'm just a plane ride away. So let's make her L.A."

Eloy stalled a tad, pretended some more. "Yeah, they's lotsa *raza* out there. Course they won't be many of us Tex-Mexes, but they'll be Chicanos and other-side Mexicans, both. But I don't cotton to you out there layin around on your ass."

"I'll get a job, I promise!"

"You know what?" Eloy said, picking his words like emeralds and sapphires out of cow pie. "There's a trainer out there I heard about, feller name a Cooley."

"Coolie?" Chicky blurted out. "What is he, some kind a Chinaman or somethin?"

"Not that kind of coolie," Eloy said. He spelled it out so the kid would remember. "This is C-O-O-L-E-Y, Irish, Dan Cooley."

Chicky said, "Have I heard of him?"

Eloy said, "Could. At one time he worked TV fights a lot."

"How do you know about him?"

"He's a top-ten, that one," said Eloy. "Feller with a bad eye. But he's a great trainer."

Eloy swallowed hard. This would be the tough one. "I want you to keep me outta this. Cooley don't need to know that you was trained by an old bum like me. I want him to take you on because he sees how good you are."

Eloy thought fast and decided to cinch it down tight. "Besides, we met once a long time ago and . . . well, we didn't get along. Fact is, bringin me into this ain't gonna do you any good."

The rain came back and slowed the go-away for a week, but Chicky had his stuff together and was ready to take off soon as there was a break in the weather. He'd grab the Greyhound bus to Los Angeles to keep expenses down. He figured L.A. had plenty of buses to get around on. He'd heard of trains and subways, too. He was sure he could hack it.

"How'll I find this Cooley guy?"

"I'd say check around the gyms," said Eloy, "or maybe call the Boxing Commission." He intentionally left out just how he had come to know Cooley. What the kid didn't know wouldn't hurt him. Besides, Cooley had probably forgotten about him.

No sense to open a can of worms.

The sun was bright enough to split your eyeballs as Eloy and Chicky headed for San Antonio. Eloy had gotten a lube and oil change the day before, and Fresita was full of gas. Chicky had six hundred dollars saved, and withdrew it in twenties and tens and fives. It felt like a lot more than it was. His two bags were in the back of the truck, the big one filled with his gym goods.

When they got to the bus station, Eloy got out of Fresita and stood by his door instead of driving into the adjacent lot.

Chicky said, "What's this?"

"Get out."

Chicky did, and crossed around to Eloy. It took everything Eloy had to keep from breaking down, but he managed a smile instead, and hugged his grandson to him, squeezed hard as he could, knew this could be the last time he'd ever hold him. He turned away for a lick to wipe his eyes, then faced the boy.

"In case for some dumb reason I don't see you again," he said. He held

out a pink Lobo Farms envelope. Inside were twenty century notes.
"Here," said Eloy, "you take this."

"What is it?"

"Take it, it ain't much."

"I got money."

"Now you got more," said Eloy. "There's enough to get you that
brand-new birthday hat out there, and then some."

"Aw, gee, Granddaddy."

Eloy said, "Now git your ass back in the truck."

"Huh?"

"Git behind the wheel," Eloy told him. "Fresita's yours now, go on."

"No way," Chicky protested. "Fresita's your baby girl."

"She's your baby now," Eloy said firmly, "so git on in 'fore I change
my dumb-assed mind."

"You sure, Granddaddy, you serious about this?"

"Seriouser than the twisty dick on a horny boar."

"But you won't have nothin to drive."

"I still got the flatbed, and I can always buy me a run-around."

Chicky choked on his words. "Whe-when should I go?"

"Go now. *Vete.*"

DAN

Chapter 23

Dan pulled up in front of an all-night Bakersfield supermarket. He slept in the backseat of the car. He checked his atlas while he had coffee early the next morning in a McDonald's. He washed up in the john, then went back to the counter and bought a large orange juice to go. He laced the juice with vodka in the car, lit a cigar, then headed out of town. He took the 58 East back through the baked desert to Mojave. From there it was more desert to Barstow, where he picked up the 40 East to Needles and on across the Colorado River into Arizona, the old Mercedes clipping along at a steady sixty, the radio turned off. The Black Mountains were on one side, the Buck on the other. His cell phone rang. He tossed it out the window of the car. He drove on to Yucca, stopped for no reason other than he had a sore ass. He stayed at the Injun Motel, a truck stop of free-standing old buildings shaped like tepees. He ate in the trucker café, greasy food, overcooked frozen vegetables, margarine on white rolls. Vodka and a Xanax put him to sleep after midnight.

He bought fuel the next morning. He checked his map. He was aiming for Phoenix by dark. He would stay on the 40 through Kingman and then on to Flagstaff, where he'd take the 17 South. In need of provisions, he walked over to a nearby air-cooled market. So he wouldn't have to stop along the way unless to pee or whatever, he bought a loaf of bread, some sliced cheese, and two packs of luncheon meat. He also placed a pack of precooked smoky links in his shopping cart, then added a squeeze bottle of mustard and a gallon of orange juice. He bought three quart bottles of water so he wouldn't dehydrate. As an afterthought, he selected some apples and grapes and bananas. On the way to the cashier, he picked up a package of sticky pastry, a large bottle of Rolaids, and a quart of milk to coat his stomach.

Outside the market, he removed two bottles of vodka from the trunk. He popped one, and drank hot vodka with OJ straight from the gallon bottle. He drank until he had the shakes under control, then headed east. After Phoenix would come Tucson, then Las Cruces, New Mexico, and after that he'd be out in the West Texas town of El Paso. Cigars would keep him company.

In Phoenix, he'd hole up in some air-conditioned beer joint until he decided where to sleep. Just a few days more. Not even a week. The old car was a winner. Too bad he'd have to torch it. Make one more phone call to Earl. That would be it. Another round of drinks.

It was early afternoon and Dan sailed, without a hitch, through El Paso, the sprawling modern city rising on either side of a web of freeways that connected it with the prosperity of the new world and the poverty of the old.

As he passed through the parched stretches on the east side of El Paso, Dan realized his ass was sore again, so he took an exit that put him on the 20, a local road that ran parallel to Interstate 10. He decided on a beer and a burger and some Texas chili.

On a side road up ahead, a quarter of a mile, was a beer joint. A half block away, a truck stop and mini-mart that sold everything from motor oil to frozen foods. Although Dan would soon be dead, he still needed to restock a few of the same items he'd bought back in Yucca and Phoenix.

He drank two beers in the café side of the Yippee Saloon 4 Good Eats, but only messed with his food. After one more beer, he drove back to the truck stop. He'd buy fuel first, then go for the groceries. He turned off his AC, and was about to pull into the pump area, but had to stop. A big dog that looked like a cross between a bull mastiff and a pit bull trotted mindlessly straight at him. The dog had large patches of hairless, raw skin, and his dry tongue flopped almost to his chest. He was scabby white around the face and mouth, with brindle spots on his back and down one leg. The rims of his eyelids were a fuchsia pink, and glowed. Both clipped ears had been chewed on. One had been split in half.

The dog tried to swerve at the last step or two, but lost his balance and stumbled headlong into Dan's left-front fender. He fell flat down in a lump of dirty hair and bony angles. As if powered by a weak battery, he got to his feet in sections. His eyes were set deep in his head. He stumbled twice, but picked up speed and trotted on in the heat. The dog was dying, but this did not register with Dan, whose own eyes were as sunken as the dog's.

Dan filled his tank at cheap Texas prices, then hit the mini-mart. Bread, lunch meats, cheese, OJ, more water. Enough to get him where he was going. If he didn't get the job done that night, he'd do it the next.

Driving slowly east, Dan took his eyes off the road briefly to pour juice and booze into one of his paper cups. He felt the car edge toward the side of the road. As he looked up and adjusted the steering wheel, he saw a large animal in the middle of the road up ahead. Dan honked the horn, but instead of moving out of the way, the animal suddenly collapsed. Dan slammed on the brakes. He spilled juice and vodka on himself as he fought to keep from going ten feet down the embankment into a dry wash. The engine stalled. Dust swirled over and around the car. Dan sat for a minute, his heart thumping up somewhere behind his eyes. To his left he saw that the fallen animal was the big, scabby dog from back at the truck stop. It looked dead. Dan dried himself off with paper towels.

Two cars swerved around the motionless dog and kept going. Dan sat back, waiting for his hands to stop shaking. When he looked over again, he saw that the dog had several open sores, but that he was still breathing. Since no one else seemed to care, the only thing was for Dan to put the scabby-assed mutt out of his misery.

Dan thought for a moment. He didn't have a gun, which would be best. A knife could get nasty if the dog resisted.

He'd pull ahead, and then back up over the dog's head. He'd done it years before for a cat with a broken back. Once he'd dragged the dog's carcass off the road, he'd get on with his own death. Dan drove slowly past the dog. He knew he should keep his eyes up and away from the animal, but like an idiot he had to look down at the last instant. The dog's tongue was touching the hot pavement, but his bloodshot eyes were staring straight into Dan's.

"Aw, fuck!"

Dan pulled over to the side of the road. He walked back to the downed animal. The dog squinted into the sun. The raw rims of its bloodshot eyes looked ready to bleed. The dog wagged its bare tail across the pavement. He was big and raw and starving. His paws were bloody and he seemed half melted into the road. Another car swooshed by. Dan covered the sheepskin passenger seat with paper towels, muscled the scrawny dog into the front seat of the Mercedes, then turned the car around and headed back toward the truck stop. The dog was a fifty-pound sack of bones, and limp as a worn pillow. He melted into the seat the way he had melted into the road. Ticks big as a thumb feasted on what was left of him. Dan was suddenly afraid that the dog would die before he could get back to the truck stop and find out where to locate a vet. He pulled over and the dog raised its head, fear in its begging eyes. Dan grabbed the first stuff he could from the backseat and fed the dog bits of bread and cheese and leftover sausage. The dog swallowed without chewing. Dan loosened the top of one of his quart water bottles so a small stream would flow. He cupped one hand and dribbled water into it.

The dog dropped his snout into Dan's hand, but was unable to drink. Dan spoke to the collapsed animal, but it didn't respond. He cradled the dog against himself, then drizzled water down its throat. The dog coughed a few times, then learned to open his throat to allow the water to trickle into him. Dan got close to a full bottle into the dog, then fed him more bread and cheese and lunch meat. The dog licked Dan's hand.

Dan said, "No, no, none of that licky business with me. Your ass is going to the vet, and then you're on your own. What the hell happened to your feet?"

At the truck stop, the cashier told him that the nearest vet was in the pink stucco office complex on the right about three miles down the road. The dog was already looking better, but was clearly helpless. Dan couldn't stop himself. He petted the dog, scabs and all. He wished he had adrenaline for its oozing feet. The hair around the dog's neck was worn and matted where there had once been a wide collar. Scars in the loose skin, only partially healed, looked like bite marks.

"How does somebody lose a giant fookin dog?"

The dog blinked.

The pink office complex was off the frontage road and up a short, cobbled driveway. Several trees had been planted among various cactus plants, but the trees hadn't grown much. The vet's office was in the second building on the left, and had a redbrick sidewalk and steps. Over the entrance was a small sign in black and white.

GONZALEZ PET & VET HOSPITAL
Emergencies 24-7
Meows to Cows

The dog continued to melt into the paper towels and sheepskin. Dan tried to lift him, but the dog's loose skin stretched like bubble gum, and his legs hung at odd angles. When Dan was able to get his arms up under him, he hugged him to his chest. He lugged the dog toward the vet's office, and felt the animal's complete surrender. He carried it inside and placed it on the cool red-tile floor next to a heavy Mexican colonial chair made of dark wood and thick leather. The dog began to shiver. At the desk, a young Latina receptionist gave Dan an information form to fill out. He wanted to hold on to his cash, so gave her his driver's license and a credit card to run. Given the way he looked, he figured she might check to see if the credit card was stolen. Besides, he would be dead anyway, and no one would connect the dog with the burned-out old car. He couldn't supply much on the dog, and left most of the questions unanswered. The receptionist saw the blanks.

"Dog's name?"

"Unknown."

"Age?"

"I don't know. Maybe six, eight? He looks like he's got a lot of miles on him."

Dan explained his connection to the dog. She began to enter his data directly into a computer. She printed out an info sheet for the doctor, rang a small metal bell, and placed Dan's paperwork in a basket marked "Emergency." There was an outburst of animal sounds. The dog tried to crawl into a corner. Cats in cages paced or slept. As if in a bored long-distance conversation, several dogs from cubicles down the hall barked back and forth with dogs at the rear of the building. An unseen animal howled mournfully.

Dan waited. A well-groomed white woman with a dead cat wrapped in a Gucci silk scarf hurried out. "It's not fair, it is not fair," she sobbed.

A big parrot rocked in his cage. Between whistles and caws, it sang of Mexico's beauty. "*¡México lindo! ¡México lindo!*" It occasionally flapped its wings and in a deep voice croaked orders "*¡Ven acá! ¡Ven acá!* Come here! Come here!"

The dog looked up, its good ear cocked. Dan patted him, rubbed his half ear. Dan sensed someone standing behind him. He turned to see a woman in a white smock removing the dog's paperwork from the basket.

She said, "Hi, I'm Doc Sally."

Dan wasn't sure he'd heard her correctly and figured her for a nurse. "Is Dr. González in?"

"I'm Dr. González. How can I help?"

She spoke with a touch of border in her talk, and her shortish blond hair was perfectly styled for her face. She clearly had a larger ratio of European blood than Indian, as evidenced by her Texas blue eyes. Dan reckoned she was in her late forties. She was tall and still shapely, and she dressed in jeans and a red-and-white-checkered cowboy shirt under the smock. She wore polished black boots, and on her right wrist was a stainless-steel-and-gold Rolex. Dan figured her for a southpaw. He also saw that she noticed his bum eye.

"Is that your dog?"

Dan said, "No, I'm just the dummy who stopped to help." He explained the situation.

"Never save nothin what eats."

"Huh?"

"It tells the world you're easy."

Dan said, "I don't know about that, but I couldn't let him get squashed."

Dan helped Doc Sally get the dog on a gurney and they wheeled him into one of the cubicles. She checked the dog's paws and pasterns, and the mark the collar had made. She spoke kindly to the animal as she examined him. He didn't respond. She checked his ears and teeth and throat. She used a stethoscope to check his chest cavity and the arteries down his hind legs. She felt for broken bones, tugged on the dry, hairless skin, examined the dog's eyes.

"Why are his feet bloody?" Dan asked.

"He's been running nonstop on pavement of one kind or another for days, maybe weeks. The pads have worn through in his search for his master."

"First thing I noticed was his lost-dog look." The second and third things he noticed were the outline of Doc Sally's full lips and the clean line of her perfect ears.

"He'll need to be sedated so he can be fed and hydrated intravenously, and so he won't lick off the medication for his paws and hide. He has to be bathed and have the ticks removed. He probably has worms. A dog with less heart would have been dead a long time ago." She spoke directly to the dog. *"Oye, tú. ¿Cómo te llamas?"* Listen up. What's your name?

The dog wagged his tail halfway. *"Gnuff,"* he replied weakly.

Dan said, "Sounds like he's got a harelip."

"Your dog, Mr. Cooley, has had his vocal chords surgically removed."

"He's not my dog."

"I should also mention that he speaks Spanish, and doesn't understand a word you say."

"He's Mexican, too?"

Doc Sally smiled wryly. "It's not so bad, I assure you."

"Maybe not for you, you speak the lingo."

"Does that mean you're keeping him?"

Dan ducked the question. "How could someone lose a dog this big?"

Doc Sally said, "He may have been dumped. See the scars on him? Somebody's fought him, looks like. He may have been stolen and given to pit bulls to practice on. He might have been trained to fight, too. Fighting dogs are treated cruelly by their masters during periods of conditioning, as in endless hours chained on a treadmill, but they love their masters blindly. For many, their world is a treadmill and the pit, and they are so starved for love that they adore anyone who shows them the slightest kindness."

"Does that mean he'd be vicious to others?"

"Not likely. But I wouldn't want to mess with someone he loved, if he was around."

"What about the cut vocal chords?"

"People will sometimes do that if they use a dog for home security.

By the time an intruder is aware of a dog like this, he's already got teeth in his ass."

Dan liked the way Doc Sally talked. He nodded to the prostrate dog. "Will he survive?"

"Good chance. He's much younger than he looks, four, maybe five. And he's a fighter."

Fighter. The one word that could still break Dan's heart. Dan said, "So what's the tab gonna be?"

"Not as much as where you hail from, but enough. That is, if that's what you want."

"What I want?"

"Well, with the proper treatment, to include medication, food, vitamins, and twenty-four-hour supervision, we're talking roughly a hundred dollars a day."

"How many days?"

"A minimum of three days, and that's only because dogs heal faster than we do. He would still need a safe place to recuperate for some time after that. But in all truth, he'll probably need to stay here five or six days anyway, maybe a week."

"Damn."

"Or, I can put him out of his misery and out of your life for a fast thirty-five dollars. Make it a twenty, and I'll do it right now."

"See, I can't wait around."

Doc Sally said, "Like I say."

"Won't the pound take him?"

"They'll put him down on day one, but not as nicely as I," she told him.

"Ain't this a bitch?" He looked at the dog again. The dog looked back. "Hit me for a three-day pop to start with. You got my card number."

Doc Sally promised, "If he doesn't make it, I'll only bill you for the time he lasts."

"You mean he might not?"

"All I can say is, look how weak he is. He must have lost thirty-five pounds or better."

"What if I don't come back in three days?" Dan asked.

The vet shrugged and said, "I suggest you come in at least once a day every day, for the dog's sake."

"And if I disappear into the hills?"

"I won't bother with the pound," Doc Sally told him. "I'll just put him down."

"Well, you got three hundred, anyway."

"Will you not return, Mr. Cooley? If not, we're only adding to the dog's suffering."

Dan touched his eye. "Look, Doc, I can't say right now, okay? But if I don't make it back in three days, do what you gotta do and add it to my tab." He rubbed the dog's neck. The dog flattened out even more. "You do what the doc says, hear?"

"He only understands Spanish, remember?"

It was getting late as Dan returned to his car, the sun dropping quickly and the light going pink and flat. He checked the Texas map in his atlas. Eighty-ninety miles up ahead was the small town of Van Horn. Head south from there on the 90, driving between the Van Horn and the Wylie Mountains, and he'd be into the higher Davis range. A couple of left turns past Valentine, and he'd be on the dirt roads and trails up around Mount Livermore, which peaked at almost 8,400 feet—no-man's-land, where death was all part of growing up.

"High and bone dry."

He pulled in at the Yippee Saloon again, this time for some bourbon. Thought he might change his luck if he switched back to whisky, hoped for a different alchemy. He knew better, but the idea of being lit on Kentucky Straight instead of grain vodka sounded good to his sagging insides. Four shots later, he was back in fighting trim. He got in his green car. "Promises to keep," he thought, "and miles to go before I sleep." The long, big sleep.

Dan arrived in Van Horn, a Texas town where folks said "tar" for tire. He bought a six-pack of Pearl longnecks, and a gallon of orange juice in a convenience store. He used a phony name and address to check into the Horn of Plenty Motel and BBQ Shack. He paid cash in advance for three days, though he'd probably need only two. Once in his room, he drank three beers with one of the thawed frozen meat-loaf dinners he'd bought back at the truck stop. At midnight, he had to drink the other three beers to get to sleep. He had more on his mind than he thought he'd have—Earl, the dog, finding the right spot for his version of the Molotov cocktail. What if it fizzled? He took more Xanax.

Fortified with a breakfast of vodka and OJ and beef jerky at ten o'clock the following morning, he took Highway 90 south and headed forty-three miles down to Valentine, passing through Lobo on the way. He needed calories, and found a diner. He sat at the counter and had to use both hands to drink his coffee. He then ordered biscuits and gravy, fried potatoes, tortillas, grits, Polish sausage, and buttermilk. He poured on the house's blistering homemade fresh salsa.

The Mexican waitress was also the cook and she wore a white outfit, and a high white hat that covered her gray hair. She wrote swiftly. "You wan' no egg?"

"Too high in cholesterol."

Dan ate less than half of his food, but drank the buttermilk to coat his stomach. Some ten miles past town, he turned onto the narrow 505. It wound its way up toward the spiky dark crags and dry washes near the base of Mount Livermore. White clouds raced across the peak. Three circling buzzards worked something dead beyond a far ridge. After another ten miles on the 505, Dan swung onto the 166. He took the first dirt road, hardly more than a fire trail, and followed it up even farther into the bleak landscape. He parked the car and scouted, the trail allowing him to later drive even deeper into the desolation. He sat awhile and drank and felt comfortable. No one would see, no property but his own would be destroyed. Win-win.

He listened to a kicker station for two hours, would have waited until night and torched himself right there, but having thought that it might take a few days to find the right spot, he'd left personal items in the motel room that could ID him if he didn't toast himself just right.

"Mañana."

The wind came up and Dan dumped what was left of the OJ. He filled the white plastic bottle with dirt so it wouldn't blow away, then set it against some rocks as the beacon he'd aim for the next day.

In Valentine, he bought another gallon of OJ and more beef jerky. Back in Van Horn, he packed all his stuff, except for his toothpaste and toothbrush, and set it on a small table next to the door. He felt both queasy and hungry, knew he had to eat something. He stopped by his car, then returned to his room with the second defrosted meat-loaf dinner. It smelled a little off, but he ate it anyway, scooping the meat and gravy and mashed potatoes into his mouth with his fingers. His sweet tooth got loud, so he had a piece of berry pie with ice cream at the BBQ Shack, but halfway through it, he remembered Tim Pat eating berry pie and ice cream back in San Pedro. Dan left the rest of the pie, along with a full cup of coffee, on the counter, paid on the way out. He wasn't sure how he got back to his room.

He woke up with puke in his mouth from food poisoning. He stumbled to the bathroom and threw up until he thought he was empty. He tried to get back to bed, but was then convulsed with dry heaves. In the middle of clutching the john, his ass went loose with diarrhea. Each time he got back to bed, he'd start up with the pukes or the squirts. Sometimes they both hit him at the same time. He passed out on the messed tile of the bathroom floor.

He woke at daybreak, showered to clean himself of himself, then slept for thirteen hours. He went back to the BBQ Shack and ate half of a cherry pie and drank a quart of buttermilk. He put his stuff in the car and tried to drive to his white OJ bottle in the hills, but he was still so weak that he had to return to his room in the motel. He watched a TV news-and-weather station the rest of the day and late into the night. A handful of Xanax put him to sleep until dawn. He was still sick and whippy. He tried to remember how long he'd been in Van Horn, but couldn't. He tried to go back to sleep, but couldn't. He thought of the dog and tried to put it out of his mind, but couldn't.

On the afternoon of the third day, the dog's paws were healing well, but he was still sick and scrawny. He was off the IV, and Doc Sally continued to prescribe medication, but she doubted that Dan would return. The dog was so helpless and sweet that it would be no small matter for Doc Sally to do to him what she knew she'd have to.

"*Eres tan lindo,*" she cooed to him. You're so pretty.

By the time Dan showered again, made instant coffee in his room, and took aspirin and drank spiked OJ, he was able to check out of the motel well before the noon deadline.

He went to the pay phone and called Earl.

Earl said, "Where the hell you been, where the hell you callin from?"

"Well, I'm way up here in Mendocino. To get here from Frisco, you have to drive through the redwoods, imagine that, redwood trees tall as the sky."

"Huh," said Earl, wondering if Dan was jiving. "Redwoods and sinsemilla, side by side in the boo capital of California. I thought by now you'd be drinkin Canadian beer, not smokin weed."

"Yeah, well, I had a few hits and lost my way, you know how that goes."

"When'll you be back?"

"I'm not sure. See, I ran into this dog."

"You ran over a dog?"

"No, but there was this one in the road who was in trouble. I helped. It's a long story."

Dan didn't sound right. Earl pressed. "So, when you comin back?"

"Soon," Dan said, lying again. "I'm getting tired of this wet weather."

Earl let Dan know how he felt. "I miss you. We all do."

"Same for me. So look, maybe next time I call, I'll be on my way home."

"You do that," said Earl. "Everything's jake around here, so don't worry none. You okay?"

"Oh, yeah."

Earl said, "Hurry home."

"Will do."

Dan hung up, dropped his chin to his chest, covered his eyes with one hand.

The old Mercedes started right up. There was no rush, so Dan let it warm up slowly. He pretended that he was doing it so all the fluids would circulate properly. He really did it because he needed some time to separate his concern for the dog from the implications of the empty OJ bottle waiting for him up the hill.

Why did he feel shitty? He was running on empty, but he knew that wasn't what was on the front burner. The scabby-assed dog was on the front burner. He liked dogs, sure, but he didn't have any ties to this animal except that he'd gotten him to a vet in an emergency. Besides, he hadn't been with the fucker for even an hour, so what was the big deal if he forgot about him? He'd already forked over three hundred dollars, hadn't he? What more was expected? Besides, the mutt was probably dead. Then again, what if he wasn't?

Dan drove out of the motel parking lot and headed for the 90 junction and Valentine. A left turn, and he'd be on the mountain in an hour and a half. The more he thought about it, the more he realized that he should have backed over the dog's head and been done with it. He never should have picked up the dog, never should have fed or watered his rag-gedy ass, and he never, *ever* should have looked him in the eye. Shit-bird dog had ruined his plan.

So why should I care? Dan wondered. *One shot from Doc Sally and the dog'll be in fireplug heaven.*

"Aw, fuck this!" Dan said so loudly that he looked around for some-one else in the car, as though that person had said it.

He blinked a few times, then saw himself three days back cradling the dying dog. The bastard licked his hand and then looked up at him in gratitude and hope and faith. It was a look that reminded Dan of the one Tim Pat had given him when he fought and won in Carson. Dan won-dered what was happening in his head.

At the junction of the 90, Dan kept going west instead of turning south toward the OJ bottle. He eased the old car up to seventy. If he didn't get to Doc Sally's in time, the dog was sure to get whacked. He didn't know why, but he suddenly felt he had to get the dog through the next few days, even though there was another part of him that hoped the dog was already dead. He got back on the road and kept going west to Doc Sally's. There was plenty of time for the mountain.

Chapter 24

Doc Sally had fed the dog his third light meal that day, including another dose of antibiotics. The whites of his eyes were clearing up and he'd already gained back nine pounds. He'd gain more weight by the next day, and more each day to follow. As he lay flat and sleepy, she rubbed his neck and ears and scratched his back with her fingernails. One of his hind legs sprung up involuntarily to scratch the air near his pink belly. Doc Sally hated animal shelters. She knew they were necessary, but seeing the pathetic eyes of lost and deserted animals with no chance of survival was hard on her. She'd continue to feed this dog his meals, and pet and rub him and make him feel loved. And tomorrow she'd kill him. Dogs and donkeys were the hardest for her to put down. She knew that after twenty-five years it shouldn't matter, but it did.

Dan Cooley entered the office and rang the bell. A moment later he saw Doc Sally in her white smock approaching from down the hall.

Talking Texan, she said, "Look what the cat drug in."

She ushered Dan back to the dog. What was left of his ears pricked up, and he eyed Dan quizzically. Dan could see the improvement, saw that the dog was filling out and that his coat was already growing back in. He rubbed the dog's neck and scratched the top of his head. The dog flattened out on the floor of his cage and closed his eyes. Dan could still see the heavy ridges of his ribs.

Dan said, "He looks good."

"He'll look better in three, four more days."

"That long, huh?"

"Ballpark."

"Damn!" He wasn't sure what he thought about the whole mess, except that throwing good money after bad didn't make much sense, especially if she was going to ice the dog when he didn't show up for him.

"You were hoping he was dead?"

"I'm not sure what I was hoping, to tell the truth."

Doc Sally said, "If you have a clean and quiet place for him to recuperate, I could, in a pinch, provide his medication and the proper food, and you could take him now. But you'd still have to bring him in at least two more times."

"Here's my credit card again. Nail me for another three days."

Doc Sally ran the card. "You'll be in for sure?"

"Same deal as before. If I can, I will. Otherwise, you can, well, you know."

"I want you to know something, Mr. Cooley," Doc Sally said. "It pisses me off to have to kill other people's unwanted animals."

"He's not my animal."

"He's not mine, either."

Dan said, "Once he's healthy, isn't there anyone who'd take him?"

"Well, he only understands Spanish, so that cuts his chances with the white population. And he's too big to feed for most Mexicans in these parts. That pretty much points to a dog fighter who'd sacrifice him to some big pit."

"And if you turned him loose once he was strong enough?"

"Same thing. He'd go back to the road looking for that lost master. Or he might go looking for you."

"I don't want that, for God's sake."

Doc Sally slipped into Texan again. "Then I'd say that you was up a unsanitary tributary without sufficient means of locomotion."

"You have a way with words."

"I want you to say something after me, slowly, okay?"

"Sure."

"Dah may lah pah tee tah."

One sound at a time, Dan said it without trouble. She had him repeat it several times, then told him to stress the *Dah* and the *tee* in "*Dah* may lah pah *tee* tah."

Dan stressed *dah* and *tee*.

Doc Sally said, "Do you think you can say it a little faster?"

Dan sped it up. The dog opened one eye.

"Now say it as if you were in conversation."

Dan said, *"Dame la patita."*

The dog struggled to his haunches and held out a front paw.

Doc Sally said, "You just told him to shake hands."

"Ah, Jaysus."

Head down, Dan rushed down the red-tiled hallway for the front door. He had a lump in his throat the size of an avocado. He hit the porch running. He raced to the Davis Mountains and the white orange juice bottle. But instead of immediately lighting up, he carefully laid out his suicide gear and took himself through a practice run so there would be no screwups when the whistle blew. The only things he didn't do were spread out the charcoal and fill the gallon bottles with gas. He got in the backseat and arranged everything in its proper place. He had a cigarette lighter in one hand, and the green plastic pack of single-edged razor blades in the other. If one lighter didn't work, he had backups. All this planning would pay off, he told himself. He felt good.

Dan put his makings back in the trunk of the car and slept in the backseat wrapped in his sleeping bag. It was so cold on the mountain that he had to start the car and put on the heater to keep from freezing. The next morning, he took the 166 all the way back around to Fort Davis. He stayed at a roadside park after he'd spent the day walking around town and going to a restored frontier army post that dated from 1854. In these parts hombres died fighting, white and Apache and Comanche. Dan felt like a pussy among their ghosts and edged out the door. He shaved with cold water at a gas station to make himself halfway presentable, and slept in the car again. The following day he took the scenic road to Alpine, stayed on it all the way to the town of Marta. He bought another gallon of OJ, and ate market tortillas and jerky and pork and beans from small cans with yank-off lids. He kept drinking. He had no choice. He crapped out in another roadside park. He had the place to himself, but wished there were some kids playing. He tried repeatedly, but had trouble remembering how many days were left before the dog would hit the pump.

He woke early and cold. He jump-started with two glasses of vodka and an OJ chaser. He drove on to Valentine and ate in the diner again.

He bought gas afterward, but instead of turning back to the mountain and the white bottle, he drove straight through to Doc Sally's.

One look at him as he came through the door and she said, "If it isn't my favorite homeless advocate."

"Yeah, well, I hope you're happy, 'cause I'm not."

"Then why did you come back?"

"That's what I'd like to know."

Doc Sally ushered Dan out the door of the office. "Close the door all the way, and then come back in."

Dan followed the instructions, came inside, and closed the door behind him.

"Now, what are you doing here?"

He barely managed to get out the words. "I'm here for Barky."

———

Barky had a new bright blue collar and was proud of himself as he tugged lightly at his leash. His legs were wobbly, and he walked with a slight limp, but he still managed a touch of strut. He made sure he stayed close to Dan as they walked toward the green Mercedes. Dan smiled as the dog kept brushing against his leg. Most of Barky's coat had grown in, and Dan was surprised by how much the dog had filled out in such a short time. Dan knew he had done the right thing in taking the dog on, if only until he could shuffle the mutt off on to someone else. At least Doc Sally wouldn't have to kill him. Dan also knew he had done the wrong thing, knew there would always be a white plastic OJ bottle lodged somewhere in the Davis Mountains that had a pull on him like the Bermuda Triangle.

Dan opened the front-passenger door to his car, and with no urging, Barky climbed slowly in. He was still too weak to jump, but he sat up on the passenger side and stuck his snout out the window and waited for the wind. Dan heard something behind him, and turned to see Doc Sally pushing a dolly down a side ramp. It was loaded with a carton of canned dog food and a monster bag of dried food.

"On the house," Doc Sally said.

As they loaded the dog food into the backseat of the car, Doc Sally said, "Feed him twice a day, no more. Put half of a can on top of the dry at night, but be sure to walk him. Run him, if you can. If he gets spooky, add a cup of brown rice at night. But that's it, and no people food." Doc Sally stood and stretched her back, her ample breasts on near vertical display. "Why aren't we puttin all this in the trunk?"

"Trunk's loaded with my travelin stuff."

Doc Sally could smell the sauce on Dan, and raised an eyebrow. "Loaded is rat."

Dan ignored her look. "My kids always had fox terriers. They got scraps from the table."

"This ol' boy'll eat your table."

From a plastic bag looped over one wrist, Doc Sally produced a large bright blue divided plastic dog bowl big enough to hold food and water at the same time. She also held out an opener for the canned food, and a five-by-eight card with a handwritten list.

She said, "You can buy him a cheapo blanket at Wal-Mart that'll keep your sheepskins from getting all doggy."

"I will, and thanks for the stuff."

"You're welcome, I'm sure," she said. "Say, where you two cowpokes headin to?"

"Just headin," said Dan. He held out Doc Sally's list, his face a question mark.

Doc Sally talked more Texas still. "That's the secret decoder'll give you access to the wondrous Spanish-speaking world of your Messkin dawg."

Above the top red line of the card, Doc Sally had printed categories in letters neat as a draftsman's.

English Command	Spanish Command	Sounds Like
(Stress the underlined sounds.)		
Come here	Ven acá	*Ben* ah-*cah*
Let's go home	Vamos a casa	*Bah*-mohs-ah-*cah*-sah
Hungry?	¿Tienes hambre?	¿Tee-*yeh*-nes *ahm*-breh?
Water?	¿Agua?	¿*Ahg*-wah?
Eat	Come	*Coh*-meh
Drink	Bebe	*Beh*-beh
Git	Vete	*Veh*-teh
Shake	Dame la patita	*Dah*-may la pah-*tee*-ta
Pretty boy/Good boy	Eres tan lindo	*Air*-es tahn *leen*-doh

Dan eyed the list. Hungry. "¿Tee-*yeh*-nes *ahm*-bre?" He said it slowly a few times, then sped it up.

Barky went on immediate alert.

Doc Sally said, "Not bad. Need more practice?"

"If I do, I'll grab hold of some Mexican."

"I'm a Mexican."

Dan wanted to kiss the shit out of her, but got in the car instead. "You're not like any Mexican I ever knew."

Doc Sally went to the dog and scratched him between his poor ears. "*Eres tan lindo, mi Barquito.*" She looked at Dan. "In Spanish, *barquito* means little boat."

Doc Sally crossed to Dan, then leaned down and kissed him on his undamaged eye. Dan had forgotten how the soft lips of a woman could make him shiver, could make him melt. He cleared his throat with difficulty.

Dan said, "Well, listen, thanks for all your help. I guess."

"That's okay, easy."

"It isn't as if I was set up by a certain border lady, rat?"

"*¿Quién sabe,* who knows?"

"Yeah, well, how'm I supposed to afford an eighty-pound dog?" Dan saluted. "See ya, Doc."

"*Váyanse con Dios,* go with God."

Instead of hunting for a Wal-Mart, Dan bought an army blanket in a surplus store to keep Barky warm and his sheepskins clean. He also bought a six-pack of Negra Modelo beer in a convenience store, and some Mexican food at a taco stand next door. Two pork tacos; a beef tamale with thick red sauce and melted cheese; rice and beans; guacamole, or mashed avocado salad; corn tortillas. He planned to snack along the way on what he didn't finish, wash it down with the rich beer. But once Dan was back in the car, Barky smelled the food and leaped around as if he were electrified.

"Sit down, you fuck. I'm trying to eat." Dan looked straight ahead, but talked to the dog through rice and beans. "Just don't get any ideas about this deal bein permanent, okay? I'll get you lookin fat and sassy, but once somebody takes a shine to you, I'm hittin the bricks, get me?"

"*Gnuff.*"

Dan looked over. Barky slobbered and begged. He licked Dan across the face, the long pink tongue quick as a champion's jab.

Dan wiped himself with a sleeve. "You been fed once today."

"*Gnuff-gnuff.*"

Dan said, "I want you to understand that this will be the last time I ever eat in your presence."

"*Gnuff.*"

"Lucky for you I don't understand Spanish."

Dan got out of the car, let the dog out, and put half of the tamale and one of the tacos in the blue dish. Two gulps and both were gone.

Dan checked Doc Sally's list. "All right, wise guy. *Bebe,* drink."

Dan poured half a bottle of the foamy dark beer into the blue plate. Barky inhaled it, no hesitation, his tongue a scoop. He belched. He licked his chops. He wanted more. Dan dragged his drunken ass back into the car, opened another beer for himself, then went back to the trunk of the car where he could eat and drink out of Barky's reach. The dog settled down, began to nod from the beer, then flattened out. He was snoring by the time Dan got back in the car.

"You lush."

Dan drank more vodka, and had to stop to buy more OJ. He missed some turns, got turned around, and drove around awhile somewhere on the east side of El Paso. He passed a small park where little boys and girls were playing. He stopped to watch and pet Barky. He heard the sounds of his own children mixed in with the laughter of these little Mexican kids.

Dan pointed. "Barky, see? Kids?" He spelled it out. "K-I-D-S. P-L-A-Y-I-N-G. Understand?"

Barky didn't understand a damn thing, especially since he'd never heard any part of the alphabet in Spanish, much less in English. But he made a sound that was somewhere between a whine and a wheeze, and Dan understood that the dog had to pee, understood that Barky couldn't whine right because he had nothing to whine with.

Dan hooked up the leash and let Barky out of the car. He ran straight for a pole and peed, but he was careful not to let all of it go. He ran to a tree. Then he ran to another tree.

One of the little kids tripped over another, who dropped his faded yellow tennis ball. All the kids began to pipe Spanish words like little birds. Their playfulness was infectious, but their words were unintelligible to Dan. But not to Barky, who bounced around and tugged at the leash. Dan allowed himself to be pulled along, grateful to be near the joy of children. They ran and tumbled and when the ball rolled free again, Barky snapped it up. The kids swarmed after him, and he ran in a tightening circle until he was stuck fast against Dan's legs. As the kids squealed, Barky rolled on his back and pawed the air and they jumped on him.

Dan realized that Barky had been part of a family. A family was where he belonged, not with some old man. When one little girl got the ball back, the kids scampered away, each laughing and piping. Barky wanted to keep on playing, but his tongue was hanging out and Dan could see that he was already tired. As Dan untangled him, one of the children's mothers got between them and the unknown dog, and worriedly moved them farther away. She smiled at Dan. He smiled back. Both nodded.

Once Dan got the dog unwound, Barky immediately tugged the leash in the direction of the children. Dan tugged back, and headed for the Mercedes. Barky remembered his bladder and knew he had to finish in a hurry. As they walked back to the car, he let go full bore against another pole. As Dan waited, he noticed the weathered sign.

GUADALUPE PARK

"Damn."

Guadalupe was that girl's name, Lupe's name, Guadalupe Ayala. He hadn't thought of her since way back. Now he saw her face, and then he saw Tim Pat's face. He leaned against the park's old iron fence, his hands covering his eyes in shame. He wept for the first time since the accident. Half cowed, Barky huddled behind Dan's legs. Snot and drool rolled out of Dan, tears soaked his hands and sleeves. As the sobs trailed off, Dan felt some of the bitterness that he'd felt toward the girl come back. He didn't want these feelings, but if he had to have them, it was better here than in Los Angeles. He didn't want to hate the girl. Tim Pat's death was not her fault, it was his. His mind told him that, but he realized that there was something still bubbling inside, and that troubled him. The fire he'd planned for himself would have ended all this. He patted the dog, who was suddenly happy again. Dan wasn't.

"Forgivin's a bear when you got nothin holdin you up inside."

Dan Cooley took a good, hard look at his face in the rearview mirror. What stared back at him was an aging alcoholic, gray bristles on his cheeks and chin, red-rimmed and bloodshot eyes. "I'm a fucking wreck," he muttered.

Dan drank more vodka to stay loose and to forget. He pulled over and fished out a coin. Heads, and it was back to Los Angeles through Las Cruces, New Mexico. Tails, Miami, Little Havana. Both had plenty of people who spoke Spanish, didn't they? Somebody would take Barky, why not?

Dan didn't flip the coin. Lit as he was, even if tails came up, Dan knew he would be heading for Los Angeles. He wasn't kidding anybody. At least in Los Angeles there was the shop. Once he got Barky installed there on the pretense that the business needed a watchdog, he could always go finish the job on himself that the four-footed fuck had interrupted.

The sun started down over the desert. Dan got back on the 10, and soon passed through the adobe town of Las Cruces. He stopped at several motels, but none took dogs. He tried the Motel 6.

"Is he housebroke?" asked the desk clerk.

"He better be."

"Fill out the form."

Dan fed the dog Doc Sally's formula, and took him for a walk on the leash. Barky stayed close to Dan, pulled away only to go off to do his business. When he came back from a tree or a pole or a squat, he'd nuzzle Dan's hand.

"*Air*-es tahn *leen*-doh." Dan felt like a dummy speaking Spanish so poorly, but the dog didn't seem to mind.

Dan had his usual vodka and OJ to start the day, bought a six-pack of Bohemia, then drove to a Taco Bell. He got one burrito for himself and two for the dog. The dog looked up for more. Dan checked the list. There was nothing on it that said "No more," or "That's all you get," or "Look there goes a cat."

"*Ven*," come.

Barky had gained a little more weight, and he tried to jump into the car, but he still didn't have the legs for it. He climbed into the car instead, and his snout poked out through the window. As they rolled along, he would look from time to time over at Dan to make sure he was real. Dan practiced from Doc Sally's list. Maybe he should give the dog lessons in Gaelic. He took a little sip of the raw, clear stuff. Tried out some of the few words in Gaelic he remembered. Barky looked at him, cocked one eyebrow, and went to sleep.

A wave of self-disgust washed over Dan. All of this dancing around, this grand "plan"—pure bullshit. If he had really wanted to kill Lupe, he would have blasted away at her while she stood helpless on the sidewalk. If he had wanted to kill himself, he would have done so sitting on the cool concrete floor of the garage. Whatever happened, he had a life sentence—and he had to finish out that sentence as best he could. He turned around and looked at Barky sleeping on the backseat. Then he reached under the seat and pulled out the road atlas. He could make L.A. in two days. Easy.

But he didn't want to show up looking like someone who had just crawled out of a flophouse. He had to get his shit together.

Dan decided to stay a week in Del Mar. He'd eat seafood and fresh fruit, and take long walks twice a day with Barky, and try to dry out some before heading back to the shop to face Earl.

Chapter 25

When Dan showed up, he was still bloated and had a touch of a lush's stink on him, but he was upright, and Earl was grateful to God that he was still alive.

"How's business?"

"I could use another pair of hands."

"I can do my best."

"That's good enough for me."

"And this is our new watchdog."

"So that's what that is."

Dan had planned to take Barky and live in his house on Cahuenga, but its mirrors reflected things that were no longer there, and he quickly decided to move back into his bachelor apartment above the gym. The place was too small for Dan and a big dog, so he bought a forest green, extra-large dog cushion for Barky and placed it in a big closet downstairs. He banked the wall behind the cushion with old blankets and installed an electric heater that worked off a thermostat to make sure Barky's room would always be cozy.

Barky, however, decided to sleep upstairs with Dan. To make his point, the dog spent six fucking nights scratching and leaping at Dan's door. Dan decided that it was time to show the dog just who was boss, and bought earplugs for bedtime. But Barky was relentless, and no earplugs could blot out the sound of the leaping and wheezing dog. Dan tried putting Barky outside to teach him a lesson, but he immediately suffered profound Irish Catholic guilt when the dog rolled on his back and looked up with the eyes of a second-century martyr.

Earl delighted in this battle of wills, knew that the fight was fixed, even if Dan didn't. When Dan finally capitulated, red-eyed and bitter, it was no surprise to Earl or the dog. Barky was magnanimous in his forgiveness, however, and smothered Dan with unconditional love.

Earl said, "Man's best friend."

"That's what you hear, anyway."

"What's happenin with that watchdog shuck you laid on me? Only thing your dog is watchin for is when it's time to eat."

Dan said, "Yeah, well, that's gonna change, I guarantee you."

"Sheeuh," said Earl, talking like a brother in a high whine. He loved the dog for his sweetness, but most of all for his effect on Dan. "Bark be workin by the *book,* man."

"Earl, dogs can't read, you forget that somehow?"

"I'm talkin 'bout *workin* by the *pimp* book. You furry buddy there, he be pimpin off you, man. Dog a stone pimp."

The boozing was way down. Dan was working, if only to drive the truck on runs to suppliers or to make deliveries with Momolo. But at least he was out in the world, instead of shit-faced in his dark room. Most important, he'd begun to laugh again, especially when telling some story about Barky chasing deer in the Hollywood Hills, or licking some kid's ice-cream cone. Damn dog made everybody laugh.

Earl cupped his hands to his mouth. *"Gnuff-gnuff."*

Barky cocked his good ear and wagged his loopy tail.

Dan said, "Don't try to alienate the affections of my dawg."

Earl was scheming. If he and Barky could only get Dan back into the gym, and then start going to fights. Earl knew that Dan was staying out of the gym because of the mirrors and the White Fox. But he didn't know about the stuff locked in the trunk of Dan's Mercedes.

Dan made an appointment and drove to Plunkett's office. He left Barky in the pickup to sleep off his latest plate of chiles rellenos, rice, and beans. Plunkett reached for the bottle of Booker's and two glasses.

Dan said, "None for me, but you go ahead."

Plunkett poured for himself, made a ritual of the way he set the glass down and held the bottle.

"I want you to change my paperwork on Earl," Dan told him. "Everything's to be the same, except for the automatic three-year part. Simplify it to go into effect at the time I punch out."

"Anything else?"

"That's it."

Plunkett finished the first hit and poured another. He said, "It's good to have you among us."

"Did I leave?"

"Did you really think I wouldn't figure out what you were up to?" said Bobby P. He raised his glass to Dan and this time sipped slowly. "We're an island people, Danny, and there are those of us who can't keep from jumping off the cliffs."

"Thanks, Plunk."

"Strictly confidential, of course," said the lawyer.

"Strictly."

Plunkett raised his glass again. "You'll get my bill."

Dan could not bring himself to get rid of the deadly stuff in the trunk of his car. He never gave a thought to what might happen if someone rear-ended him.

He doubted that he would ever use it, but the idea that he *could* gave him a feeling of control. Having gone back to bourbon, he'd picked up a bottle of Basil Hayden's, and would sometimes take a drink, but usually he'd head to Canter's for pastrami and Dr. Brown's cream soda and chocolate marble cake, all to go—one order for himself and one for Barky. They'd eat in the parking lot. Dan tipped the soda bottle and the dog guzzled from it, his head upright. Barky weighed seventy pounds and wanted to weigh ninety. He would belch from the cream soda and plop down, ready for beddy-bye. Dan knew the dog liked beer better than soda pop, but he figured that if he had to cut down on the sauce, so did Barky.

"You pig."

"*Gnuff.*"

Dan showed no interest when Earl invited him to watch TV fights. When Earl mentioned fights in Indio or Palm Springs, and asked if Dan wanted to go with him, Dan begged off, saying it was too far. When Earl suggested local club fights at the Santa Cruz Sports Arena in Montebello, or at the Hollywood Park Racetrack Casino in Inglewood, or at one of the local Marriott hotels that held fights under chandeliers, Dan would say he'd be too busy taking Barky for his run in the hills.

"See, Barky'd miss pissin on the Hollywood sign."

"A lousy fight once in a while, what the hell."

"Naw," Dan would say, his eyes looking off, or sometimes deep within.

The phone rang during one of these conversations. Earl answered, and yelled for Dan. "It's Louie, from TJ."

Dan picked up the phone. "Louie fuckin Carbajal."

"Dan *culero* Cooley."

Dan said, "What you sellin this time?" He winked at Earl.

"No, no, I ain't sellin nothin, I'm comin to Al-*lay.*"

"I didn't know they let undesirables across the border."

"That's you. Down here they got posters with you *foto* to warn *las madres.*"

"How can I help you, you Luigi?" Dan asked.

"I'm comin for the featherweight title fight at the Olympic Auditorio. I got a piece of the promotion, and one of the fighters, but don't tell the goddan Commission."

"Everything you do is 'don't tell the goddan Commission,' " said Dan. "Who's your boy?"

"Bazooka Flores, out of Hermosillo, champ of México. See, I think maybe I promote sontine in Al-*lay* by myself, but for now I wan' you to work Flores's corner, you and Errol."

Dan had to sit down. A title fight. The Olympic. Memories, all good but one. Dan remembered the low ceilings of the concrete dressing rooms, the exposed pipes, and he remembered the photo displays of old-time strong men out front that had so fascinated him as a boy.

Dan said, "I thought they only had *norteña* bands and that hip-hop shit at the Olympic these days."

"Yeah, but you can still promote fights," Louie told him. "All you gotta do is pay the rent, and the licenses for the Commission, and all the city and state shit, too."

"Why don't you promote it at the Auditorio in TJ?"

"Title fight. Lots of Mexicanos in Al-*lay*. Dollars instead of *pesos.*"

Dan said, "Thanks, Lou, but I'm busy here at the shop and all."

"No, no, I need a good cut man for my boy, and besides, I wan' a white man and a black one in the corner to make it look good for the fookeen gringos and the *maiates* in the crowd."

"Louie, you're a beaner racist fuckin pig."

"Of course!"

Dan got the details and hung up and told Earl about the fight, and working with two of Flores's regular corner men. "I'll be workin cuts, you work the bucket. The kid's trainers'll handle the grease, ice, and conversation. Title fight, so four can work the corner."

"Rainbow coalition," said Earl.

"You're in, right?"

"Naw," said Earl, "my old lady's bitchin I don't spend enough time at home. Besides, I got stuff to do around here."

"Bullshit," said Dan, "we're partners, right?"

"Well, yeah, I guess I could work it."

Dan stood up and threw three short right hands into his left palm. Earl bit the inside of his cheek to keep from smiling. Dan didn't know that Earl, at his wife's urging, had put in an SOS call to Louie.

Louie's boy won. In the seventh, he got a jagged rip at the corner of his right eye, but Dan stopped the blood and kept it stopped. Though subordinate to Flores's trainers in the corner, Dan and Earl worked the fight as smoothly as ever. With Louie the next day, they sat on cushions and enjoyed a long lunch in Little Tokyo. Having a champion meant that Louie suddenly ranked large in the fight game. He got drunk on hot sake and cold beer, and threw money around as if he was in a whorehouse. Earl ate so much sushi that he asked if his eyes had changed shape. The eyes that had started to look different belonged to Dan Cooley, and Earl was grateful for a wife who had men figured out so well.

After the Olympic fight, Earl got Dan to watch TV fights. Eventually, Earl finessed him into going to club fights in and around town as well. Dan ran into fight guys he hadn't seen in a long time, and they laughed and scratched and told war stories, and lamented the deaths of old friends.

New times were never as good as old times, but to Dan's surprise, he found himself wanting more of both. So Dan got Earl to go with him to venues as far away as Palm Springs, even down to Louie Carbajal's venue, the Auditorio in Tijuana. They traveled northwest out to the Marriott Hotel at the Warner Center in the Valley. Or they'd head down south to the Arrowhead Pond, home of the Mighty Ducks, in Orange County. They often took Momolo along, wanted promoters to get a look at him.

Momolo learned things by listening to Dan and Earl as they discussed the lights and shadows of boxing, the angles and the curves and the dead ends that could make careers disappear like sweat socks in a dryer.

Momolo got four fights in quick succession. He went two and one, with one draw and no KOs. No matter how hard Earl worked with him, Momolo was as deliberate in his movements as he was in his speech: Earl told Dan that he thought Momolo's chances of making big money in boxing were limited. "He's in great shape, he works hard, he has the desire, but he doesn't throw in combinations. And still no hook."

Dan didn't want to write the kid off. "You never know."

"Yeah," said Earl, "but when he starts to move up one side of the pyramid, the guys on the other side will be moving up, too."

"He'll know it's time to quit before we do."

When things slowed down a bit, Earl started worrying again. So he was relieved when Wardell called him and asked him to come to the Sports Arena and watch one of his top fighters in action. Earl accepted the invitation for both of them without bothering to even ask Dan.

When he got around to telling Dan about it, Dan just smiled faintly and said, "Well, hell—why not."

Two days later, battling commuter traffic, Earl and Dan headed for the Sports Arena, Earl in his van, Dan in the company pickup. They drove separate vehicles because they would be taking different freeways home. Barky had his nose out the window of the pickup and couldn't care less about smog or the stop-and-go, as long as he was with Dan. His weight had leveled out because of his runs in the hills, and he was all muscle and bone and sass.

Detective Nájera, from West Traffic, would also be going to the eight o'clock fight. He'd leave for the eight o'clock fight at seven-fifteen, his home in South El Monte just a few miles away.

Earl and Dan picked up the tickets that Wardell had waiting for them. They were in the first row of the stands, where it was better to watch than from down close. They were used to working ringside, but that was different. From the stands in the small facility, they could see a fighter's foot position as well as his punches.

It was seven-fifteen, and instead of going to their seats, they went back to the dressing room to talk shit with Jolly Joe and their cronies. Jolly Joe was working a fight down in El Centro, across from the Mexican border, and Earl and Dan were disappointed that they'd missed him.

Then Dan saw Wardell and his fighter.

"Who the fuck dyed that kid's hair?" he wondered.

Chapter 26

hicky Garza left San Antonio on 10 West and drove through El Paso and Tucson, then crossed the Colorado River into California at Blythe. Up ahead ninety miles was Indio, where there were two Indian casinos that periodically held boxing matches, one indoors, one out. All of it was hot, most of it dry. It was the same into and past Palm Springs, and didn't begin to green up until around Ontario, well to the east of Los Angeles.

As he got closer, it was starting to get dark and a few lights were coming on. The sun was setting as Chicky drove toward it, and the sky was all purple and orange and dark blue with black splotches and streaks of silver. Smog hovered over the sprawl. Coming down a steep hill near a big cemetery, Chicky felt himself entering a foreign land where folks would tell you to go take a flying fuck and not look back. Chicky would show 'em.

To save money on the road, and to be safe while he slept, Chicky had pulled into truckers' stops to nap. He ate plastic-wrapped ham-and-cheese sandwiches he bought in gas stations and washed them down with Pepsi. His red '81 Chevy pickup, with "Fresita" painted in beautiful script on both doors, had held up like a champ. The map had looked simple enough—keep his ass on the I-10 all the way smack into down-town L.A. Back in San Anto he couldn't have imagined what it might be like, but here he was.

"The winner, and new champion of the world, Eduardo *Chicky* Garza! Garza!" Chicky was serious when he said that out loud, but had to laugh as well.

Crossing into California, Chicky'd called information, but there was no Dan Cooley listed in the Los Angeles area, and no Cooley's Gym. All Chicky knew about California was what he'd seen in the movies. He would have to get the lay of the land before he started to track down Dan Cooley. Chicky felt sure Cooley was still a trainer, still ran or worked out of some kind of gym. It only made sense. It's what old fight guys did. He'd ask around. Somebody'd know. He wasn't worried. He still had about $2,400 from the $2,600 cushion he'd left San Antonio with. A for-tune. First thing, once he got situated, he'd buy him that Stetson. Then get him a picture of him wearing it standing in front of Fresita with Dan Cooley, and send it to his *abuelito*.

"Look out, Al-*lay*, ol' Garz's ridin into town!"

He checked the map as he drove, his eyes flicking to the blue high-lighter he'd traced along the map's red line of the highway. He was com-ing into Baldwin Park, still part of the arid sprawl on the east side of Los Angeles. Big green 605 Freeway signs began to appear, along with off-ramp signs that hung alongside the road. Chicky squirmed in the seat of the truck, his behind sore from the long drive.

He checked the map, his eyes darting in the fading light between the blue highlighting and the traffic. The north/south interchange of the 605, the San Gabriel River Freeway, had to be close. He could almost taste Al-*Lay*. He wanted something good to eat, that was for sure. He wondered what the City of the Angels would look like all lit up.

There were sure to be cheap motels in L.A., but now he wondered where to find one. He looked down to check the map again. When he looked up, he had to slam on the brakes. There were four lanes of cars, and lit-up brake lights stretched all the way out to the Pacific Ocean, as far as Chicky could tell. It wouldn't take Chicky long to know why Angelinos called their freeways the longest parking lots in the world.

"*Estamos a puro chingazo,*" Chicky mumbled. We're fucked for sure in this mess.

Chicky waited with the others for the police and ambulances to take away the wreckage up ahead, human and machine. But as cars got closer to the site of the accident, he got detoured onto 605. After a half hour of stop-and-go, he saw the blinking lights of a half dozen patrol cars up ahead. After another fifteen minutes, he could see the overpass of the 605.

He checked the map again, and saw that the parallel East and West 60 was just a few miles to the south by way of the 605. He'd swing south on the 605, and then west again on the 60 into Angel Town.

But he had to put up with even more stop-and-go traffic on the 605. Stuck in the mud of traffic, Chicky glanced over and noticed the brightly lit red and yellow of the Santa Cruz Sports Arena. He only got a glimpse of it, but damned if it didn't look like a bullring there among the trees and the pylons. He'd never heard of bullfights in California.

"Course you never can tell in Califa."

Chicky finally got a break. Afraid that he was lost, he took the Firestone Avenue exit and headed west, thinking that would get him back on track. It wasn't long before he passed over the dry concrete banks of the L.A. River, and could see the illuminated cones and cubes of downtown Los Angeles ten-plus miles away. He was completely turned around. He got off Firestone at Atlantic, then turned right toward the towns of Bell and Vernon. As he crossed Florence Avenue into Bell, he immediately felt he was deep into the Westside of San Anto, though this was upscale a notch or two. Except for street signs, virtually everything was written in Spanish. Doctor, dentist, and lawyer signs were in Español, as were the billboards. Cars smoked, sombreros were proudly worn. Mexican cafés offered all kinds of seafood. Food stands sold tacos, enchiladas, *tortas,* and all classes of *antojitos,* or snacks—¡*Tacos joven, todas classes de antojitos!*

Chicky saw a motel sign over a drab 1930s stucco building, and his anxiety leveled out. At a corner stand next to the motel, he parked and ordered a Pepsi and a *torta* made on a crusty, wide roll with cheese and avocado, or *aguacate.* Jalapeño chiles were free, all you could eat. He had a *pan dulce* for dessert, dunked the sugared sweet roll in scalding-hot *café con leche*—espresso and milk served in a tall glass—latte Mexican style. Then he drove into the motel's parking lot and checked in.

"Well, I made 'er, *abuelito*," Chicky said from deep in his throat. "Almost anyway."

Chicky woke for the third time at noon, but he wasn't sure where he was. He parted a brown curtain and looked out on a dusty asphalt parking lot, but still wasn't sure. He doused his face with cold water, then remembered checking into the Bell Motel, but he had no real idea where that put him relative to downtown L.A. He showered, gave his short hair a quick wash with hand soap, and went down to the office, where an old white woman with paper-thin skin informed him that he was in Bell, California.

"This town used to have a different complexion," she said, "no offense intended."

"How far are we from downtown L.A.?"

"On a good day, and at the right time, twenty minutes."

"How far on to Hollywood?" Chicky asked.

"Another twenty minutes, you're lucky."

At the food stand next door, Chicky had Mexican scrambled eggs, with beans and tortillas, and another *café con leche.* He walked for a half hour trying to get his bearings, and, after a good look-see, asked people on the street and in shops if there was a boxing gym nearby. No one knew.

A police car was parked on the street and the middle-aged policeman inside looked Mexican. Chicky greeted him politely and asked about fight gyms and a certain white trainer. The cop thought Chicky was putting him on, then realized he was serious.

"Where you bringin that accent from?" said the cop.

"San Antonio, just got into town, and I'm lookin for a Mr. Dan Cooley, who lives in these parts."

"What, you a fighter?"

"Yessir."

The cop hadn't heard a "Yes, sir" in a long time, and smiled. He thought a moment, then gave Chicky the names of several gyms and general directions to them.

"I don't know the addresses, but start with these. They can give you more places to check if you don't find your man there. The nearest one is the El Indio, and that's just a few blocks over at the corner of Florence and Bear."

"Bear?" said Chicky, the sound of it tugging at him despite his self-control. "How you spell that?"

The cop looked at him closely, thought he might be a smart-ass after all. "B-E-A-R. Like in *Teddy* bear."

Chicky was disappointed. "I thought it might be spelled B-E-X-A-R, that's the county San Antonio's in. Down there we say 'Bear County' for Bexar County, like in Teddy bear. Yeah, well 'bear' kinda took me back."

The cop understood, saw that the boy was showing signs of homesickness. "Well, good luck, cowboy."

"Much obliged."

Walking, Chicky took Florence over to El Indio. He passed by the ass-end of Bell High School and saw the football field and track, and noted that this could be a convenient place to do roadwork. Chicky would learn that El Indio was known among L.A.'s Mexican fight guys as *el taco roto*, the broken taco. But it was clean and presentable and the walls were covered with photos and posters of legendary Mexican fighters, going back to Mexico City's Raul Ratón Macias of the mid-50s. The gym was nearly empty, most pros having finished their workouts by one o'clock. They'd run early, then slept. Now they'd sleep again, then walk after dinner. Fighters would waste away if they didn't get their shut-eye and lots of it. An old guy playing dominos told him that the manager, Tony Velasco, would be back around five.

Chicky bought a street map of Los Angeles, and back at his room called information for the addresses of the gyms the cop had given him. He used his blue highlighter to mark the routes he'd take. The blue lines looked like grapevines twisting senselessly through the grid of the map, but Chicky knew that once he'd been to one place, then the next one, the ones after would be easier to track down.

Thinking that Dan Cooley would have a gym closer to downtown and in a white neighborhood, Chicky headed for the gyms that sounded Anglo to him.

Huntington Park Gym, on Soto, sounded white. It was fairly close, but it was all Latino. Though everyone in the gym could pronounce "Cooley" all right, the *cholos* had fun joking with the name, saying *culero* instead of Cooley. One of the old-timers woke up from his nap and said he'd known Dan for years, but that he hadn't seen him working in corners lately. Fight guys are always polite to strangers, but they are closemouthed around people they don't know, for fear that they might somehow rat someone out.

Hollenbeck Gym, east of downtown, was a cop gym for amateur kids, mostly Mexican. The amateur coaches weren't familiar with Dan's name.

Hoover Street Gym was south of downtown, near where the Rodney King riots had erupted. Black and Latino fighters and trainers worked at Hoover. One of the old-timers said that Cooley had once had a gym in Hollywood, but that it was closed as far as he knew.

"It name Hard Rock," another old man said.

"No," the first said. "It Hard *Knock*. Hard Rock be a Hollywood up-town club for spo'tin folks."

Broadway Gym, at the corner of 108th Street, deep down in South Central L.A., had some Latinos working out, but it was mostly black. The old black men playing checkers knew Dan Cooley, all right, and knew that he'd had a gym some time back, but were not sure of its name or where it had been. The owner, Wardell Purdy, walked with a limp, had lip whiskers and a full head of steel gray hair. Wardell added that he'd known Dan Cooley forever, but hadn't seen him in a while, and had heard that Dan had closed his gym.

"It was called the School of Hard Knocks," said Wardell, "somethin like that. I ain't sure, but I think it was on Wilcox, in Hollywood near Melrose someplace. Cooley could fight, I can tell you that, and he did it so pretty you wished you had the same daddy."

Wardell also suggested the Boxing Commission. Chicky called, and spoke to a polite secretary, but she informed him that the last time she'd tried to call Cooley for her boss the phone had been disconnected.

Chicky said, "Can you tell me where his gym is?"

"Sorry, we don't keep that information on file."

Chicky checked with information, but there was no listing for the School of Hard Knocks, and none for Hard Knock, either. By the time he got back to Bell, he was bushed and returned to the motel instead of to the Indio. He had Pepsi and another *torta* next door, and fell asleep watching grainy TV in his room.

The next day, he was offered a deal at the motel. If he paid for the room a week in advance, $210.00, the rate would be thirty dollars a day instead of $42.50. He was also offered a deal of $500.00 a month if he paid in advance, and that included maid service and clean sheets and towels once a week. Chicky realized that finding Dan Cooley was going to take some doing, and went for the monthly deal. He could always move after thirty days. He'd done the numbers and felt that he was saving money, but paying out five hundred in one chunk hurt. He hoped that he'd find

Mr. Cooley, who could surely help him settle into a cheapo $200 bachelor apartment somewhere close to his gym. Without realizing it, Chicky was still operating at San Antonio prices, but he would soon realize that in L.A., his fortune of $2,600 wasn't going to last long.

Chicky'd picked up the names of several other gyms along the way. Someone confirmed that Cooley's gym had been in the vicinity of Melrose and Wilcox, but that Cooley had somehow dropped out.

Chicky asked, dreading the answer, "He couldn't be dead, could he?"

"Could be, I suppose."

Chicky checked his map, marked the L.A. grid with his blue highlighter, and lit out. He circled the area for an hour, passing the Hollywood division of the L.A. Police Department twice, but he saw no sign of a gym. He was ready to head back for Bell when he noticed an old building set back from the street, its front dirty and neglected. Dry eucalyptus leaves and bent weeds had claimed the yard. The door and windows were boarded up with slabs of weathered plywood. Chicky pulled over and got out, leaving his truck to idle. A man dressed in a dirty T-shirt and plaid brown-and-green bell bottoms was watering his lawn next door. He had a drinker's nose; the veins looked like they were ready to burst. Apprehensively, Chicky asked if the adjacent building was the Hard Knock Gym.

"I don't know if it had a name. Used to see people comin and goin that looked like fighter types, but not in a while, now."

The boozer set the hose down, motioned Chicky over to a patch of weeds, and pointed down. Lying there, half covered with hard dirt, was Dan's small hand-painted sign: "GyM."

"¡Ay!" Chicky said. "You know what the owner looked like?"

"Is he a black man?"

"White, far as I know."

The neighbor said, "I only saw a black man, that I recall."

"That rips it."

Even though he was tempted to give up, Chicky decided that he might have one more shot, and returned to the Hollywood division PD.

He spoke with a female desk officer, "Payson" on her name tag, and asked her if she knew of a Dan Cooley.

Officer Payson said, "Seems like there was a Cooley involved in a traffic death a while back, but that's all I remember."

Chicky said, "I was afraid of somethin like that. Thanks."

He drove back to Bell, his options exhausted, his mind blank. That night, he dreamed that he couldn't sleep, and that was worse than not sleeping at all. He was exhausted the next day, and slipping into despair. He'd spent five hundred on the motel for nothing, in addition to the money for the trip. He'd been ready to go to New York or Philadelphia alone, but now he was alone in Al-*lay*. A new kid in town. He thought of the El Indio.

Chicky wore his straw Resistol hat. He entered the El Indio gym at ten-thirty, knowing that most of its fighters would have already arrived. No whites, no blacks, all Latinos. Some were warming up, others were still changing into their gym togs. Chicky could tell that most were four-round fighters, but he could also see that others had the moves and weariness of bust-out, ten-round pros. Trainers worked the punch mitts, or stood coaching boys on the body bags. It was too early for the *bippity-bippity* of the speed bags, or the *yop-yop-yop* of the leather jump ropes. Two fighters stood in opposite corners of one of the rings. They wore protective cups, mouthpieces, headgear, and gloves. Their corner men greased them with Vaseline. It wasn't Bexar County, but Chicky felt at home.

A kindly looking man, one who reminded Chicky of a smoother version of his grandfather, was on the phone at a desk against a wall. Owner of the gym, the man at the desk also trained and managed fighters. He had a bit of a gut, but otherwise looked in good shape for his age. Gray hair, dark, dark skin, frameless glasses. Tony Velasco smiled and pinched a thumb and forefinger together, indicating to Chicky that he'd be with him in a moment. The ring timer was on. When the thirty-second whistle sounded, Velasco hung up the phone. He hurried over to Chicky and smiled again. Given Chicky's straw hat and boots, Velasco couldn't be sure where he was from, but newcomers from the other side of the border often wore the same outfit. Velasco figured Chicky for Mexican of one kind or another, despite his light complexion. Some of Velasco's fighters wore the *vato* baggy shit from the barrio. Others, having assimilated more than the younger guys, wore standard white-bread clothes. When Chicky got to the desk, Velasco held out his hand.

Velasco said, "You speak English?"

"Yessir."

"Hey, I'm Tony Velasco, can I help you?"

"Hi'ya," said Chicky, shaking hands. "I hope you can. I'm lookin for a trainer, white feller name of Dan Cooley?"

Velasco heard the accent and figured Chicky for a hayseed, but he also noticed the flattened nose and scar tissue. "You a fighter?"

Chicky said, "Yessir. You know Mr. Cooley?"

"Why you want Cooley?"

"I want to turn pro. You know of him?"

Velasco knew Dan Cooley. Cooley had kicked Tony's ass at the Olympic in the old days. In a rematch, Cooley kicked his ass again, only worse. Cooley's fighters always whipped Velasco's fighters as well. But that was expected by insiders, given Velasco's reputation for supplying "opponents"—inexperienced, unprepared, or worn-out fighters who could be offered to promoters looking to build a favored fighter's record. "Opponents" could also be fighters who could aspire only to being "opponents." Just being in the game was enough. Maybe they'd catch a break, who could tell? And the "opponent" sometimes got paid more than the favorite. Such fights weren't "fixed" fights, in the sense that the outcome was predetermined; but they were "rigged," meaning that the playing field had been seriously tipped. When insiders saw Velasco in some boy's corner, the smart money usually went down on the opposite corner.

Tony Velasco looked into the exposed rafters of the old building. "Cooley? You say Cooley?"

Velasco seemed legit to Chicky, and he grew hopeful despite himself. "Yessir, that's Dan Cooley?"

Velasco loved to lie, cheat, and steal. "Older guy, right? Like my age?"

"I guess."

"Well, I hate to be the one to say it," Velasco told him, "but I think I heard he was dead."

"Shucks," said Chicky.

"Yeah," said Velasco, "seems like it was a while ago. Maybe it was he retired and moved, but I think I heard he bought it."

Chicky said, "It's about what I'd come to."

Velasco said, "What's your name? Where you from? What's your amateur record?"

"Chicky Garza. San Antonio. Fifty-six and seven, with twenty-nine KOs."

Velasco knew that having a good amateur record didn't guarantee success in the pros, but he was looking for bodies, not success. Velasco appeared to be considering something, but he already had a plan, the same plan he'd always made his living by, and he was sure he could make some quick money off this hick.

Velasco said, "That's some record. I got connections, you know. Maybe you should come train here, see how you like it, you know? I could turn you pro."

Chicky hadn't had a better offer, but at this point he was thinking more about whip-out money. "How much'll you charge me?"

"If me or one of my guys trains you, there's no charge. But you got to be good, and always ready to fight, no excuses like the bullshit punks come in here lookin for a sugar daddy. Otherwise, it's thirty a month, your towels," said Velasco. "I could find you a cheap place in one of my apartments close by, bed and stove and that, for maybe six hundred and fifty."

"I already got a place at the Bell Motel for a month, and cheaper, too."

"That's even better, *mano*," said Velasco, slipping into an Us-Versus-Them tone of voice. "I take a lot of boys up to Vegas, eh? Or I take 'em down to Mexico, you know, along the border, so they can make quick money and no taxes and fight in their hometowns or at least in front of *raza, ése*. My cut is the standard one third for manager, and one of my guys gets the standard ten percent off the top for trainer." Velasco didn't mention that the "trainer" was washed up, slept in a back room for his pay, and bombed himself out every night on a bottle of Wild Irish Rose.

Chicky said, "You know any places where I might get a job, too?"

"Might. Could take me a little time," said Velasco. "Ehy, I like a guy ain't too proud to work. Is it a deal?"

Chicky hesitated. "Don't we need a contract, or somethin?"

"Naw, I trust you. A handshake's good enough for me."

Velasco held out his hand. Chicky shook it.

Chapter 27

At the El Indio Gym, other fighters assessed Chicky, checked his skills without challenging him. He did likewise. Trainers, egged on by Velasco, tried to convince Chicky to spar. Chicky knew he needed time running at the high school track first. When Chicky worked the mitts and bags and rope, boxing guys saw that he knew something about the game, and they silently respected him when he said he was working on his wind.

Velasco didn't care if the kid had wind or not, only that he would look respectable for two rounds before losing, and Velasco figured the only way Chicky could do that was to spar. If the kid lost, he lost. If he won, all the better, because he'd stay at it a little longer. If he didn't like Velasco's deal, fuck him.

Velasco said, "When'll you be ready to get in there?"

"Gimme a couple of weeks."

"I thought you wanted to make some money."

"Yeah, well, turnin pro and all, I want to be ready, right?" But, for all his confidence, Chicky felt a need to run this by his *abuelo*.

For the first time since he had arrived in L.A., Chicky telephoned his grandfather. He explained his situation, and how he'd come to train with

Velasco. He soft-peddled the part about Dan Cooley being dead. "It's what some people think."

The old man sighed, "I'd hoped for better. Well, maybe it'll be my turn next."

Chicky said, "Don't say that. I got to know you're in my corner."

"I ain't quittin on you, if that's what you're thinkin. You need some money?"

"No, sir."

"Don't lie."

"I ain't."

"Well now," his *abuelo* said, "call regular."

"I will."

Chicky called weekly at first, but when things began to hit the shitter with Velasco, he called only once a month so he wouldn't have to make up stories.

The first day Chicky sparred, he took an ass whipping, not because of his wind, but because his hands and eyes were out of sync. The second day was the same, Chicky missing and the other guy landing. The third day was better, and the wise eyes at ringside could see the improvement. By the end of the week, Chicky was handling four-round pros, guys his weight with six and eight fights, but Chicky could sense they lacked his amateur experience. Velasco put him in with a ten-round fighter from another gym who'd come in for work. He tried to intimidate Chicky. He stung Chicky, but Chicky was able to sting him back, because he was in shape and strong. Chicky knew he wasn't learning anything, and that troubled him. Not from Velasco, and not from Velasco's wino trainer. Chicky would realize in hindsight that nobody learned much at El Indio, which was why so few of Velasco's four-round fighters had careers that lasted much more than six to eight fights.

Velasco said, "Lookeen goood. You ready to turn pro?"

Chicky said, "So soon?"

"Vegas in two weeks, homey."

Chicky said, "What about that job we talked about?"

"I'm workin on it, but fight money is quicker and sweeter."

With his funds running low, Chicky knew he had to shit or get off the pot. "Book it."

Vegas was scary and cheap. Chicky's dislike for it began at the tits-and-ass airport. The wall-to-wall casino come-ons and the long stretches of dinging slot machines assaulted the senses and the soul after the flight across pure desert. But Chicky needed money and he wanted to make it as a professional fighter, so he saw Vegas as just one of many packages he'd have to tie a ribbon on.

For this fight, he was to receive $100 a round, standard for four-round fights, but $400 was nothing like the tens or hundreds of thousands he would have made if he'd won a medal in the Olympics before turning pro. He was down to $1,100 and change, and the $400 paycheck would give him a cushion until his next fight. But $400 a fight wasn't going to be enough to keep him going. He needed a job soon if he was to keep from spending the money his granddaddy had given him for the Stetson.

Chicky couldn't imagine Velasco getting him more than one fight a month, though he knew that it was not uncommon for fighters from their twenties through their fifties to fight once a week, sometimes more—they kept in shape fighting. His grandfather blamed the IRS for the brain damage that too often afflicted modern-day fighters. In days past, many boxers had 150 fights and more. They fought often, but were able to take their money home, less the 10 and the 33⅓ percents that went to trainers and managers. "The Gray," gangster Frankie Carbo, ran boxing for a time, but the great thing about mobsters is that they die, kill each other off, or go to jail. The suits who make up Government Commissions go on forever. They always need more and more money to fund seminars in exotic places. Pals replace pals, each doing less and less while demanding more and more. Dishonesty becomes institutionalized, the best hustle of all, since government crooks seldom lose their jobs, regardless of shortages or excessive expenditures. Eloy would take gangsters over government crooks anytime.

Chicky said, "But don't Commissions and sanctioning bodies help fighters?"

" 'Bout the way a hook'll he'p a catfish," his grandfather replied.

He went on to explain the connection, that when the IRS began to take such huge chunks of boxers' purses, the champions and other big-money fighters had to start taking fights based on how much they could *keep* in a given tax year, instead of how many big-money fights they could *get* in the same year. Consequently, if they had a big fight early on, they would lie around on their asses for six to ten months, get out of shape, and chase trim until they were cross-eyed and bow-legged. All this to beat the tax man.

Problems arose. Training for a fight typically lasts only six to eight weeks, but this is only temporary shape, not long-term conditioning. During the lengthy periods between fights, fighters would balloon up like hogs in a fattening pen, and would have to lose twenty pounds of blubber, maybe more. Their bodies had to suffer the shock of sparring, the grind of roadwork, the punishment of the exercise table—all this while fighting an appetite the size of a forty-foot tapeworm.

Gaining and losing weight makes gaining easier and easier, and losing it harder and harder, particularly in a matter of weeks. Add nose candy and carbohydrates and the lack of exercise and how much fighters are in love with their dicks. The human body breaks down. Neurons in futile search of neurons, blood in the piss from kidney shots, eyes with blood in the whites. The greater the fighter's wits—guys like Benny Leonard and Kid Azteca—the less susceptible the fighter is to being hit. Being hit increases the number of dead spots in the brain that stem from concussions, and dead spots lead to more dead spots, lead to more dead spots, and lead to more dead spots.

"Hit and don't get hit," said Eloy.

"Hit and don't get hit," Chicky said. "But I heard of folks who get Parkinson's and Alzheimer's who never got hit even once."

"Doctors, pilots, all kinds. It's the same with detached retinas. Some folks get 'em walking down the street. It's the cards what you get dealt."

Chicky couldn't resist. "What about that big ol' belly you got there?"

His *abuelo* smiled and lied, "Boy, that's somethin you got to earn."

Chicky was aware that today's fighters didn't have the opportunity to fight as often as the pre-TV fighters, though he also knew that in the last few years more club fights were being held. Even so, he wanted that job Velasco said he could get for him. Chicky wasn't shy about applying for a job, and if Velasco didn't come through, he'd try for busboy jobs, or even stand on street corners with illegals and wait to be picked up as casual labor. But it had to be part-time, otherwise he wouldn't be able to train or run properly. Chicky figured that anyone Velasco knew would understand that, so he had been willing to wait for part-time employment. He didn't care what kind of job it was, so long as it was honest work and it paid enough to get him from fight to fight. If he could rack up a string of knockouts in a hurry, and word about him got out to promoters, he could make enough money fighting to quit work and focus only on becoming Champion of the World.

He hoped for ten, maybe twelve strong wins as a four-round fighter, and then move up to six- and eight-round matches before becoming a ten-round fighter. If Velasco had the juice he said he had, Chicky felt he'd be on his way in a year and a half. He knew that most fighters didn't move up that quickly, but he also knew that most fighters didn't hit as hard as he. Being a southpaw was an advantage he was grateful for.

His grandfather would have told him not to count his chickens before they hatched. Only the best managers in the world could move him the way he hoped to be moved, and that meant he would need a promoter backing him as well, one who would invest time and money in him, with the expectation of big gates. Promoters were antsy about fighters, since pugs were known to turn to smoke, figuratively and literally. Promoters weren't standing in line to back unknowns. And what about the kind of training Chicky would need, now that Dan Cooley was dead? And what if Chicky lost? Could he handle that? Or was hurt? Or if the people in his corner were crooks, or simply incompetent?

But Eloy wasn't there to talk horse sense to Chicky. The kid was all alone. The last thing Velasco cared about was teaching his fighters to win. How was an eighteen-year-old kid to keep himself from dreaming his dream?

Chapter 28

It had been a month since Chicky had called home. When he called from his room in the motel, his grandfather sounded drunk, and the conversation was one-sided. Once Chicky got a good payday, he would send his *abuelo* money for an airline ticket to L.A., or maybe he would make a quick trip back to Poteet. He knew his granddaddy was hurting, and he missed the old man, but Chicky also knew that his first goal was to get himself going as a pro. It's what his granddaddy would want, too.

But why did Velasco keep telling him to punch hard, and not to worry about catching and slipping and blocking punches? Fuck, he could already hit hard. Good fighters could do that and more, were taught the head game of boxing, and Chicky wanted slick as well as power. A puncher could take you out with one shot, but the real boxer would usually win. Chicky hoped to become a boxer-puncher. Maybe Velasco would bring in a better trainer once he saw Chicky fight and win big, maybe get a KO his first time out, maybe get it in the first round. This fight in Vegas might be the make-or-break.

Aside from Chicky's $400, he also got a nonrefundable round-trip plane ticket, room in a squat motel for three days, and meal tickets for the motel buffet. The morning before the fight, he got his medical exams and blood test. At the noon weigh-in, he came in at 145¾ pounds. His black opponent weighed 147, even, and would fill up on carbs and fluids and weigh 158 by fight time. Chicky would only hit 148¼. Along with the local boy's experience and KO record, the 9¾-pound weight difference gave him a clear enough advantage that only the Mexican busboys bet on Chicky.

The Vegas promoter and Velasco were in cahoots. The promoter backed the local boy, who was eleven and zero, with eight KOs. Seven of the eleven wins were rigged fights, though the black kid didn't know it. He didn't know that his manager would one day sell his contract, either, or that he had to keep winning big—otherwise, *he* would become the "opponent."

Commission guys are good for the most part, and they will seldom sanction fights in which one fighter has considerably more experience than the other, if for no other reason than to cover their asses should the boy with less experience get killed in the ring. But records can be doctored by crooked managers and hungry fighters, who inflate or deflate their records depending on the circumstances. Promoters will go along with it, even instigate it, especially if they have trouble putting a card together.

Velasco and the promoter told the Vegas Commission that Chicky was eight and one, with six KOs, and that all his fights had been in Alabama, Georgia, and Ensenada, Baja California. Back at the gym in Bell, Velasco had told Chicky that his opponent was only three and two, and had no knockouts.

Chicky said, "Yeah, but that's five fights to my none."

Velasco said, "Don't worry about it. He don't have your amateur experience."

The fight was held at the Black Canary, a third-rate casino on the west side of Vegas, blacktown. Chicky wore his maroon-and-white shorts from the Regionals. The crowd was predominately black, some white, and a scattering of Latinos who bought lottery tickets and played the nickel slots. Velasco, acting as chief second, worked the corner with a local cut man.

At the introduction, the ring announcer called the fighters' names, weights, and gave their ring records. When Chicky heard his opponent's record of eleven and zero, with eight KOs, he did a one-eighty to face Velasco.

"What's with this dude's record? And they got me with fights I don't have."

Velasco was silky, spoke in a confiding whisper. "The fuckin promoter changed the card on us at the last minute, *m'hijo,* and I had to make you look good to the Commission, that's all."

Chicky said, "I don't lie."

"This ain't lyin, this is business."

"Hail, this's like cuttin me off at the knees."

Velasco had plenty of practice in handling this particular situation. "I only went along with it so you could turn pro. That's what you said you wanted, right? What about all your amateur fights, and you're a southpaw? You can take this nigga easy." Velasco was again guilty of the sin of omission, failing to mention the other guy's amateur record of sixty-four wins out of seventy-two amateur fights, thirty-one of those wins by knockout.

Chicky said, "This don't smell right."

"A skunk's ass don't smell right to a wolf, but it smells right to a skunk," Velasco said. "Look, quit if you have to, but you can forget about getting any more fights, okay? When the promoters hear about you goin dog, that's gonna be it."

"*Me* goin dawg? *Me?*"

The referee waved the two fighters to the center of the ring for the last instructions and to touch gloves. Chicky's opponent rocked from foot to foot, his blood-red gloves and pearlescent shorts and his greased body glinting under the lights. He could hit, the Vegas boy, but so could Chicky.

The bell rang and Chicky went out and did his best. His fight was first on the card. The arena was half empty. Loud fans were straggling in, paying more attention to the ring girls than the fight.

Chicky lost. Not by much, but he lost. He gave as good as he got in the first two rounds, but his bigger and more experienced opponent used his size and savvy to finally wear him down. His years of dreaming of a big win in his first pro fight and of having an undefeated pro career were smashed in four three-minute rounds. Fifteen minutes overall.

He shared his dressing room with three other prelim boys. They already knew about his defeat, and looked away when he came through the door, his bruised face as long as a leg. None of the other fighters spoke to him. They feared the taint of a loser's stink, and pulled even tighter into themselves than before.

Chicky got his paycheck while he was pulling on his first boot. He stood up and signed for it before noticing the amount. Instead of $400, the total was $20. The deductions, listed on the check stub, were explained in a monotone by the promoter's money flunky.

"Purse was $400. Less $240 for your physical, and blood tests that include HIV and hepatitis type C. Less another $115 for your optical. There is an additional $25 deduction for your Nevada boxing license. So, $400, less the combined $355 medical and the $25 for your license—that's $380 in deductions and leaves you a net of $20."

Chicky stood there, one boot on, one in his hand. "Say again?"

Back at the motel, Velasco reminded Chicky that he still owed the trainer 10 percent of the purse "off the top."

Velasco added, "That's $40 for him. And don't forget that I get a third of the other $360, and that'll be $119.88, but you can forget the 88 cents."

"How can I still owe you when ever'thin's been taken?"

"Because I'm your manager," said Velasco, "and because I'm the one what got you the fight, remember? At least you don't have to pay income tax right now, but the promoter will send your 1099 in the mail."

"I still got to pay income tax, too?"

"On the whole $400. And your FICA. It's the law. And you owe me another $50 that I paid from my pocket to the cut man, so that's $209 you owe all told. But the fans liked your heart, so the promoter's gonna give you another shot soon. If we fight before the end of the year, you won't have to pay medical again or get a new license."

"So I have to fight a ape with eleven straight wins, and still end up on the short end of the stick? We don't treat hogs like that in Texas."

Velasco spoke honestly for the first time. "Hey, it's the same fees for everybody their first fight."

Chicky said, "Tell me again that you didn't know I'd be fightin a ape."

Velasco said, "No, no, only at the last minute, homes, when they switched on us. You didn't have to fight, I told you that in the ring."

"Yeah, but only at the last minute, and you shouldda told me I'd be up to my ass in debt."

"How'm I supposed to know how much you don't know unless you say somethin?" Velasco said. "Don't get pissed at me, I'm the one in your corner you can depend on, ése. Get pissed at the Commission, not at me, that ain't fair."

"This's donkey's dick."

Velasco said, "Listen, kid, I thought you was gonna take him out. You caught him with some good shots."

Chicky looked at himself in a mirror, touched the lumps and discoloration. "He caught me with more."

Velasco said, "Don't be hard on yourself, chiquito. The all-time great, Henry Armstrong, he held three titles in different weights back when titles were titles. Feather, light, and welter. Henry, he lost his first fight, too."

Chicky didn't know that Velasco had given the same little speech for years.

Aside from the $119 he made off of Chicky, Velasco also made $400 cash under the table. The payment came from the manager of Chicky's opponent, a common practice that was used to get reluctant managers and fighters to take fights they would otherwise not sign for. That the fighter might not see any of the money was the fighter's problem. Velasco would sometimes supply three fighters on the same card. He loved boxing, Señor Velasco did, and he knew that he must be doing something right by it. After all, he was a property owner, wasn't he?

Chicky paid Velasco the $209 dragging from the Vegas fight when they got back to Bell. He had to dig into his dwindling kicker, and Velasco saw how unhappy he was about that. To divert Chicky, Velasco made a call and quickly got him a job in a slaughterhouse working the gut wagon. It was something Velasco could have done all along, but now the timing was right.

The stink and the shrieks were bad for the first few days, but like everyone else, Chicky got numb to them, had to. Twenty hours a week, animal juices leaking in a silent wail. Five dollars an hour under the table. He had to buy a floppy rubber hat, a body apron, and boots to keep the liquids and solids of death off of him. Chicky had always worked hard, and though this was far from the best job he'd ever had, at the end of each week he would be able to pocket a clear $100.

By the time they'd returned to the dressing room immediately after the Black Canary fight, Velasco already knew that Chicky was not the usual farm or slum boy he was used to dealing with, and realized that his time to milk Chicky was short.

Okay, punk, so I only get you for one more pop. Son cosas de la vida.

Velasco telephoned a promoter he'd done business with up north, and agreed to one fight with the local favorite, a Mexican national with sixteen wins, no losses or draws, and nine KOs. Because there was no way for the California Commission to verify the Mexican's record, the promoter only had to cop to the boy's U.S. record, which was five wins, zero losses, and three knockouts. Velasco would make only three hundred *chueco,* crooked. A small-town fight, but you took what you could get. It was business.

Velasco sat down with Chicky in a beer joint. Chicky had water.

"I got somethin good for you," said Velasco. He explained a six-fight deal that was bogus from the git.

Velasco said, "I got this promoter who makes fights up north. Salinas, San Jose, Watsonville, Merced, Fresno, Stockton, places like that. Not big for now, but steady. He heard about how tough you was in Vegas and he called with a offer. You interested?"

"Yeah, I am."

"Here's the deal. You bitched that I didn't tell you about Nevada licenses and medical exams and shit. Okay, I was wrong for not asking, okay? I'm telling you everything now, so don't bitch later on, or because you don't like the deal. You don't like it, forget it, that's what I'm sayin. But medicals and licenses, that's standard, okay?, and they're always up at the end of the year for everybody. It's the Commission, not me, check it out."

"Okay, but what's the six-fight deal?"

Velasco said, "This California guy's Mexican, like you'n me, so we can trust him. My Vegas guy's got nothin until January, and that means another Nevada license and shit next year. But my *raza* guy up north, he can get you goin now, but the only way I can move you is if you're licensed."

"I am licensed."

"Yeah, right," said Velasco, "but you're licensed in Nevada, not in Califa, *ése.* So if you want to wait it out for Nevada, that's okay by me, but that's a long time, and sooner or later that means you pay for another Nevada license. You follow this?"

"I s'pose," Chicky said. "So how much'll a license and all go for here in California?"

" 'Bout the same as before, but you'll get all your money back, and more, on the next five shots, get me? And the medical and license come off your income tax same as the stuff in Vegas, see? That's standard, too, so don't think I'm screwin you, okay?"

"How much does the *raza* pay?"

"Four hundred the first two four-round fights, but then it's five hundred for the next two. Once you're ready to move up to six and eight rounds, it's a hundred a round. That's six and eight hundred big ones. More if you're a KO puncher." Velasco let it hang.

Chicky sipped his water. "When's all this supposed to happen?"

"Couple a weeks. Plenty of time for you to rest, and get sharp."

"Do it."

"You want the six-fight deal?"

"The whole nine yards."

The fight was held in Watsonville, just a few miles up and west from Salinas. The arena was a converted produce warehouse with folding chairs. It was set off from the strawberry fields and two miles in from the sea. It drew mostly Mexicans, the field-hand fans coming in from as far south as Soledad, home of California's Soledad State Prison, and also from the sea town of Monterey.

On the way to the fight, Chicky saw the strawberry fields, and homesickness loped through him. He swallowed hard, then told Velasco to stop the car.

"How come?"

" 'Cause."

Chicky picked strawberries from four different rows, careful not to damage the plants. He inspected and tasted each berry, allowing the red flavor to linger in his mouth. He got back in the car feeling better.

"Not too bad," he said, "but we grow 'em bigger in Texas."

Chicky lost his second fight for the same reasons he lost his first, but this time he was wobbled in three of the four rounds. He left the ring bleeding from the mouth. The fans booed him. After all, this *pinche tejano* was not one of their own, not from Mexico, not a true Mexican from the other side.

In the dressing room, Chicky stared at Velasco. "You sure this monkey only had five fights?"

"You heard the ring announcer."

Chicky's license with the California State Athletic Commission was $65, $40 more than Nevada, but the medical fees, including blood, eye, and the complex neuro were less, at $175, for a total cost to Chicky of $240. His trainer got $40, the local cut man got $50, and Velasco still got his $119. The total cost to Chicky was $489 out of a purse of $400. Velasco made $419, no taxes.

Chicky began to live more and more on *pan dulce* and *café con leche*. He also began to lose weight. Ounces at first, but then three pounds, a significant amount for a walk-around welterweight. Other welters usually walked around closer to 160, if not more.

A week after he'd returned from Watsonville, Chicky's rent was due, and he had to dig deeply into his kicker again. At least he had a clean, dry place to live. With his six-fight deal, he figured that things would work out. He did the numbers on his next five fights. Twenty-eight hundred, less his corner men and manager, would still buy him time, especially if he kept working the gut wagon. Once he fought again, he could start eating good, maybe even move to a nice place. Despite his losses, he knew he was a better fighter now, but two losses in his first two fights was something he could never have imagined. He began to wonder if he was as good as he thought he was. He'd have to fight harder, that's all. Maybe he'd get an easier fight the next time out, especially now that he had a promoter backing him with a six-fight deal.

But Velasco had a surprise for him two days after Chicky paid his rent. "Look, *carnal*, I'm sorry, but the Watsonville promoter, he called me. He has to go back to Mexico because his wife died, so he won't be using you after all. I think it's best anyway, homes. You lost bad this last time, so I'm not goin to manage you no more. You're a nice kid, but I don't want you gettin hurt, see? You can still work out here at the gym, but I got to charge you dues, you know how it is."

Two days after that, Chicky was laid off at the slaughterhouse, was told that there was a slowdown. He sold his rubber boots and other gear on his way out to a new kid from the gym, coming in.

Chicky felt like climbing into Fresita and heading home, but knew he should have beaten the second guy, and maybe even the first. If he'd only known how to move. He had the right questions, but wasn't getting the right answers. Getting hit was sure as hell not the way to the money he'd need to bring the farm back into shape for his grandpa, not the way for his own future wife and kids to live decently once he retired. Maybe it was time to pack everything in, including college. The idea of going back to school made no sense to him now, the four-year wall of college suddenly too high for his mind to climb. Maybe he was just a dumb-ass, small-time beaner after all, and he'd better quick get himself back to hoeing rows like he was supposed to.

He'd lie to spare his granddaddy the shame. He'd say that, since Dan Cooley was dead, he had given up boxing to chase girls, that he'd worked in a hardware store in East Al-*lay*. Since his face hadn't gotten cut up, Chicky figured the old man would buy it, or would say he did, even if he didn't. If only Dan Cooley had been alive.

Ay-yai-yai.

Chapter 29

Part of Chicky flat wanted to head home pissing sideways, his tail between his legs; but another part, the stupid part, still hoped to fight one more fight—to maybe win at least one, before having to face his granddaddy and the folks in Poteet. If he lost, he could always lie. But if he did lose, the grave for his dreams would surely be dug, and time nigh to shovel in the dirt.

But he had another three weeks left on his rent that he couldn't just dump, so he went looking for a job. His eats money running low, he began to worry about affording that Stetson his granddaddy told him to buy. He'd starve before he'd go through his hat money. At least he'd have something shiny to take home.

Because he was an eager, clean-cut kid who spoke good English, he found a busboy job his second day out. He'd be working the night shift in the coffee shop at the Bicycle Club casino in nearby Bell Gardens. He was paid minimum wage, but got good tips nightly from the waitresses because he cleared and set tables and bussed dirty dishes as if he was getting twenty dollars an hour. He ate one hot meal during his shift, and while the manager purposely looked the other way, the thick-ankled old gals he worked for tipped the cooks into slipping him another hot meal to go when he punched out at eight A.M. In a few days, he gained his weight back, but he still felt weak. He wasn't sleeping properly because of his shame. He needed to get back to the gym, but where should he go? Certainly not the Indio. And at what time of day, now that he was working nights? Being dumped as a loser by Velasco still hurt. He couldn't stop thinking about Vegas, or Watsonville, nor could he stop thinking about his lost passbook in San Anto. He needed sleep like a sumbitch.

He worked three weeks at the casino. He saved everything he made, except for gas money and a few dollars for *pan dulce* and *café con leche*, the hot and the sweet waking him up after fitful sleep. He paid another month's rent, had money left over, and realized that if he kept saving, he could add to Eloy's money and buy the kind of Stetson that would make his grandpa proud. The job also paid enough that he could pull up stakes anytime he wanted and haul ass for home, not that he'd have that much left over after gas and such on the road. But that wasn't what he wanted. What he wanted was what he'd always wanted, to be Champion of the World, the best champion there'd ever been.

He also wanted some pussy, damn. A thirty-something chip girl from the casino, known to all and sundry as Blond Darleen, took care of that. She fed him Sara Lee pies, and gave him bubble baths, and rubbed Kama Sutra oil into him. She bought him a wide, tooled belt with a heavy silver belt buckle that depicted a longhorn steer. She peroxided his dark hair to a yellow blond. She taught him to eat pussy, and gave him blue-ribbon head. She had him do her with a vibrator. She put strawberries in her pussy. She made him forget boxing.

"You're so beautiful," she'd whisper on her water bed, dragging her decorated nails across his twitching back. "Look at you, you're so beautiful, oh, ah, God, I'm coming on your cock!"

Pussy, and sleeping again, and eating, and not going to the gym . . . Chicky went up to 151 pounds, 4 pounds over his fighting weight, the most he'd ever weighed. The weight went into his neck, and shoulders, and back and didn't show, but Chicky didn't like the idea of being overweight.

He paid another month's rent. In the Sunday newspaper, he saw an ad for a yearly sale at the Hat & Boot Bonanza in Hawthorne, which was almost on a straight line west, across South Central, from Bell. He took care of business with Blond Darleen the next day in Downey, put his Resistol straw back on, and then took the 710 and the 105 and got off at the Hawthorne Boulevard exit near Imperial Highway. He added some of his casino money to what he still had from his granddaddy's money, and shelled out $487.17 for his El Patron 30X beaver, light tan in color, known as a "Silver Belly," the light off it like the first silver streaks of a Texas dawn. He'd hoped to buy such a Stetson with his granddaddy at Paris Hatters in San Anto, but the Hat & Boot Bonanza would have to do.

He wore the 30X beaver out of the Bonanza. At least he'd done one big thing in California. He just wished his granddaddy had been there to see it and touch it and try it on. Even so, Chicky dwelled on what ate at him most—was he a loser?

"Please God, no."

Chicky liked the hot tricks Blond Darleen was teaching him, but he missed the action of the gym, missed the kind of work that daily made him a better man. He'd gained another two pounds. That scared him, so he began dipping more so he'd start spitting more, and lose water weight. He didn't.

On the way back to Bell, he remembered that the Broadway Gym was not far off his route. Mr. Purdy at the Broadway had been courteous and helpful when he'd been there asking for Dan Cooley. Courtesy was not all that common in Califa.

Chicky drove in a leisurely fashion through moderate, black middle-class traffic for several miles. Once he crossed Western Avenue, things began to change, took on a desolate cast. Used tire stores. Failed cafés. Stacked barbecue ovens, all rusted, made from welded oil drums.

Chicky signed up for $20 a month at Broadway that same day. He began training the next. He'd sleep after work, sleep again after training, and then run a mile or so before going back to work the same night.

Wardell Purdy had remembered him. "You never found Dan Cooley?"

Chicky said, "Looks like he passed."

"I'da gone to Dan's funeral if I'da known, and I don't usually go to funerals."

Chicky worked out a week at Broadway and lost two pounds. Darleen pursed her lips when he turned down her frozen pumpkin pie, and was clearly pissed when he began to sleep some at his place instead of mostly at hers.

Wardell had liked Chicky's polite ways the first day he'd come in. He admired Chicky's raw talent, too, and appreciated how hard the boy worked. Watching Chicky in the full power of his youth made Wardell remember all the times he'd brought kids like Chicky along. Black and brown and white. But the whites weren't hungry anymore. Not so many blacks were, either. The truth was that the fights had gone mostly Latino, of one kind or another. Now it was the Latinos who outnumbered the rest of the ticket buyers at the gate. Promoters saw where the money was, and the result was more Latinos in the ring.

The Russians and the Armenians were tough fuckers these days, so were the Japanese. The same in South Africa, Australia, and in the British Isles, particularly now that the Brits had a heavyweight champion. Boxing was big again in Germany, as well. So there was indeed white blood, aside from the marines and such, who would still fight. And some of those boys were big, too. Wardell had always wanted a white heavyweight, didn't care if the muhfuh came from outer space. White + heavyweight = $.

"Wardell, you wanna train me? I'd pay," Chicky said after a couple of days.

"Naw, son," said Wardell. "Too old. Catchin all those punches cripples up my back and bad leg so bad I walk around like I got a stake up my ass."

Chicky said, "Any of these other trainers any good? I could use some slick."

"Some'r good. But they'll want to know how long you'll be around, so their time ain't wasted."

"I'd be lyin if I said I knew," said Chicky.

"You decide to hang around, let me know."

"How much'll they charge?"

"You're good enough, they won't charge but their righteous ten off the top, not long's you stay good enough."

Hawaiian-Japanese trainer and first-class cut man Mack Takahashi was in L.A. preparing his Japanese junior-welter for an upcoming ten-round HBO fight in Vegas. Mack stood five-foot-four and weighed 141, up 30 from his 111-pound fighting weight back when. He had a full head of dyed black hair he wore in a ducktail, and sported stringy gray chin whiskers. He had bad eyes and wore thick specs with oversize black frames. Mack always showed respect, but should someone try to stiff him, he'd cuss their mamas as if he stood six-foot-five, and dare their ass to move on him.

"I got somethin for you, bastahd fuckkah!"

Mack got up at three-forty-five A.M. every morning but Sundays to run his fighters. He had followed this schedule as a fighter, and had never dumped it, no matter how much hot sake and cold beer he'd had the night before.

Mack had started out with two sparring partners at Broadway, but one boy couldn't take the pounding, and he quit. Needing another, Mack watched Chicky work. From Wardell, he learned that Chicky had just turned pro. Mack didn't think he could get much out of Chicky except a moving warm body, and wasn't sure if Chicky would even take the deal, but he offered him ten dollars a round to spar two rounds a day for ten days.

Chicky took it, more to learn than for the money. Wardell coached him from the floor because he couldn't climb the ring steps. Chicky got popped good the first day by Mack's Japanese fighter. He was out of gas after the first round and a half, but the second day he was better. Being a southpaw helped. By the third day, his wind carried him the two rounds, and from then on he stayed with the Japanese boy bell to bell.

Mack liked that. "Hey, brudduh, you pretty good."

He offered Chicky four rounds a day, $40.00, no taxes. Chicky took it, got into shape inside the ropes, bruises and lumps meaningless to him at this point.

Mack upped it again two days later, fifteen dollars a round. "You a tough fukkah. We go Japan, blondie, you make mothafukkah big money."

Getting paid for learning was the sweetest money Chicky had ever made. This was the kind of training he'd needed before his first two fights.

Chicky made the daily trip in from Bell after only three hours of sleep, but he wasn't tired until the drive home. Darleen wanted him to spend more time with her.

"I would," Chicky said, "but I'd be all jiggle-kneed and get hit too much."

"You could quit boxing and move in here."

"No, I couldn't."

"Getting hit in the face doesn't make much sense to me."

"Like my granddaddy says, 'It's more fun to play with girls than fight with boys, but you don't get paid playin with girls.' "

"No?" Darleen said, and gave him a sly smile. "Move in here rent free, and you do. Think about it, hon."

A call came to Wardell from a small-time promoter. He'd put together an all-Latino card across town at the Santa Cruz Sports Arena in Pico Rivera, but a prelim boy had pulled out because of a bad hand. The fight was to honor César Chávez, and the promoter found several black fill-in forty-seven-pounders, but not a Chicano, and was calling every gym in town because he couldn't afford to fly someone in. Wardell motioned Chicky into his office. He covered the phone with his hand. He explained the promoter's problem, and laid out the deal in simple terms while the promoter hung on the line.

"Your guy's from East L.A. He's four, three, and one draw, with no KOs—seven fights. His trainer's a dummy. You want it? I said five hundred, since it's a last-minute pop. Promoter's goin for it on my word you can fight."

"Five hundred? Damn," Chicky said. "But I'm zero and two. Will the Commission go for it?"

Wardell said, "I'll call my man Jolly Joe and tell him you been sparing with Mack's Jap."

Chicky said, "You think I can take this *cholo?*"

"Take him like you take a shit."

The fight was made and would go off three days before Chicky's rent was due.

Chicky said, "You'll be workin my corner, right, Wardell?"

"I don't hardly work 'em no more. Rushin up wobbly ring stairs knots up my old hip."

"You hurt it fightin?"

"Korea."

Chicky said, "Can you get me somebody good as you?"

"Yeah, for half a yard. He'll be your chief second, and I'll work the bucket and the stool from the floor."

"What if I get cut?"

"It'll take a while, but I'll come up."

"I'll pay you what you want."

"Just pay my gas."

Chicky hadn't moved in with Blond Darleen, but he'd been tempted, especially with his rent coming up. Sleeping alone had been tough. But getting to sleep while thinking about games with candles and hot wax, or flipping a coin to see who'd be on top and such, that had been tough, too. Seeing her at work had been awkward. She'd smile as always, but lately she didn't stop to chat the way she had before. After he had taken the Sports Arena fight, he made a point of stopping her in the lobby so she couldn't get by.

"You're gonna come to the fight, ain't you? It'll be over before your shift. Afterward, we can be together like before."

"That's so good to hear."

"So you'll come, right?" Chicky asked.

"I didn't exactly say."

"But you didn't say no, so I'll get you a ringside ticket, okay?"

Chicky continued to sleep alone. No pie, no poon. It was lonely in bed, but that was better than being lonely in the middle of the ring. He stayed at 147¼. The day before the weigh-in, he drank no liquids from noon on.

At the weigh-in he came in at 146, even, a pound under.

"Eat," Wardell ordered him.

On the morning of the fight, Chicky had the jits. He felt that he hadn't had enough time to be in top shape, and was preoccupied with losing.

Wardell had warned him to be on time. "We'll most likely fight first. Don't be late."

"No way."

Chicky tried to eat breakfast. Bacon and eggs and hotcakes with butter and syrup. Couldn't get it down. He called Darleen from his room. He called her three more times between one o'clock and two, but no answer. He left messages and hoped she was all right and could make it to the fight. He had something for her afterward, but as much as he'd missed all that trim, he knew he was right to stay away. Once the fight was over, Blond Darleen would have to pull him out of her with a team of Clydesdales.

Now that he'd made weight, there was no rule against half a pie and a quart of milk, and maybe gaining a few pounds before the fight. Besides, a nice rest on the water bed would calm him some if he could get some shut-eye, a nap taking his mind off of losing again—sprawled on the twisted sheets of his own bed, losing was all he could think of.

He called Darleen again. Still no answer. Since her condo was on the way to the arena, and since he had to get her ticket to her, he decided to pack his fight gear and drop by her place. If he missed her, he'd stick the ticket in her door and call later. Surely she'd understand about his staying out of her knickers once she saw the kind of shape he had to be in to be a boxer. Maybe she'd pick up some more Reddi Wip and have him shave her pussy again.

He parked at an angle across from Darleen's condo. Her car wasn't in her carport. He hoped there was nothing wrong. Maybe she'd just gone to the market, or had to pull a double shift. Or something. He was setting his emergency brake when Darleen's door opened. She was wearing a kimono that hung open down the front. Her white hooters glowed in the shadow of the doorway. Standing with Darleen was one of the other busboys from the casino, an illegal from Zacatecas. He tried to pull the kimono closed, but she pulled it open again. They laughed and kissed, and played some grab-ass, and then the busboy rode off on a bicycle. He waved and she waved back, and she closed her door without noticing Chicky.

Chicky tore up the forty-dollar fight ticket and drove the fifteen minutes back to his room. He carried his clothes down to his truck, then went back to his room for the rest of his stuff, which wasn't much. He pulled off his belt and silver buckle and dropped them in the toilet. He left the room for the last time and went to the office to check out.

The old lady at the counter said, "No refunds on early departures. House policy."

"I only wanted to give you my key."

He drove to the casino, and spoke to the restaurant manager. "You folks been good to me, and I don't like hangin you out like this, but I'm goin home tonight after my fight. Sorry, sir."

"You were the best ever," the manager said, "and we'll miss you. It's Darleen, right?"

Chicky nodded and looked away.

"You weren't the first, and won't be the last. So don't take it personal."

"Yessir."

Chicky drove to the arena. He'd fight because he'd signed a contract to fight, and because Wardell had put his name on him, but not because he wanted to. He felt like all his blood had been drained and wondered how he could last one round with a midget, much less duke it out for three minutes times four with some hothead from the barrio.

Fucking Blond Darleen had nutted him. Fucking cunt-whore bitch-pig. This would be one more thing he couldn't tell his *abuelito*.

He arrived at the arena at five-thirty. He'd haul ass home right after the fight. He parked over by one of the pylons so he wouldn't get blocked in. Electricity sizzled through the high-tension wires. A dazzling, triple-black lowrider decorated with streaks and whorls and flames of piercing blues and yellows and greens and fuchsias cruised the lot, the three beefy occupants sullen-eyed and covered with jailhouse tats.

Several lunch wagons had already arrived and the drivers were setting up. Chicky bought a *pan dulce* and hot coffee, the only food he'd had that day. Dunking the sweet bread into the coffee, he realized he no longer cared whether he won or lost. Getting paid was all that mattered now. He was tempted to just take off and forget the money, but the five hundred, less fifty, was a cushion he could use on the road in case of a breakdown. Besides, losing again was just another round of drinks. He'd go through the motions, collect as soon as he could, and then head for home.

The aroma of cooking *carnitas* and chile reminded him of home. He'd pig out on Mexican food back in Poteet, and he'd never leave home again. Fucking Al-*lay y su chingada madre*. He thought about Blond Darleen despite himself. Why should he care so much? He'd always known they were just screwing each other, so why was it so hard to breathe? Why did he want to break something? Why did he feel like hiding in the reeds instead of going for a win that would make him real again? Why did he care so much that another pair of balls was sitting in his saddle? He didn't know whether to kill or die.

"Old Darleen's Winchester kicks as good as it shoots."

DAN AND CHICKY

Chapter 30

The soft dirt floor of the Sports Arena had been tamped down and covered with two-foot by four-foot interlocking plastic mats. Metal folding chairs were set in rows around the ring. Mariachi music was already blaring through maxed-out speakers. Ring officials had arrived. A few fans, all Mexican, were taking seats high in the stands. When Chicky inquired about the stables and horses, he was told about the Sunday *charreadas,* and he wished that he had known about them before. Maybe he would have met a nice little sloe-eyed *pocha* instead of that *gabacha* whore from the casino.

Chicky entered the dressing room. Some of the other fighters were either napping or talking softly. Most had trouble looking anyone in the eye. It had become popular for some Chicanos to peroxide tufts or even all of their hair, and no one thought anything of Chicky's yellow mop. Many thought he was white, until they heard his name.

Wardell said, "How you feelin?"

Chicky said, "Somewheres between low and flat."

"Wass that about?"

"I'm goin home after the fight, Mr. Purdy."

"How come?"

"Pussy."

"Boy, you went and got some pussy on you before the goddamn fight?"

"No way. Darleen's fucked me, all right, but I ain't fucked her."

Wardell said, "Put the bitch out you head, boy, we got us a fight to win."

"I know," said Chicky, "but I keep lookin for my nuts and I can't find 'em."

"They'll grow back, same as when you prune a tree, only bigger."

"This ever happen to you, Wardell?"

Wardell said, "Why you think I walk funny?" Then he saw Earl and Dan headed his way.

"Hey, Dan!" yelled Wardell. He was laying out the gauze and tape for Chicky's hands. "I thought you was dead."

"Bullshit!" he shot back. "Nobody this pretty is allowed to die!"

Wardell slapped hands and laughed. Earl saw the gauze.

Earl said, "I heard you stopped working corners, slick."

"That's right. I'ma just he'pin this boy for tonight," said Wardell. "This here Chicky Garza wit the blond head. He black-headed first time I see 'im."

Chicky nodded and smiled, but then thought of Blond Darleen and his face darkened. Dan and Earl shook Chicky's hand, noticed his height and weight, and the bright shine of good conditioning in his eyes.

Wardell said, "Chicky, this here's Dan Cooley, the one you was lookin for."

Dan said, "Me you were lookin for?"

Hearing Dan's name, Chicky's heart began to thump. Now he was tongue-tied. Too much was happening in one day. He wanted to unload his whole story on Dan, but knew better, and just nodded, his mouth dry, his eyes wide.

Wardell said, "Boy from San Antone. He come lookin for you to train him while back."

Dan shook his head. Barky was all he could handle these days. "I'm outta trainin."

Chicky said, "That's what I kinda heard."

Dan said, "You're from Texas, how come you know about me?"

Chicky knew he couldn't tell him the truth, what with his losses and another loss sure to come. Three strikes and you're out in any ball game. He'd brought enough shame on himself, what with Blond Darleen and all, but there was no way he'd put a black mark on his grandpa.

"How'd I know about you?" Chicky said, stalling. "Somebody at one of the gyms said you were good. I got other names, too."

Wardell said, "He trained some with Tony Velasco."

"Aw, shit," Dan said. He turned to Chicky. "Garza, huh? You ever hear of a old-time lightweight named Eloy Garza? He was from Texas someplace. Stay on your ass like a goddamn wolf with blood in his eye."

Chicky lied, "Can't say I have. See, there's lots a Garzas in South Texas."

Chicky didn't know at first why he was telling the lie but later figured it out. He didn't want his pitiful record associated with his grandfather's achievements in the ring.

"Yeah, well, Wardell here'll steer you straight now you're here."

"Me'n him only a short-notice deal," Wardell told Dan. "He be leavin right after he get paid."

Dan said, "With a name like Garza, what you doin with all that blond hair?"

"I had me a ol' gal what sung me a cunt song."

Once Wardell had wrapped Chicky's hands, Chicky got a look at his opponent, who made several quick trips to the men's room. Chicky was wondering if he should call his granddaddy from somewhere on the road, or just walk in on him. At least he'd have his El Patron to show off. Other than the Stetson, he had bragging rights on nothing.

The arena was filling rapidly, the sounds of humans muffling the roaring music. Chicky felt disconnected. From boxing, from home, from himself. There were no Mexicans he could turn to, and he hadn't heard any Texas talk since he'd left El Paso. He thought of his grandmother. He clung to her memory and he yearned for his grandfather's rough hand on his shoulder.

The referee checked and signed Chicky's wrapped hands, and the promoter came in to wish everyone luck. Chicky was then told he'd fight third instead of first. Now he had to wait in line for his ass whipping. As he sat brooding, he remembered what Dan Cooley had said about the way his granddaddy fought. Chicky flushed Blond Darleen from his mind and vowed to go out there with blood in his eye, like his granddaddy had.

Earl and Dan watched the fights quietly, their eyes trained to see each combination of red punches as distinctly as cherries in a basket. The first two bouts were dull, the opponents short on skill and long on fear. The crowd hooted, but everyone knew these were just warm-up fights, and accepted them as such.

Earl said, "Best all those boys hang 'em up soon, maybe after tonight."

"It's a hard game," said Dan.

Chicky and his opponent, Pepe Reyes, made their way to the ring, Chicky looking bony to Earl at 143. Reyes was well over the 147 limit, having eaten steadily since the weigh-in. When the announcer introduced Chicky as hailing from San Antonio, many in the crowd booed.

Dan said, "Let's see what Tex's got."

Chicky lost the first two rounds, but only by a slight margin. When the East L.A. boy began to tire early in the third, Chicky's work with Mack's boy paid off. Once he was able to force his southpaw stance on Reyes, the balance of the fight changed. With Reyes backing up, Chicky let his power loose, fueling it with his hurt and shame, and his grandfather's honor. The barrio boy was tough, and only backed up when Chicky knocked him back, but Chicky felt himself slip into a dancing, bob-and-weave rhythm, and suddenly the punches were throwing themselves. Chicky won the third round easily, but halfway through, a shot to his nose started bleeding severely. He breathed the way Eloy had taught him. Through his mouth, so he wouldn't swallow blood coming down from the back of his throat or snort air into the aperture of torn nasal tissue and inflate his face.

Wardell wobbled up to the ring apron between the third and fourth rounds. He couldn't waste time climbing through the ropes, so he worked from outside. He stopped the blood flow with adrenaline chloride and pressure, then cleaned and greased and watered his fighter and got it all done in less than the allotted sixty seconds.

Earl said, "Nothin stop Wardell."

Chicky knocked Reyes down near the end of the fourth, but was unable to put him away because the last bell rang, ending the fight. Both boys raised their arms in victory. The crowd cheered what was clearly a two-point round for Chicky. Along with most fans, Dan and Earl saw Chicky winning his third fight.

But two of the three judges gave the fight to Reyes, the third calling it a draw—a majority decision going to the local boy. Most of the crowd hooted, but not the fans from East Al-*Lay*.

"Home-town call," said Earl.

Dan said, "What's new?"

Wardell stopped by with his bucket. "Kid's about to die. Two Velasco setups, now this mess."

Earl said, "We thought he won."

Wardell said, "Damn straight he won! Only now what we got is a good young fighter jobbed into three losses."

"He's better than zero and three," Earl said. "He don't know how to fight, but he's got those fast, heavy hands that came from somewhere."

"Yeah, but he's got a wide-ass stance that shortens his reach and forces him to lean in to land," Dan said. "Leaning in puts him inside the other guy's reach. He wants to be inside, he'd best know how to counter instead of fuckin stand there and trade."

Wardell said, "Why don't you take him on?"

"Nooo," Dan said, "I already lost too much to this game."

Wardell nodded. "Like the rest of us."

Chicky changed clothes and waited in silence as whoops of victory came from Reyes's friends down the hall. Wardell emptied water bottles, dumped ice, and began to put all his gear together.

Chicky spoke to himself, the words falling dead in the air. "When you can't even win when you win, then you ain't never gonna win."

Chicky wanted his check so he could go, but nobody showed up from the Commission. The bell ending the fourth fight rang, but Chicky had heard none of it. The ring announcer shouted out the winner's name, and then called for the intermission. The music blared while beer drinkers headed for the urinals. The commission guy arrived, had Chicky sign, and then gave him a check for the full five hundred. The promoter, a local Chicano, left the noise down the hallway and glanced in on Chicky.

He said, "Too bad, homes, losing after coming on like you did."

Chicky said, "This kinda shit could make a Mexican hate Mexicans."

Dan checked his watch and turned to Earl. "Time to take ol' Bark out to pee."

"How do you say pee in Spanish?" Earl asked.

"I haven't got to that lesson yet."

"That dog's more trouble than a kid."

"Yeah," said Dan, "but he don't listen to loud music or need braces."

Chicky paid off his corner man, then turned to Wardell. "I 'preciate what you done out there."

"Glad to do it. Too bad you're leavin."

"Deck's stacked against me, pods."

Chicky palmed a folded, crisp hundred-dollar bill he'd taken from his kicker, and shook hands with Wardell. The old man felt it and knew right off it was more than gas money.

Wardell said, "No good, son. I be happy if I don't make nothin workin wit you."

Chicky said, "God bless you, Wardell, but I want you to have it. California ain't all bad."

Chapter 31

Dan moved through the crowd toward the main exit. He saw Detective Nájera leaving the men's room. Dan caught the cop's attention.

'Well, it's Mr. Cooley."

"You remember me."

"How could I forget?" Nájera said, with a faint smile.

"Like the action?"

"Club fight, you know," said Nájera. "But my Texas brother got robbed for sure."

"I know what you mean," Dan said. "Listen. Somethin's been botherin me ever since when I, uh, well, you know, I want to apologize for the crap I said to you."

Nájera smiled. "Oh, hell, I'm a cop and we don't always see folks at their best."

"I just wanted you to know."

"I 'preciate it, Mr. Cooley. And I understand."

Chicky had carried his gear out to Fresita. His hat was off and he was studying his map for a place to stay later on that night. He saw the town of Indio, located east of Palm Springs, but it brought the Indio Gym and Velasco to mind, and he decided to just drive as far as he could. Tired as he was, maybe he'd just konk out along the road like before and save money. He'd need it. If he had enough left when he got home, he'd haul his grandpa to the Paris Hatters and buy him an El Patron, too. The old man was due for something splendid, and the idea of buying a Stetson for his granddaddy made Chicky feel good for the first time in a spell.

Barky went on alert as soon as he heard a noise outside the truck, then bounced around when he saw it was Dan. Dan unlocked the door on the driver's side and the dog dashed out, selective in his sprinkles only after he let his main load go.

Dan said, "I got some dog treats for you, and then I'm goin back inside with Earl, hear? You stay in the truck and sleep, and then I'll take you out again."

As they returned down the lane leading to Dan's truck, they saw three dark figures hovering near the driver's side of the vehicle. Off to one side was the triple-black lowrider that Chicky had seen earlier, its trunk open. Dan didn't connect the car with the dark figures until he heard glass shatter and sudden bursts of Spanglish slang.

"*¡Wátchale estúpido!*" Careful, stupid!

Barky wheezed once, then tore into all three *pandilleros*, his teeth ripping into ass and balls. Desperate hands tried to drive him off. One of the gangbangers took off through the stagnant pools and muddy bottom and into the reeds of the shallow river, Barky right after him.

"Stop him! *¡Socorro!* Help! Please! *¡Por Dios!* In God's name!"

Dan tried to stay away from the other two as they checked themselves for blood and punctured flesh beneath the rips in their leather jackets. When they saw him, they began to bellow in Spanish, and they knocked him down and began to stomp him. Dan got in a nut shot that slowed one of them, but they kicked him back down. The second pulled a knife, and Dan scuttled away, his ribs aching and one thigh cramping in a charley horse that made his eyes water.

Chicky heard the ruckus, then saw Dan on the ground, the two 'bangers on him. Chicky moved into both from the side, firing lefts and rights into their faces and bellies, and then he cranked a one-two combination that knocked one of them over the hood of an adjacent car. He stopped the second guy with a shot to the liver that made him drop his knife and grab his guts. Chicky slid across a fender to the first, who wobbled to his feet. Chicky dropped him again, this time with a right hook that left him twitching in the dirt, his eyes blinking in spasms.

Dan was up and drilling the second attacker when Barky came racing back. As the punk started to raise a fist to club Dan, Barky got it between his teeth and crushed the thumb and fingers. As the *pandillero* began to howl, Chicky kicked his knee sideways, and he went down on his side, his hand still locked in Barky's jaws.

"He's eating my hand get him off me *hijo de su chingada madre el pinche perro me está comiendo* fuckin dog's eatin me alive!"

As the first 'banger pulled himself to his knees, Dan kicked him in the stomach so hard that shit filled his Jockeys. Barky gave up his hold on the second one's hand, and went for his face. Dan was afraid Barky would kill him and pulled him off, blood splashing and flesh hanging loose from the torn cheek and neck.

The two *pandilleros* saw a chance to escape and took off in a stumbling run, both falling along the way. Barky stayed on them through the mud and reeds and up the embankment and into the darkness. Dan called him back.

One of the running 'bangers shouted back through the darkness, "Ain't fair havin a silent dog, man!"

Barky returned, pumped on adrenaline, slobber all over, his eyes bulging. He snorted and jumped around for approval, and then sniffed Chicky. He looked to Dan for instructions.

"This is Chicky Garza, he's okay," Dan said. He patted and rubbed the pooch and fondled his ears. "Good boy, good dog. You're so pretty."

Chicky wasn't sure he'd heard right. Dan turned to him.

"Hey! Thank you, thank *you!*"

Chicky rubbed his hands, "I don't much identify with truck thieves."

Dan saw the knife on the ground and picked it up. "Who were those guys?"

Chicky pointed to the lowrider. "Earlier on, I saw 'em in that."

Dan crossed over and knifed the tires, then got Barky into the pickup. He put the truck into low, and rammed one side of the lowrider with his reinforced-steel push bumpers. He backed around and got the other side, then bashed in the customized grill and the rear end, the open trunk tilting off to one side.

Dan said, "We better clear out of here."

Dan drove to a nearby truckers' café where they served homemade pie. Chicky, wearing his El Patron, followed in Fresita. They ordered pie and coffee and then they began to laugh. They finished their pie, laughed some more, and then ordered more pie.

Dan said, "That's some red truck you got."

"Belonged to my granddaddy," Chicky said, feeling crossways with himself. Things were complicating up. He wanted to say more about his grandfather, but didn't feel he could now that he had denied knowledge of Eloy. "This pie's good stuff."

"They make great bread pudding, too."

When they finished, Dan took a double order of bread pudding out to Barky, who was still charged and shivery and going *gnuff-gnuff.* The bread pudding disappeared in one gulp, and then Barky sat politely back and licked his chops.

"Some dawg."

"He's my baby boy."

Chicky said, "I had more fun back there than I've had in a coon's age."

"Me, too," said Dan, knowing how lucky they were not to have been killed. "Say, cowboy, you can crack."

"Yeah," said Chicky with a sad smile, "not that it matters much now."

"What do you mean? You could get somebody good to train you. Hell, I'd work cuts, if you wanted me to." Dan wobbled back. *What? Did I say that?*

"Much obliged, Mr. Cooley. But see, I already quit my job and all."

"Well, uh . . ." Dan could see what he had in mind, but he couldn't come right out and say it. "You could leave tomorrow same as tonight, right?"

"Not really," the kid said, rubbing his hands again. "See, I already checked out of my room, too."

"Look," Dan said, "you saved my ass. I owe you."

"No, you don't"

"Yeah, I do. So why don't you follow me back to my shop?"

"Now?"

"Half hour this time of night. You can check out my gym."

"I was fixin to leave, Mr. Cooley."

"Tell you what. If you don't like what I might have in mind, I'll put you up overnight at the Four Seasons Hotel on Doheny Drive in Beverly Hills."

Chicky said, "Let's do it."

Dan used his cell phone to call Earl.

Earl said, "Where the hell are you?"

"I got into a beef with some thieves tryin to steal my truck. That Garza kid saved my ass."

Earl said, "Where you callin from?"

"We're on the way back to the gym, uh, to the shop."

Earl smiled, had a hunch his partner was near healed, but was careful not to sound too interested. "Can you trust the kid in the shop?'

"Hell, Earl, the kid saved my fucking life!"

Earl put his hand over his mouth in glee and bobbed his head.

Dan showed Chicky around the shop, but didn't mention the shot-up Caddy under the tarp. They moved out to the gym, and Chicky saw how it could be entered from the shop. He quickly understood that this was a holy place to Dan, sensed that Dan was revealing something of himself that not many were allowed to see. He also saw the hand-lettered signs on the wall: "Good Fighters Don't Need Water and Bad Fighters Don't Deserve Water." "Learning's Hard, Doing's Easy." "The First Rule of War Is Don't Shoot Yourself." Chicky understood them all, and saw their sense.

Dan also told the kid about Earl and Momolo and how he had several Mexicans working for him. He also mentioned that he'd been out of the game awhile, but didn't say why, though he did explain briefly how he'd come by Barky in El Paso.

Chicky said, "I like that ol' dawg."

Dan said, "And he talks Spanish better than English."

"No."

"Talk some lingo to him."

"Naw."

"Say somethin in his native tongue."

"*Dame la patita.*"

Barky sat back and held out a paw.

Chicky took it, and shook it, and doffed his Stetson. "Well, if that don't beat all."

Dan hemmed and hawed. Against his better judgment, he blurted out what he'd been bubbling to say. "I got to clear this with Earl, so maybe I'm talking too soon, okay?"

Chicky didn't understand, but said, "I guess."

"What I'm getting at, is that you could work for me and Earl in the shop."

"I'm a country boy, Mr. Cooley."

"You could learn a trade so you'd make a good living outside boxing."

"Outside? I don't have no *inside*."

Dan said, "You will if you train with Earl and me."

"You joshin, Mr. Cooley?"

"I'm serious," Dan said, his mind racing ahead, gamboling now, having fun as things suddenly fit as tightly as a wrapped hand in a fighting glove. "You could work part-time in the shop. Say twenty hours a week so you could rest and train. Ten dollars an hour, under the table. That's two hundred a week to start, clear. You could take over my room here, no rent. If you're not happy in six weeks, you'll have a thousand dollars in your pocket to go back home on, plus what you already got. But you gotta run in the morning, five days a week. After work, you train in the gym five days a week, plus a light workout on Saturday." Dan hesitated. "You turn out to be a flake, I give you a free week's pay just to get rid of you, and you're outta here quick as you came in."

Chicky smiled. "What if I ain't no flake?"

"I don't see you like that or I wouldn't be talkin to you. See, I have to hedge here a little, because I can't tell the future. But if you're happy, Earl and me'll be happy. You'll get fights that are matched right, and you'll start to make money once we get you up the ladder a ways." Dan hesitated briefly. "I got to say this. At any time, either side can pull out, no questions, no hard feelins. That sound okay to you?"

"Yessir."

"If you stick, whether you get a title shot will depend most on you, but also on a thousand other things neither one of us can think of right now. But you'll have somebody in your corner who's got some juice and who gives a fuck about you, I can guarantee you that. But if you screw around, this ain't Santa Claus Lane, and you're outta here."

Chicky said, "Goshees, all a this is comin outta nowhere, Mr. Cooley."

"Like I say, I got to clear it with Earl in the morning."

"Where do I stay tonight?"

"Four Seasons, like I said before, or you can bunk with Barky in my room up those stairs."

"Where'll you sleep?"

"I got my house a few blocks over."

"You got clean sheets upstairs?"

Dan drove home. He opened all the doors and windows to air the place out. He pulled the bedspread back and fluffed the pillows. He washed up, removing the wrapper from the new bar of soap on the washbasin. He closed all the doors, but left some of the windows open. The crucifix was still on the wall. He thought he'd taken it down. He began to take off his shoes.

Chapter 32

Dan and Earl sat in their office drinking coffee. Chicky waited in the customers' lounge downstairs.

Dan said, "Believe me, this is some kid, so if you don't have nothin against it, I thought we could take him on. He could run with Momolo at the golf course, and they could give each other sparring once we fatten the kid up."

Earl was happier than he'd been since before the death of Tim Pat, but he didn't feel he could show his hand yet. "Well, it sounds all right, maybe, but it's a big step, what with me workin and trainin Momolo alone. I'm not so sure I could make time for someone else."

Dan said, "I was thinkin that I could start doing my regular work in the shop again, and the kid could drive the truck part-time, somethin like that, work clean up, you know." Dan hesitated, then jumped in with all four feet. "That way I could train him, instead of you havin to do all the work."

Earl had to look the other way to keep from busting up. "What, you're already cuttin me outta this deal?"

"Hell no! You're in fifty-fifty like always, I just didn't want it to be too much for you, that's all."

"He's left-handed, right? Getting him fights won't be easy." Earl pretended to have doubts. "You think he's worth it?"

"Maybe you could switch him from left to right."

"But not if he don't want to."

"Shortcake switched you to the right side," said Dan.

"I wanted to."

Dan felt dread. Maybe Earl was opposed. Dan couldn't blame him, and thought about vodka for the first time in a while. "He's a tough hombre, Earl, with one hell of a amateur record. And he's as smart and nice as he is tough. I see grit in the kid, like in your dad."

Earl missed his daddy every day. Fucking Dan. The Irish could talk. Like the brothers, they could go to the body with words. Earl swallowed hard, but kept bobbing and weaving, countering with his own shots. "Lotta work, him bein a lefty and comin from other trainers, and all. What if he's locked into his old ways?"

"At least he can make a living if he stays with us," said Dan, feeling it all slip away. "Or he'll have the money to go back home, and still have some when he gets there. But suppose we catch a break and he gets to be somebody? You never know, right? Suppose he starts to cash in? Suppose he gets a title shot, maybe wins a belt? A title, that's what all this's about, for him and for us."

"How do we know he's that good?"

"We don't. Not yet. But he can hit, Earl. Kid can crack."

"That's a start," Earl said, pretending to still hold back. "Where'll he live?"

"I already got him stayin in my old room."

Earl had to look away again. "*Old* room? So this is already a done goddamn deal?"

"No, no, not if you don't want it."

Earl couldn't keep it in any longer. He slapped his thigh and busted out laughing.

Dan said, "Ya fuck, ya, makin me dance, your own white brother."

Earl clapped his hands and laughed some more and held his belly and slid along the wall. Dan loved him.

They went downstairs, where Chicky was waiting. Tired as he was from the night before, he had slept little. Barky had made things worse at five A.M. when he wheezed to go out to pee.

Earl and Dan tried to look serious, but Chicky could see they were happy about something. He hoped to God that Earl saw something good in him, too.

Earl said, "Why'd you say you were going back home?"

"My piss-poor record. And money."

"Who'd you lose to?"

"Black feller in Las Vegas who was eleven and zero with eight KOs. The other one, a Mexican supposed to be five and zero with three knockouts. Once I was in with him, I could tell he was way more'n that. Tony Velasco set the first two up."

"Setup is right," said Earl. "Did the first two kick your ass?"

"Hail, no!"

Earl had to smile. "Where'd you do your farming?"

"For my granddaddy in Poteet, that's the strawberry capital of Texas."

"You think you'd like shop work?"

"What with trainin with y'all, it's soundin better'n better, yessir."

Earl extended his hand, and shook the gentle, fighter's handshake. "Hard Knock's got a new fighter."

Dan had returned to Los Angeles three months before Chicky shook hands with Tony Velasco. He wished that he had met the kid earlier, that he could have saved him from being fucked over. Well, they'd just have to make up for lost time.

They went through the door at the back of the shop and entered the gym.

"But there's one more thing, since you're stayin here. No girls upstairs," Earl insisted. "Whores steal and nice girls squeal."

Chicky smiled at the idea of nice girls squealing.

Earl said, "Not that way. To the police. Lawsuits."

Chicky frowned. He hadn't thought of that. These old guys were no dummies.

Dan said, "You got a steady girl?"

"Not no more."

"If you get one, that's your business," Dan said, "and she'll be welcome here to visit, but not upstairs."

"I ain't likely to go fishin in that ol' pond for a spell."

Earl winked at Dan. Both smiled.

Chicky was so grateful and so proud to be working with Dan Cooley that he thought he'd bust his buttons. He wanted to call Eloy right off about the good news, but decided to wait at least a week, maybe two, for fear that he might somehow mess up large and get his dumb ass run off. How would he ever explain that one? Tony Velasco and Blond Darleen would be hard enough to talk about. He thought on it some more. Yeah, he'd come clean to his granddaddy about Velasco and his defeats—his three losses were sure to come out in the wash, anyway. But Blond Darleen's dirty drawers he'd keep tucked under his Stetson.

He fit right in to the shop, with Momolo and the other guys. This was the closest thing to family he had experienced since he'd left Eloy and the farm.

Dan and Earl trained Chicky the way they had trained Tim Pat. They trained all their fighters the same way, starting with balance, movement, and how to torque ass for power. Because Dan was getting old, Earl worked the punch mitts. Dan was involved with everything else, especially movement, angles, and distance, but he also worked the mitts if Earl wasn't there.

Once Chicky'd settled into the routine of his new job, and the hump-busting training sessions in the gym, he began to believe in himself again, especially when he heard the *pop, pop, BANG!* his gloves made when he fired jabs and leads and hooks into the mitts, Earl calling the combinations like a drill sergeant.

"Come off that hind toe! Do it! 'At's my baby! Do it again! Do it *pretty* for me!"

Chicky found himself slipping punches, and catching punches, and countering punches, and suddenly understood that he was learning boxing from Doctors of the Philosophy of War. Dan taught him about breathing, too. It was hard at first. Chicky could coordinate it with the jab as he shot forward off the back foot, but breathing as he threw combinations flummoxed him. Dan walked him to a big bag. He instructed the boy to only slap, rather than punch, and to breathe and slap in slow motion with both hands, one after the other, four punches per combination.

"Start with the head and end with the body, like this. Now start with the body like this, and end with the head. Breathe as you slap. Slow. Slow. That's it. Do it slow until you can combine the timing and balance and slaps with your lungs, until it's all one thing, simple as a yawn and a stretch."

It took a few days. Chicky practiced with the doorjamb in his room. *Slap, slap, slap, slap.* One night he got it. He ran downstairs, Barky on his tail. He went slowly, only slapped, and then he began to punch and to breathe, slowly at first, slowly, and then he let it rip, and then he punched for a solid five fucking minutes and knew he could punch for another ten. Sweat streamed from him, the best sweat of his life.

"Hot damn, look at Chicky Garza now!"

The next day he was breathing *and* punching, and never in his life had he worked so fast and with such force, never had he had such wind and legs. His body worked for him instead of the other way around. He was suddenly separate from and free of himself. Fifteen three-minute rounds, one minute rest between each. Aside from Earl and the mitts, his routine included the big and speed bags, the jump rope. It also called for sit-ups, five sets of thirty reps each. It meant he was working at the max, and he was losing four to six pounds of water weight during his seventy-plus-minute workout, about what he'd lose during a fight. He'd be up the next morning to jog through the wooded old golf course. He would shower afterward, eat a light breakfast, and then nap for an hour and a half. He'd lie around watching TV until time for lunch, and then he'd work off his meal in the shop until it was time to hit the gym again. After that, it was salad, chicken or fish, green vegetables, and either steamed spuds or brown rice—no salt, light butter. Fruit, sleep. Up and running the next day. Sunday he'd go to the park or the movies, or sometimes out to Venice Beach to watch girls. His Stetson and boots seemed to put off the local stuff. He didn't understand that he needed a volleyball and baggy shorts. Or have bodybuilder bitch tits and strut, half whacked, with steroid-fueled rage. He understood the thongs up the cracks of babes' asses, all right, but he didn't know how to get those thongs down to their ankles. He'd think about Darleen, have to rearrange his shorts, and then head for a movie with lots of stunts and explosions. Fool movies. But they took him away from being lonely until he could set his mind back where it belonged.

"How'm I doin, Mr. Cooley?" said Chicky, turning away from the big bag at the bell.

"Not bad."

"Not bad? You didn't see me tearin it *up*?"

"Yeah, I did. And you'll do it better once we close that wide-assed stance of yours."

"I just don't seem able to get the knack."

Dan smiled. They'd been working at it since day one. Dan knew how simple it all was—once you understood it. But some boys never would get it, even fighters who made it to a title. "Let's give her another shot."

Dan waved Chicky into the ring, thinking he'd try to reach the kid by using different words, different moves, something new. He instructed Chicky to take his regular fighting stance, feet wide, and to stand midway between two corners of the ring, his left shoulder next to the top ring rope connecting the two. When he threw his straight left hand, it would slide along the top of the rope.

"Good," Dan said, facing Chicky. "The wider your feet, the shorter your reach." Dan rested his open hand on the top rope. "Now go easy and in slow motion. Slide your left glove along the top of the rope and make contact with my hand same as if you was punchin."

Chicky stepped off his right, or front foot, but as always his back foot remained rooted in the same rear position. That meant that in order for Chicky to make contact with Dan's hand, he would have to lean in and bend forward. With his head and shoulders down and stretching, it meant that Chicky's upper body was out past the balance point of his right, or front knee, a problem that had deviled him from the very beginning of his boxing career. Stripped of balance, and his reach shortened due to improper mechanics, Chicky was unable to make contact with Dan's open hand.

"You're too far away."

"Not when you do it right," Dan told him. "Like I keep tellin you, the problem is that you're stepping off on the heel of your front foot, instead of pushing off with the toe, or ball, of your back foot. Simple as that."

Dan instructed Chicky to rest his left glove on the top rope the same way Dan had rested his right hand. Dan, as a right-hander, made the move he'd instructed Chicky to make. Not only did Dan reach Chicky's glove, but his fist moved six inches past it.

"How the hell you *do* that?" Chicky asked.

"Make the same move as before, only this time push off the ball of your hind foot as if you were jumping a puddle with a snake in it."

Chicky pushed and damned if both feet didn't move forward on their own. "No snake bite."

"No snake bite," Dan repeated. "Now, do it again, but turn your ass and left shoulder while you do. No reaching or leaning, just a little flexing of your front knee as your weight shifts forward."

Chicky followed instructions. Not only did Chicky's glove make contact with Dan's hand, but it also shoved Dan's hand back another eight inches.

"Damn!" said the kid.

"Now do it with your jab, coming off that back toe in the same way."

It worked again.

"Now give me a one-two, rotating your ass and shoulders."

Chicky thought of the snake in the puddle. Both feet moved. Both punches landed.

"This here's magic, Mr. Cooley."

"I told you you'd get it. Now it's practice. Repetition until you're blue in the face."

"What shade of blue you want?"

Dan had to smile. "Now let's move around the ring. Use your back foot to move forward, your front foot to go back, your left foot to go right, and your right foot to go left." Dan kept circling. "When you're in position to fire, come off that back toe for me so both feet move. Soon you'll be able to fight inside, outside, left side, right, any fookin side you fookin want."

These were the dreams Chicky had dreamed back in Texas. He could feel his life changing.

"See, boxing ain't street fighting where strength alone can make a winner," Dan explained. "Boxing's a game of little things, like the links in a bicycle chain. It ain't about big or strong, it's about speed times weight bein equal to *force*, not to strength. It's about respect and heart, and all this comes from your mind and legs, not the muscles in your arms, and sure as hell not because you think you're some kind of tough. Now the question is whether you can execute under pressure."

"I can execute," Chicky said confidently.

"I believe you."

And Chicky believed Dan. Everything his new trainer showed him how to do made sense. It worked, all of it.

Dan was friends with the greens master at the nearby Wilshire Country Club. He was the father of an amateur boy Dan had once trained. Dan's fighters had run there for years, running the paths and under the trees at five every morning except Saturdays and Sundays, and leaving by the back gate before most golfers teed off on the first hole. Now Chicky ran with Momolo and Barky every morning. After breakfast, Chicky cleaned floors in the shop and hauled trash to the Dumpsters. He cleaned toilets and painted the fence. He kept the gym looking bright and spare, the mirrors polished. He finished his duties so quickly that Dan and Earl gave him work making pickups and deliveries. He wanted to work more hours, but Dan made him rest. Chicky was getting strong again, inside and out, and he knew it.

Dan and Earl could see it, too. They'd known the boy was solid after only three days, knew he'd be there when the rockets came ripping in and things got thrilling.

Chicky made the call back home to Poteet and held his breath for fear he might not say things right. But there was no need, because things between him and his granddaddy were the same as always.

Eloy said, "Well, well, if it ain't the ol' strawberry man himself."

"Guess what, Grandpa," Chicky said, "I found Dan Cooley and he ain't dead."

"Huh?"

Chicky related the story of his losses and how he'd come to meet Dan Cooley, about the fight in the parking lot, about Earl, about Barky, and about his part-time job and where he was living and training.

Eloy was so tickled by the good tidings that he forgot the bellyful of tenpenny nails in his guts. "From what you say, this Velasco was bad medicine."

Chicky said, "More like poison."

Eloy said, "Cooley'll cure you."

"It's what I'm thinkin, too."

"You wait and see," said Eloy. He spat some dip juice down into a Pyrex measuring cup, the liquid pungent and grainy as it soaked into a balled-up paper napkin. "Cooley, he, uh, does Mr. Cooley know about me?"

Chicky said, "He asked if I heard of a Eloy Garza from down Texas, and I'm sorry, Granddaddy, but it just come out that I said I didn't."

Eloy smiled, was glad there was nothing to connect him to Chicky for Dan Cooley. He remembered the smashed side of Dan's face and winced, closed his eyes. "You done good, boy, like always."

"See, Granddaddy, I said I didn't know of you 'cause I was losin my ass off out here, and I didn't want to bring shame on your good name."

Eloy set the measuring cup down, used the handle to give it a half spin. "*Mi querido chiquito,* my beloved little one, you could never bring shame on nobody, least ways not on me."

I'm the one that brings shame. I should be dead.

Because Trini Cavazo always insisted, Eloy Garza had to meet him at the Cathedral of San Fernando. Like every other time, Trini had made his drop and gone. Eloy remained in a pew, where he read an article on Psycho Sykes's professional career in the San Antonio *Express-News*. Eloy shook his head, then dropped his right hand to press his swollen liver. In his left hand he clutched a paper bag of small, boxed brown bottles he'd just bought from Trini. Every time Eloy saw the dope dealer, he remembered the deal with Chicky's passbook. But now Eloy was able to think of Chicky working and training with Dan Cooley in California, and Eloy was grateful to God. He'd complained to Trini about doing business in the cathedral.

"Ain't nothin safer than the bosom of the Mother Church, *m'hijo,*" Trini said. He checked the cathedral again for narcs, and then pinned Eloy with his black eyes. "So Chicky's still goin school, eh?"

"*Claro,*" Eloy said. "He calls home all pumped about new science and stuff."

Trini added, "He been comin back into town some, *¿ése?*"

"Nooo," Eloy said. "He can't afford to take off from his books, and ain't no way I'm up to drivin to College Station."

Trini nodded, but didn't remove his eyes from Eloy's. "It's best he stays up there. Ain't that right?"

"I know."

Trini left the church smiling. Scoring was better than anything, especially in a cathedral off a dead man.

Chapter 33

No, I'm not askin for too much money," Dan Cooley said into the phone. "Garza'll fill the auditorium."

Dan listened to the Mexican promoter's complaints while he savored a reddish brown Montecristo robusto with a fifty-two ring. When the promoter finished, Dan jumped back in.

"It's not too much money, not when Chicky Garza can knock your dick in the dirt with either hand."

"*Ya, ya,* but nobody wan' Garza," said the Auditorio Municipal promoter in Tijuana. "Garza fight at welter, but he hit like a goddan middle, and from the lef' goddan side."

"So I pay 'em extra."

"They don' wan' extra."

Dan winced as he nipped at the end of the Montecristo. Except for being a southpaw, a kid like Chicky was Seabiscuit, Whirlaway, and Man o' War all rolled into one.

I got no more juice, Dan thought. He looked in the mirror on the opposite wall across from him, saw himself and his white hair. *Why keep tryin, old man? You had your run.*

But being in his sixties had never stopped him before, so he gave the promoter's nuts another squeeze. "Louie fuckin Carbajal."

"Dan fuckin Cooley, *el culero*, the butt-fuck," chortled the Mexican promoter.

Dan came back with, *"Póg mo hón."*

"Eh, what's that you say, *culero?*"

Dan laughed. "I said kiss my ass in Irish."

Carbajal enjoyed this rough talk between old friends. "Dan, you know I'm sorry."

Dan touched his ruined right eye unconsciously, a habit he'd years before given up trying to kick. "Louie, we go back a lotta years. Garza's a KO puncher, he's what all fans want, specially you fuckin Mexicans, c'mon, talk to me, gimme some love."

"Dan, you was always good to me when I start out," said Carbajal, "but Garza's got that hebby left hand, and managers don't want they pre-lin boys knocked on they ass. I got ten-round fighters for you boy, but you don't want that."

"Garza's only had seven fights and he lost three of those, for chris-sakes," Dan said. "He's not ready for ten rounds."

The promoter said, "Maybe on my next card, okay?"

"I'll pay 'em extra outta my own pocket, what do you say?"

"Nobody wan' the extra, that what I'm sayin."

Dan said, "You could bring in somebody from Mexico City who don't know about Garza."

"Costs too much for me, plane tickets and all that shit. Maybe next tine."

Dan said, "Yeah, okay, Louie, maybe next *tine.*"

Dan hung up the phone and glared at it. He'd called three U.S. promoters before he called Carbajal, got the same answer each time. He left his soundproofed office and started downstairs to the main floor of his body-and-fender shop. It was his crew's afternoon break, and they were kicked back eating junk food from the coffee wagon. Only Earl was on his feet. He stroked his Dizzy Gillespie lip whiskers and looked up.

"I lost my juice," Dan said, ready to spit. "I had it, and I threw it away."

"You still got juice," Earl said, wiping a speck of dust from a shiny tail fin with a polish cloth he held in his bad right hand. "Makin fights for a lefty's like findin a free ho house."

"Yeah, but me stayin out of the gym all that time didn't help none. We lost some good fighters. And they spread the word around about me. 'Cooley's a burnout.' " Dan spoke through his nose somewhat, like people who have suffered broken noses and such. "I shouldn't a taken time off."

"We could still get lucky with Garza."

"I wish he was right-handed."

"Me, too," said Earl.

The two partners stood admiring Dan's newly restored, factory-red 1959 Cadillac Eldorado Biarritz convertible, its high whitewalls gleaming. Under Earl's supervision, Chicky Garza had restored Dan's car from the hubcaps up.

Dan sighted down the fenders of the Caddy for wrinkles and warps; checked the chrome for pits and flaws; eyeballed for defects the leather upholstery Chicky had chosen to be installed. Dan looked up to Earl. "You find anything wrong at all, at all?"

"Not a thing I could see," said Earl.

"Me neither," said Dan. "Chicky on his break?"

"He's deliverin that 'forty-one Ford woody he helped me with to Universal. Momolo followed in the pickup."

"You and Chicky did a good job on that one, too," said Dan.

"What say we raise Chicky another two dollars a hour?" Earl suggested.

"Why not?" Dan said. He again thought about getting Chicky a fight and decided to give it another go. "I'm going to try the promoter for the casino in Indio," he said.

Earl nodded. "It's a shot."

Dan returned to his office, which had been enlarged several times over the years. Dan and Earl's two desks took up most of the space; the rest was jammed with filing cabinets and shelves that overflowed with paint and fabric catalogs, and dusty cartons full of faded receipts. In the bottom of one of the cartons were some old scrapbooks. One wall of the office was glass and it looked out on the shop. Two walls were covered with before and after photographs of whacked vehicles that Shamrock Auto Body had returned to showroom condition. A fourth wall was covered with fight photos, many of them of Earl when he fought at 160, Dan in his corner. There were fight photos of others as well, blacks and Chicanos mostly. There were a few whites, but not many. There was a Philippino fighter, Buzzsaw Magallanes, out of Manila, a bantamweight champion in whose corner Dan had worked as cut man when Buzzsaw came to the States. He'd worked corners of several other champs as well, but he'd never had one of his own. There was heavyweight Luther Willis, now a paramedic, and featherweight Petey Rosas, now a sergeant with the San Ysidro PD. Schoolboy Tommy Ryan, just an average kid with a big dream and a bigger smile, always fought his heart out, but heart wasn't enough to bring him back from Vietnam. There was one small photo of Dan winning the featherweight finals of the California Golden Gloves at the Olympic Auditorium.

Dan checked his card index, but before he could place a call, the phone rang. "Hello," Dan said, "Shamrock Auto Body."

"Yessir," a deep male voice said in greeting. "Is this here where Chicky Garza works? I'm callin long distance from Poteet, Texas?"

Dan smiled at the accent, thought it must be the Tex-Mex grandfather Chicky had sometimes mentioned. Dan had been delighted to learn that there were many Tex-Mex Mexicans who talked just like good ol' South Texas boys, and in the beginning he would bullshit with Chicky just to hear the kid talk.

"Yes," Dan said, "Chicky works here, but he's makin a delivery. Can I help you?"

"Yessir, you can. This here's Coach Harlan Oster. I was his football coach, and I been knowin him and his granddaddy ol' Eloy Garza a long time. See, the Wolf's terrible sick and I need to talk to Chicky, 'cause this here's a emergency."

Stunned, Dan sat back. "I'll have him call as soon as he comes in, shouldn't be very long."

"I surely do 'preciate it."

Dan took Oster's number, said good-bye as calmly as he could, and hung up. He stared at the phone.

"Well, fuck me."

Eloy Garza, the Wolf, the Lobo Tejano.

Dan's face felt funny, felt as if all the blood had gone somewhere else.

It fit! Dan understood, some of it, anyway. He also wondered how much the kid knew, wondered if maybe the kid didn't know anything about any of it. He thought about dialing Chicky's cell phone, but decided to wait so he could be there when the kid called Texas.

He was about to go back down to the shop when the pressure hit his chest. One knee came up, and he caved forward. Kogon had warned him. An angioplasty solved the problem temporarily, sometimes for an extended period. Then it either had to be redone—or you were off to the races with a coronary bypass. Dan figured that the pain meant he was headed for a rematch with Kogon. It would start as an escalating pain over his left tit. He'd never had anything wrong with him except for his eye, and he kept hoping that the tit pain would just go away. Which was like hoping that your opponent in a fight who was slamming you with head shots would ease up on you.

Dan's knee came down and he pressed hard on the left side of his chest with both hands. He momentarily summoned up what he thought open-heart surgery would be like. It would make the angioplasty look like a day at the beach.

He took an aspirin, his second that day, hoping to further thin his blood. Aspirin was part of the long-term treatment he'd begun once

Chicky came into his life, along with medication to lower his cholesterol. At night he took half of a .5 Xanax to keep him asleep once he fell
asleep. He was off the sauce, thanks to the dog and Earl and Chicky. But
the call from Coach Oster had been like an arrow through his ears. He
touched his eye.

In less than a minute, the pressure subsided. He waited a few moments more, caught his breath, then found excuses to climb and reclimb
the stairs to his office, dared his heart to kill him. No more pain. He told
no one about the incident.

Because of the Texas phone call, Dan let everyone off early. Earl knew
something must be wrong.

Earl said, "You need me to hang around?"

Dan shook his head. "I'll cover it."

"I'll stay if you want," Earl offered.

"I gotta talk with Chicky."

"I hope it ain't bad," Earl said.

"Me, too."

It was four o'clock when Momolo and Chicky got back from deliver-
ing the woody, and Chicky was surprised that Dan was alone in the shop.
Dan told Momolo that he could take off, too.

"Is there somethin up?" Chicky asked.

Dan waited until Momolo left, then gave the kid Coach Oster's phone
number.

"He said it was about your grandfather. If I remember right, Oster
called him the Wolf."

Chicky said, "Lordy," and stood a minute not knowing what to think
or do. *Cat's outta the bag,* he thought.

Dan said, "Use the office phone."

Chicky ran up the stairs, and Dan hurried up behind him. Still no
recurring chest pain, so Dan conveniently forgot that it had ever happened.

Chicky telephoned Oster, and the coach told him that Eloy was in bad shape and needed him. Chicky was as stunned by the call as Dan had been, but for different reasons. "I knew he was hurtin some when I left," he told Oster, "but I been callin him regular like since I been out here and he never said nothin about feelin bad."

Oster said, "Bad enough that if I'da known about it two weeks ago, I'da called and said come home then."

"I'll get the first plane out."

"Ain't no plane until tomorrow. I checked," Oster told him.

"I'll be on the first one I can get. Thanks, Coach, God knows I mean it."

"Glad to he'p you, boy."

Chicky hung up and turned to Dan. "I gotta go home tomorrow. Is it too late to get a ticket?"

"There's a travel agent open late in the Beverly Center. Ticket won't be cheap, comin so close to the flight."

Chicky kept his savings in Dan's safe. "Take whatever you need outta my stake."

Dan said, "Traffic and parkin' over there'll be a bitch, but you go pack anyway, in case we can get you out of here tonight. Maybe do a connecting flight or something."

Chicky said, "I guess you're gonna wanna talk to me some, huh?"

Dan said, "Is there a *T* in Texas?"

"Yup, an'ere's a *T* in Tennessee, too, but I figure that ain't gonna he'p me much."

Dan could talk some Texas, too. "Rat."

Chicky's insides were hanging upside down, and he was filled with a shitload of wouldda-couldda-shoulddas for leaving his granddaddy alone to come to California. It didn't help that Eloy himself had backed this move. Now there was this *T* for Texas business.

He sat on the bed in his room. Packing wouldn't take but a lick, but Chicky had the heebie-jeebies. What would he do until tomorrow if there were no red-eye flights? How would he get through the night? He decided to warm up and go ten hard rounds on the big bag, bust himself up, mash his nerves down, jump rope till his knees buckled and his skin sizzled.

Nailed to one wall of Chicky's room was a clipping with a photograph from the San Antonio *Express-News*. It had been sent to Chicky by his grandfather, and featured Houston's Cyrus Psycho Sykes, rising junior-middleweight star, whose record was nine and zero, with six knockouts. In the photo with Sykes were his two smiling trainers, San Antonio "boxing legends and trainers of champions," Trini and Paco Cavazo.

According to the article, the Cavazo brothers had such faith in Sykes's dedication to boxing and the clean life that they often sent him to the city for a few weeks of R & R after a fight, ". . . because it provided the Houston native with the best comfort zone to rest prior to returning to the wars of his skyrocketing career."

The article added that the two San Antonio Chicanos training an African American "was but another example of how wonderful it is when members of different ethnic and racial groups cast aside real or imagined differences to work toward a common goal."

Chicky said, "I got your common."

He glowered at the clipping at least once a day.

While Dan was buying the kid's ticket for a nine A.M. flight the next morning, Chicky pushed himself to exhaustion in the gym. When Dan returned, the kid innocently asked him if he would drive him to Christ the King Church.

Dan hesitated, then said, "You want to take the Caddy?"

To drive the old Cadillac was tempting, but Chicky said, "I don't much feel like messin with traffic, is all. Or bein alone."

Dan had come to loathe the lovely old church and its newer school. He didn't want anything to do with the place, hated God and the Catholic faith. But because Chicky sought solace there, Dan kept his mouth shut and drove him over.

Christ the King had been built in the mid-twenties, stood on Arden Boulevard just south of Melrose. The church was only a few blocks from Dan's house on Cahuenga, and another few blocks from Shamrock Auto Body. It had a high, red-tiled roof, and inside there was dark wood—a beamed ceiling and old pews. Stained, leaded-glass windows brought shafts of springtime light to the quiet interior all year round. High above the simple but majestic altar was a brilliantly colored triptych of Christ as King.

Dan entered the dim, cool interior of the church reluctantly, someone venturing into enemy territory. But despite himself, Dan's hand moved toward the holy water and he remembered how he had knelt before the statue of St. Pat for consolation in his worst times—all but that one time, that last time. His instinct, ingrained for over sixty years, was to kneel, but his anger and bitterness kept him upright, standing at the rear of the church and watching Chicky kneel in a pew right in front of him.

He could hear Chicky whisper, "God, don't let my granddaddy die, please. Virgencita de Guadalupe, *ayúdame* Little Virgin of Guadalupe, help me.

Dan heard it, felt the old hatred, and immediately left the church, stood out front cursing while he waited for the kid.

"Fuck the Virgen de Guadalupe, the Virgen de Fatima, and fuck the Queen of the Angeles, too."

Chicky followed in five minutes, and looked better than when he'd gone in. They had dinner at Mario's, a Peruvian seafood restaurant owned by a Peruvian-Japanese. Chicky wanted to pay the tab, but Dan waved him off. They drove in silence back to the shop.

Dan knew that Chicky was itching to talk, but now that he'd seen the kid in church, Dan wasn't all that sure that he wanted to.

Chicky coughed and cleared his throat. "Uh, did I have much left after the ticket money?"

"You started with nine hundred in the safe. The late ticket cost you five-ninety and change." Dan offered Chicky a thick brown envelope. "Here's some extra."

It was eight-thirty after a nerve-wracking day. Dan and Chicky had entered the gym through the entrance at the back of the shop. The gym's license had been renewed and it was officially listed as the School of Hard Knocks, Inc. For tax purposes, Dan had always had one license for his auto business, a different one for the gym. Moonlight filtered in through the crusted skylight and made patches on the worn hardwood floor.

Dan touched his bad eye, then held out the envelope again. "You might need it."

"Makes me feel gawky," said the kid.

"Malarkey," Dan growled.

Chicky could use the extra dough, but he wasn't sure taking Dan's money was right, especially since Dan had caught him in a lie. He was afraid this might be kiss-off money.

Dan offered the envelope a third time. "Take it. If you and me stick it out, you can pay me back from wages, or outta your next fight."

Chicky's chin lifted. "You mean I still got a job?"

"Yeah, you do, but lie to me again and you won't."

"I don't like to borrow, Mr. Cooley," said Chicky, his Tex-Mex South Texas drawl gone all to cotton in the dim light of a bare, sixty-watt bulb.

"You got no choice," said Dan. When the kid called him Mr. Cooley, Dan knew things were as serious for the boy as they were for him. "And this isn't like you're on a vacation, right?"

Chicky took and opened the envelope. It contained his ticket home and back to Los Angeles, plus ten hundred-dollar bills. "I ain't gonna need all this."

"It's walking-around money."

"That's a lot of walkin."

"You can rent a car," Dan suggested.

"Granddaddy's got a flatbed I can use."

"So buy the old man a new suit." Dan caught himself too late, wished he hadn't said it.

"Think he might need it?"

Dan shrugged, not wanting to say more.

Chicky coughed again. "We still gonna talk?"

"Oh, yeah."

When Dan had gotten the call from Coach Oster, he was taken back some forty years to that night when he and the Wolf got to know each other inside the squared circle of L.A.'s Olympic Auditorium. Except for a few blacks, and a handful of blue-collar Poles and Italians, the essential mix was Mex and Mick, close to fifty-fifty. All five rounds still flickered black and white in Dan's memory. He replayed this fight in his imagination almost every day. It had been an elimination bout that should have taken him to a title shot. Near the end of the fifth, the referee stopped the fight and Dan watched himself go to one knee, his crushed face cradled in his shiny gloves.

Dan wasn't one to look for excuses, and surely he wasn't one for self-pity, but it was obvious that he hadn't been tough enough to hang with the Wolf. His weakness had cost him a shot at the Lightweight Championship of the World back when there was but one champ for each of eight weight divisions. As a pretty, stand-up boxer-puncher, what still baffled Dan was that he should have easily beaten the Wolf, a flat-footed slugger who came in face-first. He should have been able to pick Garza to pieces with his punishing jab and then taken him out in the later rounds. What hounded him still was his absolute certainty, given his speed and fighting style, that he would have gone on to beat the flat-footed champ, as well. It wasn't to be.

Dan felt better when he looked over at Chicky. The kid had a narrow strip of scar tissue in one eyebrow, and a slightly flattened, hooked Mexican nose. This boy was tough enough, for sure. Dan's hope was that he could get the kid smart enough, and keep him smart enough.

The kid said, "I'll square up soon's I get back to work."

"I'm not worried," said Dan. But he was dealing inside with a wound that had scabbed over years ago. Oster's call had opened it up again.

"Your granddad was a hell of a man. He was a hell of a fighter, too."

"Was he really that good?" Chicky asked.

Dan said, "He was damn good. He beat me, didn't he?"

"Huh?" said Chicky, feeling his mouth hang open, his skin flush hot. "I didn't know y'all'd ever fought Granddaddy."

"Oh, yeah, I did. You didn't know about that?"

"No, sir, I didn't."

Dan shook his head to clear it, couldn't separate his feelings from his thoughts and memories. "I don't get it," he said. "When I asked you early on about a old-time Texas fighter named Eloy Garza, you told me there were a ton of Garzas in South Texas, but that you hadn't heard of him. That's right, right?"

Chicky wiped the sheen from his face and nodded shamefully. "Yessir, I did, I plumb lied."

"Why did you have to lie to me?"

Chicky hung his head, rubbed the toe of one boot on the back of the opposite pants leg. He wanted to tell Dan that Eloy had told Chicky not to mention him because he had locked horns or something with Cooley a while back.

He decided he wasn't going to open that can of worms, so he tried to come up with something close to the truth.

"After my gran'pa told me to come out here and hook up with you, I couldn't find you, no matter how hard I tried. That's when I didn't know no better and took those first fights I lost. I was afraid I might shame myself workin with you, too, and I didn't want to put a black mark against my granddaddy's name on account of me losin again. I was fixin to head on home after the third one, only took it 'cause I was next to bust-ass. I did tell you that."

Dan said, "That's what you said, anyway."

"I wasn't lyin 'bout that," Chicky said, sitting up straight. "If I hadn't met you, I'd a gone straight home that night with my tail tucked between my legs. I wasn't even gonna tell Granddaddy I had any fights out here so's not to shame him from my losses."

Dan sat back, lost in the tangle of what passed for the kid's logic. This had been a hard day for Chicky, but it had also been a bitch for Dan. "Your grandfather told you to look me up?" asked Dan. "The *Wolf* said that?"

"Yessir," said Chicky. "See, he said you was the best."

Dan felt as if he'd been hit with a Garza left hook. "The *Wolf* told you that? Why didn't you say so, for chrissakes?"

Chicky hung his head again, and Dan saw that the kid's lower lip quivered. "I'm sorry, Mr. Cooley. I never meant to hornswoggle."

"I'm sorry, kid, but that kind of thinkin makes you a screwup."

Chicky was clear-eyed again. "Yessir, I know that now, but no, sir, I ain't really. See, once you and Earl worked with me, I could see how good I was gettin to be under y'all, could see I wasn't just some no-account Texas brag-mouth or a dumb-ass Messkin who fights with his face. That got me to thinkin that I could be *some*body if I just hung on."

Dan wanted to believe, but he didn't know what to believe, yet he was pretty much persuaded by the kid's explanation and wondered if it was the Tex part or the Mex part that was talking. "Chicky, you was livin a lie, and you made me and Earl live it with you. Hell, Earl's got a wife and three little girls he could be givin his attention to, and one of the kid's a heart patient."

"I was only waitin for the right time to come clean, and I could see it comin." The Tex and the Mex were both talking. "All I needed was one good payday. See, I was savin so's to bring Granddaddy out here so y'all could meet up, and so y'all'd be proud of me and so I could thank y'all together, and so I could take you and Earl and Granddaddy to some famous Hollywood hot spot for a fancy spread."

Dan said, "Hell, I'd a loaned you the money to bring the goddamn Wolf out, I'd a given it to you, for chrissakes."

Chicky still felt shame, and again had a hard time looking at Dan. His granddaddy had been the only father he'd ever had, and Chicky'd come to think of Dan almost in the same way, had felt downright saved when Dan told him he still had a job.

Chicky tried to explain "See, when you asked about Granddaddy, I didn't know how you knew him personal. I'd a told you if I'd a known, I truly wouldda."

"Whatever the hell reasons you had, it kept me'n Earl in the dark."

"But I always trained and worked hard as I could for you," said the kid, "and I never once cheated or stole off you, and I never would, Mr. Cooley, and I always fought my heart out."

"Follow me," Dan ordered.

He led Chicky from the gym to the shop, then took him to the coffee machine and the sink, where the crew always left their unwashed cups and spoons and such.

Dan said, "See that stuff in the sink?"

"Yessir."

"Wash it."

Chicky grinned, knew things'd worked out. He got right down to it, even dried everything and stacked it proper. But all the while his mind was on his grandfather back home in Poteet, Texas.

Chapter 34

Chicky took his time driving as Dan showed him surface-street shortcuts to LAX from Hollywood. When they hit the 405 Freeway off of La Cienaga Boulevard, there was an unexpected break in traffic, and Chicky took the Caddy up to sixty-five for the last open stretch before the Century Boulevard off-ramp.

He drove the Caddy into the airport entrance and Dan guided him to the upper level. Instead of parking downstairs and having to walk a half mile, Chicky could carry his one small bag through one glass door.

Dan said, "You got your ticket?"

"I got her."

Dan said, "Take all the time you need back there."

" 'Preciate that," said Chicky. "Don't be surprised if I bring Grand-daddy back out here with me."

"Do it," Dan said, and Chicky knew Dan meant it.

Chicky nodded and touched the brim of his hat. Dan waved good-bye as Chicky headed through the glass doors.

———

Dan edged into airport traffic, made the big loop that took him back to Sepulveda, part of early California's El Camino Real, the Royal or King's Highway that was originally built by the missionaries. Cars crawled, this was maybe worse than the freeway, but Dan liked this piece of road, knew it had once passed between pastureland and bean fields, and decided to take it instead of the freeway. Earl needed him back at the shop, but by now Dan knew he had to make one stop along the way.

Before exiting the airport, Dan put the Caddy's top up so people couldn't see his face.

He looked at himself in the rearview mirror. What he saw was still the same old man he'd seen in the office mirror, but the strange thing about getting old was that you never saw yourself aging from day to day, even year to year. Despite his bad heart and family heartache, Dan hadn't deteriorated like so many his age. He weighed 20 pounds over the 135-pound fighting weight of his twenties and was always taken for younger than he was. His hair had gone white early, that had happened on both sides of his family, as it often did with the Irish, but like many men who go white early, he had kept most of his hair. He sometimes thought of Bette Davis's line, *Getting old ain't for sissies.* Dan agreed. Of course he could have dyed his hair, back to the the wavy sable of his youth, but he would have been embarrassed; women dyed their hair. His only concession to vanity was the plastic surgery he'd had on his eye, but mostly that had been done so he could see better.

Dan drove thirty minutes north on Sepulveda, then turned right onto Venice Boulevard and headed east. A wide median had once separated east- from westbound traffic. Railroad tracks had run down the middle of it. Red "interurban" trolleys had taken thirty minutes to shoot people from downtown L.A. all the way to the beach. The "red cars" had been scrapped for buses after World War II, in the name of progress, but buses took an hour and more to make the same trip. He could still remember riding on them and the faint metallic smell of lubricating oil.

Memory was a strange thing. He could remember the long-gone trolleys. He could even remember back to age four, maybe earlier, but now some of his short-term memory had begun to slip away, and it pissed him off that he sometimes had to go to the kitchen twice to remember why he had gone there in the first place. He also wondered about Alzheimer's disease, wondered if he was prone to it. Both of his parents had died of heart disease—his mother at sixty-two, his father at fifty-eight, both before the miracles of angioplasty and open-heart surgery—so he had no way of knowing if Alzheimer's came programmed in the hard drive of his name. The Cooleys in Ireland had died too young, from work and disease and hunger, for Alzheimer's to sink its teeth into them. Having inherited a bum ticker, like his parents and two of his brothers, Dan figured he'd check out like they had, which he hoped would be a long time before he went dotty. Until then, he'd always remember the day he bought this very car for Brigid, and how Brigid drove the Caddy from the showroom, the backseat full of red roses and the six bunches of shamrocks he'd had flown in from Dublin. And he knew he'd always remember the laughter and tears of those who had left him behind.

Dan knew almost every inch of L.A., had even driven a cab for close to a year after his boxing career had crashed. But it was Brigid, a former domestic in a Bel Air Estates mansion, who'd convinced Dan to open his own body-and-fender shop.

Brigid, with three other Irish girls, had shared a two-bedroom apartment in an old Spanish stucco building on Curson Street near Hollywood Boulevard. Dan had met her at a Sinn Fein St. Patrick's Day picnic in Griffith Park. The first thing Dan attempted, after thickly spreading his usual cheap line of blarney, was to try to ply her with poteen and get her in the bushes. Her refusal kept him interested. What she did a few days later was march him to confession and communion at Christ the King. He loved her for it.

Dan checked himself in the rearview mirror again, mentally moved back in time, and focused on his right eye. Four of the six muscles that extended from the socket to the right eyeball had been damaged in his fight with Chicky's grandfather. Dan's eye had been repaired somewhat, but he'd been left slightly wall-eyed on the right side. He could see well enough to drive legally, but during the beating he'd taken from the Lobo Tejano, part of his eye socket had been shattered and bone fragments had pierced his sinus cavities. Several surgeries had repaired part of the zygomatic arch, but the lumpy edges of the smashed brow and socket could not be made entirely round. Most of the feeling on the right side of his brow and cheek returned, but not all. Stony left hooks from a lesser puncher had retired him.

Chicky had a snack of tasteless airline food, then napped. When he woke up and peered out the window, he saw that the plane was over the low hills and mesquite of South Texas. The massive hole of San Antonio's old cement quarry, now a ritzy golf resort with mansions on its bluffs and a high-ticket shopping center, signaled that the plane would land shortly, and that Chicky would be almost home after living and fighting in Los Angeles for a year. Sitting up, his hat nearly slipped from his lap.

Getting down to Poteet, thirty miles south from San Anto, wouldn't be a problem, what with *el bus* Greyhound leaving every few hours for the small town of Pleasanton, on the way to Corpus Christi. What did worry Chicky was the condition of his sick *abuelito*. Chicky couldn't understand this weakness in Eloy—hell, Eloy was a *fighter*! But when he was fourteen, Chicky had caught Eloy drinking bottom-shelf vodka straight from the bottle.

The old man shrugged, rubbed a stubbled cheek, said, "Boy, you know us Mexicans."

It was then Chicky understood that his grandfather was drinking himself to death, and turned away near tears.

While Chicky worried on the plane, Dan worried in the Caddy, wondered if he could indeed drive on to that place that he was always afraid to go back to. At La Brea, "Tar Avenue," he should have turned north to Melrose and then east to Cole and the shop, but here he was, still on Venice Boulevard. Continuing eastward toward old Los Angeles. At some point Dan stopped thinking. He just let the car drive itself where it wanted to go.

As Dan passed Hollenbeck Park, he felt his pulse quicken. He parked the car on Breed and stared at Lupe's house. It was still the same parched pink and green from three-plus years earlier, the same color it had been for twenty years, or more. Although he knew he was absolutely wrong, something in him still wanted to blow the fucking pink house away, still flirted with the trigger in his mind.

Dan didn't know that he was being watched as he sat there. A nineteen-year-old Chicana cowered behind the faded, striped kitchen curtains of the pink house. She had seen the Caddy as it coasted to a stop at the corner of Sixth. She couldn't see the driver, but she knew it had to be the same old white man who had driven the Caddy the last time she'd seen it. She shook her head to clear it, the same way she shook it almost every morning as she struggled up through the black sea of sleep, at once rattled and numbed. She shook her head again, now in dismay, for she had convinced herself that she wouldn't see that red car ever again, but now realized that she should have known better.

Little Boy, I'm sorry, lo siento tanto. *Please, Little Boy, tell him that I never saw you, tell him that I pray to God for you every night, that I would give you my own life this instant if there was a way to bring you back.*

As Dan slouched in the Caddy, he had no idea that Lupe also had frequent nightmares in which her dreaming mind replayed the accident. And the music jingling out from the truck:

> *Mary had a little lamb, little lamb, little lamb . . .*

Each time the dream came, she would wake up. Her teeth and jaws ached, and she knew she would not be able to get back to sleep. Lupe waited for the sun to rise and for the clatter of life.

Dan stared at the pink house for a quarter of an hour, then pulled a U-turn and drove off.

The girl crossed to a little shrine where a candle burned. She made the sign of the cross. There was a photo of a man and two teenagers, her father and two older brothers, each wearing a straw hat. Smiling proudly, they stood next to a brand-new pickup truck, outfitted with all the tools of the roofer's trade, manual and electric—coiled orange power lines, saws, staplers, shovels, rakes, push brooms, a heavy-duty vacuum unit for cleanup.

It had taken the family six years to save enough to pay for it. They'd always had to work for someone else. Now they'd work for different contractors if they had to, but they'd also seek their own accounts. From now on, they'd be their own bosses. They would work seven days a week, if that's what it took, to make it in the roofing business.

The photo had been taken the week before all three were killed on the Sixth Street Bridge. A speeding carjacker had plowed into them head-on during a police pursuit. The carjacker survived. The girl's mother told her how the driver's bar-owner brother and several gangbang buddies from the bar showed up in court to give their homeboy support, how they laughed and cupped their crotches with their hands and defied anyone to fuck with them.

The girl hung her head.

Kyrie eleison. Christ have mercy.

Dan headed for a green hump of hilly land near a bend in the Los Angeles River, the site of St. Athanasius Cemetery, the last home of so many of those who had made their way from the clouded skies and vivid green of Ireland to the sunshine and prosperity of California.

Brigid had chosen St. Athanasius Cemetery because of its Celtic crosses and the Gaelic inscriptions. She made of it a special piece of what she called the "ould sod," Ireland. Every space in the small cemetery had since been sold, and most graves had long been filled. Mexican gardeners kept the place "daycent," as Brigid would say.

When Dan saw the wide iron gate, he felt like turning back. Traffic wouldn't allow it, but neither would the need that had come so powerfully over him at the airport.

Ah, Jaysus!

The top part of the Cooley family headstone was a high, white-marble Celtic cross, Celtic because it had a ring intersecting each segment of the shaft and crossbar, a design dating from the eighth century and Irish Viking times. The base of the cross was a dark green Irish-marble cube four feet high that stood at the head of eight burial plots. Only Dan's plot was empty, and it would remain so. As much as he yearned to lie forever with his darlins, he'd not be buried ever in any place Catholic or in any way religious. He'd thought of cremation for himself, but gave up the idea, not knowing anyone who would flush his ashes down some toilet for him.

Names and corresponding dates were chiseled in Celtic lettering an inch deep into the slick green base of the gravestone. On either side of the names was a perfectly reproduced Irish harp. A six-inch border around the face of the green stone framed the names with the intricate Celtic latticework and forms, both human and animal, found in the Book of Kells. It was the last name he stared at—and began to weep.

TIMOTHY PATRICK MARKEY   1986–1997

When Dan got back to the shop, Earl was on the phone at the downstairs counter ordering supplies.

Dan said, "You miss me?"

"Naw, we just had to hire ten new men to fill your place, that's all."

"I had to make a stop," Dan explained.

Earl nodded. "Ain't no big thing."

Dan smiled. Earl knew him better than he knew himself. Dan nodded in the direction of Earl's paperwork. "Want me to handle it from here?"

"Naw," said Earl. He knew that Dan's offer was an apology for being late, but he could also see that Dan's eyes were red, and that his mind was off somewhere. "Why don't you take off?"

"You don't mind?"

"I'll take a day off next week," Earl said.

Dan climbed the stairs to the office, then sorted through several cartons of stored receipts until he found the two scrapbooks he wanted. He dusted them off, put them in a paper bag, and hurried down the stairs. He waved to Earl, then drove the Caddy home.

Inside the house, he placed the scrapbooks on the coffee table in the living room, then went to the kitchen and poured two fingers of Basil Hayden's Kentucky Straight bourbon into a Waterford crystal tumbler, no ice in whisky this good. He took the drink and bottle back to the scrapbooks. He sat on the couch, which, like all the other upholstered furniture, was covered in custom-fitted clear plastic. Brigid's call. The plastic got hot and stuck to you, but beneath the plastic, the thirty-five-year-old fabric was like new, the colors of the leaf design sharp and clear.

Dan sipped the whisky, noticed wistfully that "whiskey" with an *e* on the bottle was spelled incorrectly. It was Brigid who'd taught him that only Irish whiskey was rightfully spelled with an *e*.

The house was a two-bedroom 1922 Spanish stucco. It had a red-tile roof and hardwood floors. There was a large service porch at the rear, but there was only one bathroom. That made for hectic times when the kids were little. It was worse when Mary Cat was learning about makeup and boys. Dan had lived his happiest days here. Now it was worth ten times what he'd paid for it, but he had no one to leave it to.

Dan opened the first scrapbook. Pages of photos led him through his amateur career. A forgotten Manila envelope contained photos of Tim Pat as a baby in the arms of his mother and father the day he was baptized at Christ the King; as a toddler peeking out from under the kitchen table; and as a freckle-faced, green-eyed tyke in his first-grade school uniform, two front teeth missing. Dan touched his eye. At the bottom of the stack, one photo showed Tim Pat wearing golden headgear and a pair of huge boxing gloves. He was in the ring during the Silver Gloves tournament at the American Legion Hall in Carson, his hand raised in victory. His was the only white face in the picture, the mostly Mexican crowd in the background on its feet applauding him. It was the last photograph of him ever taken. He'd won with his hook.

Dan had to put the photo of Tim Pat away. He tossed off the last of his whisky, and reached again for the bottle, wanted more burn, was about to fill the tumbler full.

Dan took the bottle and glass back to the kitchen, rinsed the glass. He returned to the couch and the second scrapbook, and then sat for a half hour before he opened it. Then he quickly flipped through the photos and clippings of his pro career. Next came the shots taken of him in the dressing room of the Olympic Auditorium prior to his fight with Chicky's grandfather. Brigid had saved the program. There were two ten-round "main events" scheduled that night, his fight the second one, the one people had come to see, the last fight of the night.

Dan took a deep breath, then turned the page. The next photo showed him standing alone in his corner waiting for the opening bell. In the corner across the ring from him, also standing and waiting, was Eloy Garza, the Lobo Tejano. As in all main events, both fighters were wearing new gloves, pristine red things that glistened under the lights.

The black-and-white film played out in his mind. Suddenly it was sharper than ever, as if a new, fresh print had been made from the negative of his memory.

Cooley threw and connected with the first six shots of the fight. He knocked Garza back into the ropes, where one of Garza's knees buckled. Cooley thought for sure that he'd be going home early, but Garza used the ropes to launch himself back into Cooley's face with a stiff jab. Garza also began firing power shots without caution, one after the other after the other, bang, bang, bang. Cooley slipped and countered, stuck and moved, and Garza was unable to tag him cleanly.

Garza looked like a four-round fighter in there, not a ten, and missed three more power shots that tangled his feet and made him stumble. He took two more stinging Cooley jabs, but slipped the third, and like a football player, Garza used his shoulder and elbows to force Cooley into the corner. He threw more power punches, landing punishing shots where Cooley's shoulders and chest joined, then landed a left hook that almost knocked Cooley's mouthpiece out. This was a Tex-Mex street fight.

Cooley tried to look over to Shortcake, his trainer and chief second, who squatted on the steps leading up to Cooley's corner, but Cooley's eyes were scrambled and he couldn't line up the lights and the shadows. The line on Garza was that he fought with his face; that he waded in throwing punches from all angles, but lost power from lack of balance and leverage; that his relentless attack took opponents out with an accumulation of punches rather than with one big shot; that he'd fade as the fight wore on. But the line on Garza was no longer straight, and Cooley couldn't decipher the rules of the new game. Pain stung him like a bamboo cane to a bare leg.

Garza was so busy throwing punches that he hadn't seen Cooley's body go slack, hadn't realized that he'd missed an opportunity for a quick KO. But his corner men, Trini and Paco Cavazo, had seen it, saw Cooley as a toasted marshmallow, and congratulated each other.

"Está a puro chingazo, mano." He's fucked completely, my brother.

"¡Ay-yai-yai!" whooped Paco.

Shortcake saw it just as the Cavazos had, and signaled with his pumping left hand for Cooley to jab out of the corner. Cooley stuck his jab and moved free. He pivoted, then fired a lead right hand and then a left hook behind it that hurt Garza, but Garza came on anyway. Cooley had been hit in his career, all fighters get hit, but he had never before felt as if a tenpenny nail had been driven into his jawbone. He shoved his glove into his cheek as if he had an abscessed tooth, looked for his blood on the glove, saw none, and went back to work. Hit and don't get hit, Cooley reminded himself, yet he was not at all sure how Garza had even hit him, much less hurt him so badly.

But this is the first round, Cooley also told himself, the round in which fighters are most easily knocked out, that time in the fight where they are not yet *completely warmed up, when they are most vulnerable to shock, when they can lose their legs. He got on his bicycle, pivoted off the front leg, off the back, thought that Garza would tire himself from throwing and missing so many heavy punches, that Garza's legs and wind would go from the movement Cooley imposed on him.*

Garza continued to miss, and Cooley put bumps on him with his peppering jab and solid right hands, but Garza would come on in a crouch and shove Cooley into the ropes with his elbows and fire his heavy artillery. Cooley, if for only two or three seconds, was unable to block or slip all of Garza's punches, especially the body rockets that tore into his liver and ribs and edged illegally around to his kidneys. Cooley knew he could take a shot with the best, had learned that time and adrenaline would erase damage, that the desire to win overcame pain, knew that pissing red looked worse than it felt, believed that he could always go one more round.

Survive this, *Cooley told himself,* then go out and fuck this Mexican up.

But the body shots in the next round left him gasping, the ball-peen hammers in Garza's fists made Cooley's ribs and sternum creak, caused spasms from his knees to his elbows. He was in the best condition of his life, so how could this be? Pain usually came after the fight was over, the delay of pain part of what made fighting possible. Pain had good manners, normally waited until after the dance before it came to collect, waited for the dressing room or the hotel before it invaded the jaw or the knuckles or head or lower back, then throbbed all night, diminishing with codeine when available, or diminishing with the heart rate as it ambled back down to its usual forty to fifty beats a minute. Pain could disappear overnight, or last for days, or maybe you went to the hospital for two weeks, or maybe the ring doctor stretched you on the floor in the back room of an old arena and stitched an eye that was cut to the bone, the hole long as an eyebrow, pain paying its visit only after the hypodermic needle's wet miracle had worn off, and then even your teeth hurt.

But Cooley was in torment now, and this didn't make sense. Cooley's distraction allowed Garza to pound him with more hammers. Cooley fought back, cut Garza's eye, but then he felt his first bone break as Garza caught him with a right hand to the face just before the end of the third round. It broke Cooley's nose, set his face on fire, felt as if hot coffee had been thrown into his eyes. His nose went sideways, spurted raspberry down and across his chest that mixed with sweat collected in the hair. The cracking-bone sound banged against Cooley's eardrums, warned him that it might be best not to engage further in this activity.

Shortcake was able to slow, but not completely stop, the blood, and Cooley began to doubt himself. As long as a boxer can fight back, he can hang—can keep on if he believes that he can give as good as he gets. In that equation, his body tells him it won't betray him—his trusted, beautiful body—the body that has been as loyal to him as first love. But when damage is not returned to the other fighter in equal measure, pain conquers. It leads to fatigue and to doubt and to despair and to loss. And suddenly the other guy's hand goes into the air. And then the beaten fighter goes home feeling lower than whale shit.

The only thing for Cooley was to jab and pivot off the ropes, get to the center of the ring and stay there. He caught Garza with a right hand as Garza came in with his Mexican hook wide as a barn door. Since Cooley landed first, it was Garza who went down on his ass, but Cooley knew it could have been the other way around. His vision was still blurred from the cracked nose, and he couldn't make out how badly Garza was hurt, but he pressed with his own power once Garza was up, fired a power hook off a jab. Garza managed to slip under Cooley's hook, and pie-eyed as a stumbling drunk, grabbed and held. Cooley struggled to pull free, could now feel how badly Garza was hurt, suddenly knew again that he could knock him out. But Garza clung to him like paint, held on stumbling and grappling to keep Cooley from knocking him out with another straight right.

The bell rang, and the ref checked Cooley's bleeding nose, then allowed him to return to his corner.

Cooley said, "They won't stop it, will they?"

Shortcake said, "Naw!," but he was guessing and hoping more than stating a fact.

Cooley's cut man first cleaned him, then went after the inside of the busted nose with adrenaline-drenched swabs. He saturated number 2 cotton rolls, the kind dentists use to absorb a patient's saliva, with more adrenaline using some *of Cooley's blood to camouflage them, he bent them double, and then shoved one up each nostril and illegally left them there. The adrenaline woke Cooley up.*

The cut man said, "Don't breathe through your nose."

Cooley said, "I can't anyway."

Shortcake said, "What if the cotton come out and the ref shit?"

The cut man said, "I tell him I forgot 'em up there, what's he gonna do?"

The cut man slapped an ice bag over Cooley's eyes and nose and applied pressure to his upper lip, and for the time being, stopped the blood cold.

Shortcake knelt in front of Cooley, spoke quietly. "You gotta stay away from him, baby, this a hard man, fight him from outside, hyuh?, keep him at the end of your punches."

Dan said, "Somethin's fishy, right?"

Shortcake said, "Yeah, dass right, he too slow to be hittin so hard."

"He don't feel slow."

In the fourth, Garza tried to stay in Cooley's nose, but Cooley bobbed and weaved, countered and slipped. The bent cotton rolls remained lodged in place, and the blood flow was reduced, but the pain was as sharp as ever, and Cooley's tear ducts kept his vision goofy, and having to breathe improperly sapped his strength. When the shots kept coming to the face, and Cooley tried to block them, Garza went to the body with the ball-peen hammers again. Cooley felt something give in his ribs, wasn't sure if it was a separation or a break. Garza came back with another left to the ribs, and Cooley felt something crack on his right side, sensed it in his spine, gagged, had to fight off shock like it was another opponent. Cut flesh doesn't hurt like broken bone. Stab and horn wounds cause delayed hurt, but broken bones are quick as a bumblebee bite, and Cooley's face twisted as he lost his ability to keep his right hand up for protection.

This time Garza saw that he had Cooley hurt. He began to fire wildly, mindlessly, left himself wide open again. Cooley felt the opening more than he saw it, came up with a Philadelphia hook—half uppercut, half hook—put Garza down again. This time Garza stayed down until the last second, the count of nine. While he was down, Cooley looked to one of the time clocks that hung on opposite walls of the old arena. Visible time clocks were still common, there to help the crowd judge the progress of the fight, but fighters would cop looks hoping that the round was about to end. Cooley looked. A whole minute remained. The first two minutes of the round had felt like twenty. The next one minute loomed like sixty, and dreading that, he began to wonder if Garza had somehow fooled the ring officials, wondered if Garza'd slipped rolls of dimes into his gloves, or maybe steel roller bearings. Cooley shook it off. A roll of coins could fracture a dirty fighter's knuckles and metacarpals as quickly as he could break his opponent's jaw, maybe sooner, and the gauze and the tape around the knuckles and palms would prevent him from closing his hands properly, especially if he was a lightweight who had small hands.

The crowd bellowed and roared and crowed, Mick and Mex together, but Cooley heard only Shortcake yelling for him to finish Garza off.

"Get him, Danny, put him asleep, baby, one-two hook to the body come back hook to the head knock him out le's go home! Do it!"

The ref waved the fighters together. Cooley knew he had to get Garza, knew it because his body had turned to broken glass inside, knew that he could never go the distance hauling the damage Garza had done to him. Garza, demoralized himself, couldn't understand what was holding Cooley up.

The bell rang, ending the round. Both men coughed from deep in the chest. As Cooley wobbled to his corner, he thought again of the rolls of dimes.

Cooley sat on his ring stool and said, "Somethin's wrong, Cake, somethin's hard in those gloves."

Shortcake said, "Boy, you been hittin him more than he been hittin you."

Cooley said, "Look at me and look at him. Gotta be somethin inside the gloves."

Shortcake yelled at the ref, said Garza had loaded his gloves, said he wanted Garza's gloves cut off. He knew the ref wouldn't delay the fight, would think he was trying to steal some rest for his fighter, but he wanted the complaint on the record.

The referee scowled. "I been doin Cooley a favor lettin it go this long, right? Now take that packin outta his nose, you think I didn't see it?"

Shortcake squatted back in front of Cooley, "Muhfuh," he said, and picked out the cotton. "You got to fight him, kid."

Both fighters made it to the fifth, and both were used up, but it was Cooley who was broken and lumpy and turning blue in spots. He couldn't believe Garza was breaking him down. Cooley knew he was the better fighter, knew that he hit harder. He'd known that Garza was no chump, but he also knew that his own style should have sapped Garza's will, should have siphoned off his wind, should have stolen Garza's ability to hang. Yet here they were, in round number five, and it was Cooley who was sucking wind, it was his five-and-six-punch combinations that had been stolen. He knew that he should have stopped Garza by now, but he hadn't, and now all he had left to go on was tit.

They were halfway into the fifth when Cooley was turned sideways by a left hook to the body that frightened him for the first time in his fighting life. He felt more bones creak and shiver, and the stabbing pain of the rib that was already broken caused him to groan. He instinctively dropped his right hand in an effort to protect his body, but then a hook to the head landed and he heard the bones breaking at the outside of his right eye, the sound like a cracked claw. Sweat and blood from his nose headed sideways again, and so did the vision in his right eye. The white area of the eyeball turned crimson from internal bleeding, and the eye and right side of Cooley's face swelled immediately, looked like a sweet potato had been slipped in under the skin. Pain tore through the eyeball and the shattered socket and into Cooley's soul. Blind in one eye, Cooley fought on, as fighters who are fighters will, fought a brown shadow and a smear of black hair, but Cooley's legs were almost gone and he knew he had only seconds left if he was to win.

Garza had forgotten defense early on, and Cooley was able to catch him with a liver shot that made Garza keen. Cooley thought he might still win if he could catch that liver again, but another Garza left hook from Cooley's blind side broke more bones in the eye socket. Cooley sagged, caught himself. Because of the busted rib, he had to use one glove to lift the other up to protect the socket from more damage. But he also covered part of his left eye in the process, and was clearly unable to see the punches Garza was throwing at him. The referee slid in to stop the fight, and Cooley dropped to one knee as Garza raised both hands in victory. The Cavazos rushed in to lift the Lobo Tejano into the air.

The side of Cooley's face continued to swell, looked like something dead alongside a country road. His cut man sat him on his ring stool, wrapped his head in the icy wet towel from the bottom of his ice bucket. The glove attendant removed Garza's gloves, then removed Cooley's, and left the ring. Cooley was exhausted, almost in shock, but even before the ring announcer could proclaim Garza the victor, Shortcake yelled for the ring doctor. Shortcake also called to the referee and demanded that Garza's hand wraps be inspected. The ref waved Garza over while the Cavazos were still cutting off the wraps. Shortcake and the ref examined them.

The ref said, "You satisfied?"

Shortcake said, "No, I ain't, I wanna see them gloves."

The ref sent one of the Commission guys for the glove man with instructions to bring Garza's gloves.

Trini Cavazo said, "What the fuck is this shit, man, what you sayin about my boy?"

Shortcake said, "Look at my boy face, that the shit I be talkin 'bout, what you think?"

Garza was announced the winner, and the Mexicans in the balcony began to hoot and to pegar sus gritos—"¡Ay-yai-yai-yaaaai!"—and to piss in their beer cups and shower them gleefully down on ringside.

Garza's gloves were produced. They were wet with sweat, but they were the same as new and neither had been altered, and both had clearly been used only once.

Shortcake made a last try. "Ain't no goddamn blood on 'em."

The glove guy said, "I wiped it off, like always."

Cooley, the icy towel still around his head, was already thinking of a re-match. With only one good eye, he could see Garza's gloves well enough from his stool to believe that Garza had won fairly. But he wouldn't concede defeat—as he saw it, he had beaten himself. Given the fury of the fight, and the way he had covered up, if only for an instant, Cooley realized that he had thrown in the towel on himself, had accidentally signaled the ref that he was defenseless. He hadn't meant to, had in fact believed that he could still win, yet he was the dummy who, in the blink-second of lost concentration and a broken rib, had forced the referee to stop the fight.

That one moment would eat at Cooley. It would whack him more than missing his shot at the title. It would torment him more than having to retire from boxing. It was a nightmare he could never wake up from, and he would live the rest of his life brooding about being too soft for the hard game.

Chapter 35

Chicky's plane landed at two-thirty P.M. San Antonio time, and he immediately called Greyhound for the Corpus schedule. The next bus wouldn't leave for two hours, so there was nothing to do but head for downtown and wait.

He took a city bus from the airport to the Main Plaza, the Plaza de las Islas. He stopped to pray for Eloy at the Spanish colonial Cathedral of San Fernando, where a marble sarcophagus held the remains of Travis, Crockett, and Bowie. Afterward, he thought about walking over to the San Ignacio Gym, where he'd won many of his trophies. He decided against it, because those *pinches* fuck brothers, Trini and Paco Cavazo, might be back from Houston, those *hijos de la gran chingada puta madre*, sons of the great fucked whore mother. So he strolled over to the bus station, sat on a bench, and tried to steel himself against the shock that might be in store for him in Poteet.

Chicky's bus left the blue-and-white Greyhound terminal in San Anto about the same time that Dan opened the first scrapbook. Before heading down to Corpus Christi and the Gulf, the bus would stop at the country towns of Floresville and Pleasanton, both big growers of peanuts. Eloy's farm in Poteet was some sixteen miles down from Pleasanton, off of Highway 16 and at the end of an oil-soaked private road. Poteet was smaller than Pleasanton.

A sign on the road read "Don't Mess with Texas." Chicky could feel in the air that he was getting close to home, and he began to remember little things and big. But mostly he remembered the day when things began to change, the day his grandfather was late coming back from the doctor. Chicky realized that he was almost back to where he'd started. Nonetheless, he thought back to how mortified he'd been when Dan discovered his connection with his sick granddaddy, the Wolf.

"You come a long way, cowboy," Chicky whispered.

When *el bus* stopped at the Exxon station in Pleasanton, Chicky put on his El Patron. There were no cabs, so he took Texas highway number 242 and lit out on foot. Poteet high school was some nine miles off, but it was on the way to his granddaddy's farm, and that was a good six to seven miles more. Chicky figured he could make the high school in an hour if he humped, but it turned out that he didn't have to walk. He got a ride from a weathered peanut farmer in a frazzled straw farm hat and faded bib overalls.

They passed the Atascosa River, narrow and all but dry, and then the farmer headed down empty roads and let Chicky off at the high school. Chicky took off straight for the football field. Practice was winding down. Coach Oster waved him over. Though Chicky had been small for football, the thick, big-bellied old coach knew him as one of the hardest-hitting defensive backs who had ever played for Poteet. Hitting hard wasn't something a Texas football coach forgot.

Coach Oster shook Chicky's hand and asked, "You need a lift, boy?"

"Yessir," said Chicky. This was Texas, and in Texas you talked Texas. "If it wouldn't be no bother."

"Hail, no."

The coach blew his whistle, spots of brass showing through the worn chrome plate. He waved his players to the showers, then motioned Chicky over to his sun-bleached '82 pickup.

Oster shook his head, said, "Big bad Wolf ain't the same, son."

"No?"

"Y'all'll see."

They drove to Eloy's peeling, white clapboard house. It was set between low trees and trimmed in layers of buckled green and strawberry red. It sagged at one corner, and one end of the big "Lobo Farms" sign out front hung loose from its rusted frame. Part of the sign depicted a smiling wolf in bib overalls standing upright in the faded reds and greens of a strawberry field, but now the wolf had become a dull gray. The front section of the picket fence was on its side. Prairie dogs had taken over the lawn. The barn door was closed, the chicken pen empty, and every other animal was gone as well. Eloy's dirty 1964 Chevy flatbed, his first truck ever, was parked near the open side door of the house. Chicky stood at the door and called out, "¡Abuelito!"

Eloy's voice sounded weak as a poisoned cat. "Door's open, ain't it?"

Coach Oster looked back to Chicky. "Wont some help with this here deal?"

"I better handle it."

"I understand," said the coach, a sigh in his whisper. "Ya'll call me, hear?"

"Yessir," Chicky said. He hoped he could handle it, but wasn't sure.

Oster heard the doubt. "Maybe I better hang around, just in case?"

Chicky said, " 'Preciate it."

Chicky walked in and Oster followed him. What was once as neat as a priest's parlor was now strewn with newspapers and unwashed tin cans. This was not the place Chicky had grown up in, the place he had learned to keep respectable, the place where he had learned to scrub floors. The kitchen sink was full of dirty paper plates. Uneaten food had gone to garbage on the tile counter. Roaches scurried, and the place stank of black bananas. Fruit flies hovered like a lace fan, and the place smelled like death.

"Grandpa?"

"I'm here."

The voice came from the bathroom, located down a short hall. The floor tiles and those in the shower had always sparkled, but now the grout was gray and there was black mold halfway up the shower wall. Eloy sat on the toilet wearing long johns. His head was in his hands, his face had caved in, and his bent body listed into the wall.

Between the toilet and the wall was a rusted old pink oval waste-paper basket. In it were several used syringes and six of Trini's empty twenty-milliliter squat brown morphine bottles. They were Eloy's last, and he was ready to die. He tried to flush the toilet, but didn't have the strength. He smiled bleakly and with shame at Chicky, his gums showing instead of false teeth. He mixed Spanish with English, and Chicky answered him likewise.

"Lost my teeth somewheres." The whites of his eyes were a dull yellow, and so was his skin. His diseased liver had caused his feet to swell so badly that he hadn't worn boots in weeks, forcing him to drive to and from the hospital in flip-flops. "I figure I've had about all the fun I can stand."

"How long you been on the stool?"

"Been sleepin here is all I know. Can you get me to bed?"

"I can he'p ya with him," said Coach Oster, standing off to the side just in case.

Chicky got the old man to his feet. He was emaciated except for a bulge in his stomach the size of a pumpkin. Chicky buttoned the flap of his grandfather's soiled underwear, then picked him up, not needing Coach Oster's help after all. Eloy didn't weigh ninety pounds. His skin was flaky, and his sparse gray hair was greasy and long. Chicky eased the old man down to sheets that hadn't been changed in months, then made the sign of the cross.

"We got to get you to the hospital."

Eloy said, "I was in the Santa Rosa two weeks ago."

Chicky said, "Then what the dickens you doin back home?"

"Checked myself out once me'n Doc Ocampo had us a sit-down."

"What'd Ocampo say?"

"Same's before. *Que me han chingado el hígado y el pinche corazón.*" That my own liver and fuckin heart have screwed me.

"You never told me," Chicky said, looking away.

Eloy shrugged his bony shoulders, tried to smile. *"Son cosas de la vida."* He winked at Oster. "Coach, I wonder if you could dump that trash basket in the crapper for me? I think I got me a varmint loose in it."

"Glad to," said Oster.

When Oster saw the syringes and morphine bottles in the pink can, he understood why Eloy had asked him to remove it.

"Don't worry, Eloy," Coach Oster said under his breath. "Chicky'll never find out from me."

Oster dumped the bottles and the needles into a black plastic bag, and stashed the bag in the back of his truck. He reached for his can of Copenhagen, and figured it was best to remain where he was, but then he put the dip away and decided to go back inside. He winked at Eloy, and Eloy understood.

Eloy said, "How you like trainin with Mr. Cooley?"

"A lot."

"Psycho Sykes is up to eighteen and zero with eleven KOs," Eloy said. "I been followin the boy's career somewhat close."

Chicky said, "You'n me both."

"Got too big for welter. He's fightin at one fifty-four now."

"Don't I know it?"

Eloy squinted, his yellow eyes dull. "What's your record again?"

"I'm nine and three, with six KOs. The three losses come before Mr. Cooley. I'm six knockouts out of nine with him."

"I told you he was good."

Chicky couldn't shake the smell and returned to the bathroom. The reeking toilet was full of white feces and coffee-colored urine. Chicky gagged as he flushed the toilet, then opened the bathroom and bedroom windows for ventilation.

Chicky gave his grandfather a sip of water. "Why didn't you stay in the hospital?"

"Because home is where my wife died."

Chicky thought of his Mamá Lola, her Indian eyes and nose, the copper in her skin. He lowered his eyes as he remembered how tenderly she had cared for him. Swinging his eyes back to Eloy he said, "But now we got to bundle you up good, and get you back to the Santa Rosa."

"*No'mbre,*" no man, the old man said. He looked away from the kid, then back again. "You really okay with Mr. Cooley?"

Chicky nodded. "Next to you, he's the best."

"Naw, he's better'n me," said Eloy. "He figured out who we was to each other, didn't he?"

"It was Coach's call what did it."

Eloy said, "How long't take him?"

" 'Bout a minute, once Coach called you the Wolf," Chicky said. "How come you didn't tell me about how you knew Mr. Cooley?"

Eloy evaded the question, wheezed out a snicker. "I got the Cavazos thinkin you're up College Station goin to A & M. They think you gave up *el box.*"

Chicky said, "Ain't you the slick old dawg."

"*Wolf,*" Eloy said slyly, "slick old *Wolf.* Game ain't played out yet, rat?"

Chicky locked hard on Eloy's eyes, repeated his earlier question, "So how come you didn't tell me about you and Mr. Cooley?"

Eloy hacked, his lungs shot. "I wanted you goin to him clean, son, and I wanted him to take you on when he saw how good you are."

Chicky said, "That he did."

Eloy said, "How hard is it getting the right fights out there?"

"Hard, now that I been winnin."

"I warned you 'bout bein a lefty in the pros, rat?" Eloy watched as

Chicky nodded, then said, "You still got a hard-on over that Psycho Sykes deal?"

"Hail, yeah," said Chicky, "and will have for a spell. But each dawg has his day, and rat now you're what counts."

Eloy pointed to a card table on which there was a large package. It was amateurishly wrapped in shiny paper, and tied loosely with ribbons and a stick-on bow, all used Christmas wrappings saved from years before. "It's for you."

"What is it?"

"You'll see later." He pointed to a thick brown envelope sealed with clear tape that set next to the alarm clock.

Chicky picked it up. Two words, "DAN COOLEY," were scrawled large.

"That's for Mr. Cooley," Eloy said. "Don't you never open it before you give it to him, hear?"

Chicky said, "You'll give it to him yourself. We'll get you fixed up and I'll take you on back to L.A. with me."

Eloy dismissed the idea, turning down his mouth. He spoke formally. "You don't open the envelope, understand?"

"Yessir."

Eloy struggled to get the words out. "You put it in Mr. Cooley's hand directly. You say it is from me. Use my name, say the Lobo Tejano sent 'em, Eloy Garza, you understand?"

"*Simón*," Chicky said, but uppermost in his mind was how to keep his granddaddy alive.

Eloy said, "Coach Oster's helped me with my paperwork, and all. The ranch'll be yours to do what you want with. There's some money left if you want to jump-start it after fightin."

"I only care about getting you back in the saddle."

"And I only care about you."

————

Eloy died in the night. His legs were off the bed, but bent up underneath him, as if he was trying to beat the count. Chicky had Eloy's rosary and funeral mass held at the little carrot-colored brick church of St. Philip Binizi in Poteet. Eloy went into the ground next to his Lolita, at the First Memorial Cemetery, where there were names like von Uffen, de la O, and Indian Pete. Chicky wept openly as he sprinkled dirt on the coffin, bronze and snazzy, an image of Our Lady of Guadalupe etched the length of the lid. Inside was Chicky's 30X El Patron.

"Don't forget me, Grandpa," said Chicky. "Be good to him, Virgencita," he added, touching the image of Guadalupe. He looked heavenward. "Have mercy on him, Lord. On him and on me."

Chicky wondered where all this would take him. He thought of the Cavazo brothers and Psycho Sykes. He thought of his passbook. He clenched his teeth and felt rage run through him like a powerful electric current.

Chapter 36

Sitting by himself in his office, Dan listened to the two short tapes that he'd found in the package Chicky had brought from the Lobo Tejano. Eloy had recorded them on a mini-cassette recorder he had borrowed from Coach Oster.

The voice on the tape frequently faltered, and Dan realized that Eloy was often turning away to cough and hack things up, but the words came from a soul so long without God that even Dan, despite himself, felt a chill.

"Dear Mr. Cooley. This here's Eloy Garza. Used to be the Texas Wolf, remember me? No wolf no more.

"I was afraid of you, Mr. Cooley, and I wronged you. See, I didn't think I could beat you. So when a way come to me outside the rules to get at you, I took it. I never shouldda done it, but I did. It's 'cause I wanted so bad to be champion. But I stole my title shot from you, so it never done me no good. You know how I got whipped.

"See, what I did, I let the Cavazo brothers take the padding across my knuckles out from the inside of my gloves. That's how come I was able to bust you up. Afterward, the glove guy at the Olympic switched good gloves for mine, so nobody'd know. For a price."

On the first tape, Eloy explained that he had bought the farm just before his fight with Dan. He was flushed with confidence after all his wins as a barnstorming young boxer fighting his way across northern Mexico, through Texas, and west to New Mexico, north to Nevada, and west again out to California. He hadn't started to make real money until he hooked up with the Cavazos, and when he did, he thought he'd died and gone to heaven.

From the time he was a boy, he'd worked the fields, but he'd also, with his daddy's help early on, raised *ganado,* cattle. Cattle money, along with money he'd earned in the ring, had helped him buy the farm in Poteet. After the ass whipping he took in his shot at the title, he'd retired from the ring to raise strawberries full-time.

But now, he admitted, there was very little left of the farm, and nothing left of him, only shame and the expectation of a slow liver death. The farm had been good—he'd built it with his own hands from a weedy field into acres of something respectable.

But there was that one moment of *traición* in Los Angeles when he'd bought Trini's guarantee for a win over Dan Cooley, that moment of treachery to steal a title shot when he'd sold his *huevos,* when he'd become *un vendido.* The way Trini had put it, Eloy could slip around behind the rules—it was just once, after all—and then he could go back to being the same man he'd always been.

There was a long pause at the end of the tape. In the background Dan could hear some noise. Maybe a toilet flushing, he thought. Then Eloy came back on.

"I can't ask you for forgiveness, Señor Cooley. I can't lay it all on Trini or Paco. Hell, I coulda said no to the whole damn thing. Or I could have told you a long time ago."

Eloy was wracked by a spasm of coughing before he could continue.

"Course I knew, and all these years I ain't ever been able to live it down. You'da had me out in four rounds if I hadn't done what I did. You'da clean knocked *out* the champ. Yessir, I'm who ruined your life, Mr. Cooley, I took the title from you before you ever even got your shot.

But I want you to know that I ruined myself, too. It don't matter about me. I got what I had comin. But not you. You deserved better. I acted yeller, Mr. Cooley. I tried not to own up to it forty years now, 'cause I couldn't face it like the man I once was, like the man my Chicky is.

"God bless you for what you done for him. And please forgive me for what I done to you, if you can, for I am dreadful sorry for it. Please, sir."

Dan sat silently for five minutes, and then his laugh came out like a bark. There was glee in it, not fury and spite, no desire to desecrate the Wolf's grave. "Yes! They had to cheat me to beat me, the sonsabitches! I *was* hard enough! I'da won the goddamn title, I'da won three fookin titles!"

Dan felt no bitterness toward Eloy. Instead, he wished he could call him and thank him for telling the truth, for letting him know at last, but of course it was too late for that. He wanted to pray for Eloy, too, but he couldn't do that, either.

Dan played Eloy's second tape.

"It's me again, Mr. Cooley. It's about Chicky getting a shot at Psycho Sykes. No way'll he fight a southpaw, and no way'll the Cavazos let him fight somebody with a good record. And no way'll they fight Chicky Garza. What you gotta do is turn Chicky *Irish*. You know how light-skinned he is. See, his other family name is Duffy, comes from the Irish side that goes way back.

"And switch Chicky to a right-hander, too. Dye his hair blond or red. Call him Irish Eddie Duffy.

"It's just a idea, and I don't wont seem like I'm buttin in. But I know you could switch the kid to the other side if anybody can. Just three, maybe four rounds of it. Once everyone's into the fight, and maybe it looks like Sykes is winnin, let Chicky switch back to lefty. I don't see it as too tricky a deal, but Sykes and the Cavazos won't know they been reamed until it's too late. I wont 'em reamed, Mr. Cooley. Wont 'em reamed bad, both the Cavazos and Sykes, too.

"So you'll know, and Chicky, too, if you let him hear this here tape, Trini and Paco stole Chicky's passbook, and that's how they kept him out of the Texas Regionals so Sykes could win. I knew about it, but kept my trap shut 'cause I was afraid for Chicky, but most 'cause I was a fuckin' coward. Sykes won from my kid on a walkover, and went on to the Nationals, but Sykes couldn't make it to the Olympic team. Chicky wouldda *won* the *pinche* Olympics.

"I can only imagine how low you think I am by now, but this is my last chance to square things, so I'm pukin it out.

"*Que Dios te bendiga,* may God bless you. Thank you again for what you're doin for my kid. I just hope you can, well, you know, maybe not think too bad of me.

"*Adiós* . . . old . . . friend."

Eloy's voice held until the end, then broke just before he hit the stop button.

Dan made up his mind right after the second tape finished. Chicky had no need to know about any of Eloy's confession, how the Cavazo brothers had screwed him, then screwed Chicky all those years later. The passbook scam—all that was in the past and nothing could be done about it now. Chicky was riled up enough about Sykes; telling him *how* he had been screwed was just going to make the boy crazy. And that was the last thing anybody needed. It was going to be hard enough to pull it off. He needed a fighter who could think, not a fighter who would go into the ring like some mad bull.

Eloy had given him the answer. The more he thought about it, the more he was convinced it would work. He began to lay out a plan, first about how much to tell Chicky, then about the Wolf's idea. He wondered if Earl would buy into it. Wondered if Earl should know anything about what was on the first tape. Not now, he decided. Maybe someday, and only if he couldn't avoid sharing Eloy's shame with his partner.

Dan stood up and put both tape cassettes on the floor. He stomped on them, crushing the black plastic. Then he stripped out the tangle of brown tape. He scooped up the wreckage. Later tonight he would take some gas, douse the tapes, and set them on fire. For the moment he stuffed them in the bottom drawer of his desk.

Suddenly the familiar pain knifed through him. He couldn't seem to catch his breath and felt dizzy. Ah God, not now, Dan thought. He sat down in his chair and inhaled—long, slow breaths through his nose. Then he breathed out through his mouth, letting it come out in a gentle stream, his lips pursed as if he were whistling. He gripped his left wrist in his right hand and took his pulse. It was high, skipping beats. Kogon had warned him about arrhythmia. Not a good sign. He forced himself to continue the breathing exercise until his pulse rate slowed down and the dizziness seemed to recede. But when he stood up, he took two steps before he collapsed back into the chair. Not now, damnit! Not now! Give it time. Buy time.

Dan walked down the stairs clutching the railing. Chicky was sitting on a wooden crate, looking out into space. When he saw Dan, he jumped up.

"What . . . ?"

Dan held up his hand.

"Sit down and listen up. Your grandpa told me all about the bad luck you had, how they lost your passbook and then this bum Sykes got a walkover. You want another shot at Sykes?"

"Sure do! But how's that goin to happen?"

"Well, Eloy just told me how!"

Dan cleared out the gym, sent the other fighters off to work elsewhere, and began to train Chicky to fight from the right. The switch was smooth and quick. Now that he had someone who knew how to teach him the science of it, Chicky's feet began to make the right moves without his mind even having to think about it. Momolo was there to spar with him, run with him, cheer him on.

Two months later, Dan took Earl off to the side. "It's now, or never, what do you think?"

"It's now."

Dan and Earl put Chicky into a half dozen fights, spacing them a month to two months apart, depending on the competition. Most of them were down in Mexico, two in Colorado. No fight tapes. Each fight was tougher than the last. The last of the six was a ten-rounder that only went eight. Chicky won them all, three by KO, which gave him a record of only five and three, but his real pro record added up to fifteen and three, and eleven KOs. Chicky fought four more ten-round fights as Eddie Duffy. Dan's instructions were to go for decisions instead of knockouts.

"Too many KOs and Sykes'll duck us."

Following Eloy's scheme, Chicky would eventually be able to meet Sykes for a NABF title, a minor title, but one that would position him subsequently for one of the three majors, WBC, WBA, IBF. But having a plan was one thing; making it work was something else.

Jolly Joe would be able to justify Chicky's "official" record, should there be an inquiry of some kind. Seldom are there inquiries when the underdog whips the favorite.

Aside from going "Irish," Chicky covered himself with removable tattoos. Stars, snakes, panthers, barbed wire around his biceps, a devil's head, etc. And fake body jewelry in his ears and navel. For his fights, he colored his hair green. He wore a Kelly green robe, with a golden harp on the back—the real Irish flag. White fans, especially the Irish, were thrilled, and younger fans of all colors loved him for his outlandish look.

Jolly Joe of the Commission agreed to look the other way after Dan told him about his plan and how Chicky had been set up. The Commission is required to reveal a fighter's real name to the opponent only if the opponent requests it. Virtually no one ever asks for real names, since the press usually puts them out. But because Chicky had had so few stateside fights before the Sykes fight, and would be seen as an "opponent," the press would not catch on until after the sting had stung.

Dan roped in Louie Carbajal to serve as a cutout. It wasn't hard to persuade him after Dan promised Louie the lion's share of the money if "Eddie Duffy" won. Chicky Garza had become a nonperson.

The Cavazo brothers were lured to California on the premise that Eddie Duffy had limited experience, because of the big payday, and because Carbajal, promoter of record, was *raza*. When they first spoke by phone, Carbajal had driven up from Tijuana and was calling from Dan's office.

"*Un maiate y un gabacho*," should draw a big crowd. "Otherwise I wouldn't make the fight. Blacks want another Hurricane Carter, and the Irish are crazy for a new Billy Conn. The rest of the card'll be *mejicano*."

Trini said, "So is it kike or dinge money behind you? Maybe drug money out of Culiacan?"

Louie laid it on, his background information on the Cavazos and Sykes coming from Chicky. "Forty percent my money, but I got the other sixty from gangster Irish guys and their lawyers, who want to take over boxing from the *prietos* and *judíos*."

Trini went for it. "I got me two Texas white asses back here that want the same thing for Texas."

Louie said, "Then you know what I'm talking about. *Pendejos*."

"Fuckers don't even know when they're getting fucked, *ése*. But listen, fifty thousand isn't enough for my boy, not with his name. We gotta have more. And I gotta check out Duffy's record, right?"

"Why not?" Louie said. "And maybe the two of us can share the *salsa*, know what I mean? But that's just between you and me, eh?"

"*Claro.*"

"But Sykes can't fuck around or foul out on me, or it's my head in my ass with these micks, *¿comprendes?*" You understand? "For these Irish *hijos de la chingada*, he's got to fight *a huevo*."

"The nigga'll fight, all right," Trini assured him. "He knows what'll happen to his dick if he don't. Listen, *oye*, can you get me ninety?"

"*Tal vez.*" Maybe.

"Give me your phone number," Trini said, "and I'll get back to you about Duffy's record. If it's what you say, we'll do business."

Louie hung up and shook hands with Dan, who'd been listening to Louie's side of the conversation. Louie said, "He's all shit, *pura mierda*, like you say."

Dan loved it—the icing on the cake. The fight would take place in L.A. Full circle. The Wolf would have been pleased.

With Dan and Earl backing Louie, and putting up all the money for personal expenses and Sykes's big purse, the fight was made for the Olympic Auditorium at sixty-five thousand dollars for Sykes, plus ten thousand dollars for training expenses, under the table to Trini, that was to be split with Louie. Sykes would never know about the "training expense." And Chicky would never know that Dan and Earl were putting up most of their savings plus a secured loan from the Bank of California. They were literally betting the business on Chicky's winning.

Chicky would get twenty-five. "I'd fight him for free, just to get my teeth into him."

"Naw," Earl said. "A man works, a man gets paid."

Chapter 37

Dr. Kogon, Earl, and Chicky were standing in the hall when Father Joe came toward them carrying a small, black, leather-covered case.

"I would have come sooner, but the housekeeper at the rectory doesn't always get messages to me on time. Guess she thinks us old retired guys shouldn't be disturbed."

"Well, *padre*, we just thought . . ." Chicky began to explain.

"Dan isn't doing so well, Father," Kogon said. "We expect a certain percentage of patients to have a rough time after a quadruple bypass. But Dan's problem isn't physical, as far as we can tell. The psychological part of it is another matter. He went into a depression after the angioplasty. This is different. He just isn't fighting—and if he doesn't fight, we can't win."

It was nine days after the match with Sykes. Dan had been in intensive coronary care for six days after the bypass operation. He was now in a private room on the coronary-surgery floor.

"I understand. I have seen this before, many times," Father Joe said with a sigh. "But is he willing—prepared?"

Earl rubbed his eyes; he had not clocked a lot of sleep in the last forty-eight hours.

"Prepared. Well, I don't know. But what he needs is sumpin they don't have here."

Kogon simply nodded his head in agreement and left.

"You must understand," Father Joe said quietly. "This is also a sacrament of healing for many. But only if there is a desire to be healed."

He turned away and went through the door into Dan's room. The blinds were halfway closed, leaving the still figure on the high hospital bed in a kind of twilight. Above the bed was a bank of monitors, green traces running across the screens. In a kind of counterpoint, a faint but regular beeping noise could be heard in the background.

Dan's eyes were closed. An IV bottle was hanging on a stand with a clear plastic tube leading into a butterfly needle in Dan's arm. Another tube was feeding oxygen into Dan's nostrils.

Father Joe pushed aside a carafe of ice water on the top of the table beside the bed. Slowly unzipping his case, he removed two candles and a container of oil for anointment. Before he could remove all of the contents, Dan's eyes suddenly opened. A prayer to the Blessed Mother went through the priest's mind: "Be with us . . . *nunc et in hora* . . . now and at the hour of our death."

He bent over the bed and grasped Dan's hand. He was careful not to touch the tubes running into him.

"My dear friend, can you hear me?"

"All too well. What's that you're up to?"

"I think you know."

"Not now!" Dan seemed to rally and his voice became stronger, more insistent. "So it's my time, is that what yer thinkin?"

"That's in God's hands." The priest paused and then added, "And in yours."

Dan's free hand stirred restlessly on the sheet that covered him.

"No. Not mine!"

Father Joe thought for a moment and asked, "Do you want to make a general confession? It's easy enough. Just ask God's forgiveness for all your sins. Which are probably not as many as you think."

"Ah, I could use a shot of that top-shelf bourbon Brigid used to pour for you, Father!" Dan managed a brief smile. "But it's not God's forgiveness I seek."

Dan had been working with Chicky right up to the week of the fight with Sykes when he'd keeled over with a massive coronary infarction. What saved Dan's ass, at least for the moment, was Earl's giving him mouth-to-mouth. And the paramedics getting there in record time.

Dan had no memory of the lightning bolt that had hit him.

He remembered waking up and looking around. It was a different environment from the "storage room" of the angioplasty. He saw what looked like walls made of dark stripes of amber and black and umber glass separated by strips of gray tilting at a forty-five-degree angle. Where was he? What kind of room would be constructed of umber and amber glass?

Sometime—hours? days?—later he opened his eyes again. The room looked the same. Suddenly the pain was so intense that he could not protect himself from it, could not find a way to slip it, to block it, to counterpunch.

He closed his eyes again, and this time tumbling cubes and cylinders and spheres and rectangles and triangles, isosceles and otherwise, came shooting at him from deep space. He opened and closed his eyes several times to drive off the angles and curves, but they were immediately replaced by other bizarre objects that came hurtling toward and past him in absolute silence.

Once again Dan opened his eyes and tried to survey the room, desperate to focus on something peaceful and familiar, like a typical hospital room. But all he could see was the surrounding space enclosed by the ominous slanted dark glass walls. He closed his eyes. More hurtling geometric objects bursting forth from a black beyond triple black. He sensed that he was hallucinating, but didn't understand that it was caused by drugs. The deadening chemicals flooding his body and brain were no match for this new pain. It was like an animal chewing its way through him.

He wondered if this was the way he was going out, all pissy and cringing. Was this to be his final round? Was this hyena thing rooting inside him what life had had in store for him from the beginning? Why had it waited so long? He'd known from early on that he'd end up six feet under, no surprise there, but in his conceit, he'd always thought he'd be man enough not to whimper and cringe.

Dilaudid had knocked him flat, left him strung out and numb and wet with cold sweat. Oxygen up his nose. An IV in his veins. Heart monitors and electric leads. But none of it helped break the jaws of the thing gorging on his entrails.

Time eluded him. *How long had this business been going on, for Christ's sake? No! Not* Christ's *sake, and not* God's *sake. Not* nobody's *sake, least of all a fiction's.*

The postsurgery pain was so bad for a while that he no longer wished to live. Yet those first days, right next to his bed, there had been an apparatus with a miracle push button. It flooded his IV with sticky sleep, and he willingly used it as often as the pain jolted him awake. If only he hadn't squandered that morphine! If only he had enough left to OD.

Dan was alone with some animal gnawing at his guts. The hallucinations multiplied, and as their hurtling onslaught of unearthly shapes increased, so did the pain. Calvary flickered on and off amid the geometric items.

Christ sure as hell could never have suffered the fucking cross if I can't suffer this. It's lies, all of Him. No one could take that.

Images of thorns and spikes and the mockery of INRI—Jesus of Nazareth, King of the Jews, the crown of thorns, the cup of gall, the spear in

Christ's side. "They have pierced my hands and my feet. They have num-
bered all my bones."

*No, I will not think of this. Fuck Christ. Only I am here, I only. I am God,
yes! But no, no, how could I be God when I am unable to endure this thing that
is happening inside me.*

Dan brushed away the memory of those horrors, returning to the present, to the anxious priest still standing beside his bed, and he looked up.
His mouth was suddenly very dry, but he managed to croak, "Not a general confession, Father. Just one thing."

Afterward, Father Joe came out of the room and walked over to where
Chicky and Earl were slumped in two uncomfortable plastic chairs.

"Who is Lupe?"

Chicky stared at Earl, who was blowing on his steaming-hot coffee, sitting at a table in the nearly deserted hospital cafeteria.

Earl heaved a sigh and said, "She was drivin the car that hit Dan's
grandson. Wasn't her fault—just a damn assident. Tim Pat stepped in
front of her car, no way she could have stopped and not hit him. But he
blames her. Jus' can't stop blamin and they ain't no one to blame in this."

"So why does Dan want to see her?" Chicky asked. He sensed there
was a lot more to the story.

"Well, quite a time 'fore you showed up, this all happened. After the
little boy, Tim Pat, was killed, Dan went kinda crazy. He'd start leavin
the shop all kinds of hours and driving around. I didn't have no idea of
where the hell he was a lot of the time."

Earl paused and took a long gulp of coffee. "You unnerstan' that I was
gettin worried. Then came the mornin I find Dan sittin on the floor
with the Caddy all shot up and I found out what's goin on." Earl didn't

mention the shotgun and the drinking and the suicide stuff. Chicky didn't need to know about that. Nobody did.

"Then he tells me that he's going off on a trip. I figured that be for the best if he went away for a while. I figgered, he wouldn't be . . . well, anyhow, he went off, called me once and a while, said he was in this town or that. No way I could be sure where he really was, but I was pretty sure he was nowhere near L.A. I was still 'fraid that he . . . well, I guess I was afraid *for* him."

Earl told Chicky that he had gone to see Raul Nájera and gotten a copy of the accident report.

"Nájera—he's a good cop, jus' like he was a damn good fighter. He tole me that there was no way this was the girl's fault. Tole me about Dan's makin noises about a cover-up. Dan was lucky—Nájera cut him some slack, 'cuz he understood that kind of crazy grief. Then, all a sudden, Dan, he comes back, lookin like hell and thin enough to see through."

Earl yawned and stretched, then went on. "And then *you* showed up. Well, you was just what Dan Cooley needed. Now he need somebody else."

"Lupe?"

"Yeah," Earl replied. "But I reckon she's not gonna be all that innerested in seein Dan Cooley."

Earl yawned again and shook his head, trying to get rid of the fog of his fatigue.

"Well, we ain't gonna know 'less we try. I got her address," Earl said. "Let's go. You drive. I'll tell you where to go."

Earl stood up and shoved his chair against the table. He wasn't sure just what kind of reception they were going to get when they showed up. But one way or the other, they would persuade her to come.

Earl and Chicky stood at the front door of the Ayala home and pressed the doorbell. They had to wait a long time before the door opened and Lupe's mother confronted them.

She stared at Earl and asked, "Do I know you?"

In that particular close-knit part of L.A., it was unlikely that anyone knew him, a black man where he was not supposed to be. He was glad that Chicky was standing there with him.

"No, ma'am, but I think you know about Dan Cooley."

Chicky removed his hat and said, "Ma'am, this here's Earl Daw. He's Dan's business partner. I work at their shop. My name is Eduardo Garza. We sure would 'preciate a chance to talk to your daughter."

When she heard Chicky's accent, she seemed to relax a little and asked, "What's the reason you want to talk to her?"

Chicky thought fast and said, "Mr. Cooley's real sick and he asked us to send a message to your daughter. I swear to you it ain't nothin bad. If she would just hear us out."

"Well, I have to ask Lupe. It's up to her if she wants to see you."

Before she closed the door, she said, "You just wait here."

Ten minutes passed before the door opened again and Lupe, her mother hovering behind her, appeared. Chicky was almost struck dumb. She was so beautiful. Even the shadows under her eyes, the signs of strain on her face, nothing could hide her radiance.

"What is this message from Mr. Cooley?" she asked, her voice low and hesitant. Chicky addressed her gravely, formally, in his Tex-Mex version of correct Spanish in order to show his respect and, he hoped, create some kind of bond with her.

"*Señorita, Señor Cooley está muy enfermo. El quiere verte. Yo sé que es difícil . . . pero tú le harías un gran favor.*"

Chicky hoped his genuine conviction came through; Dan was very sick. Chicky knew it would be difficult for her, but she would do Dan a great service, *un gran favor.*

Before she could reply, her mother broke in.

"*¿Exactamente cuán grave es la enfermedad?*" Just how sick is he?

"*Puede ser que vaya a morir. Pero creo que si su hija viene a visitarlo en el hospital podría hacer una diferencia bien grande.*" Even as he told the two women that Dan might die, Chicky refused to believe it could happen. But he was also firmly convinced that what he said was true—Lupe's visit really *could* make a great difference, and turn the tide currently running against Dan.

Her mother looked at Lupe and spoke to her softly.

"*Escucha, mi amorcita, tienes que hacerlo. Tal vez puedas ayudar a que este hombre se quite el odio del corazón.*" The decision was up to Lupe; but she must go, try to help Dan get rid of the hatred in his heart.

"*Sí, Mamá, tiene razón. Debo verlo aunque sea para pedirnos perdón.*"

She turned to Earl and explained, "I think my mother is right. I will go with you. Perhaps we can forgive each other."

It seemed to take forever for the elevator to reach the fourth floor. Patients, doctors, and nurses, people pushing food carts, got on and off at every floor. A late afternoon calm had fallen over the hospital. The evening shift was about to come on.

Earl gently took Lupe by the arm and guided her down the hall.

"He don't look so good, Miz Ayala, but don't you worry—he's a tough ol' bird."

He ushered her through the doorway and withdrew. Father Joe sat on the room's only chair, head bowed, stole still around his neck. The priest looked up and said, "*Buenas tardes,* Lupe. I am so very glad that you came."

Dan had been propped up in the bed. The board taped to his arm to support the IV butterfly was sticking out at an awkward angle. Father Joe got up, moved the chair closer to the bed, and invited Lupe to sit down. Gathering her long skirt, she gracefully sat in the chair and looked directly at Dan.

"It's been a long time since I've seen you," Dan said.

"Yes, Mr. Cooley. But long overdue."

"Yes, long overdue."

Each waited for the other to speak. Lupe broke the silence.

"O, Señor Cooley, por favor, perdóname. En el nombre de Dios, perdóname."

Dan did not try to brush away the tears that began to stream from his eyes.

"No, darlin—please forgive *me*."

Slowly Dan extended his hand and Lupe grasped it in hers. They sat there in silence for a few moments and then Lupe gently replaced Dan's hand on the bed.

"You knew I was watching you, you saw me. I was just crazy, just sick with hate. But the truth is, I couldn't forgive myself. Had to blame you. Had to blame God. Put it on anybody but me."

"But I did blame myself," Lupe said, her voice trembling. "I knew what you were feeling, I knew your sorrow."

Leaning close to Dan, Lupe told him about the collision on the Sixth Street Bridge between her father's truck and a stolen car driven by a carjacker. He survived; her father and her two brothers did not. She told him about the trial and its outcome.

"It was for us as for you—a sadness for which there are no words. So when . . ." She hesitated and then gathered her resolve. "When my car hit your grandson, I felt the guilt, the sadness all over again. A thief killed my father and my brothers. But I . . . I was just as guilty. I took the life of your grandson."

Dan saw tears starting to roll down her cheeks and took her hand again.

"Darlin, we can help each other. We can learn to bear the sadness and that blaming ourselves is pointless. For your dad and your brothers . . . for Tim Pat . . . we have to honor them by living and remembering. Child, you have a whole life ahead of you. Don't let grief or guilt or anything stop you from livin that life to the hilt."

Lupe was in a daze when Earl, Father Joe, and Chicky took her down to the hospital cafeteria. As the elevator descended, Lupe looked over at Chicky and asked, "Do you understand what has happened?"

"No, I don't. 'Preciate it if you'd tell me."

The four of them sat down at a table and Father Joe went to get coffee and a pastry for Lupe.

"You know about the accident?"

"Yeah, Earl told me all about it."

Looking directly into Chicky's eyes, Lupe began to talk about the days that followed Tim Pat's death. Without thinking, she switched into Spanish, and the well-worn, informal style of the culture they shared. As he listened, Chicky was thinking of the words one used to speak grandly, from the heart, words he had never uttered to any girl:—*¡Ay-yai-yai, no me dejes así morenísima de mi alma!*—

Neither one noticed when Earl and Father Joe left them sitting alone, together.

Later that evening, up on the fourth floor, the usual background noise of the hospital had died away. Tracy, the RN on the unit, had checked Dan, given him his meds, and told Earl that he should go. "Mr. Cooley needs to get some rest."

"Jus' another half hour, then I'm gone," Earl promised.

"Okay. But no more." She fussed with Dan's pillows, tucked the thermal blanket around him, and left.

Earl was beyond tired. He was grateful he didn't have to drive. Chicky would come back to the hospital and pick him up after he took Lupe home.

For a few minutes both men remained silent. Then Dan hunched himself up a little higher in the bed.

"You know, when I came round the first time and you told me Chicky had won, my first thought was that I hadn't been there when he needed me the most."

"Naw, don't be goin on with that stuff. Chicky told me he knew you was there for him, every round," Earl said.

Dan waved his free hand impatiently.

"I let Chicky down, damnit. Hell, I let you down. It's all my fault for not doing what Kogon told me. I knew he was right—I had a time bomb tickin away inside me. But I just couldn't face it, couldn't deal with it. Didn't even eat right for months, damn near drank myself to death."

Earl got out of the chair, stood up, and crossed his arms over his chest.

"None of that mean a thing, Dan. Chicky told me he reckoned that you and Eloy figured out how to set things right."

Dan grinned ruefully and said, "Yeah, I guess we did at that."

"Damn straight. I wish you could a seen it go down. First of all, we had a sell-out crowd. I walk in durin the prelims and I can smell it—everybody lookin for Sykes to just roll over this guy nobody ever heard of."

Earl chuckled. "Oh my, it was sumpin. Sykes, he come out first, strutting down the aisle to the ring like some damn pimp. Even wearing those shades. Lucky he take 'em off by the time Chicky come in. He don't get it at first. Nobody ever said that boy is swift. But when the ref starts to call him and Chicky over to give 'em the usual bullshit instructions, then Sykes looks close at Chicky and, swear to God, I think his eyes gonna pop right out of his head."

Earl started laughing, and slapped his thigh with his hand.

"Trini and Paco figgered it out just about then, too. The Cavazos threw a shit storm when they saw who they was fightin. Trini, he jus' goes nuts. He jumps down from the ring and starts screamin that the Commissioner got to stop this fight."

Dan grinned and said, "So Jolly Joe did right by us."

"Yessir, he sure did. He tells Trini the Commission was stickin to the rules: 'Hey, this dude really is named Duffy. An', yeah, his record is for real. An' your guy's gonna have to fight him. Or else it's a walkover.' "

"Any chance they'll try to contest it?"

Earl shook his head and laughed.

"Well, I hear Trini and Paco got other things to worry 'bout. Seems them two candy-ass lawyers who been backin Sykes got real mad at them 'cause they find out from Mr. George that Sykes don like trainin too much. And Trini, he lets Sykes off doin roadwork."

Dan shook his head. "Now that surprises me. Trini may be lower than a snake's belly, but he knows better."

"Jus' wait a minute," Earl said. "It gets better. Sykes got hisself a taste for nose candy. Guess who his supplier turn out to be?"

"My God—Trini?"

"You got it. Those legal eagles not too happy when they find out how much of their money bin goin up Sykes's nose. Trini, he makin money both ways."

Earl sat back down in the chair and leaned over to Dan.

"Jus' picture it. Those dudes came spectin to see their boy make his move for the big time. 'Stead, they end up watchin a train wreck."

Earl could still hear the mounting chorus of boos that started in the second round.

"Sykes just couldn't think what way to go. Wanted to get in shots to the head. Chicky didn't let him land but two. You want to get to the body, well, you got to go to the head first, get the other guy to get his hands up, Sykes figures. That way he can use his gangbanger shit. But he never got no chance. When Chicky went lefty, Sykes look like he gonna shit in his pants. It was jus' kick ass all the way. Chicky gave Sykes three rounds. First two, he took him apart. Piece by piece. Sykes get tired out real fast. Like they say, you can't run, you can't fight. Then round three and he put Sykes down for good."

"What do you mean, 'for good'?" Dan flashed back to the terrible injuries he had sustained in the fight with Eloy.

"I mean for good, pardner. A clean KO. Ain't no way Sykes is going to have the balls to get into the ring again with anyone for a long time. Maybe ever. He's history. I reckon our boy is set up for the next shot at the championship."

"You sure?" Dan was no longer on oxygen. His color looked good and his eyes were clear, and shining with happiness. And pride.

"Yeah, right after the fight, I got a call from a promoter talkin about a fight with Pizzaro. Chicky's ready. All we gotta do now is cut the deal. So you betta get out of this place pretty quick."

Dan looked over at the bedside table. He could still see the image of Father Joe's instruments of salvation sitting on it, the candles unlit, the holy oil untouched.

"Book it! I'll be there. You can count on it," Dan said.

ACKNOWLEDGMENTS

We, the children of F. X. Toole, would like to express our deepest gratitude to Nat Sobel and James Wade, who made the publishing of this book possible. Their work was done in honor of and to pay tribute to a writer, our father, whose last words were, "Doc, get me just a little more time, I gotta finish my book." They have accomplished this endeavor, and we are forever thankful.